Call to Arms

Blood on the Stars II

Jay Allan

Also By Jay Allan

Marines (Crimson Worlds I)
The Cost of Victory (Crimson Worlds II)
A Little Rebellion (Crimson Worlds III)
The First Imperium (Crimson Worlds IV)
The Line Must Hold (Crimson Worlds V)
To Hell's Heart (Crimson Worlds VI)
The Shadow Legions(Crimson Worlds VII)
Even Legends Die (Crimson Worlds VIII)
The Fall (Crimson Worlds IX)
War Stories (Crimson World Prequels)
MERCS (Successors I)
The Prisoner of Eldaron (Successors II)
Into the Darkness (Refugees I)
Shadows of the Gods (Refugees II)
Revenge of the Ancients (Refugees III)
Winds of Vengeance (Refugees IV)
Shadow of Empire (Far Stars I)
Enemy in the Dark (Far Stars II)
Funeral Games (Far Stars III)
Blackhawk (Far Stars Legends I)
The Dragon's Banner
Gehenna Dawn (Portal Wars I)
The Ten Thousand (Portal Wars II)
Homefront (Portal Wars III)
Red Team Alpha (CW Adventures I)
Duel in the Dark (Blood on the Stars I)

www.jayallanbooks.com
www.bloodonthestars.com

Call to Arms

Call to Arms is a work of fiction. All names, characters, incidents, and locations are fictitious. Any resemblance to actual persons, living or dead, events or places is entirely coincidental.

ISBN: 978-1-946451-01-9

Chapter One

Orbital Platform One
Archellia, Cassiopolis III
308 AC

"Commander, I understand *Dauntless* was badly damaged when we returned, but it's been four months. I've read all the status updates, but frankly, they are somewhat vague regarding dates. I really need to know when she will be fully operational." Tyler Barron stood next to the clear hyperpolycarbonate wall of the space station, looking out at his battleship. *Dauntless* firmly attached to the station by a series of massive docking cradles. He'd been her captain for over a year now, and he had led his ship in one of the most desperate and deadly battles imaginable, yet he realized now that he'd rarely seen her from the outside.

The battleship was almost four kilometers long, whitish-gray metal with huge structures projecting out on each side, her landing bays. She was beautiful in her own way, almost symmetrical, but with just enough irregularity to give her charm. At least in her devoted captain's eyes. Especially now that her wounds had been healed—the outer ones, at least. There had been long gashes in *Dauntless*'s hull when she'd arrived back at Archellia, and half her laser turrets had been blown to bits or melted down to slag.

Barron could see small specks on her hull, barely visible from this distance. Suited technicians, he realized, working all along *Dauntless*'s exterior. There were repair boats moving around her too, some of them hoppers carrying supplies, others work ships extending giant robotic arms to repair various damaged areas. Near the bow, two larger craft were easing a large turret into place, a replacement for one of *Dauntless*'s destroyed secondary batteries.

"Captain Barron, I have three full crews working around the clock. We are a remote base, I'm afraid, and our priority for supply requisitions is quite low…especially since the war began. We've had to improvise some workarounds for replacement equipment we just didn't have. That takes time." Commander Farnor stood facing Barron, clearly slightly intimidated by the captain's renown, both inherited from his grandfather and, since his return from the battle at the edge of the Rim, newly earned. Farnor was the officer in charge of Archellia's base repair facility, and the target right now of Barron's impatience.

"So, you've heard the Confederation is at war, have you? Perhaps there might be a use for another battleship at the front, don't you think?" Barron knew he wasn't being fair. Farnor's statements were nothing but the truth. From the reports they'd been receiving from the front, things weren't going very well. He had no doubt every spare part and new system had been diverted to damaged vessels far closer to the front. But he didn't care about fairness now. The Confederation was at war, and he and his people were sitting it out in some backwater, lightyears from the action. It was intolerable.

"Captain Barron, I know you're anxious to get underway, but it takes time to repair the kind of damage *Dauntless* suffered." Farnor paused, exhaling hard as he turned to look out at the great battleship. "One month, Captain. I will add another crew, and we will do everything possible to have her ready in…"

"Two weeks, Commander." Barron looked back at the frustrated officer standing next to him. "*Dauntless* will depart in two weeks, so I trust you will get everything necessary done by then."

Farnor returned the stare, no mean feat when the eyes glaring at you were those of Rance Barron's only living descendant. "Captain…"

"I'll make it easier for you, Commander. In fact, I can offer you some assistance. *Dauntless*'s entire engineering team has selflessly volunteered to cut their shore leaves short, and report for repair duty." He glanced at the small chronometer on his comm unit. "Commander Fritz should be here any minute." Fritz was *Dauntless*'s chief engineer, widely considered the best—and most terrifying—in the fleet. She was a legendary taskmaster, and Barron could see in Farnor's expression that her reputation had spread to Archellia.

"Captain, I'm not sure that's such a good idea. Meshing our operating styles on a project already this close to…"

"Don't worry, Commander. I think you will find that Commander Fritz is tireless. I'm quite certain she can help you reorder your workflow and…expedite…the work here." He looked over the stunned officer's shoulder. "Fritzie," he called. His engineer was stepping out of the lift on the far side of the bay. "Come join us." He waited until the diminutive officer was closer, and then he said, "I was just telling Commander Farnor that I thought we could get *Dauntless* ready for action in two weeks. Do you have any thoughts on that?"

"Absolutely, sir. I'll have to have a look at the duty logs, and of course inspect the work that has been done, but I'm sure we can meet that deadline." She smiled crookedly. "At least no one's shooting at us now…that's *got* to make things easier."

Farnor shifted nervously on his feet. He looked like a caged animal trying to find a way out of a trap. He opened his mouth to say something, but Barron spoke first.

"Then it's settled." He looked right at Farnor. "I think you will find Commander Fritz and her people to be a dynamic force, one that can't help but speed the project along."

Farnor looked for a moment as though he was still going to offer some protest or argument. But finally, he just let out a breath and said, "Yes, Captain. I'm sure they'll be an enormous help.

*   *   *

Atara Travis sat quietly in the back of the ground car, staring at the countryside rolling by. She knew Archellia was a bit of a backwater, a sparsely-populated world lacking the sophistication of the worlds closer to the Confederation's core. But it was a beautiful planet, lush and green, almost totally unspoiled. Compared to the industrial hell world that had spawned her—and that she'd escaped from with herculean effort—Archellia was a full-blown paradise.

Travis had a reputation as a bit of a cold fish, one she knew she deserved, at least in part. But much of her hard edge was simply intense focus on her duties, on achieving excellence in everything she did. Unlike most Confederation officers, she'd had to claw her way up from the gutter. She'd done some dark things to make it to the Academy, and from the moment she had graduated, she'd been determined to make sure it had all been worthwhile, that the career she'd fought so hard to attain was all it could be.

She'd always resented privileged officers, especially the brats of the great naval families, who'd held court at the Academy and who'd viewed their future promotions and command prospects as their just due, no more than the passing of rank and station from one generation to the next. She'd hid her disgust—showing it openly wasn't something likely to improve her prospects. She'd even flirted with them from time to time. It was amazing what a smile or a toss of her hair could accomplish, though she'd have cut her throat before she'd done any more than that with any of those self-entitled assholes. Those types were so used to getting what they wanted, she relished the ability to deny them something.

But Tyler is different.

The Barrons were the ultimate naval family, and Tyler stood at the very top of the pyramid of privilege, the grandson and only living heir of the Confederation's greatest hero. Everyone wanted to be Tyler Barron's friend, and she could only imagine how he could have peddled his influence if he'd wanted to. But he hadn't. As far as she could tell, save perhaps for demanding the mission to the Union border, Barron had never used his position to advance his career. He was young for a capital ship captain, but he was damned good too. He rated the posting in every way.

Travis still remembered the first time she'd reported to him for duty. He'd been second officer on *Illustrious*, and she a lieutenant hot on the heels of her lieutenant commander's insignia. She'd been attracted to him at once, and she'd decided to suspend her usual policy of rejecting advances from other officers. But the seduction she'd expected so confidently never came, and over the past three years she'd come to love Barron in a different way, as a best friend, almost a brother. The two shared a close bond, and the officers they'd served with had always been stunned at the almost telepathic link between them. She trusted him with her life, and she knew he felt the same about her. On *Dauntless*'s bridge they were a team without compare, as they'd proven out on the Alliance border.

My God, how far out did he go?

A small laugh escaped her lips as she watched the endless kilometers of countryside pass. She'd seen Barron's efforts to avoid the spotlight before. It had surprised her at first. She'd come from nothing, and she'd watched in stunned shock as her friend who had everything ducked and dodged and generally tried to escape the fawning crowds everywhere he went. Every step she had taken in her life had been a struggle, and everywhere Tyler Barron went, people thronged around him, wanting to meet the grandson of the greatest hero in Confederation history.

As she'd come to know him better, she began to understand. Her background had made her envious of those for whom life and advancement were easy, but she'd come to realize the toll it extracted from her friend and commander; the incessant attention, the need to act like a long lost friend to local dignitaries he'd just met, the unyielding spotlight that followed him everywhere he went. She knew now that Tyler paid his own price for all the privilege and opportunity that was his by birthright.

Still, she shook her head as the kilometers rolled by. Barron sometimes took his quest for privacy too far. He'd spent three days terrorizing the work crews on the orbital platform, driving them every way he could to speed their progress…and finally, in a sort of nuclear option, sicking Anya Fritz and her pack of engineers on them. Then, satisfied he'd done everything possible to accelerate the repairs on *Dauntless*, he'd taken off to go camping in the hills outside Archa City, dashing off a quick message to Travis to tell her where he'd be—and leaving his comm link sitting right in the middle of the table in his hotel suite.

Travis had made his excuses, advising the local VIPs that Captain Barron was busy with repairs, catching up on tactical reports from the front, even fighting off the ravages of a local bug he'd lacked the natural resistance to avoid—anything to cover for him. Over their years together, she'd adopted somewhat of a role as the guardian of his privacy, and she damned sure wasn't going to let anything interfere with the closest thing to a vacation she'd seen her workaholic captain take. Even if he *was* just hiding out in the woods.

But now she had to disturb him. Admiral Lowery wanted to see them both, as soon as possible. His exact words…*as soon as possible*. Her first thought was that the admiral wanted to talk about some minor issue with the repairs, or even more likely, some member of *Dauntless*'s crew who had enjoyed shore leave a little too enthusiastically. The ships fighter pilots especially had been partying like there was no tomorrow, though after the losses they had suffered at Santis, she didn't have the heart to come down on them too hard. But she'd spoken to the admiral herself, and he'd repeated his order with enough emphasis to convince her there was something far more important going on. It had to be the war.

She stared down at the small screen in the dashboard, watching as the blinking dot moved closer to the center. Barron had left his comm unit behind, but fortunately, he'd still worn his location transponder. Otherwise, Travis knew she'd have had to scramble the whole crew to search the woods for their lost commander, a debacle she was just as happy to avoid. Especially since she had no idea what the admiral had to say, not even whether it was classified or otherwise sensitive information. Until she had a better idea what was going on, the fewer people involved the better.

The car slowed to a stop. The car was designed for rough terrain, but now it sat in front of a wall of trees, an impenetrable obstacle for a vehicle of its size. Travis sighed, and then she allowed herself a smile.

"Of course, Tyler…you would find the most inaccessible spot possible, wouldn't you?"

She reached down and pulled the tracking unit from the dashboard. Then she popped the gullwing door and climbed out, setting out into the words on foot.

* * *

Tyler Barron sat on a rock, looking out over a small brook. The stream twisted its way all through the area, the water gurgling over boulders and fallen logs as it worked its way toward the lowlands to the south. It was idyllic, peaceful, and he sat listening to its calming sound, trying to sooth his tired psyche.

But calm was a difficult target now, and despite his best efforts to clear his mind, troubling thoughts still gnawed at him. The war, of course, and whatever role he and his people would be called upon to play in it. They would face danger, but now he'd had a taste of war in all its unrestrained brutality, as had his crew. How would they respond when they were again moving toward the enemy? How would they deal with the memories of their struggle at Santis?

Faces drifted in and out of his thoughts too, those who'd come back to Archellia with him, scarred by the terrible battle they'd endured. And those who hadn't come back. Sam Carson, the young engineer, whose heroism had saved *Dauntless* and her crew. The fighter pilots lost in the cataclysmic melees deep in space…and the others, hundreds in all. His people had been like a family, close knit, trusting and relying on each other. He wondered if they could regain the feeling of easy camaraderie they'd once had, or if his crew would harbor resentments against him, even subconscious ones they didn't realize were eating at them.

His thoughts wandered even farther, into unexpected places. He couldn't get Katrine Rigellus out of his mind. She had been his enemy—she had attacked *Dauntless*, killed his people. On one level, he despised her, cursed her for the damage she'd done to his ship and its crew. But there was more to it than just that, and he found himself wondering about her, even sympathizing. She had been a creature of duty, even as he was. The ideals of the Alliance were repugnant to him, but the more he thought about it, the more he understood them.

He'd read everything the Archellian base library had on Alliance history. It wasn't much—the Alliance was far away and not very well known or understood in the Confederation. He was struck by the history of Palatia, the primary world of the Alliance. The Palatians had been subjugated, their world ruled for almost a century by invaders from another planet. And from the few accounts he'd been able to find, that occupation had been anything but gentle. The Palatians had become warlike, bloodthirsty, even cruel…but Barron was far from sure his own people would have been any different.

He tried to imagine his grandfather breaking free of servitude rather than leading fleets in battle. How would he have reacted, what would his bitter experiences have made of him? What would the Confederation be if it had grown from that kind of nightmare? It was already a morass of corrupt and incompetent government, with more than one planet that sustained virtual caste systems and huge poverty-stricken underclasses. What if it had been born in fire, in a rebellion against those who had enslaved and tortured its people?

It was easy to pronounce judgments, to make grand moral and ethical gestures, but reality often presented itself in far more complex ways. And Barron suspected his adversary had indeed been a complex and intriguing woman. For all the damage his people had suffered at her hands, he found himself mourning her death.

He was startled out of his introspection by something behind him, someone walking through the woods, snapping branches. He turned, letting out a loud sigh, wondering how someone— a reporter, an Archellian admirer, a local functionary who just wanted "one picture with the hero"—had found him.

"A sigh? I came all this way for a sigh?" Atara Travis stepped out of the foliage, and she walked toward Barron's perch.

"Sorry, Atara." Barron smiled. He was relieved to see his first officer. For an instant. Then he realized there had to be a reason she'd come looking for him. "I figured it was one of the Archellians. It was bad enough before...but now every-body wants to hear about the battle, about how *Dauntless* saved Archellia."

Travis walked over and sat on one of the stones near Barron. "And you're not ready to talk about it."

He nodded. "No, I'm not. And now I wonder how my grand-father put up with it for so long. It's a story to these people, Atara, something exciting and heroic. But our friends *died* out there. They died following my orders. Would these Archellians like it if that were the story I told? About the bodies all over the ship? About the blood on the walls, the severed body parts, and the pilots blown to atoms?"

"They're civilians, Ty. You can't expect them to understand." She looked down at the ground. "I can't say I did myself. Not really. At least not before everything that happened out there."

Barron nodded. The Confederation had been at peace throughout his career. He'd seen some minor action chasing down pirates and poachers in the Badlands, but the battle out by Santis had been his first taste of all out, brutal warfare. He wasn't sure what he thought of it all, not yet. But he was certain of one thing. It had changed him.

"I understand that. It's not reasonable to expect them to know what we went through. And yet, every time someone wants me to come to dinner and tell stories, or they want to pose for a photo, I can't help but think of the men and women who fought with us...and never made it back."

Travis just nodded. Then she said, "I feel the same way you do, Ty...but I didn't come to ruin your solitude because of that.

It's Admiral Lowery. He wants to see both of us. As quickly as possible." She stood up. "I have a ground car just outside the woods."

Barron jumped up. "The war? Orders?"

"I can't think of anything else it could be."

"Maybe he has news from the front."

"That's possible. He wouldn't tell me anything over the com. He just told me to find you and get over there."

She turned and reached down, starting to help Barron pack up his kit.

"As soon as possible."

Chapter Two

Base Command Complex
Archellia, Cassiopolis III
308 AC

"Captain Barron, Commander Travis, please come in. Have a seat." Admiral Davis Lowery was a tall man, almost two meters, and his impeccably-tailored uniform hung neatly from his rail thin frame. Lowery had a reputation as a humorless martinet, but Barron had come to feel the base gossip did the admiral a bit of a disservice. The base commander had let more than one of *Dauntless*'s disorderly fighter pilots off the hook for their various offenses with nothing more than a stern talking to.

"Thank you, Admiral. I apologize that it took so long, but I'm afraid I indulged in a little trip to the woods and neglected to bring my comm unit with me."

"Neglected?" Lowery smiled, or at least his own version of that gesture. "I can't say that I blame you, Captain. My memories of battle are over twenty years old now, but I can surely understand the need for some time to yourself after what you have been through."

"Thank you, sir." Barron suspected he knew more of Lowery's history than the admiral would have guessed, including the fact that, as a young officer, he had spent most of the Third Union War on convoy duty, protecting supply shipments. Ser-

11

vice, certainly, and dangerous at times, but no match for the meatgrinder he and his crew had just come through. Still, he could excuse the admiral a small boast or exaggeration, especially since he seemed to be willing to overlook the fact that command officers were required to have their comm units with them at all times.

"You must be wondering why you're here, so let me get right to the point. Our forces have suffered a string of defeats on the battle lines. Losses have been heavy, and we've been driven back at all points of contact. Five Confederation systems have been occupied."

Barron stared back, the surprise obvious on his face. "I'd heard there had been a few minor setbacks, but nothing like you're describing, sir." He paused. "I'd never have gone off like that if I'd known."

"You don't know because everything I am telling you is highly classified. The information released to the public and the news organizations has been tightly censored."

Barron shook his head. He didn't like the sound of that. The Confederation was *supposed* to be a republic, a free society distinct from the dictatorships and oligarchies that surrounded it. He understood why the Council would want to withhold such information, but he still wasn't sure how he felt about it.

"I know, Captain. My first reaction was similar to yours. But there will be no Confederation at all if we don't win this war. It's clear the Union intends complete conquest, the subjugation of all our worlds."

"I understand, sir." He didn't, not really. The admiral had repeated the kind of line that was frequently used to justify one dubious act of government or another. But was national security really served by such secrecy? The people might be upset by such news, even scared. But then they would rally. Patriotism was a strong motivator…and fear could be an even stronger one. Most citizens, save perhaps for a small fringe group of radicals and fifth columnists, had an idea of what life under Union rule would be, just how much they had to lose if the Confederation fell.

His grandfather had railed against just this sort of thing, and the virtual revolution he had led swept away a layer of calcified generals and admirals who'd seemed more interested in covering up their failures and preserving their careers than they had in winning the war. The elder Barron had embraced the people and brought them to his side. He made speeches that were transmitted to every world in the Confederation. He rallied the citizens in the streets, the factories. Cheering crowds lined the streets as new recruits marched toward the depots to report for duty. Workers on dozens of worlds labored around the clock, producing arms and armament, and the convoys flowed to the front, turning the output of a mobilized and energized people into military force. Into victory.

I wonder if the navy grandfather created is backsliding to what it was before, hidebound, run for those in high positions and not for the protection of the people? Of the Confederation itself?

He snapped his focus back to the admiral, who had continued on. "In any event, Captain, what is and is not released to the population is not our decision, nor our concern. Our orders, however, most definitely are."

"Yes, sir. Of course." Barron might disapprove of the withholding of information from the public, but there wasn't a doubt in his mind he'd follow his orders to the letter.

I wonder if Captain Rigellus had similar thoughts when she was invading Confederation space, killing my people...

"*Dauntless* will be leaving as soon as possible. Your trip to the orbital station the other day, as it turns out, was opportune." He paused, and his eyes caught Barron's, and the look of not-quite-surprise they held. "Yes, Commander Farnor...mmm, how shall I put this...advised me of your visit."

Barron had no doubt Farnor had cried like a baby to Lowery, especially after he'd had a few hours of Commander Fritz. "Perhaps I should have checked with you, sir, before I went up..."

"Not at all, Captain. *Dauntless* is your ship, and you were right. Commander Farnor is a good engineer, but no one would call him the quickest worker. Commander Fritz's willingness to cut her leave short will no doubt have a significant effect on the pace of work up there." He glanced down at a small tablet on his desk. "And that coincides well with your new orders, Captain. And mine." He paused, a sour look passing over his face before he squashed it. "I have been ordered to assign Marines and fighter pilots from the garrison to bring your vessel up to full strength." He hesitated again. "I'm not sure how I'll defend Archellia if anything threatens us, but orders are orders."

Barron just nodded. He doubted Lowery would need the transferred personnel any time soon. The Alliance had shown no signs of hostility in the months since *Dauntless* had engaged *Invictus*. The diplomatic mission sent to Palatia in the wake of the incident had been greeted with nothing but steadfast denials that *any* Alliance ship had entered Confederation space, and repeated assurances the Alliance had no intention of initiating hostilities. Barron tended not to speak the language of diplomats, a dialect he typically referred to as "bullshit," but it seemed unlikely that Archellia would face any more threats from the Alliance, at least not in the near future. And if the Union got there in force, it meant most of the Confederation was already gone.

"Yes, sir," he finally said. There was nothing to be gained by offending Lowery. Barron had come to realize that admirals were touchy creatures, best handled with care. At least by those of less exalted rank.

"I've already prepared the transfers. The fighters will be loaded as soon as Commanders Farnor and Fritz give the word. The pilots and the Marines have already been notified and given forty-eight hours to pack up and prepare to ship out."

"Thank you, sir. What are our orders, if I might ask? Where are we going?"

"Admiral Winston is rallying segments of the fleet to make a stand somewhere along the front line, probably at a major choke point like Arcturon or Belatar. He's looking to fight one massive battle to stop the enemy invasion and turn them back. You are to leave Archellia in ten days and proceed at maximum speed to join this force. You will go to Corpus, where a courier ship will be waiting to meet you with further orders."

"Yes, sir." His voice was crisp, loud. Barron didn't relish the thought of leading his people into combat again so soon, but he hated it a damned sight less than standing by out on the Rim while the navy fought for its life. For the Confederation's very existence.

He turned and looked over at Travis, and he could see immediately she felt the same as he did. They had just returned from one nightmare, but it was time to go back.

"With your permission, Admiral, I will shuttle up to the orbital platform and check on Commander Fritz's…and Commander Farnor's…progress with the repairs."

"By all means, Captain." Lowery stood up slowly, waiting an instant while Barron and Travis did the same. Then he continued, "My best wishes to you, Captain, Commander. And to those who serve with you."

"Thank you, Admiral." Barron flashed another glance at Travis. Then he snapped off a salute and turned to walk out of the room.

* * *

Barron walked down the corridor, inhaling deeply. The smells of burnt machinery and leaking chemicals had been replaced by those of sealant and freshly welded metal. *Dauntless* wasn't the newest ship in the navy, nor the biggest, but she'd been reborn, at least after a fashion.

Dauntless wasn't one hundred percent, not yet. Her primary and secondary batteries were fully functional, though Barron was, as usual, a little worried about the temperamental primary guns and the patchwork repairs that had put them back in working order. Her reactors had been repaired, though he knew Fritz would have preferred to replace at least unit B if there had been any spares available. They both functioned at one hundred percent, but Barron knew their age and the punishment they had taken could rear their heads at any time.

Despite the best efforts of the base staff and his own engineers, his ship still carried scars from its great struggle. The repair teams had focused on structural issues and vital systems.

There were still areas where walls were battered and bulkheads blown to twisted wrecks. But in every way that was truly important, his vessel was ready.

Ready to go back into battle.

He'd just dropped his kit in his quarters. He'd been surprised to see his rooms had been fully repaired. They'd been gutted and completely rehabbed, every surface brand new and gleaming. He'd felt a twinge of guilt when he walked in. He knew Fritzie had meant well, that she was only showing her dedication to him by making sure the captain's suite was in top condition. But there'd been little time for repairs to most of the other crew quarters, and truth be told, if he'd thought about it, Barron would have told her to leave his as they were as well.

He walked down the hall toward the lift. The senior officer's quarters were almost directly below the bridge, three levels above. Barron stepped into the intra-ship car. "Bridge," he said softly.

"Bridge," the AI repeated back as the car began to move up. A few seconds later the door opened, and Tyler Barron stepped onto his bridge. For the first time since he'd nursed his broken and bleeding ship back to base, his bridge crew were all at their posts. More than one of them, he knew, had spent good portions of their "leave" in the hospital, recovering from the wounds suffered in battle. He had the utmost respect for his crew, for the courage they had shown in battle. But the officer inside him, the commander who would be leading *Dauntless* back into war, couldn't help but wonder how they'd been affected by the brutal fight at Santis. And whether any of them blamed him for the losses they had suffered. He'd grown close to his people in the long months patrolling the Union border. Had the nightmare at Santis changed that?

"Captain on the bridge." Travis's voice was sharp, crisp, and it took Barron by surprise. Announcing the captain's entry and exit onto the bridge was a procedure definitely buried somewhere in the regs, but most ship commanders tended to eschew the custom, following his grandfather's example and running their ships less formally. Still, not all officers were created in the elder Barron's image. Tyler's first commanding officer had been an officious martinet who had enforced every pointless show of outward respect for his rank, and all he could remember was the caustic resentment of the crew, the nicknames and nasty comments that whipped back and forth, all behind the captain's back, of course. He'd promised himself then and there that when he rose to command rank he would never forget his experiences as a junior officer. And he liked to think he hadn't.

Would you know if you had?

Barron turned toward Travis, but before he could hit her with a questioning glance, the entire bridge crew got to their feet and began cheering. Barron was surprised again, and he stopped and stood motionless in the center of the bridge. He hated it, every second of it, and he knew Travis had been well aware that he would. But he also understood. His first officer knew him better than anyone else, and this was her way of assuring him that the crew didn't share the recriminations he'd insisted on directing against himself.

"Thank you," he finally said. "All of you." He stood where he was for another few seconds, and then he moved to his chair and sat down. It was a signal for the cheering to stop, though it was some time before the raucous welcome finally died down entirely.

"I'm pleased beyond words to be back here, with all of you."

Except all of you are not here...

There were new faces, but not as many on the bridge as he knew there were in the fighter squadrons and among the gunnery crews. He'd known for months, of course, how many people he'd lost, and he'd spent a lot of time brooding about it. But being back onboard was throwing fuel on that fire, and he knew every time he looked at a new face at a station, the daggers of guilt would hit him again.

"We fought a desperate battle together, and we came through victorious. We paid a terrible price for that victory, and I wish I could tell you all that the pain and loss is behind us...but it is not. We leave now for the battlefront. The war we have so long expected is here. The Confederation expects much of us...it *needs* us. And we will answer that call."

He glanced over at his first officer. "Commander Travis, are we ready?"

"Yes, Captain. All systems report one hundred percent operational. Both reactors are functioning normally. Commander Fritz is awaiting your command to activate the engines."

"Very well." His eyes moved to the right, to another station. "Lieutenant Darrow, please request authorization from Archellia base for *Dauntless* to depart."

"Yes, Captain." Darrow leaned forward, transmitting his request. A few seconds later, he turned back toward the command station and said, "*Dauntless* is authorized to leave, sir."

Barron nodded approvingly. He had rescued the communications officer from undeserved disgrace, from the misfortune of having served under the only captain in Confederation service ever to turn traitor. The taint of his superior's treason had smeared Darrow with suspicion, all of it without any basis whatsoever in fact. The injustice of it had disgusted Barron, and he'd specifically requested Darrow for his own crew, not only giving the wrongfully-tarnished officer a job, but also throwing the Barron protective umbrella around him. But it was only at Santis, he realized now, seeing Darrow's utter dedication to duty, that the doubts he himself had subconsciously harbored had been entirely dispelled.

"Commander Travis, bring us out of space dock, if you please. Thrust at one-quarter of one percent."

"Yes, Captain." Travis turned to her station and relayed the command. A few seconds later, *Dauntless* shook as the station's locking bolts released.

Barron watched on the main screen as his ship floated slowly away from the docking cradles and then turned, positioning its main engines to exert the thrust that would push *Dauntless* clear of the station. It wasn't the first time he'd sat at his command post and watched his massive warship leaving port. But it still felt new, exciting. His entire career had been a journey to this command, and for all the fear, and the trepidation about going back to war, he knew he was right where he belonged.

He watched his people at work at their stations, the smooth efficiency of *Dauntless*'s operations, and a smile slipped out onto his lips. He was proud of these people, all of them. And he almost felt sorry for the enemy.

Almost.

Chapter Three

The tension was thick on *Repulse*'s flag bridge as the men and women, among the best the Confederation had to offer, prepared for battle. There was a noisy hum, the combined sound of almost two dozen officers and spacers speaking into headsets, shouting orders and reports back and forth, banging away on keyboards. The Confederation's flagship was about to move forward, into battle.

Admiral Arthur Winston sat in his chair, projecting an image of confidence personified. The gray-haired, steely-eyed officer seemed almost like a statue, a representation of some ancient god of war, without doubt or fear. But it was all an illusion, and it was taking everything Winston had in him to maintain. His stomach was twisted into knots, his back and hands were clammy with nervous sweat. Winston was scared, as terrified as the rawest recruit deep in the bowels of his massive flagship. He was a hardened veteran, accustomed to battle, but now he knew there was more at stake than his own life and the lives of those he commanded. He carried nothing less than the future of the Confederation with him into the fight, perhaps its very survival.

The war that had so long been expected had finally begun, and for all their preparation and readiness, the Confederation fleets had gotten the worst of it. Everywhere on the contested front, Union forces poured into Confederation space, more numerous than expected…more ships, more ground forces. The intelligence reports on enemy strength had proven to be wholly inaccurate, and the men and women of the Confederation's navy faced overwhelming odds everywhere. They had done all they could—fighting savagely, falling back, selling their lives dearly. But nothing had stopped the vicious Union onslaught. And now Winston had drawn a line at Arcturon. Here the retreat would end. Here the massed fleet would make its stand.

Winston was the navy's senior combat commander, a member of the dwindling old guard of officers who had served under Rance Barron, the hero who had led the Confederation back from the brink of ruin almost half a century earlier. Winston had been green then, one of Barron's cadre of young aides, and he'd cut his teeth in the battles that had saved the Confederation. Now he was old—too old, he feared—and he felt almost as if he'd come full circle. After the disastrous first months of the war, it was almost as if he had traveled back in time, that once again he stood alongside Admiral Barron, fighting to save the Confederation from ruin. But this time he was more than a junior officer following a commander he idolized; this time he was in command, and he suddenly understood the true weight of the pressure his mentor had borne.

"All fleet units report ready for action, Admiral." The officer's voice was firm, but Winston knew it was as much a façade as his own grim confidence. Isaiah Beltran was Winston's senior aide, a captain who'd given up his command to stand alongside his admiral, to help direct the largest military formation the Confederation had ever deployed.

"Very well, Captain." Winston paused, staring at the massive tank in the center of the flag bridge. Hundreds of floating specs of light represented his forces, and those of the enemy. He dug down, drawing courage from that mysterious place deep inside that was its wellspring.

Here I am, Admiral Barron…what you made me, sitting here trying to fill your shoes…

"The fleet will advance. All units engage thrust at 4g."

"Yes, Admiral."

Winston listened as his aide repeated the command, sending the orders to the various task forces and sub-units of the great armada. A moment later he felt the thrust on him, four times his weight pushing him back into his cushioned chair.

First Fleet was an immense force. Its three dozen battleships held more than fifteen hundred fighters, and they were backed by over one hundred support vessels. It was the greatest concentration of military might Winston had ever seen…except for the one it was facing.

The array of Union ships displayed in the tank was sobering, almost fifty ships of the line, backed by clusters of support units. Winston didn't know precisely how many fighters all those motherships carried, but it was a good bet his pilots were going to be badly outnumbered. And when that battle line advanced to firing range and its primaries opened up, the amount of destructive force that would be directed at his ships was almost incalculable. His people would give it back, every bit of it and more. One on one, he had no doubt his Confederation spacers could defeat their enemy, but outnumbered as they were, he knew the battle would be a near run thing. And a costly one too.

"Our lead elements are within five hundred thousand kilometers of the enemy vanguard, Admiral."

"Very well, Captain. Bring the fleet to battlestations."

"Yes, Admiral." Beltran tapped the side of his headset, activating the fleetwide comm. "All vessels to battlestations. Alert status red."

The aide stared down at the large board in front of him, his eyes fixed for perhaps ten seconds. "All ships confirm, sir. The fleet is at red alert."

Winston nodded. He sat unmoving, almost like a statue, staring at the tank for another half minute. Then he snapped his head up and looked toward Beltran. "All battleships are to scramble fighters, Captain. I want launch operations begun in three minutes."

"Yes, sir." Beltran turned back to his station. "Fleet order… scramble all fighters."

Winston had already sent out his pre-battle instructions. His capital ships had been instructed to deploy their fighters in accordance with standard procedures. One-third of the birds had been equipped as bombers and tasked with closing on the enemy battleships and conducting attack runs. The other two-thirds had been armed as interceptors, half assigned to protect the strike force and the other half deployed to combat space patrol, defending the motherships against enemy fighter attacks. It was a conservative formation, right out of the book.

He'd considered something bolder, more daring. Perhaps sending half or more of the fighters at the enemy capital ships. But in the end, he'd decided to play it straight. This battle was crucially important. If his forces were victorious, if they held here, the Union invasion would be blunted, and the battered Confederation forces would have time to recover and reorganize. But if he lost in Arcturon…

This is not what Rance Barron would have done.

Winston's old commander had utilized an almost constant series of unpredictable tactics. Barron had led the revolt against the old high command, a reaction to the aged officers and hidebound procedures that had almost lost the Confederation.

I am *an aged officer now. Rance was younger when he won his glory in the second war. He died early in the third, before he had to fight as an old man…*

Winston had considered some aggressive plans, even a few that seemed borderline crazy. But he'd decided in the end to rely on the skill and dedication of the Confederation crews and not on wild and risky maneuvers. His people faced half again their numbers, but Winston was willing to gamble they could overcome that. His confidence said his people were that much better than their enemies, and he'd bet the battle on that.

His eyes glanced down to the screen to the side of his workstation. It displayed a small network of local systems centering on Arcturon. He'd chosen the place for his stand carefully. Arcturon was along the line of advance of the main Union fleet, and he had to defeat that force to blunt the enemy invasion. There were three other transwarp lines in the system. Two led deep into Confederation space. They lay behind his fleet, and they were the primary reason he'd made his stand at Arcturon. The other line led to Copernika, and from there to Ghallus, where Admiral Marionberg and her Second Fleet were deployed in a blocking maneuver, to protect Winston's flank.

"Range to enemy vanguard, four hundred thousand kilometers, Admiral. All vessels report ready to launch fighters."

Winston took a deep breath and held it for a few seconds. Then he said, softly, "Launch all fighters."

* * *

"I've got the spot picked out on my throttle, Mustang. There's room for at least half a dozen more marks, and I'm looking to get them all today." Dirk Timmons was cocky, as usual. The commander of *Repulse*'s elite squadron, he and his people had seen a lot of combat time over the past few months. A *lot*. Enough for him to score ten kills, which placed him in the top three of the fleet—a fact he'd been only too willing to share with his shipmates. At least, to those he outranked or managed to trap long enough to tell the story *again*.

"Just make sure no Union pilot's carving one for you, Warrior...or whatever they do to celebrate a kill." Charles "Mustang" Aires, Chuck to his comrades when he wasn't in the cockpit, was Timmons's rival in *Repulse*'s strike force, and his friend. The two men had different personalities, but they were the closest of friends, and two of the deadliest pilots ever to climb into a strikefighter. Aires wasn't far behind his comrade, with eight kills of his own, though the styles of the two men couldn't have been more different. Aires was meticulous, cautious...he flew his bird almost like a computer. Timmons, on the other hand, at least as far as everyone who knew him would attest, was crazy, as certifiably insane as they came.

"Never happen, Mustang. Never happen. Those Union

pukes haven't bred the pilot who can take me."

"Maybe not, but what about the two pilots? Or the ten? I'm serious, Warrior, watch yourself. We're outnumbered here, probably by a good bit. So be cool, man. Don't get yourself shot to pieces."

"You either, buddy. The drinks are on me when we get back to base. Now let's earn our pay…two hundred eleven credits a month doesn't grow on trees, you know. The Confederation's expecting a return on its investment." Timmons let out a bloodthirsty howl, and then he closed the line. Aires shook his head, fighting back a laugh. Warrior was like a brother to him, and he worried about his friend—that his luck, and his unquestioned skill, would fail him one day and his crazy antics would get him killed.

He reached out, switching the com to his squadron's frequency. "Okay, Direwolves, it's almost time. We're covering the strike force, and that means no crazy, jacked up moves. Stay in tight, and keep those enemy birds away from the bombers."

His eyes dropped to his scanner display. It was covered with small dots, so many that they were clustered together in a cloud, defying his attempts to count them. Fortunately, his AI had done the job for him. There were almost two dozen squadrons deployed to escort the bomber strikes, and six of them, ninety birds, were with his group. But he still figured they'd be facing almost double their number of enemy interceptors. And despite Timmons's confidence, Aires knew well enough that the Union ships were as good as his own. He forced a tiny smile.

Even if their pilots aren't…

He leaned forward, flipping a series of switches. The first two armed his missiles, a loud clicking sound confirming the safeties were off, the warheads ready. The other four controls triggered high-pitched whines as his quad lasers powered up. He was ready.

"Okay, Direwolves…we've got our coverage area, and nobody gets through, you got that?"

A rough chorus of acknowledgements and yessirs rang out on the channel.

"Then let's go…break!"

Aires snapped his mask across his face and moved his throttle to the right, pulling back, feeding thrust into his engines. He felt the pressure as the force of acceleration slammed into him. His pressure suit provided some relief, and his facemask forced air into his aching lungs, partially countering the feeling of nearly ten times his body weight pressing against his chest.

"Switch to local display," he said to his AI, struggling to force the words out. There was no point in staring at the long-range scans. He'd seen enough of the huge masses of fighters heading toward the Confederation fleet. Now he was interested in enemies that were closer. Enemies he could kill.

"Local display active," the eerily calm voice replied as his screen morphed into the tactical readout. There were a dozen enemy contacts, two of them almost in range.

Here they come…

He nudged the throttle, bringing his fighter right at the closest enemy. The incoming fighters were coming straight on, their formation rigid, just like a bunch of rookies right out of flight school.

His eyes focused on the closest fighter, and another just beyond it. If his course was just right, he might be able to scrag them both with his missiles.

His eyes narrowed, focused on the targeting screen. He tapped his controls again…then one more time, adjusting his course slightly, coming in at his adversary on a direct line. His hand tightened around the throttle, his finger ready, closing slowly over the firing stud. He watched the range count down. Under fifty thousand klicks now, close enough for one of his missiles. But he held firm, allowed his ship to close. Forty thousand kilometers.

The enemy fighter fired its own missile. He could see the incoming warhead, heading right for his ship. But still he held his course. Twenty thousand. Then he pressed hard, hearing the loud click as the missile disengaged from his bracket and took off toward the enemy fighter. He nudged the control to the side, angling his bird toward the second target…and then he launched his other missile.

He whipped his hand hard to the side as soon as the second weapon cleared its cradle. He pulled back on the control as far as he could, blasting his fighter at full thrust, stifling a grunt as the massive g-forces slammed into him. He angled the throttle, and then again, changing the vector of his thrust wildly, randomly. According to intel reports, Union missiles only carried enough fuel for one hundred fifty seconds of active thrust. Once that was expended, the weapons would continue on a straight-line course, unable to match his evasive maneuvers. They would be useless then, unless a fighter had the appallingly bad luck to wander right into the flight path of one.

His eyes darted to the display, checking quickly on his own missiles. The weapons were moving directly toward the enemy fighters. The pilots were trying to escape, but their moves were too late, too slow. Aires felt a wave of excitement as he realized he had the Union pilots, the first one for sure. An instant later his scanners confirmed the kill.

Yes!

Aires was far calmer than his friend Timmons, more deliberative. But those terms were relative, especially where pilots were concerned, and the kill filled him with as much excitement as it would have any other fighter jock. Then he felt another wave of satisfaction as the second target winked out of existence.

Stay cool, Mustang…you've still got to break free of this missile…or you're going to be some cherry's first—and last—kill.

He pushed the throttle forward hard, cutting his thrust to almost nothing. Then he moved it to the side and pulled back, firing up the engines again. He looked back at the display, watching as the enemy missile overshot him and began to try to decelerate to reacquire him. But it was too late. He watched the countdown clock move past one hundred thirty seconds. The missile had less than half a minute's fuel left, far too little to bring itself around and make another attack run.

He glanced back at the display, looking first for any threats, enemy birds that had targeted him. But there was nothing. The Union fighters were mostly ignoring the Confederation interceptors. They were pushing right through toward the bombers, ignoring the losses they were taking.

Damn.

"Direwolves, let's tighten up and come around toward coordinates 280.120.310. These bastards are after our bombers, and we can't let them through."

He gripped the throttle again, his hand tight around the worn leather covering the control. Then he brought his bird around, his eyes fixed on the dozens of enemy fighters heading right for the strike force.

Chapter Four

FSS Victoire
Arcturon System
In the System Oort Cloud
Union Year 212 (308 AC)

Hugo D'Alvert sat in his chair, staring out over *Victoire*'s flag bridge. His seat was raised on a dais, a meter above the other stations, as was standard in the Union service. D'Alvert was no ordinary commander. He was a fleet admiral and a member of the Presidium, which gave him power in both the military and the political spheres. It was a rare straddling of two of the primary branches of power in the Union, and it was one he intended to ride all the way to the First's Chair, especially after his forces conquered the Confederation.

"The fleet is to arm all weapons and prepare to advance." His words were imperious, his very demeanor dripping with arrogance. He was a creature of the Union in every way, driven since childhood to rise to the highest levels of power. It was the nourishment he fed upon, the very air he breathed. And his ruthlessness in protecting it, or in acquiring more, knew no bounds.

"Yes, sir," came the nervous response. D'Alvert's crew were acutely aware that he could—and potentially would—throw any of them out of the airlock if they displeased him in any way.

The Union navy was a highly professional force, led mostly by career officers who enjoyed certain levels of privilege but who were also limited in the heights they could attain. The Presidium was paranoid of the prospects of a military coup, and the officers of the navy performed their functions surrounded by a virtual swarm of political officers and spies tasked with watching for any signs of rebellion.

Admirals like D'Alvert were far from the norm, more political animals than career officers, and they didn't receive the same respect from the rank and file…not that any spacer on *Victoire*, or any other Union ship, would dare express anything but razor-sharp obedience.

D'Alvert had already sent his fighters forward, over one hundred-fifty squadrons. Enough, he was certain, to overwhelm the Confeds' wings. The two forces had already engaged midway between the battle lines, and a massive struggle was underway.

His intelligence reports had warned him that Confederation pilots were well trained and highly skilled, but he had disregarded them as overly paranoid. In an even fight he might have been concerned, but he had an advantage in numbers of almost two to one, and he didn't doubt for an instant that would be enough. Still, he wasn't about to take chances. If enough enemy bombers got through his interceptors, they could hurt his battleships. Badly.

If the fighters can't stop them, I'll give them something to attack…

"The first line is to move forward, thrust at 4g."

"Yes, Admiral." Sabine Renault was a career officer, one D'Alvert knew had risen to command rank without starting with any political influence or patronage, just as he had.

For all his power and arrogance, D'Alvert still remembered his early days, picking through the garbage for food in one of Picardie's worst slums. His home world had been a poor one, even more so after a rebellion against Union authority that had prompted an immediate and brutal response. He could still remember the orbital bombardments, and the soldiers, turned loosed on the survivors in an unrestrained orgy of rapine and murder.

He had suffered as much as any of the Picardans, losing both of his parents and his home. But he'd learned a different lesson than his friends and neighbors. They had harbored resentments, anger. They'd preserved notions of renewed rebellion, tempered in their actions only by fear. But D'Alvert watched the officers of the occupation force, the operatives from Sector Nine, the new governor and his political aides. They had power, *real* power. They lived well, many of them very well, even amid the smoking ruins. He decided then and there, that would be his future. And for fifty years he had single-mindedly pursued that goal, with a level of success the young and hungry man he'd been could hardly have imagined.

D'Alvert pushed the memories aside. They had no place in his mind. Nothing did, save the pursuit of victory he planned to leverage into absolute power. He turned his eyes to the main screen as the ten ships of the vanguard moved ahead, their thrust accelerating their movement vectors, pushing them out in front of the main fleet. The lead vessels were smaller than the rest of his battleships and, as far as he was concerned, they were also expendable. The task force had come not from the massive Union shipyards, but from the newly-subjugated Blue Star Duchies, and its greatest value to D'Alvert was he didn't care how many of its ships he lost.

The Duchies were on the far side of the Union, a group of worlds that had been loosely allied, ruled for over a century by quasi-independent merchant princes and drawing great wealth from trade with the less-advanced planets farther out. At least until Union forces overwhelmed their defenses and forcibly annexed them, executing the ducal families and seizing control.

Now the wealth of ten generations of traders served the Union, and the surviving vessels of the Ducal navy had been conscripted to serve in the war against the Confeds. It was a strategy that made sense all around. Losses didn't matter. In fact, they were a positive. D'Alvert and the rest of the Presidium wanted to get rid of the potentially troublesome Blue Star forces anyway. Their ranks were riddled with former nobles and others with the most reason to resent Union rule. They were a liability, best eliminated. And heroic death in battle was easier to explain away than mass executions.

The conscripted spacers knew that as well, but their families, their entire homeworlds, were effectively hostages for their loyalty. There were Sector Nine operatives all over the Blue Star planets, and the ruthless reputation of the Union's spy agency had reached the farthest reaches of human-occupied space. The Blue Star spacers had been left with little doubt what would happen to their loved ones if they failed to serve the Union with courage and obedience…even to death.

D'Alvert watched the screen as casualty figures from the fighter battle began to come in. They weren't good. The Confed pilots were taking down three or four of his birds for every one of their own they lost. He dismissed it at first as a series of isolated incidents, perhaps an elite squadron or two engaged with his green pilots. But the numbers were the same across the enormous engaged area. Confed interceptors were blowing through his escorts and moving against his bombers. D'Alvert had expected his numbers to prevail, for his bombers to break through in force and savage the enemy battleships. Now it looked like his strike forces were going to be slaughtered thousands of kilometers from their targets.

"The advance guard is to increase thrust to 8g and move to engage the enemy fighter wings."

"Yes, Admiral."

"And send an order to all interceptor wings assigned to attacking the enemy strike force. They are to break off and move to defend our bombers."

"Sir…that will allow the entire enemy bomber force to attack without…"

"I am aware of what it means, Captain. I trust you are also aware of how orders work."

"Sir!" Renault snapped back, properly chastised. D'Alvert didn't like being questioned, and certainly not by a subordinate in battle. He might have come down harder on another officer—his reputation for casual brutality had been well-earned—but he liked Renault, and there was just enough left of the young man he'd been to respect someone who had clawed their way up, as he had.

D'Alvert stared at the display. He knew his order would open up the way for the Confed strike to break through and launch their attack runs unimpeded. But he didn't care. The enemy bombers would encounter the advance guard, the Blue Star battleships. They would savage those vessels, no doubt, but he didn't care. He would let the bombers expend all their ordnance ridding him of the troublesome Blue Star contingent. Then he would send in his main battle line...and destroy the Confeds.

*   *   *

"Mustang, you've got one on your tail." Timmons leaned back, his seat retracted as far as it would go. The ace pilot flew his fighter from a position as close to lying down as he could. Every one of his comrades who'd seen the pose had remarked on how uncomfortable it looked and wondered aloud how anyone could fly that way. But no one could argue with the results. Timmons had more kills than any other pilot on *Repulse*, more than twice as many as anyone else except Aires.

"They're all over the place, Warrior. They're coming in from all sides. It's almost like..." Aires's voice stopped abruptly, and Timmons saw his friend's fighter thrust hard to port, then again a few seconds later back to starboard. But the bird pursuing him was locked on, unshakable.

"Stay cool, Mustang...I'm on my way." Timmons took a deep breath. His vector wasn't ideal for trying to bring his ship around to help his friend. He was going to need all the thrust he could get. He reached down and flipped off the safeties, and then he pulled the throttle hard, back and to the left. His engines roared, the sound almost deafening in his cockpit, as he was slammed back into his seat, 18g of force overloading his dampeners and hitting him like a sledgehammer.

He gasped for air, even the forced flow from his mask too little to fight the crushing pressure bearing down on him. He tried to ignore the pain, the feeling that his ribs were going to force their way out of his chest at any moment. Mostly, he struggled to stay conscious. His friend was in trouble, and that was all that mattered to him. He'd stay awake and focused because he had to…because if he didn't, Mustang would die.

He was soaked with sweat, his pressure suit sliding around uncomfortably on the slick wet sheen, rubbing the skin beneath raw. But none of that mattered. Through all the physical torment, the wave of blackness threatening to engulf him, there was nothing in his mind save Mustang's ship. And the fighter on his friend's tail, firing at the wildly gyrating Confed bird.

Timmons' ship was screaming toward the enemy now. His course adjusted, he pushed back on the throttle, cutting the acceleration. He felt the relative relief as the force dropped to 6g, and he felt his hand moving more freely on the ship's controls.

He tapped the throttle to the left, then again once more. His eyes narrowed, focusing on the targeting screen. The enemy fighter was there, still tight on Mustang's tail, even as the Union pilot began his own evasive maneuvers in response to Warrior's approach.

Damn, this guy is good…

Timmons had been among the many pilots in the Confederation service who'd been vocal in their disrespect for their Union counterparts. The initial battles of the war had been disastrous for the Confed forces overall, but the fighter duels had been largely one-sided affairs, with victorious squadrons rearmed and relaunched again and again as their overmatched motherships retreated.

However, this pilot was no rookie, and no one's fool. If Timmons could have admitted it to himself, he'd have acknowledged this enemy to be his equal, even his superior. But he didn't have it in him to do that, so he simply whispered to himself, "Be careful, Warrior…this one is dangerous."

He flipped on his laser cannons, and he moved his finger to the firing stud. He'd burned his missiles already, so he'd have to do this Union ace the old-fashioned way…at close range. He stared, his eyes following every move his enemy made. The fighters were moving at nearly 0.005c, and that limited the range of evasive maneuvering. He'd expected his target to give up on Mustang, to focus on escaping his deadly assault, but the Union bird stayed stubbornly on Aires's fighter, the repeated laser blasts coming uncomfortably close.

"Damn...this guy's got balls..." Timmons surrendered his mind to his targeting, falling into an almost trancelike state. He was digging down, reaching for the intuition, the inner strength that made him the pilot he was. His friend was going to die... unless he blasted this fighter now.

He pressed down on the stud, his cockpit echoing with the whining sound of his lasers firing. He was wide. He stared straight at the display, adjusting the throttle, bringing his ship around ever so slightly. Then he fired. And again.

His blasts were close, within a hundred meters of his target. But that wasn't good enough. He watched the scanner as his enemy's shot came so close to Mustang's bird he thought for an instant his friend had been hit.

There's no more time...

He took another deep breath and held it, his concentration fixed, unbreakable. He stared at the small dot on the scanner, the enemy fighter seven hundred kilometers ahead. He had to hit now. If he didn't, it would be too late. He was here to save his comrade, not avenge him.

He watched as the enemy bird wiggled back and forth on the display, the moves seeming almost random. Most pilots allowed patterns to creep into their maneuvers...and that was when they died at the hands of attentive pursuers. Predictability was death in the cockpit. But the fighter in front of Timmons was gyrating wildly, all the while maintaining its grip on Mustang.

Timmons was still, unmoving, his held breath screaming to escape his lungs. He nudged his throttle, trying to anticipate his enemy's next move rather than reacting to the last. It was risky. No matter how good he was, how careful, he was guessing. It was a gamble. And the bet was Mustang's life.

* * *

The cockpit was hot from the constant heavy thrust of the engines. Union fighters were effective in combat, but they lacked the kinds of luxuries the more expensive Confederation craft had. Like proper insulation for the cockpit.

Aurore Lefebrve was normally as cool as they came. The Union fighter corps tended to lack skilled, experienced pilots. The personality types that most often excelled in the cockpit tended to do poorly in the rigidly controlled Union society. The men and women who would have been most likely to rise to the top of the Confederation's squadrons often found themselves imprisoned at an early age or, worse, they fell into the hands of Sector Nine, weeded out as risks to the tight social order. But Lefebrve wasn't a typical cocky pilot. She belonged to the much smaller group that also excelled in the cockpit, the cold-blooded automaton, the emotionless, stone cold killer.

Even so, her cool was failing her now. Many of the Confederation pilots she'd fought—and killed—since war broke out had been highly skilled. But the one on her tail now was something else again. She'd tried a dozen evasive maneuvers, but he was still on her like glue. He hadn't managed to hit her yet, but she knew it was only a matter of time…and there wasn't much of that left.

She'd almost run her target down. The pilot she'd selected as her victim was clearly also highly skilled, if a bit more predictable than the devil on her tail. She'd almost had the kill…but then her own pursuer had come out of nowhere. She'd had to respond to the new threat, but she'd refused to give up her prey. The kill was hers, fairly won, and she had no intention of surrendering it. But she hadn't been able to lose her own pursuer, not while constrained by the need to stay with her own target. She'd managed to avoid the incoming fire, but now she realized it was a losing battle. She was stubborn, strong-willed, but she prided herself on her logic, her rationality. The pilot on her tail was too good. The payoff of a single kill wasn't worth the risk.

Break off…get away from this pilot. The battle here is far from over.

She took a breath and moved the control hard to the starboard, pulling back and increasing her thrust to escape, allowing her victim to escape. But she was too late.

She heard the sound first, a loud crash followed by the shrieking of metal twisting, structural supports snapping. Then the hissing of air escaping from her ship. Her visor slammed down automatically, and she could hear the emergency air supply pumping into her helmet. Then the cockpit went dark as her reactor kicked out.

Her fighter was careening out of control now, spinning end over end. The hit had been a glancing one, which was the only reason she was still alive. But her ship was dying. Without thrust she couldn't alter her flight vector...and that made her a sitting duck. She'd never been defeated in a dogfight before, but she knew now she had no choice but to eject.

She reached down, her hand hovering for an instant over the large red lever. Then she pulled it...and she felt herself being thrown upward, even as the top of her cockpit broke away.

She was pushed out into space, her emergency cocoon activating, expanding all around her. It would keep her alive, even in the frozen, airless vacuum of space. For a while, at least. Long enough to be rescued, if the Union forces won the battle.

And long enough to die slowly, watching the defeat if they do not...

Chapter Five

"I don't understand. It's almost as though they sacrificed those ten battleships just to absorb the impact of our bomber strike. But who would do something like that?" Winston spoke softly, to himself as much as anyone, watching the display as his bombers savaged the enemy advance guard. Four of the battleships were already gone, and the other six were badly damaged, bleeding air and fluids into space from their broken hulls.

Winston had been elated when he'd first seen his attack waves going in, scoring hit after hit. But then he realized the enemy had let his squadrons through. They'd put up a fight at first, a nasty one, but then their interceptors had moved en masse to the support of the Union's own strike force. His fighter pilots had begged to follow, but he'd gone by the book, and ordered the escorting squadrons to remain and continue to support the attack force.

That's where you dropped the ball...

He stared at the display, at the constant flow of scanner data reporting hit after hit on the enemy capital ships.

They're decoys...

It didn't make sense. The advance guard ships were smaller than the units the enemy had held back, but they appeared to be reasonably new, well-armed vessels. He'd panicked for an instant, wondering if it was all a trick, if the ten battleships were actually freighters or some other kind of dummies, using ECM to pose as capital ships. But those concerns vanished when his bombers closed and the vessels opened fire. They had formidable anti-fighter batteries, far more powerful than those any freighter could mount.

It was hard for him to believe even a Union admiral would sacrifice ten line battleships just to blunt his bombing strike. But that was exactly what he'd just seen unfold.

No, not just to blunt our strike...

The incoming enemy attack was moving into range of his own Confederation line and, courtesy of the enemy's vastly reinforced escort squadrons, it was arriving far more intact than he'd expected.

They sacrificed their advance guard so they could hit us harder...

"All ships activate anti-fighter defenses."

"Yes, Admiral."

"Combat space patrol...advance and engage enemy bombers." Winston had ordered a portion of his fighters held back in reserve—again, a "by the book" maneuver—but his CSP was woefully inadequate to face what was coming...especially since there was still a phalanx of enemy interceptors in the lead of the approaching formation.

He watched the cloud of tiny icons in the display moving toward his ships, and the much sparser cluster of his own CSP units. He felt the urge to recall the rest of his interceptors, but he held back. There was no point. Those squadrons were far too distant to intervene before the enemy bombers launched their attack. His own bombing strike might be expending itself on some kind of enemy decoys, but he was already committed to his course of action there.

His CSP fighters moved forward, accelerating hard, trying to hit the enemy attack before the bombers were able to launch their torpedoes. It was a hopeless effort. There were too many enemy interceptors still screening the assault force. Winston knew that, and he was certain his pilots did too. But that hadn't stopped him from ordering them into the fight. And it hadn't prevented them from following that command.

Winston stifled a sigh. He'd long known war was coming, and he'd been just as sure he would have the top command when it did, but now he felt out of place, unprepared. He'd always prided himself on his devotion to duty, but he'd never wanted to run as badly as he did now. He wasn't hopeless of winning the battle, quite the contrary…his forces had a good chance. But watching his bombers continue to savage the enemy advance guard, he came to appreciate the brutal ruthlessness of the Union. It was sobering, and it triggered something deep within, a primal fear of an enemy so utterly indifferent to the loss of human life. Even total victory in this war would be almost unimaginably costly. Defeat was unthinkable.

"CSP engaging." Beltran's tone suggested the aide had come to many of the same conclusions.

He watched as the Confederation fighters hurled themselves at the enemy strike force with unbridled fury. The pilots, too, realized what was at stake, and they ripped into the defensive screen of interceptors. The defenders were outnumbered, but they had one advantage. They were fresh, and they still had their missiles. They used them to devastating effect, and it seemed that hardly a warhead failed to find a target. Whole Union squadrons seemed to vanish from the display as the Confed pilots drove forward, relentlessly moving toward the approaching bombers.

Winston saw his wings moving directly ahead, leaving enemy interceptors on both flanks. His fighters could have defeated the Union escorts in a protracted dogfight, he was fairly certain of that. But they knew their primary mission was to hit the bombers—even if that meant flying into a trap, allowing the surviving enemy escorts to close in behind them.

He'd been a warrior for decades, for his entire adult life. But he was still taken aback by displays of selfless courage like the one he was witnessing now. His pilots sliced into the bomber squadrons, racking up kills. They weren't going to get them all.

They weren't even going to destroy most of them. But every one of the enemy destroyed was one less to ravage the Confederation battleships.

Repulse's bridge was almost silent, every eye on the display or on workstation screens, focused on the epic fighter duel. Dozens of enemy bombers were destroyed or disabled. Hundreds. But hundreds more pushed forward.

The surviving attackers moved into range of the battleships' defensive batteries. On thirty-six capital ships—and on dozens of smaller escort vessels—laser turrets opened up, rapid bursts targeting the incoming bombers. More enemy ships were destroyed, but the strike force kept coming, moving closer. A handful of interceptors had come about, following after the bombers, taking down a few more of the strike craft, but most of his surviving fighters were trapped in a dogfight as the bombing group's interceptor escorts closed in from their flanks.

Winston stared at the cloud of enemy craft, definitely thinned out from what it had been, but still substantial. His own people had almost finished off the ten ships of the Union's advance guard, but the rest of the enemy battle line was untouched. If the Confederation capital ships could come through the bombing runs with minimal damage, it would be close to an even match. The Union ships still had numbers, but Confederation skill and élan could make up for the modest difference. But getting through the approaching strike without extensive damage seemed an unlikely prospect.

His hands moved subconsciously to his chest, checking that his harness was attached. He looked around the flag bridge, his eyes passing over his people, double-checking that they too were belted in, like some grandfather looking over his grandchildren. He realized it was an odd thing for a fleet admiral to do, but he valued his staff, and he wasn't about to lose anyone to something as profoundly stupid as getting thrown from a chair into a bulkhead. Besides, it gave him something to think about besides the battle...and the barrage about to overtake his ships.

"Detecting multiple torpedo launches, Admiral. All across the line."

"Very well." Winston sat still, like a statue hewn from the hardest marble. "Switch interdictive fire to torpedoes."

"Yes, Admiral."

Winston knew it wouldn't make much of a difference. It was hard to target a ship as small as a fighter at anything but the closest of point blank ranges, and it was even more difficult to lock onto a single torpedo. But it was the last chance to stop some of those shots from closing, and every torpedo his weapons destroyed was one less that could tear into his ships and kill his people. His gunners would only have a brief opportunity. Once the reactions triggered inside the warheads, converting the mechanisms to balls of super-heated plasma, even that small chance would be gone.

He watched his screen, feeling a wave of excitement as he saw reports of hits scroll down the side. His gunners were earning their keep, their accuracy almost uncanny. At least thirty of the incoming weapons were destroyed. But then he saw the tiny symbols in the display changing color, the torpedoes converting to pure energy.

"Laser batteries cease firing at torpedoes. Retarget back to bombers. And all ships, conduct evasive maneuvers, now!" He'd expected the enemy attack craft to break off after they'd launched their primary weapons, but the fighters were still coming on, preparing to conduct strafing runs on his battleships. It was an aggressive strategy, one likely to result in high casualties among the fighters. But it would also give the attackers a chance to close on the capital ships hardest hit by the torpedoes…and maybe push a few over the edge.

His eyes darted to the larger display. His interceptors were still locked in their death struggle with the enemy's. It was a massive dogfight, with losses high on both sides. His people were slowly clawing their way to winning the engagement, but they were still outnumbered, and unless the enemy broke off, there was no way most of his birds would get back in time. He had a few birds from the CSP and his ship's laser turrets, but that was all.

"All laser batteries targeting bombers, sir," Beltran said. "All ships executing evasive maneuvers." Then a few second later he added, "Lead torpedoes entering impact range...now."

Winston inhaled deeply. For a few seconds, nothing happened. Then his screen lit up, reports of torpedo hits coming in from the ships of the fleet. At first, it looked like the enemy barrage was hitting with deadly accuracy, one superheated plasma after another slamming into his ships. But then the frequency dropped off, dozens of the deadly weapons zipping by, no longer able, in their pure energy form, to adjust their courses in response to his vessels' evasive maneuvers.

He could hear his communications officers fielding damage reports from across the fleet. He knew Beltran would filter the raw data, relaying only the most severe to him, but he glanced down at his own screen anyway. *Excalibur*, *Galaxy*, *Illustrious*, *Renown*...all hit. *Indefatigable* and *Warspite*, hit multiple times, reporting extensive damage to primary systems. And *Dominion*...

"Admiral, we're getting a Code Black transmission from *Dominion*."

Winston went cold. Code Black was the signal that a ship faced imminent destruction. He'd known his fleet would take losses, that the massive battle to stop the Union invasion would carry a terrible cost. But *Dominion* was the first, and his mind recalled her stats. Forty-eight fighters, seven hundred ninety-four crew. Captain Becca Klein commanding. He'd known Klein for ten years. She was a good commander...and a friend.

Perhaps they'll be able to evac...

"*Dominion*'s gone, Admiral." Beltran's words hit him hard. His eyes were still focused on the display, where the blue sphere representing the battleship had just winked out of existence.

Winston heard more damage reports coming in...and then *Repulse* shook hard, throwing him forward with considerable force. He felt the straps of his harness digging into his chest, and then he snapped back hard into his seat. He winced in pain, but he knew immediately he wasn't injured, not really. His flagship was another matter.

Flag Captain Riley was off in *Repulse*'s main bridge, and Winston knew the operation of the ship was that capable officer's responsibility. An admiral in charge of a task force might also command his own vessel, but Winston was responsible for the largest Confederation fleet ever assembled. Dozens of ships and almost fifty thousand spacers served at his command. It just wasn't feasible to wear *Repulse*'s captain's hat too.

"Captain Riley reports moderate damage to port side systems, Admiral. Two secondary batteries knocked out, structural integrity lost in several outer compartments…but both reactors are functioning at one hundred percent, and there is no damage to the engines or landing bays."

Winston felt a wave of relief. Things could have been a lot worse. Still, he suspected there were casualties, in the compromised compartments and in the damaged laser turrets…and probably some fatalities in the mix.

No point in dwelling on that. They aren't the first to die today, and they won't be the last.

He stared at his screen, his eyes fixed on the damage reports. Most of his battleships were still combat-ready. And his own bombers had obliterated the enemy advance guard—six ships destroyed outright, and the other four badly damaged, bleeding air and fluids into space. Decoys or not, that was ten less line ships ready to fight his own. It was time to decide the issue.

"Captain Beltran, issue a fleet order. The battle line will advance. All ships accelerate at 6g."

Chapter Six

"I need your help, Jake. I know how you feel about these Rim garrison pilots. I know how everybody feels about them. But they're what we've got, and we're damned lucky to have them." Jamison paused. "You know as well as anyone the losses we took at Santis."

"Yes, I know. And those were friends, Kyle, comrades. These garrison jockeys are rejects, the bottom of the barrel after fleet command got its pickings. Not one of them has seen a shot fired in anger." Jake Stockton was generally considered *Dauntless*'s best pilot, in fact universally so since his rival—and now he'd realized too late, his friend—Tillis Krill had been killed in action. Krill had saved Stockton's life, and lost his own in the process.

It was something Jamison knew had been difficult for his cocky ace to accept. Stockton had been subdued for weeks after the battle, acting very unlike himself. But now he seemed back to his bombastic norm. *Seemed*...Jamison wasn't sure his friend had really recovered from what had happened out on the Rim.

"And how much action had you seen before Santis, Jake?

45

Who'd you shoot at before those Alliance pilots? A few pirates and renegades? You're good, I'll give you that, but sometimes you're an arrogant ass."

Stockton looked like he was going to hurl back a spirited response, but he hesitated. Then he said softly, "That may be true, Kyle, but you were with me out there. I'm not saying the Union jocks are going to be a match for those Alliance devils... but you know what's going to happen to these lap dogs. We might as well shoot them in the heads now. It would be a mercy."

"That's why I need your help. We're heading into another fight. We have to get them ready."

Stockton snorted. "You're asking for miracles, Kyle."

"Yes, Jake...maybe that's what I'm asking for. But what options are there? Like it or not, we lost more than half our people at Santis. Those garrison pilots are going to be our comrades, our wingmen...and if they get blown away, it'll be that many more enemy birds on your ass." He paused. "And whatever you think of their skills, do you really want to watch them die?"

"No," Stockton replied sullenly. "That's why they shouldn't be here."

"Well, that wasn't your decision. It wasn't mine either, or even theirs. But it was the right one. The fleet's not doing well, Jake...and my gut tells me things are worse off than we've been told. Those pilots are here because they're needed. Because the Confederation needs everyone right now. So, you can quit bitching about the fact that they're inexperienced or poorly trained or whatever...and you can help me whip them into shape." His eyes bored into Stockton's. "Or you can watch them die and know that you didn't try to help them out."

"All right, all right...I understand. What do you want me to do?"

"I want you to teach your new Blues how to fight. You know there was a day not all that long ago that even Jake "Thunder" Stockton didn't know how to fly. Somebody taught him...and he turned out to be pretty damned good at it. Maybe he can pay that forward."

Stockton nodded, a smile forcing its way onto his face. "Okay, you made your point. I'll do what I can."

"I want you to take the new Yellows too. Typhoon is a good man, but I had to move him up to squadron command far too soon. I think he'll handle himself well enough in action, but I'd like to see a more experienced hand trying to teach his new pilots a thing or two."

Stockton's smile slipped off his face. He stood for a moment, silent, thoughtful. Lieutenant Rick "Typhoon" Turner had been one of his own Blues, until Jamison had transferred him to command Yellow Squadron...replacing the dead Tillis "Ice" Krill. There was no question he had unresolved feelings about Krill's death, and he suspected he'd have a reckoning with himself at some point. But now wasn't the time.

He returned Jamison's gaze. "Rick will do fine, Kyle. He's a good man." He paused. "Ice would have approved."

Jamison nodded slowly. "Yes, I think he would have. But give Rick a hand anyway. You're the best we've got, and whatever you can get across to these replacements could save some lives."

"All right. I'll do my best. But I can't make any promises."

"Your best is all I ask, old friend. It's all any of us have to give."

* * *

"Captain Rogan, come in and have a seat." Barron looked over at the Marine standing just inside the door at attention. He gestured toward a vacant guest chair facing his desk. "At ease, Captain, please."

"Yes, sir." Rogan's body shifted slightly, but Barron had to stifle a laugh. If the Marine officer thought his slightly less than ramrod straight posture constituted "at ease," *Barron* decided he'd play along.

"Hello, Captain." Atara Travis was already sitting in one of the chairs in front of Barron's desk, and she turned around to face the new arrival.

"Commander," Rogan said, his body tensing slightly as he

snapped almost involuntarily back to attention before returning to his slightly less rigid pose. The Marine paused for a few seconds and then he moved toward the chair, following what he'd clearly taken as Barron's orders to sit down, though he looked as though he'd much rather stand.

"Bryan, I understand your code of conduct, and I appreciate the respect you show in my presence, but I like a certain amount of informality, especially with my top officers. I'd appreciate if you could try to relax, just a bit. At least when it's just the senior personnel present."

"Yes, sir," the Marine replied crisply.

"No, Bryan…that's not an order. Just try."

Barron caught Travis smiling, and he flashed her a scolding glance. Bryan Rogan had been having a rough time since the fighting at Santis. He'd lost almost two-thirds of *Dauntless*'s already understrength Marine contingent there, and the fact that he'd beaten a force twice as large hadn't seemed to lessen the blame he'd placed on himself for his dead Marines.

"Yes, Captain." The big Marine's voice was softer, more informal. Barron suspected it was an acting job, but you had to start somewhere.

"Bryan, I wanted to talk to you about the contingent." *Dauntless*'s forty or so surviving Marines had been reinforced by one hundred sixty-two drawn from the Archellia garrison. The reinforcements outnumbered *Dauntless*'s original cadre four to one, but Barron knew the survivors of the battle on Santis were in every way still the heart and soul of the force.

"It's difficult, Captain. Our people were always close, but the…battle…really forged them into a tight unit. You understand, sir…when a force suffers losses like…"

"Yes, Bryan, I understand completely. No need to explain."

"Yes, sir. I've been trying to integrate the new personnel, but…well, Captain, it hasn't been easy. I was going to feed them into what remains of our existing units, but if I do that, they'll outnumber our…I mean the original personnel…so much that any unit integrity will be lost."

"We're heading toward the front, Bryan, and while I expect

we'll end up in battle soon, it will probably be as part of a major fleet action. Which means, except in the extremely unlikely event that someone tries to board us, your Marines probably won't be directly engaged. That should give you some time to shake things out. Keep a core of our existing squads intact, with at least half of their strength from old *Dauntless* personnel. That should be a good chunk of one company—you can add a couple of squads of the replacements to bring it up to strength. The other company will be entirely made up of former Archellia garrison forces. I know they were drawn from different units, but try to keep them as close to their original organization as possible."

"Yes, Captain."

"If we do need your Marines, I'm counting on you, Bryan. I know it's painful to think about the losses we suffered, but you did an amazing job on Santis. From what I saw of Alliance naval personnel and pilots, I suspect their ground forces were no easy foe. Yet your people prevailed, despite being outnumbered."

"Thank you, sir." Barron had already said much the same thing to Rogan more than once, but he could see his Marine commander was still punishing himself. He sensed a whiff of hypocrisy in his own behavior. He was trying to explain why the Marine losses weren't Rogan's fault, yet he was still beating himself up over *Dauntless*'s casualties, spacers and Marines both. He understood the inconsistency, but he ignored it, deciding that wallowing in guilt was a command prerogative.

"Just do your best with them, Bryan. And let me know if you need anything."

"Yes, sir. Thank you." The Marine sat restlessly, looking back at Barron tentatively.

"Dismissed, Captain," Barron said, realizing after a second what the Marine was waiting for.

"Yes, sir." Rogan stood up, snapping into the rigid posture he seemed to find more comfortable than any other, at least in the exalted presence of *Dauntless*'s captain. The he saluted and turned on his heels, marching out of the room.

Barron waited until the Marine was gone. Then he turned

toward Travis. "What do you think, Atara? I have tremendous confidence in Bryan—and in Kyle Jamison as well—but both the Marines and the fighter wing were shattered out at Santis. I think the garrison forces take a little more grief than they deserve…but they're not a match for the men and women we lost. And if anything, we're probably going into a worse fight the one we had before. You know as well as I do, if they're censoring things as widely as it appears, the real situation is even worse than what we were told."

He glanced down at his desk, at the small tablet that held the orders Admiral Lowery had given him. His expression was a somber one, his thoughts not really on the orders but rather on the great gaps in *Dauntless*'s roster, the crowd of new faces in the ship's corridors. He'd been diving into his duties, obsessing over every decision. But he was troubled, and for all the outward appearance that *Dauntless*'s captain was at the top of his game, he wondered how he would react when he had to lead his people into battle again.

"I'm afraid you're right, Ty. But I don't see anything we can do about it. We've got the pilots we've got, and the Marines too." She hesitated. "Maybe when there's a problem you can't solve, you just do what you can and then move on. It's pointless to worry about what you can't change. I think both Captain Rogan and Commander Jamison understand the situation, and they're both talented, reliable officers. Now comes the 'move on' part. I'd like to see you worry more about making sure we have what we really need to come through the next fight…our captain." She paused before continuing.

"Ty, you've got to let it go. I know you're hurting, but you did everything you could at Santis. You won the victory, even though we were outmatched and taken by surprise. Yes, our losses were high, but if you hadn't been *Dauntless*'s captain, we'd all be dead. I believe that…completely. So, cut the self-flagellation and lay off yourself for a while. And if you won't do it for yourself, do it for the men and women on this ship. Give them their captain back…at the top of his game. You owe them—us—that much."

Barron looked back at his first officer—and closest friend.

There was a lot to admire about Atara Travis, but none of it was as impressive to him as her ability to give it to him right between the eyes when he needed it. He'd done his duty since returning from Santis, but he hadn't been the same officer who had won that brutal fight. Terrorizing engineers to speed repairs was one thing, but Travis's words had shaken loose the black shadow that had been festering deep in his mind. How would he react when he had to lead his people into battle again? When he had to send some of them to die?

"I know you're right, Atara. But…"

"No buts, Ty." Interrupting the captain was frowned upon in the Confederation navy, but it was clear Travis didn't care, not right now. And instead of being angry or offended, Barron burst out laughing.

"When you retire from active duty, maybe you can teach a class at the Academy on the proper control and chastisement of ship commanders."

Travis smiled. "Well, they need it sometimes."

The two shared a laugh, and Barron realized it was his first in a long time. "I know you're right, Atara. It's just difficult. For all my rank and years of service, that was my first *real* battle. Intellectually, I knew it would be terrible, but the reality was beyond what I'd imagined."

"It was for me too, Ty. And for all of the crew. They—we— need you now. Perhaps it's a cruel obligation of command, but you have to set the example, help them all through their own fears and loss." She hesitated, taking a deep breath. "And I know you can do it."

Barron smiled back at his first officer. "Thanks, Atara. I guess if the captain's got to set the example for the crew, the first officer's job is to set it for the captain."

She nodded. "And you know I love my job, Ty. So, pull yourself together, and we'll face whatever comes our way side by side."

Chapter Seven

CFS Repulse
Arcturon System
Just Inside the System Oort Cloud
308 AC

"Yeah! Another one...that makes five." Timmons was excited, his blood lust almost completely in control now as he gunned down yet another enemy bomber. His squadron had escorted *Repulse*'s strike force in its assault against the enemy advance guard, but that fight was over now, the target force of battleships virtually destroyed. It had been a great victory, but Timmons still wasn't sated. He'd requested permission for his Red Eagles to break off from escort duty as the attack squadrons headed back toward their base ships to refuel and rearm, and he'd received permission, along with Aires's Direwolves, to attack the enemy bombers now returning to their own launch platforms.

"Take it easy, Warrior...these bombers are easy pickings, but their interceptors are coming up now too. They'll be tougher targets."

"Bring 'em on, Mustang. I don't care how they're fitted out... we'll blow 'em away no matter what."

"Okay, Warrior, that's great. But watch your fuel status.

Mine's looking like shit. We're going to have to break off soon no matter what."

"Roger that, Mustang." Timmons glanced down at his gauges, confirming what he already knew. He had ten minutes, maybe fifteen if he was careful with his thrusters, and then he'd have to break off. And he suspected some of his pilots were even worse off.

He had a nagging feeling digging at him too. The strike against the enemy battleships had been *too* successful, one wave of attacks destroying or disabling ten capital ships. The kills had come too easily. The Union forces had practically abandoned their defensive efforts, leaving only a token force of interceptors to screen their advance guard. Timmons knew the grand tactics of fleet combat weren't his domain, but he was edgy nevertheless. *Something* was going on. If his brain wasn't telling him that, the pit in his stomach was.

He fired his lasers, and he felt the familiar excitement as another enemy bomber vanished from his display. He couldn't see it, of course. Fighter battles were close-ranged affairs compared to capital ship duels, but his victim was still hundreds of kilometers away.

He pulled back on the throttle, accelerating, bringing his bird around to track another target. It was an interceptor this time, and as soon as he angled toward the fighter, it launched into its own evasive maneuvers.

Timmons's hand moved to the side, by instinct as much as deliberate thought. As with most pilots in Confederation service, his battle experience before the war had been extremely limited. He'd been considered a gifted pilot since his days at the Academy, but it was only over the last couple months that he'd seen heavy combat. He'd adapted well, handling the stress and fear, and racking up an impressive record since the Union forces had streamed across the border. He knew not all pilots had. Some that had been considered highly skilled had found themselves overwhelmed, unable to remain focused in the massive dogfights that had characterized the fighting so far. And those who could not adapt had died. Even his own Red Eagles had seen their share of losses, and only half the pilots he'd started with on day one were still there.

Timmons stayed with his target, his hand moving back and forth, matching the enemy bird's maneuvers. He knew he had the edge, even beyond piloting skill. The Union interceptors had escorted their bombers all the way to the Confederation battle line. They had traveled farther than his people had, and the Union fighters had slightly less operational range. That meant his enemy couldn't sustain the wild evasive maneuvers that were keeping him alive.

Timmons hadn't fired yet. His energy reserves were low, and he wasn't about to waste it on wild shots at long range. He stared at the display, adjusting his course, closing steadily, relentlessly.

He knew he had to break off in another few minutes. It was more than his own fuel status…he had his squadron to think about. He'd ordered them to break formation, to pick and choose their own targets. But now it was almost time to lead them home. His losses had been mercifully light, a fact he confirmed with another quick glance to the small screen on his control panel. Two ships lost…and at least one of the pilots had managed to eject before his ship was destroyed. All casualties hurt, but Timmons and his squadron had been in almost non-stop combat since the war began. Losses had become almost routine.

He tried not to think of the pilots who'd been killed. That wasn't the way in the fighter corps, at least not among *Repulse*'s six squadrons. The dead were gone—you drank a toast to them in the officer's club after the battle, maybe told a story or two about their exploits…and then you forgot they existed. The next morning, they were gone, ancient history. It was war, total and brutal, and there was no place for weakness.

He knew people outside the fighter service considered it a harsh custom, but as far as Timmons was concerned, none of them had any idea how many more pilots would die if they climbed into their birds distracted, thinking about lost friends. No, as far as he was concerned, it was how it had to be. He wasn't about to trade a living, breathing pilot for memories of one already dead.

Still, it was hard to ignore the damage his squadron had taken, the slots taken up by replacements. Some of those new pilots were blooded now, veterans of the terrible fights along the frontier. Others were raw, including two who'd launched as Red Eagles for the first time today.

One, he reminded himself. Davis Clarkson had been one of his rookies…and now he was one of his casualties, the one who hadn't ejected. Clarkson had one of those rounds of drinks coming in his honor…before the name his comrades had fleetingly remembered was forgotten. And then another fresh face from the Academy would take his place.

Until we run out of them too. How long can we fight like this before there's nothing left?

Timmons stared intently ahead, lining up his shot. He only had four or five blasts left in his laser cannons…and he was already pushing the line on calling the withdrawal. But he stayed focused, deadly. It was inconceivable to him to let his prey escape, even as his fuel gauges screamed for him to return to *Repulse.*

He took a deep breath…and he fired. A miss. Then again. A hit!

The enemy fighter winked off the screen, and Timmons felt the burst of energy he always did after a kill. At least some version of it. After so much battle, so many dead, was the intensity waning? Was he losing the taste for it all?

He shook his head, driving away the distracting thoughts. He wasn't out here to think. He was out here to kill enemy fighters…and to lead his squadron. To get as many of them back alive as he could.

"Red Eagles, break off contact…return to base."

He watched the display, confirming that his pilots were following his orders, that none of them were in trouble. Then he angled the throttle and blasted off, back toward *Repulse.*

* * *

"Captain Riley reports the last of *Repulse*'s fighters have landed, sir. They are commencing reloading and rearming operations now. We're receiving word from the rest of the battle line as well, sir. All squadrons should be recovered within three minutes."

"Very well," Winston replied. His line was moving forward, heading toward the enemy battleships. He was edgy, but despite the nagging concerns working on the edges of his mind, he was feeling a bit of optimism. The battle was going well. The ten ships of the Union advance guard were gone, destroyed or blasted to scrap. Perhaps he had finally managed to turn around two months of nonstop defeat and retreat. Now it was time to finish the battle, to stop the enemy invasion here and now.

"All fighters are to remain in current configurations. All captains are to combine formations where necessary to create effective combat units." Winston knew his squadrons had taken considerable losses, but the Union forces had suffered far greater casualties. He'd been tempted to arm more fighters for anti-ship strikes, but converting birds outfitted as interceptors to bombers was a time-consuming process. And he wanted his fighters back in space as quickly as possible.

"Yes, Admiral."

Winston's eyes fixed on the wall of small lights in the display, the Union line moving toward his. He was still troubled by the relative ease with which his forces had smashed the enemy advance guard, but the facts didn't lie. Twenty percent of the enemy's capital ships were gone, before the two battle lines had exchanged so much as a shot. The Union's numerical advantage had mostly vanished with those ten battleships, and now Winston's fleet faced a far more manageable forty to thirty-five matchup. Granted, the rest of the Union line was fresh, untouched by his attack squadrons, while many of his own ships were moving into battle with varying degrees of damage. But, still, it was the best odds his people had seen since the massive enemy fleets had poured across the border, and he was determined to see it through. He would fight here, to the end. His people had fallen back for the last time. Here he had drawn the line.

"Captain Riley reports that his people will have two squadrons ready for launch in fifteen minutes, sir. He wants permission to launch in waves."

Winston didn't answer, not immediately. He didn't like the idea of sending his squadrons out piecemeal…but holding back fully-armed fighters didn't appeal to him much more.

"Projected time until the fleet enters firing range?"

"Twenty-one minutes, Admiral." Beltran paused, his eyes darting to his screen reflexively to double check the data he'd just reported. "Assuming both we and the enemy maintain current velocities."

Winston stifled a sigh. Getting all his fighters into space before the fleets engaged was going to be tight. "Advise Captain Riley that he is authorized to launch all squadrons as they are ready. My orders to all vessels. Launch squadrons as soon as they are rearmed and refueled."

"Yes, Admiral." Beltran turned toward his comm unit, flipping it to the fleetwide channel. "Fleet order: All squadrons are to launch when ready."

Winston sat, staring straight forward. A moment later he felt the slight vibration, one of *Repulse*'s catapults launching fighters into space, then again, one every few seconds. His flagship's squadrons were heading back into the storm, at least those the launch bay crews had managed to refit.

His pilots had done well in their first sortie. They had savaged the enemy advance guard and destroyed hundreds of opposing fighters. But the real battle was about to begin, and he had to ask more of them. He knew they would be tired now, their sharpness worn away by the hours they had already spent in combat. And he was also aware that fatigue would claim lives, that pilots who would have survived a first mission would die now, the victims of slightly slowed reflexes, of minds struggling with exhaustion.

"Captain Riley reports Direwolf, Red Eagle, and White Tiger squadrons launched. Thirty-seven total fighters."

"Very well." Winston nodded. The interceptors. The rest

of *Repulse*'s birds were rigged for anti-ship operations. Bombers took longer to turn around in the bays, and Captain Riley's people had clearly emphasized rearming the craft outfitted for dogfighting. It made sense, as long as they got the bombers out in time.

Riley knows that…do your job, and let him do his…

"Eight minutes to weapons range, Admiral."

"All ships are to activate primary batteries and stand by for the command to commence firing." The Confederation primaries were particle accelerators, at least on thirty-one of Winston's thirty-five capital ships. The weapons were long-ranged and deadly, one of the Confederation's greatest advantages in equipment and technology. But they were also fragile and highly subject to breakdown. It had been a running—and often heated—debate over the past decade as to whether the fleet was best served by the powerful weapons, or if the more durable x-ray lasers that had served two generations of Confederation warships were the better choice.

The new technology had won out in the end, but Winston, along with many of the others in the high command, had voiced concern, and even spoken out upon occasion, claiming the decision had more to do with intense lobbying by the industrial worlds of the Iron Belt, hungry for the contracts to build the breathtakingly expensive new weapons, than it did with rational military decision making.

The admiral disapproved of such corruption, at least on one level, but he was less effective at lying to himself about his own guilt than many of his colleagues were. His hypocrisy had its boundaries, at least in terms of honesty with himself. He'd enjoyed his share of largess from the representatives of the big arms manufacturing cartels, including the plush vacation home on the rocky coasts of Corellia that awaited his retirement. Indeed, if war hadn't loomed, he would already be there, spending cool, crisp mornings walking the breathtakingly beautiful shoreline…courtesy of those who had benefited from trillions of credits of his military appropriations over the years.

"All ships report primary batteries ready, Admiral. Six minutes to firing range."

"Very well, Captain." Winston inhaled deeply, holding the breath for a few seconds before exhaling it. He'd begun his career fighting desperate battles to save the Confederation, but then he'd had the steady hand of Rance Barron on the controls. This time it was on him, all of it. Perhaps even the survival of the Confederation.

*   *   *

"Primaries are offline again, Captain. Reactor A is down to seventy percent output." Heinrich Nordstrom was *Intrepid*'s first officer, a role he'd inherited two weeks earlier when the ship's longtime exec was killed in action. Commander Vargus had been very hands on, and he'd been down on the flight decks supervising the turnaround of the battleship's fighters when the bay took a direct hit. He'd lingered for twelve hours—at least the bits of him they'd managed to drag back to sickbay had. It had been long enough to say his goodbyes and to languish in pain, but there had never been any hope of survival.

"Unacceptable, Commander." Sara Eaton was *Intrepid*'s captain. She was still getting used to Nordstrom's voice in place of Vargus's. Her new exec was a capable officer, one she knew was up to the job. But going into a fight like this without Vargus had seemed like leaving one of her arms behind. "Get me Commander Merton now."

"Yes, Captain." A few second later. "Commander Merton on your line."

"Commander, what's going on down there? We haven't been hit that hard, not yet. I need those main guns."

"We're doing everything we can down here, Captain. Those damned things have so many weak points. There's no significant damage…it's just a question of tracking down the breaks in the power lines." *Intrepid*'s chief engineer was tense, the stress clear in his voice.

"Then do it, Doug. Now."

"Captain, we're on it…but it's not…"

"Don't waste time telling me what it's not. Just fix it." Eaton's hand slammed down on the comm unit, closing the line. She knew she wasn't being fair to her engineer, but she was just as aware that Merton had been with her long enough to know she believed in him. Eaton was a slender woman, medium height, her pale blond hair cut into a short bob. She looked younger than her forty-one years, a good bit younger when she was someplace less aging than the command station of a Confederation battleship. But no one who had served under her doubted her toughness, or her tactical skill.

Intrepid shook. Another hit. The enemy primaries weren't a match for her ship's, assuming the temperamental beasts were functioning, but they still packed a punch.

The battle was fully underway now, both lines locked in the final struggle. In another thirty seconds, *Intrepid*'s secondaries would come into range. Strategy had played its hand in selecting Arcturon as the site of the Confederation's bid to halt the enemy advance, and tactics had ruled in the formation of the fleet and its timing and maneuvers. But now it was down to skill and perseverance, the toughness and grit of the spacers on both sides. The willingness to stand, to fight through exhaustion, pain, fear…to ignore wounds and radiation and sweltering heat, for just that much longer than the enemy.

And the will of the commanders…of Admiral Winston's determination, and the enemy admiral's…

She knew Arthur Winston had his share of courage. Though she'd never acknowledge it in public, she thought he was a mediocre tactician. But she didn't doubt his bravery. And she'd be the first to say the man's fifty years of service and three wars earned him the confidence of his people.

Still, something's wrong…

Intrepid had fired its primaries half a dozen times, targeting two enemy capital ships, and causing what her scanners told her was extensive damage to both vessels. As well as she could follow events across the half million kilometers of engaged front, the story was the same all down the line. The enemy was inflicting a toll, their weapons tearing into the Confederation battleships. But the Union was losing the battle. *Intrepid* and its brethren pounded away, moving relentlessly forward. She wanted to believe the fleet was on the verge of victory, but something was nagging at her. As bloody a fight as it had been, one thought kept slipping into her mind.

It's been too easy.

That sounded insane, she knew. But for two months the Confederation forces had fallen back everywhere, unable to stop the Union invasion at any point. Was it possible that, all of a sudden, they would stop the enemy cold? Here? Now? She desperately wanted to believe it...but she didn't.

She watched the scanner, her eyes following as clusters of fighters and bombers zipped across the screen. The Confederation attack squadrons were moving forward, making attack runs at the Union ships, adding more destruction to that inflicted by the primary batteries of the fleet. The Union bombers were conducting their own assaults, but their squadrons had been savaged on the way back to their mother ships, and they had launched the second time at half strength, even less. And the Confederation CSPs were obliterating the approaching bombers, blowing whole squadrons away before the attackers could loose so much as a single torpedo.

That wasn't the case all along the line, of course. Two Union squadrons had broken through and closed on *Warspite*, planting half a dozen torpedoes into the damaged battleship's midsection. The old vessel was still there, but from what Eaton's scanners could tell her, she was a lifeless hulk, silent, drifting.

"Entering firing range for secondaries, Captain."

"Open fire, all guns."

"Yes, Captain." Then, into his comm unit: "All batteries, open fire."

Intrepid lurched again as another enemy blast struck her amidships.

"Reactor A down to fifty percent, Captain."

"Increase Reactor B to one hundred ten percent."

"Yes, Captain." Then: "Captain, Engineer Merton reports primary batteries back online."

Yes!

"Reroute power to primaries. Put secondaries on rolling barrages, allocating power as quickly as possible between primary recharges. And tell Commander Merton to squeeze every bit of power he can from Reactor A."

"Yes, Captain."

Intrepid, like virtually any vessel, had more systems than she could power simultaneously. With her engines shut down, even her damaged reactors could easily power the secondary weapons system. But charging the particle accelerators took almost every watt the straining power plants could produce.

Eaton looked straight ahead, even as the bridge lights dimmed. She could see the unused workstations going blank, *Intrepid*'s AI conserving power any way possible.

She sat, silently, waiting as the main guns charged. Time passed slowly, glacially, each second stretching out interminably. Then, finally, she heard the words she'd been waiting to hear.

"Primaries ready to fire, Captain."

"Lock on to target A, Commander." A pause, no more than a second. Then: "Fire."

The bridge went completely dark for an instant, not a spark of light save the red glow from the battlestations lamps. The primaries made a sound, a hideous shriek that reverberated throughout the ship, far louder than normal.

Probably the result of Merton's makeshift repairs.

Eaton looked down at the scanner, waiting to see if her gunners' accuracy had been true. Just as she saw the report, she heard Nordstrom's voice, his discipline slipping for an instant in the face of his obvious joy.

"Direct hit, Captain! Both guns."

Eaton felt a wave of excitement herself, and it grew as she watched the damage assessments flow in. It was raw data at first, energy readings, long-range optical scans. But then the AI finished crunching the numbers, and it posted the report she'd longed to see.

The enemy vessel had been torn apart, split in two by the deadly shots and the internal explosions that followed. One of

Intrepid's foes was gone, nothing but floating wreckage remaining where a Union battleship had been.

"Well done...all of you." She reached down to her comm controls and opened the shipwide line. "Congratulations, everyone. That's one down, but stay focused. We're still faced off against another battleship. Let's show them what we can do!"

Eaton was unorthodox in the way she communicated with her crew. She was prone to making shipwide announcements, and she was as selfless an officer as any had seen. She shared everything with her crew; glory, rewards, her gratitude for their tireless efforts.

"Okay, Commander...let's see about that other sh..." Her voice went silent, her eyes catching something on the long-range scanning display. It was a contact, a ship of some kind, coming in from the Copernika transwarp line. Behind the fleet.

It was smaller than a capital ship, she realized as she stared at the tiny dot.

Some kind of escort vessel...

For an instant she thought it might be the enemy, but then her scanners picked up the identification beacon. It was a Confederation ship.

But the feeling in the pit of her stomach remained, and somehow, she knew...something was very wrong.

Chapter Eight

**CFS Repulse
Arcturon System
Deep in the System Oort Cloud
308 AC**

"It's one of ours, Admiral. ID beacons transmitting...CFS *Stanton*. She's a *Wilson*-class light escort." Beltran's face was pressed against the scope at his station, reading the details as quickly as they came in. His voice changed, the tone moving from concerned to grave. "She appears to be badly damaged, sir."

"Send a message, Captain. Tell them to transmit a full report immediately."

"Sir, we're receiving a signal...I'll put it on your screen."

Winston looked down, watching as the lists of fleet stats vanished from his display, replaced by the image of a Confederation officer. His uniform was soiled and blackened with soot, and he looked like he was in pain. Winston could see at once the bridge behind him was in shambles.

"This is CFS *Stanton* to Confederation fleet command. Please respond. This is CFS *Stanton*..."

"Stanton, this is Admiral Winston. Report at once."

There was a brief delay, as Winston's response traveled to the new arrival, and then a signal returned. A look of partial relief came over the man's face. "Admiral Winston, thank goodness we got to you. I am Commander Jergen, commanding CFS *Stanton.*"

"Report, Commander." Winston regretted the curtness and impatience of his tone the instant he spoke, but he knew *Stanton*'s arrival was unlikely to herald good tidings.

"Admiral, Second Fleet was attacked at Ghallus." Jergen paused, wincing in pain. Winston realized the man was injured worse than he'd thought at first. "They outnumbered us, sir. We fought hard, sir…we really did. But there were just too many of them. Admiral Marionberg sent me to warn you."

"Warn us?"

"Yes, sir…the enemy is coming this way. They're in the Copernika system now, Admiral. Not far behind us."

Winston sat still, staring at the face on his screen. "In Copernika?" His stomach tightened. There couldn't be enemy forces in Copernika…it was impossible. "Where is Admiral Marionberg, Commander? Where is Second Fleet?" It was too much, and it was coming too quickly. First Fleet was facing the bulk of the enemy forces, he had been sure of that. Second Fleet was strong, twelve capital ships and almost thirty escorts…more than enough, he had thought, to cover his flank, especially with the main enemy force engaged in Arcturon.

"Second Fleet, it…" A burst of static drowned out Jergen's words.

"Repeat your transmission, Commander."

"Second Fleet…destroyed…"

Destroyed? The word hit Winston like a brick.

"Did you say destroyed, Commander?"

"Yes, sir. Eight capital ships gone. The others were fleeing, trying to escape."

"Admiral…" It was Beltran, and the urgency in his voice was clear. "We're picking up energy readings from the transwarp link, sir. Something is coming through."

Winston's eyes flashed toward the main display. "Zoom in on the Copernika transwarp point," he snapped to the ship's AI. The projection shifted, seeming almost to wiggle for a second.

Then it displayed a yellow circle, the link leading to the Copernika system nine lightyears away. The escort vessel was there too, a small blue dot, and closer to the transwarp link, three small red spheres. Enemy ships."

"The new arrivals are firing on Stanton, sir."

"Commander, you have bogeys on your tail. Can you accelerate toward the main fleet?"

"Negative, sir. We burned out our engines getting here ahead of the enemy. We don't have any effective thrust."

Winston could see tiny flashes in the display. Laser fire.

"Commander Beltran, who is closest to *Stanton*?"

"That would be *Starfire*, sir. But she is heavily engaged right now, and she's twenty minutes away at full thrust." The meaning in his tone was clear. *Stanton* didn't have twenty minutes.

Winston turned back to the com unit. "Commander, what happened to Admiral Marionberg?"

Jergen looked back at him from the screen and his expression answered Winston's question even before the words sunk in. "*Aspirant* was destroyed, sir. The admiral is dead." Jergen sat, staring at Winston through the com unit. A few seconds later there was an explosion behind him...and then the image vanished from the screen, replaced by a static pattern.

"*Stanton* has been destroyed, sir." Beltran's tone was grim, confirming what Winston already knew. The flag bridge was silent, the meaning of the past few minutes' events gradually sinking in to those present.

"Fleet order, Commander...the battle line will decelerate at 4g."

"Yes, sir."

"*Legion, Phalanx, Exeter, Constellation, Nova,* and *Resolution* will decelerate and come about, moving to protect the rear of the line."

"Yes, Admiral."

Winston looked down at his workstation's screen, his fingers moving across, turning the focus of the display to the battle line. As he did, *Repulse* shook hard, a hit...and a reminder his flagship was still in a desperate fight. He was questioning his order of a moment before, wondering if he should have ordered the fleet to accelerate rather than decelerate, to close and try to finish off the enemy line before whatever was going to emerge from the transwarp link arrived.

"We're picking up more energy surges, sir...ships transiting."

There was his answer. The enemy was already here in force.

He turned back to the display just as red icons started to appear, floating in the tank, moving forward into the system. He watched as the icons moved forward, unidentified as the seconds passed while scanner data flowed in. The AI crunched on it, and then small labels began to appear next to the vessels coming through, now six, with continued energy spikes signaling that more were on the way.

Winston read the small tags next to each icon. CS. Two small letters, the same near each small oval. Capital ships. All six of them.

Seven, Winston thought as he saw another symbol appear.

His eyes were fixed on the display as the AI's notation confirmed the seventh vessel was also a battleship. His mind was racing, trying to decide what to do. Second Fleet had been powerful enough to protect his flank, to beat back any peripheral force...he'd been sure of it.

How could the enemy have so many ships?

The reality of Caitlyn Marionberg's death was still sinking in. He'd known her for more than fifty years. She'd been another of Rance Barron's protégés.

And now she's dead.

His eyes were fixed on the display, watching the enemy ships stream in, even as he struggled to maintain control, to decide what to do.

Eight...Nine...

* * *

"Keep firing." Eaton's voice was calm, cold, as if she was issuing a routine command of no consequence instead of one to hold position in the battle line even as a massive enemy force was moving around behind the fleet.

"Yes, Captain."

Intrepid's commander stared at the display. She'd received the orders from fleet command to decelerate along with the rest of the line. But that wasn't going to be enough to escape the trap that was clearly developing…and there had been no word since from Admiral Winston. Enemy battleships had continued to pour into the system from Copernika, twenty-one so far. The new arrivals were moving in from the transwarp link, accelerating to cut the fleet off from escape.

What is the admiral waiting for? We have to retreat…

She hated even thinking that. The battle had been going well, and even with the pain from their losses, the hint of possible victory had been like manna to the battered Confeds. But the situation had changed abruptly. Eaton was a realist, and she understood almost at once that the fight at Arcturon was a lost cause. The enemy just had too many ships, and if they managed to get the flanking force completely in position, the entire fleet was in jeopardy.

Second fleet…gone. My God, the Confederation is in real trouble. If we lose all of First Fleet too…

She tried to shake the thoughts from her head. It was Winston's place to direct the fleet, and hers to follow his orders and command *Intrepid*. Her vessel had finished off one of the enemy ships it had faced, and only one other remained in range. She didn't have the authority to order a retreat, and she wasn't about to break ranks and flee without Admiral Winston's order. But she *could* clear out the space around her, buy some time for her ship if and when the orders to bug out came. All she had to do was destroy one more enemy vessel.

"Increase power to secondaries to one hundred ten percent." She hoped her tone sounded more like confidence than the desperation she was truly feeling. Overpowering guns was a dangerous tactic, but one that could make the difference in a desperate fight. The enemy ship opposing *Intrepid* had already been damaged when it closed, and she was sure if she kept hammering away at it, she could finish it off. Before *Intrepid* was too badly battered herself to stay in the fight.

"Yes, Captain." Nordstrom leaned forward over his workstation, staring down at the screens. "Captain, we've got friendly fighters inbound. Looks like part of our Longsword squadron and some from other strike groups."

Eaton just nodded. The fighter battles had raged all along the line, and she knew the squadron structures were hopelessly intermixed. She had the urge to order all the fighters near *Intrepid* to land, whether they were hers or not. If she waited, and the order to retreat came through, there wouldn't be enough time to get them all in. The idea of abandoning her pilots—*any* Confederation pilots—was horrifying to her, but she knew the priorities as well as anyone else, and the fighter jocks knew them best of all. Capital ships were the primary concern. If it came to a choice of saving the battle line or recovering the fighters, she knew Admiral Winston would have no choice. It made sense, in a mathematical or logical sort of way. After all, little purpose would be served by landing fighters only to have the pilots die when the mothership itself was destroyed. But there were things that made up the essence of a man or woman besides logic, and she dreaded the order to leave her squadrons behind and flee.

She looked down at her scanners. There were three other ships near *Intrepid*, two escort cruisers and a fast scoutship. One of the escorts was hers, *Astara*. Commander Jacarde was already firing alongside Intrepid, pounding away at the enemy vessel engaged with her ship. The other—*Cambria*—was just out of range. She'd been part of *Dominion*'s group, but the big battleship had been destroyed, and the escort had just been following the general battle line forward.

"Commander, get me a channel to *Cambria*."

"Yes, Admiral. On your line."

Eaton glanced down at the stats displayed on her screen. *Commander Eliot Strand.*

"Commander Strand," she snapped into her comm unit, without hesitation or preamble, "I need you to close on the enemy vessel at 132.010.200 and open fire with everything you've got." *Cambria* wasn't attached to *Intrepid*, and Eaton's command authority over the vessel was questionable at best. But she did outrank Strand, and capital ship captains were generally lofty figures in the Confederation navy, revered and respected almost without exception.

"Understood, Captain Eaton. We're on the way."

"Thank you, Commander. Eaton out." She cut the connection, turning her attention back to the scanner reports on the enemy vessel. It was big, even for a battleship, over four million tons. Her fire had definitely caused a lot of damage, but the massive vessel was still there, firing back with its remaining guns. She could take the enemy…she was pretty sure about that, at least as long as no other enemy ships moved into range. But *Intrepid* would take a real pounding by the time the fight was through, and she had no idea what condition her ship would be in when the deadly duel was over.

If the engines were down, or even damaged enough to hinder a retreat, it could be a death sentence for her crew. Surrender wasn't an option, at least not one she'd consider against an enemy like the Union. She knew enough about Sector Nine and its techniques to be certain of one thing. She'd see her people blasted to atoms in a desperate fight to the finish before she'd risk allowing them to be consigned to the torture chambers and interrogation rooms of the enemy intelligence service.

"Captain, we've got another wave of fighters inbound. Signal incoming."

"Switch to my comm."

"Yes, Captain."

"This is Captain Eaton of *Intrepid*."

"Captain, this is Lieutenant Timmons, callsign Warrior, commanding Red Eagles squadron. I've got the Direwolves with me too. We hail from *Repulse*, Captain, but we find ourselves far away from our mothership. We're forlorn and looking for a target. We were wondering if you'd like an assist with that big bastard out there."

Eaton held back a smile. Exchanges with fighter pilots were always refreshing. They were so utterly devoid of the stilted language and restrained demeanor that so often characterized ship-to-ship exchanges. And she'd heard of the famous Warrior before. There were few in the fleet who hadn't.

"Warrior, you and your people are most welcome. By all means, we would greatly appreciate your help in taking down that…big bastard, as you put it."

"Roger that, Captain. We're inbound hot."

Chapter Nine

"I will not order a retreat, Commodore Malcolm, not until the entire force can withdraw." Winston was sitting in his chair, the dense, chemical-tainted air pouring from *Repulse*'s damaged ventilation system stinging his eyes and scratching at his throat. His flagship was battered, but she was still in the fight.

"That's not going to happen, Admiral. We're too far from the transit point on this flank. But you can still save most of the battle line if you move now."

"At what cost? Leaving you behind? And *Intrepid*, *Constitution*, *Valorous*? Not to mention a huge chunk of our fighter squadrons? No, never."

Winston had looked at the display half a dozen times. The situation hadn't changed. The enemy force coming from the Copernika transwarp link was moving to cut off the fleet's escape route. They'd already trapped Malcolm's task force, and it wouldn't be long before every ship Winston had would be bracketed, attacked from the front and rear.

"Admiral, there's no choice. You *have* to pull back now. Save the fleet…or at least what's left of it. If you don't go now, no one will escape." Malcolm's voice was raw, and Winston could hear the sounds of explosions and screaming in the background. *Renown* was in bad shape, and he knew that nothing he did could save Malcolm's stricken battleship or the rest of its group. But he shook his head, grimly refusing to accept what his intellect told him was fact.

"Commodore…" Winston searched for words, but nothing came. He couldn't abandon all those ships, leave them behind to almost certain destruction. He just couldn't.

But what else can I do?

"Don't let us die for nothing, sir. If the whole fleet is lost here, the Confederation is doomed. You have to go, sir. You have to…please…"

"No, Commodore." Winston's answer was instinctive, almost involuntary. The idea of running and leaving behind a large part of his fleet was so utterly alien to his way of thinking, he could hardly imagine giving the orders. But Malcolm was right. It wasn't about the ships caught in the enemy's trap. It wasn't even about the whole fleet. The Confederation itself was at stake here. At least if he ordered the retreat now, some of the battle line would survive to fight again. If he stayed…

He sighed hard. "Very well, Commodore," he said gravely. He pushed back against the despair he felt closing in on him. He'd known Bill Malcolm since the two had been junior officers. He'd been at Malcolm's wedding, watched his friend's children—and then grandchildren—grow up alongside his own. They'd been friends for half a century, brothers in arms.

And now I'm leaving him here. To die.

"Bill," he added, struggling to keep his voice from breaking down. "I'm sorry…"

"None of that, Art. We've been friends for a long time, but we've been officers for longer even than that. You know your duty. And I know mine." The officer's voice paused. Then he added, his voice barely a whisper. "Art…tell Allison I love her."

The words slammed into Winston, almost costing him his hard-fought control. "I will, Bill," he barely managed to reply.

Then he took a deep breath. "Very well, Commodore Malcolm, my respect and admiration to you and to those who serve you… and Godspeed."

"Go with fortune, Admiral. Save the fleet. We'll hold here as long as we can." Then, a few seconds later: "Never give up, my friend. Fight to the last."

The transmission went silent as Malcolm cut the line. Winston sat for a few seconds, silent, fighting the aching sadness inside him. Then he turned toward Beltran, and he saw the pain in his aide's eyes. "We have no choice, Captain," he said softly. "The fleet will retreat through the Gamalon transwarp link." He choked on the words, but he managed to force them out. He knew he was pronouncing a death sentence on Commodore Malcolm, and on the thousands of spacers serving on the trapped ships. And the fighters. He guessed that maybe half of his fighters would be able to land in time. He would be leaving the others behind, dozens of squadrons in total, from every surviving ship in the fleet. But there was no alternative.

Beltran hesitated, looking as though he was going to argue. But he just stared across the bridge toward the admiral's chair.

"Captain Beltran, execute fleet retirement order at once." Winston repeated the order more sternly. He had all the same doubts and self-recriminations any of his crew were feeling, more even, but right now there was no time for delay. Abandoning so many ships to their doom was nightmare enough, but every moment they delayed would only add to the number of vessels stuck in the Union trap.

"Yes, Admiral." There was sorrow in Beltran's voice, but no recrimination. That tugged at Winston even harder. He felt like a coward for running, and the understanding of his aide, of all of his officers, just cut at him all the more deeply.

He waited for the vessels of the fleet to confirm the order. At least the ships that had a chance of running. He suspected the command was not being received well. It went against the grain of Confederation naval personnel to abandon their brethren. Winston understood. He even felt the same way. But it wasn't about pride or loyalty or camaraderie now. It was about saving the Confederation.

"All ships acknowledge, sir."

Winston looked around the flag bridge, imagining for a moment what was going through the minds of his staff, what they would think of him, even as he was saving many of their lives. He shook his head slightly, and closed his eyes for an instant. Then he turned and looked over toward his aide.

"Commander Beltran...execute fleet order. All units are to accelerate toward the Gamalon transit link at maximum thrust."

"Yes, sir. Transmitting fleet order now."

* * *

"Let's go, Eagles...one more strafing run on that thing." Timmons leaned back in his cockpit and reached out for the throttle. His eyes moved over to his fuel gauge, but he didn't look. He didn't want to know. Fuel status was important for fighters that had someplace to land. And Timmons had watched on the scanner as his base ship blasted away at full thrust. *Repulse* might escape from the pursuing enemy or she might not...but there was no way Timmons and his people could catch her. They were dead men and women, all except for the formality of a laser blast or slow suffocation to complete the process. And until that happened, he was going to make the enemy pay.

He'd felt a touch of resentment as he'd first watched the flagship retreating, leaving his squadron behind. Rationally, he knew there'd been no alternative, that if the battle line hadn't withdrawn, every Confederation battleship would have been caught and destroyed.

Instead of close to a dozen already destroyed, or too bracketed to escape...and thirty fighter squadrons, give or take...

"Form up on me...*Intrepid*'s been hitting that ship hard, but she could use our help." He brought his fighter around, heading right for the enemy battleship. His birds were outfitted as interceptors, which meant their laser batteries weren't hot enough to *really* hurt a capital ship, at least not one in prime condition. But the enemy vessel was wounded, and she had great gaping holes in her hull. A well-placed shot could do some damage, and every bit helped.

He looked down at the scanner. He was less than twenty thousand kilometers out, well within firing range. But he was going to go right down the throat of the enemy vessel, where he could do some real good.

"Stay in tight…we're going close. Pick your spots, and make these shots count."

They might be your last.

He watched as the dot grew larger on his targeting display. The range was under fifteen thousand kilometers now, and he was still closing fast. He punched at the controls under the display, and the image expanded, the large red oval almost filling the screen. There were light spots, areas where his scanners were picking up higher energy readings leaking into space. Hull breaches.

He tapped the thruster, and he pulled back, engaging his engines. Almost 10g of force slammed into him, as the new thrust altered his vector, bringing him directly toward the spot he'd chosen as a target. He released the throttle, and the pressure vanished, replaced by weightlessness. His fighter was directly on target, less than ten thousand kilometers away.

Close enough to smell their bad breath…

Still, he didn't fire. And none of his Red Eagles did either. They were locked on him, less than five hundred meters between each fighter. He had ten of his original fifteen birds left, all inbound. And Chuck Aires and the Direwolves were right behind, their own attack run less than five thousand kilometers behind his.

Eight thousand kilometers. His screen was almost entirely filled with the image of the enemy ship.

He'd have gone closer, perhaps even to three or four thousand, but that was too much to ask from his squadron. They were good pilots, but he knew none of them could match his own abilities…and he was just as sure every one of them would try if he led them in.

He squeezed the firing stud slowly, steadily, and then he

heard the loud whine, his laser cannons blasting away. He held his finger down, firing three, four, five bursts before he slammed the throttle back and to the side hard, 12g of thrust throwing him painfully back into his chair. He gasped for air and pushed back against the pain as his ship's vector changed from the collision course it had been on and cleared the enemy ship.

He released the throttle and sucked in a deep breath…and then he howled with excitement. He'd hit the son of a bitch, there was no question about that. And he'd put his laser blasts right through a huge gash in the battleship's hull. There was no way to know exactly how much damage he'd done, but his scanners were reporting great plumes of superheated vapor blasting out of the hull breach.

His squadron repeated his success, ship after ship targeting their lasers at the weakest points, and for the most part, hitting. The small lasers on his interceptors were a poor substitute for the bombers' plasma torpedoes, but enough of them could make the difference. He was still celebrating what looked like a particularly well-placed shot from one of his birds when another of his fighters just vanished.

The enemy ship was badly damaged, many of its defensive turrets silenced. But not all of them, and damaged or not, the Union ship had claimed another of his people.

Jute, he thought grimly, as the AI displayed the ID data for the destroyed ship. Annie Jute had been with him since before the war, another of his original roster lost to the endless fighting.

A loud buzz shook him from his thoughts. His fuel alarm. He was down to less than five percent. But he had nowhere to go, no place to lead his people. His eyes froze on the wide area displays, on the singe blue oval even remotely close enough for his people to reach with their remaining fuel. *Intrepid*.

There were going to be more fighters along the line than launch platforms, he could see that immediately. The retreating battleships had recovered their squadrons that were close enough, but the fleet's fighter wings were spread out all over the place. A lot of pilots were going to end up stranded in depleted ships, waiting to see if the enemy bothered to hunt them down or just waited and let them die slowly as emergency life support waned. But his people were close to *Intrepid*, and he suspected the big battleship had lost a good number of its own birds. With any luck, they'd have room for the Red Eagles. And the Direwolves too.

"Mustang, this is Warrior." His friend's squadron was still completing its attack run against the enemy battleship. "Fuel status is critical…we're going to head toward *Intrepid*, see if they can take in a few strays."

"Roger that, Warrior. We'll be right on your tail, old friend, so put in a good word for us too."

"You got it, Mustang."

* * *

"Keep pounding away…everything we've got. I want every watt of power we don't need for vital functions routed right to the lasers." Eaton was watching the enemy ship in the display. There was a flood of numbers on her screen, scanning reports, AI assessments, transmissions from the probes *Intrepid* had launched to monitor its adversary. But none of that mattered to her right now. She knew the enemy ship was going to go any second. She felt it in her gut. And that was something that rarely failed her.

"Yes, Captain. Commander Merton reports reactor B is nearly critical. Output down to thirty percent, and he might have to shut down even that production."

"Not until that enemy ship is gone, Commander. I don't care if Commander Merton needs to patch that system together with spit and glue, but he is not to cut power while we are still engaged."

"Yes, Admiral."

Eaton knew it wasn't that simple. Fusion reactors weren't like the old jalopies her brothers had fixed up back on Corellia. Landspeeders were complex machines, certainly, but they didn't have ten million degree reactions producing gigawatts of power, miniature suns constrained by nothing more than a magnetic bottle.

A magnetic bottle that can get very fragile when it's been beaten up badly enough...

She knew any malfunction, a nanosecond's blink in the coverage of the magnetic field, and that would be the end of *Intrepid*. Orders like she'd just given were dangerous, though not as wildly reckless, perhaps, as they seemed. After all, *Intrepid*'s AI would automatically scrag the reactor if it detected an imminent failure. That wasn't a perfect system, as the vessels that had already disappeared in their own unleashed nuclear fury attested, but it was something. Besides, how much chance did her people have of surviving the fight anyway?

She could still hear the word in her head, Admiral Winston's transmission to her vessels, explaining why he'd made the decision he had...and urging the vessels that were already cut off to fight to the end, to buy time for their comrades to escape.

That must be a hard thing to ask, to say, "sorry we have to leave you behind to die...but before you do, could you kill enough to the enemy to cover our escape?"

She scolded herself for her bitterness. Whatever Arthur Winston was, he wasn't a coward. She was sure the old admiral would have vastly preferred death in battle to the duty fate had assigned him. And Commodore Malcolm's own words were also fresh in her mind. Malcolm had taken command of the rearguard, and he'd also urged them all not to give up. To keep up the fight.

He could have saved himself the trouble, at least as far as *Intrepid* was concerned. If Sara Eaton and her people were going to die, she'd be damned if they were going to do it any way but fighting to the finish, whether some flag officer ordered it or not.

"Captain, we're getting scanner readings from the enemy vessel. Thrust zero. Energy output zero." Nordstrom turned, and in spite of the gloom hanging over *Intrepid*'s bridge, he smiled. I think it's dead."

Eaton nodded, staring at her own screen as the incoming data scrolled by. "I think you're right, Commander." Then, looking out at her bridge crew. "Well done, all of you." She slapped her hand down on the comm unit, switching to the intraship channel. "All crew members, this is the captain. The enemy vessel appears to have been destroyed. That is the second capital ship you have taken down today. I can't express the pride and gratitude that I feel to serve with a crew like you." Her praise was heartfelt, but her tone was restrained, weighed down by the fact that she knew her people were likely to die here in this system, that their "victory" would be short-lived indeed.

But it's better than no victory…

She shut down the comm and turned her eyes to the display, looking for another target. Her ship might be doomed, but it wasn't dead yet. And as long as she had a gun hot enough to heat up a cup of tea, she was still in the fight.

"Captain, we've got some of our fighters returning, requesting clearance to land."

She hesitated. It would take time to recover her squadrons now, especially with alpha bay damaged and no more than fifty percent operational. Her flight crews *might* get them refit and turned around in time to get back into the fight. But she bristled at the delay in moving against the enemy. Her destruction of the two ships she'd faced left *Intrepid* in a quiet area of the battle, at the extreme end of the line. She considered leaving the fighters behind…they were all going to die anyway. But it wasn't in her to do that. There were different ways to die, and she'd be damned if she was going to have her pilots' last thoughts be that she had abandoned them.

"Very well, Commander. Commence recovery operations at once…and tell them I want those birds back onboard as quickly as possible."

"Understood." Then, a few seconds later: "We're getting transmissions from other squadrons, Captain, fighters from some of the ships that bugged out. All requesting permission to land. Many of them are reporting critical fuel statuses."

Eaton sighed softly to herself. *Intrepid* was damaged, and the truth was, she had no idea how many fighters her wounded bays could take in. There was some room, she was sure of that, if only because of the losses her own squadrons had taken. As anxious as she was to rejoin the fight, she knew what she had to do. Those pilots out there were her comrades...and those last two squadrons that had shown up had damned sure done their part to take down the last enemy battleship.

"Advise landing control they are to accommodate every fighter they possibly can."

"Yes, Captain."

"I mean it, Commander. Every bird they can take. Put them anywhere, but we're not leaving those pilots out there, out of fuel and with no place to land."

Chapter Ten

Landing Bay Beta
CFS Repulse
Arcturon System
On the Extreme Edge of the Confederation Line
308 AC

"Red Eagle One, you are cleared to land."

"Roger that, *Intrepid* control." *And it's about time…*

His fuel status was beyond critical. By the time he'd reversed the velocity that had taken him toward his attack on the enemy ship—a course something close to diametrically away from *Intrepid*—he'd burned just about the last of his fuel. His gauges read dead empty, but Timmons knew his way around his fighter well enough to realize there was a bit of unmeasured reserve built in. He didn't know if that had been by design—the efforts of those who built the Lightning-class strikefighters to account for the insanity of so many of those who flew the birds—or if it was a deficiency in the measurement systems, but he was damned grateful for it today.

Timmons knew he had no one to blame but himself for his plight. He'd been the lowest on fuel, courtesy of his penchant for wild and aggressive maneuvering, but he'd still insisted the rest of his Eagles land first. Timmons was a hotshot pilot—

crazy, some people said—but he never let that interfere with his command of the squadron. He'd watched over his people, trained them, led them in two dozen fights…and now he'd be damned if he'd land before he knew every one of them was safe onboard.

They were all docked now, and Aire's Direwolves were coming up. It was time.

He tapped his throttle forward, just a touch of thrust. Normally, he'd have approached at a greater velocity, but he just didn't have the fuel. If he burned through more than half of what he had accelerating, he wouldn't have enough left to slow down, and he'd crash into the bay. He watched the huge hulk of *Intrepid* growing in front of him, the range dropping rapidly. Five kilometers, four, three. He was coming up on the battleship's starboard side, toward its beta bay. His vector looked good. No…he was off, just a bit. He tapped the throttle, just a tiny burst of thrust, and then, a few seconds later another, partially reversing the first.

"You look good Red Eagle One. Cleared for final approach. Reduce velocity to three meters per second."

"Roger that, *Intrepid*. Reducing thrust now." He hit the positioning jets, spinning his fighter around, positioning the engines to push against his vector. Then he pulled back slightly, engaging them again. There was a burst of thrust, enough to slow him down to twenty meters per second. Then fifteen. Ten.

Then his engines cut out, the last vapors of fuel to sustain them gone. His eyes dropped to his display, fixing on the velocity readings. Six point two meters per second…far too fast for a safe landing.

"*Intrepid*, I'm out of fuel, and I'm coming in hot." He knew procedure. A pilot unsure he could land safely was supposed to pull up, fly by the mothership and hopefully come around and make another pass. But Timmons had no thrust. None at all. And he doubted his positioning jets were enough to push him clear of *Intrepid*. If he tried it, he was as likely to smash into the great ship's hull as to clear it.

"Roger that, Red Eagles One. Stay on track. Reduce velocity

as much as possible with positioning jets."

"Way ahead of you, *Intrepid*." Timmons already had his hands on the controls for the positioning units. The tiny jets ejected compressed gasses to spin the tiny fighter around. The thrust they produced was negligible, far from enough to materially reduce even his ship's miniscule velocity. But every little bit helped.

Timmons clutched the throttle, by habit as much as anything since his engines were dead. He zipped past *Intrepid*'s bow, moving alongside the battleship, the looming gray hull no more than twenty meters from his fighter as it passed by in a blur. He hated the feeling of helplessness. All he could do was sit there, and hope the base ship's safeties could catch his fighter and slow it before he crashed into a bulkhead.

His looked ahead as the opening of the bay loomed before him, a great entryway twenty meters high by thirty wide. Beyond, he could see the cavernous bay, the emergency vehicles moving into place, around the chunks of debris and collapsed sections of interior hull…damage from the battle. His view was slightly distorted by a vague rippling effect, accented by occasional blue currents, almost like tiny bolts of lightning. The energy field kept the bay insulated from the vacuum of space, holding in air and pressure. There were actually several consecutive levels to the screen. The first would drop, only for the instant it took his ship to pass through. Then it would reactivate, and the tiny area between two sections would partially repressurize before the next one dropped. His fighter would pass through four layers in total, transitioning to the full pressure environment of the bay. Then he would be in.

He looked forward, staring at the seemingly random patterns of crackling blue light. Not just blue, but an absolutely perfect, electric blue. He'd seen it hundreds of times, but only now he noticed how beautiful it was. Normally he was concerned with landing his fighter, but this time he was just a passenger with nothing to do, waiting to see if the projectile he rode would slow quickly enough to make a rough, but survivable landing… or if he would crash into the bay and die, not in combat as he'd always imagined, but smashed to goo when his ship slammed into some heavy structural support.

His fighter zipped through the screens, and as always, he was unable to discern the four distinct levels. Even to his honed senses, his fighter appeared to move from space to the inside of the bay in an instant.

The fighter shook as the grapples caught against his wings, slowing the velocity before they detached from their moorings. The flight crew had managed to deploy three waves of the soft but tough cables, and by the time his fighter passed through the third, he was moving at less than two meters per second. Still a hard landing, but now a survivable one.

His ship hit the deck hard, and one of the landing gears snapped. The fighter twisted, skidding to the side and impacting with one of the heavy bulkheads. Timmons was thrown forward, and the harness strapping him in dug deeply into his chest. He felt a sharp pain, and he knew he'd broken at least one rib. His leg had twisted painfully as well, but he didn't think it was seriously injured. And despite the near-agony in his upper body, there was one overwhelming thought in his head. He wasn't moving. His fighter had come to a stop.

He had made it.

For whatever good it will do…

* * *

"That's an order, Captain. *Intrepid* is to break off and make a run for it. If you go now, the confusion of the fighting might buy you the time you need to find someplace to hide. That's a huge dust cloud…just maybe it's big enough to conceal a battleship, even from a serious search effort." Eaton was struck by the calm tone of Commodore Malcolm's voice, the control, despite the fact that the commander of the fleet's rearguard was facing his own imminent and almost certain death.

"Commodore, please…we can close to join the fight. We can be there in less than ten minutes." *Intrepid* was on the far end of the line, and for the moment, out of the fight. The Union flanking forces were behind her, cutting her off from the main fleet's retreat, but they were still out of range. She was over a million kilometers from the nearest friend or enemy, save for the three small escort ships clustered around her.

"Don't be an ass, Captain. I appreciate your loyalty, but there's no time for such displays. The Confederation is at war. If you join the fight here, *Intrepid* will be destroyed, along with the rest of us. If you retreat now, just *maybe* you'll get lucky and manage to disappear into that cloud…and then the Confederation will have one more capital ship still in the fight."

Eaton knew Malcolm was right. *Intrepid* had a lot of fight left in her, but by the time she could get back into the battle, half the ships of the rearguard would already be gone, and the rest would be swarmed by half a dozen enemies each. Still, the idea of running while Malcolm and his remaining battleships were still in the fight was too much for her.

"Go, Captain," Malcom added, after a few seconds of silence. "I know it's difficult, and I know you'd rather rush to our aid in some kind of heroic display, but there's nothing you can do to affect the outcome here. *Intrepid* will be destroyed, and you won't save one ship or one spacer for her loss. It won't be a legendary struggle. It will be waste. Utter waste. And the Confederation can't afford to lose another ship, not for no reason. Find a way to save your ship…and hope if its destruction comes it will be to accomplish something, to help us win this war."

Eaton struggled to speak, her dry throat defying her attempts to make the words come forth. She realized Malcolm was right, though she also knew her chances at escape were poor. But some chance was better than none. Finally, she managed to say, "Yes, Commodore."

"Good. Go now, Captain. There is no time to waste."

"Yes, sir. Commodore, it has been an honor to serve with you."

"Thank you, Captain. Now, go before…" His voice was cut off, replaced by static. Eaton's eyes darted to the display, but she knew in her gut what had happened even before the scanners confirmed it. *Renown* was gone. Commodore William Malcolm was dead.

She sat silently for a moment, trying to absorb what had happened. She wanted to leave the bridge, to go somewhere—anywhere—she could be alone and just lose it, let the tears come. But that wasn't an option. She had a job to do. There was no time to mourn Malcolm or to properly honor him, not now. Her memorial would be a simple one. She would do everything in her power to carry out his final order to her.

"Commander Nordstrom, set a course toward the large dust cloud. Advise engineering I want maximum possible thrust."

Nordstrom hesitated. Then he turned toward Eaton's station. "Captain, that will take us away from the battle..."

"Yes, Commander, it will."

"But..."

"No buts, Commander Nordstrom. It was Commodore Malcolm's order...and it is mine to you. Do you have a problem following it?" Her voice was cold, not so much out of anger at her exec but because she didn't have time to discuss it with him.

"No, Captain." The officer paused briefly, perhaps a second or two. Then he turned and began working on the course plot. When he was done, he said, "Ready to execute, Captain." There was a coolness in his own voice now, and Eaton saw that Nordstrom was still looking at his console, not turning to face her as he usually did by habit.

"Advise *Cambria*, *Astara*, and *Condor* to do the same. All ships are to engage as soon as they are ready."

"Yes, Captain."

She sat stone still in her chair. She hated what she was doing as much as her exec clearly did, though her rational mind knew Malcolm had been right. Leading her people into the fight—into certain death—would have accomplished exactly nothing. Maybe, just maybe, she could sneak out of the battle, lose *Intrepid* somewhere in the dust cloud. The enemy scanners would have trouble finding her in there, and right now the closest Union vessels were heavily engaged finishing off the trapped rearguard.

Our comrades' deaths will be our cover...

"All three escorts report ready, Captain."

She shook her head, almost imperceptibly. She'd already ordered Nordstrom to execute the order as soon as the other ships were prepared, and she knew her first officer was a fastidious man, one who'd almost certainly understood that.

He's going to make me say it again. Hoping I'll change my mind…

She *wanted* to reverse her command. Desperately. But she couldn't. If she'd been choosing only for herself, she would have plunged into the combat, seeking a glorious end. But she was responsible for *Intrepid*'s crew, plus those aboard the three escorts.

And all those pilots we rescued…

Intrepid's damaged bays were packed full of fighters, almost twice as many as her standard complement. Many of them were damaged—and others would have to be jettisoned to clear out the bay so it could function—but every one of the pilots had survived. Only twenty of her own people had made it back, but she'd collected eighty-three pilots from other ships of the fleet, men and women who would have faced certain death without her efforts. She wanted to feel good about that, but it seemed insignificant in the context of the death and destruction all around her.

She had her orders, even if the man who'd given them to her was dead. And she would carry them out, even if she hated herself for it. Even if her entire crew hated her for it.

"Commander…all ships are to engage maximum thrust immediately."

Chapter Eleven

400,000 Kilometers from CFS Dauntless
Corpus System
En Route to Arcturon
308 AC

"All right, Blues, keep it tight...and make sure those lasers are set to one-quarter percent power. This is a wargame, not a battle." The reminder was the kind of thing Jake Stockton hadn't had to say to his Blues in a long time. But half his veterans were gone, lost in the fighting at Santis, and the pilots in their places had spent their careers, such that they were, running routine patrols of the Archellia system. The toughest opponent any of them had ever run into was a freighter trying to sneak past the customs boats, and the last thing he wanted to see was some fool accidentally blasting one of his comrades with full-power lasers.

"Yellows, stay focused. And check your own lasers too. Remember, you've got a bunch of bombers right behind you, heading for *Dauntless*. Your job is to keep the Blues from blowing your strike force to bits. These guys are protecting their ship, the only place in the system they can land...so as much as they'd love to chase you all around and rack up kills, they'll blow past you if you let them. It's the bombers that threaten *Dauntless*, and they know that."

Well, some of them know that. Hopefully all of them will after this…

Stockton angled his thruster, bringing his ship around to a spot between the two converging forces. He had been *Dauntless*'s Blue leader for over a year now, but he'd set that hat aside for the moment and named one of his veterans as acting squadron commander. He was a teacher now, and an arbiter…roles he knew he was comically unsuited to perform. But he also realized these garrison pilots needed some hard lessons, and fast. Or he'd get to watch them all die when *Dauntless* reached the front. So, suited for the job or not, he was determined to teach them something.

He tapped his comm unit, flipping off the Blue channel and leaving the Yellow open. "All right, Yellows, you see the formation the Blues are in. Remember, you're the attackers. Your one advantage is initiative. The Blues are glued to *Dauntless*, they have to stay positioned to defend. But you can approach from any angle. Just remember, you have to coordinate with the bombers behind you, and the birds fitted out for anti-ship strikes are slower and less maneuverable." There were no real bombers, not right now, at least. Just a hypothetical wave of them behind the Yellows' protective umbrella.

"There are a few ways you can go. Start off by testing your enemy. Change your course and see if they react to you, or if they stay focused on the bombers. Remember, your goal isn't killing enemy interceptors. It's getting that strike in so it can do maximum damage to the mothership. Kills are all well and good, but nothing more than a means to an end here. So, if you can get those fighters to follow you away from the bombers, that's getting your job done before you fire a…"

"Lieutenant?"

"Yes, Ensign?" Stockton was annoyed at the interruption, but he was also impressed than one of the garrison pilots had the guts to do it.

"Sir, I'm sorry, but I'm picking something up on my scanner." The pilot was silent for a few seconds. Then he said, "I think it's coming from the transwarp link, sir. The one to Arcturon."

Stockton's eyes darted down to his own display. Nothing.

"Transmit your readings to me, Ensign."

"Yes, sir."

It took a few extra seconds for the data to come in. Stockton hadn't expected the ensign to be as quick on his controls as his veterans, but he was still seething with impatience when his display finally lit up with symbols and figures.

The kid was right...

There *was* something going on at the transwarp point.

Maybe that's the courier ship that's supposed to meet us.

It made sense, but something felt wrong. The courier was supposed to be in Corpus waiting for *Dauntless*, not arriving after the battleship had entered the system.

"Talon, you're with me. Cover my wing. Blue and Yellow squadrons, return to *Dauntless*. Now."

"Roger that, Raptor." Corinne "Talon" Steele was one of his oldest veterans.

Maybe the courier was just running behind...

Arcturon was a Confederation system, so the ship coming through the transit point was likely friendly, even if it wasn't the missing courier. But Stockton's instincts were on fire. Whatever was out there, he had to check it out, and he didn't want to have to worry about a bunch of rookie pilots who didn't have a single live missile and who'd burned half their fuel running wargame exercises.

He pulled back on the throttle, kicking in his thrusters. After a few seconds, his own scanners began to pick up the readings. The data was sparse at this range, just vague energy readings indicating a transit. He held his thrust, accelerating toward the transit point. His eye darted to his readouts. His fuel status wasn't great, certainly not what he wanted for a scouting mission halfway across the system. But he had the fuel to get close enough for decent scanner readings, and that was his focus now.

He glanced down at his display to confirm that the others were obeying his order to return to base. His mind told him logically the contact had to be the expected courier vessel, but his gut was screaming something different. His instincts had served him well in combat, and he wasn't about to ignore them, however unlikely their alarm.

He cut his thrust, breathing deeply as the crushing pressure disappeared. He would have liked to get his velocity a little higher, but he didn't have the fuel for that. Not if he wanted to be able to decelerate and turn back toward *Dauntless*.

He watched his scanners as he approached the transwarp point. He passed close by planet four, a cold rocky world, possibly inhabited by a few tramp miners, but of no other value. The whole Corpus system, including the more inhabited third planet, was nothing to get excited about. Its main value was that it lay along one of the two routes to the Rim.

Not that the Rim is any compelling destination...

Stockton knew the Rim as well as he cared to...whether it was Archellia in all its provincial glory or Santis, where his people had won their status as veterans.

His thoughts stopped short as mass readings began to come in. The thing was big. Three point one million tons. Energy readouts...

His gaze froze on the screen. It was no courier ship coming into the system. It was a battleship.

What would one of our battleships be doing in Corpus?

His eyes moved across the incoming data, analyzing it as quickly as he could. His fighter's AI beat him to the conclusion.

"Contact is a Union *Faucon*-class capital ship."

Chalk up one more for the gut...

He could hear his heart pounding in his ears. He'd known *Dauntless* was heading toward the front, but no one had expected a fight here in Corpus. The fleet was gathering in Arcturon. How could a Union ship have transited from there? His mind filled with possible answers to that question, but he pushed them aside. He wasn't ready to deal with the realities behind any of them.

"Warbook stats on contact?"

"Union Faucon-class capital ship," the AI replied, "three million, one hundred fourteen thousand, two hundred eleven tons. Main armament, dual bomb-pumped x-ray lasers. Secondary armament, twenty-four high-powered laser cannons, maximum output one point one gigawatts. In the most common configuration, Faucon-class vessels carry four squadrons of twelve fighters each. Point def…"

"Enough." Stockton slammed his hand down on the comm unit. "*Dauntless*, this is Blue Leader." He paused for an instant, a fleeting impulse to wait for a response. But the ship was light minutes away from his current position. They wouldn't even hear his transmission for almost a quarter of an hour. "Contact entering from Arcturon transit point, Union battleship, Faucon-class. Repeat, contact at transit point, Union Faucon-class battleship."

His eyes were still fixed on the display when new contacts appeared. Smaller dots this time, almost in a cloud.

Fighters.

"Union vessel is launching fighters. Repeat, *Dauntless*, enemy ship is launching fighters."

He watched as the range readings declined. His own fighter was racing toward the enemy ship, and the clouds of tiny dots were heading right at him.

"Talon, let's get the hell back to *Dauntless*. Fast."

"I'm with you, Raptor." There was a short pause, then: "You bet your ass, I'm with you."

Stockton tapped his positioning thrusters, spinning his ship and positioning the engines opposite his current vector. Then he pulled back on the throttle and blasted toward *Dauntless*.

I knew we were heading into another fight, but not this soon…

His new pilots weren't ready. He'd done his best, but there hadn't been time. They would pay the price…and some of the veterans would too, when their new wingmen and comrades let them down.

*   *   *

"Scanners confirm Lieutenant Stockton's report, Captain. It's definitely a Faucon-class battleship." Travis was sitting at her station, her eyes glued to the screen in front of her.

"Very well, Commander." Barron appreciated the confirmation from his first officer, but he hadn't doubted Stockton's reports. "Raptor" Stockton was a hotshot pilot by anyone's standards, often reckless with his own safety—and one of the members of the crew most likely to get into some kind of trouble on shore leave—but Barron had seen the pilot looking after his squadron in battle. Stockton didn't seem like the reliable sort at first glance, but there was no one on *Dauntless* Barron would rather have at his side in a fight than his ace pilot.

The battlestations lamps bathed the bridge in an eerie red glow. Barron had wasted no time in bringing his ship to general quarters. He hadn't expected to encounter any enemies in Corpus, but that didn't change the reality that he had...or delay his response. *Dauntless* wasn't quite as fully-repaired as he would have liked, and he knew Fritz's people had still been crawling all over the ship, finishing the last bits of work to bring the vessel back from the near-wreck it had been when Barron and his people had limped back to Archellia.

Was that really less than five months ago?

Barron wished his engineers had gotten more rest during the voyage to Corpus, instead of an endless series of double shifts under the cracking whip of Anya Fritz, but that wasn't his biggest concern. Fritz's team was the best in the fleet, a designation he'd defend against any other captain, and in the most unofficer-like and ungentlemanly manner if need be. He'd seen them in action before, and he still credited them, as much as anyone on *Dauntless*, including himself, for the victory over *Invictus*.

No, it wasn't the engineers that had him worried. It was the fighter squadrons. He was grateful for Stockton's quick thinking in sending his people back to the ship to refuel and rearm. But they had just landed, and now he had to decide whether to launch Olya Federov and her Reds, along with the raw Greens, or to wait until the just-returned squadrons were refit and ready.

He hated the idea of sending his fighters out piecemeal, but the enemy wings were already on his scanners. It was too early to tell how many were outfitted as bombers and how many as interceptors, but if he waited to launch a full flight, there'd be damned little time for his squadrons to hit the enemy before they were in range.

In the end, it came down to the same brutal calculus it always did. *Dauntless* came first, and if it was necessary to preserve the mothership, every fighter she carried was expendable. No one knew that better than the pilots themselves, who, he suspected, struggled less with the idea than he did.

"Commander, issue launch order for Red and Green squadrons. Commander Jamison is to wait and launch with Blue and Yellow squadrons." He knew his strike force commander would hate that order, but he also knew he'd follow it. Barron was sure it was the right move. "Lynx" Federov was a skilled pilot and squadron leader, more than capable of commanding the first wave...and there was no way Jake Stockton would be back in time to refit and relaunch. That meant the Blues wouldn't have their commander with them, and the Yellows were still adjusting to their new leader. Barron had complete confidence in Rick Turner's skill and capability, but he also knew the pilot was still getting used to squadron command, and his people were still dealing with the loss of their beloved former leader. Both squadrons would benefit from Jamison's presence.

"Order confirmed. Both bays report launch in progress."

Barron didn't need Travis's confirmation. The vibrations from the launch catapults were slight, at least all the way up on the bridge, but he knew his own ship well. They'd spent more than a year getting to know each other, and now she felt like an extension of his own body. They'd been to hell and back together, and *Dauntless* had become part of his soul.

He looked at the display, watching the stats pour in. He'd launched a full spread of probes, and they were sending back a flood of data. The Union vessel was a capital ship, which meant she was dangerous. But the *Faucons* were an old class, survivors of the last war, refitted and updated but still well past their primes. And small. *Dauntless* outmassed her opponent by more than twenty percent, though she was just nearly as old. But after the bow to stern rebuild his sturdy vessel had undergone ten years before, he'd bet it outmatched any of the patch and paint jobs the notoriously sloppy Union shipyards had managed.

The industrial might of the Iron Belt worlds was often ugly when viewed up close, but those sixteen planets were also the engines that had built the Confederation's military. The rapacious greed of the staggeringly wealthy industrial families of the Iron Belt was perhaps nothing to be proud of, but they ran a system that vastly outproduced the more numerous facilities of the statist Union.

There was no doubt *Dauntless* had the edge in the coming engagement, and by a considerable margin. But there was no room for overconfidence in any fight. He imagined the thoughts that had gone through Katrine Rigellus's mind, and those of her crew, raised on a steady diet of propaganda about Alliance invincibility. There was no question that Rigellus had run her ship well, like the veteran commander he knew she had been. But his people had won the fight by the slimmest of margins, and he couldn't shake the feeling that Alliance hubris had been the deciding factor. He'd vowed he would never to make that mistake himself.

He reached down, flipping his comm unit to Fritz's channel. "Commander Fritz?"

"I'm here, Captain." She sounded out of breath. Barron could only imagine what his chief engineer had been doing to prep *Dauntless* for combat. He tended to be a bit tireless himself, sleeping no more than three or four hours a night, and often lying long on his bunk, juggling a mental "to-do" list for the day to come. But he'd never seen anything like the relentlessness of his engineer, the sheer driving force contained in her diminutive body…and the ruthlessness with which she expected the same from her staff.

"Fritzie, I want you to keep a close eye on the primaries." The pair of massive particle accelerators comprised *Dauntless*'s most powerful armament, vastly stronger and longer-ranged than anything on the Union *Faucon*, but the highly-advanced guns were temperamental and prone to breakdown from even the slightest damage.

"Of course, sir. I always do."

"I know you do, Fritzie, but we've got to win this battle

quickly. We've got to get out without taking too much damage…because we may face another fight in Arcturon, and there's nothing between here and there in the way of repair facilities, save for whatever you and your people have down there."

"Well, they're definitely functional now, sir, and they outrange the enemy primaries by a good seventy thousand kilometers. So, if our fighters can keep theirs off our backs, you'll definitely get some shots in before they even get a chance to fire back and knock them out."

"Yes, Fritzie, but you know as well as I do how tough it is to get every bomber. If a significant portion of that incoming strike is equipped for anti-ship attacks—and you know it is, or they'd be hanging back farther, waiting for our own assault—some of them are going to get through."

"I hear you, sir. We'll do everything possible."

"That's all I can ask, Fritzie." He slammed his fist down on the comm unit, cutting the line.

"Red and Green squadrons launched, Captain. Lieutenant Federov reports all units in formation and moving to intercept enemy fighters."

"Very well. Do we have a time estimate on Blue and Yellow squadrons?" Barron had almost ordered the Yellows refit as bombers, but he'd decided it would just take too long. And the Blues would have had to wait too, so they could launch alongside the strike force and escort it in.

He'd been concerned about his lack of bombers in the fight, but now he was happy to have so many interceptors. If the bays could just turn Blue and Yellow squadrons around and get them launched in time to hit the enemy bombers, then maybe his people *could* get them all, and spare *Dauntless* the fighter strike. Then it would be down to a close-ranged struggle. After he'd blasted the enemy with his primaries, he knew his ship had a good chance win the victory before she took too much damage.

If his people could get the fighters launched in time.

If.

Chapter Twelve

"Let's go, Red squadron…let's clear a path for the Greens."
Olya Federov leaned forward in her cockpit, staring at the display as she increased her fighter's thrust. She'd hesitated before ordering the Greens to move forward and attack the enemy bombers. Her Reds were more experienced, more capable than the largely raw pilots of Green squadron. But she'd decided that was all the more reason to do what she'd planned. Dogfighting with the interceptors was a tough game, especially if the enemy pilots were experienced. The bombers were a far easier target, assuming the Reds could blast open a hole through the defensive screen.

Federov had given her orders, and now she set aside her command hat and returned to being just a fighter pilot. Red squadron was outnumbered, and her people were going to need every hit they could get. Olya Federov had won her ace's rating and then some out at Santis, racking up seven kills. Now she intended to add to that number.

She angled her ship toward two enemy fighters, and fired her first missile almost robotically. She'd been tempted to save the two heavy weapons until she really needed them, but then she decided it didn't make sense. A fighter handled better without the attached ordnance, and though the difference wasn't all that great, to a skilled pilot like Federov, it was significant.

Her missile accelerated straight toward the target. The enemy made a clumsy attempt to escape, but the warhead slammed into his fighter and exploded, less than a minute after she'd launched it. She wasn't looking by then—she was staring at the display, her eyes focused on the dead pilot's wingman. She flipped a switch, deactivating her remaining missile. The pilot in her sights was a newb, that much was obvious…a waste of the heavy ordnance. She closed her fingers down on the firing stud, blasting the Union ship with her lasers.

She brought her fighter around again, wincing slightly at the pain as she endured 10g thrust for a few seconds. Then she hit the missile switch again, reactivating the weapon. The wingman of her first target had been a rookie, but the bird in front of her was different. Not an ace, she decided, but a pilot with some skill. Well worth her last missile.

She angled the throttle and pulled back, engaging her thrusters again to adjust her position. The enemy fighter responded. It was quick…but not quick enough. Federov pulled hard on her ship's controller, pushing the thrust up toward maximum, bringing her straight at her target. Then she hit the firing stud, and the fighter shook as the weapon broke free and blasted toward the enemy. She'd closed to point blank range, and the missile launched with her own ship's velocity and accelerated from there.

The enemy pilot angled his fighter and fired his own engines at full, desperately trying to escape. But her missile was too close, too fast. It blasted its own engines, altering its vector, closing steadily on the target. Federov's prey tried a few last ditch evasive maneuvers, but in the end her weapon found its mark, and her kill count for the battle hit three.

She looked at her screen. Her Reds were earning their pay… there were at least a dozen enemy fighters destroyed, and as far as she could see, only one of her own.

"Holden," she muttered to herself as she scanned the roster list. *One of the replacements.*

Then she saw the transponder signal. *He managed to eject.*

She smiled. Her people were massacring the Union fighters. She knew there were rookies over there, just like hers, and from what she understood about the Union, they were helpless draftees who'd had no choice in joining the navy. But she didn't care. Any pity she might have had for those on the other end of her guns was buried deep, frozen beneath her anger. These pilots were trying to kill her people, and that was all she needed to know to blast them to hell and then go back to *Dauntless* and sleep well. They were fighting in a Confederation system, after all, and the Union was the invader.

"Let's go, Greens," she shouted suddenly into the comm unit. "You've got a hole opening up…so get in there and blast those bombers, while the way is clear."

"We're on the way, Lynx. Thanks for the assist."

"The captain's counting on us, Blaster. Now go clear out those bombers…and we'll keep these interceptors off of your backs."

"Roger that, Lynx." Larry "Blaster" Andrews was about the only veteran pilot in Green squadron, and Federov was counting on him to keep his rookies out of trouble and focused on the mission.

Federov glanced down at her display, watching for an instant as the Greens began to accelerate forward. Then she darted her eyes to the side, picking out her next victim.

"Hello, pretty," she muttered softly, as she brought the throttle around.

*   *   *

"Status of launch preparations?" Barron had been sitting silently, watching the fighter battle unfold several hundred thousand kilometers from *Dauntless*. Federov and her two squadrons had slammed into the enemy strike force. Her veteran Reds had smashed right through the enemy interceptor screen, blasting a hole for the Greens to push through to hit the oncoming bombers.

"Launch control reports that forty percent of fighter craft have been rearmed and refueled. Estimated time to complete refit twenty-two minutes."

"Very well."

Barron had been worried that the garrison transfers and rookies who had brought *Dauntless*'s savaged fighter contingent back up to full strength would fall far short of the standards of those they had replaced. But as he watched the Greens drive directly toward the enemy bombers, slicing into them and destroying one after another, his concerns slipped away. His veterans had taken the new pilots into their fold, and together they were forging themselves into a potent weapon, as the Union bomber pilots were discovering the hard way. The strike was shattered, more than half the ships blasted to bits or severely damaged. Yet, still the survivors came on.

He remembered the battle with *Invictus*, the astonishing, almost suicidal courage of the Alliance pilots. They had been his enemies, but it had been impossible not to respect them. The Union forces had nothing like the Alliance's code of honor and conduct, yet their own bombers came on, just as heedless of the losses they suffered as Katrine Rigellus's pilots had been.

Barron understood just how the Union compelled its pilots to such dedication. What the intelligence briefings hadn't told him, his grandfather had. Union military personnel and their families lived a privileged existence, at least to an extent. The pilots' families lived on massive reservations, with accommodations and rations the seething masses of the Union could only dream about. But he was also well aware what would happen if one of those pilots broke and ran for the mothership. The pilot would die almost immediately after landing, if his ship wasn't blown away as it made its final approach. Worse, far away, on whatever world the unfortunate's family resided, they would be visited by Sector Nine. Cowardice in the face of the enemy was a capital offense in the Union, not only for the guilty party but for his or her spouse, children, and parents. Entire families were exterminated, not just to punish individual cases, but to make fleeing from the enemy unthinkable, even when certain death in battle was the alternative.

Which meant even though Federov's people had inflicted over fifty percent casualties on the approaching force, there were still bombers heading toward *Dauntless*. He glanced down at the chronometer, and then back to the display. And they were going to reach launch range before his refitting squadrons were ready.

"Commander, advise launch control that all fighters are to be sent out as soon as they are ready."

"Yes, Captain."

Barron didn't like the idea of sending out his pilots in twos and threes, but there were still too many bombers coming in. *Dauntless* could take the enemy battleship, he was confident of that. Unless a few of those strike craft got lucky and scored critical hits. That was a chance he couldn't take. Not one transit from the fleet assembly point, with no sign of the expected courier. Not when an enemy vessel had come through a transwarp link he'd expected to be safely behind Confederation lines.

He felt the familiar vibration under his feet, the first fighters launching. He turned his head back toward the display, watching as the first dots appeared right next to the blue oval representing *Dauntless*. If his squadrons could keep those bombers off *Dauntless*, he could close with the enemy vessel and finish things.

He'd expected to feel tense, and of course, he did to an extent. But there was a strange calm too, a confidence in his fighter wings. His doubts about the new pilots had faded away watching Federov and her people savage the Union strike. Just as importantly, they had done it while suffering light casualties themselves. His mind had been weighed down by memories of the apocalypse out at Santis, but the Union squadrons, for all their imposed suicidal courage, were proving to be no match for their Alliance equivalents.

A small grin slipped onto his face.

Let's do it, Blues and Yellows…finish them off.

* * *

"How's your fuel status, Talon?" Stockton was staring at his scanner, doing some calculations in his head, trying to get an actual feel for how much thrust capability his fighter still had in its almost-exhausted fuel tanks. The AI had done it all already, he realized, but he also knew there was a safety factor built into those figures. And he wanted the *real* number.

"It sucks, Raptor. The same as yours." Corinne Steele's tone made it clear she knew what Stockton was thinking.

"Yeah, but there's a safety factor built into what's on your screen...and we're coming back almost right behind those enemy bombers."

"We'd have to accelerate to catch them before they launch, Raptor...and then we'd have to decelerate to land." Steele paused for a few seconds. "You're taking about cutting this *real* close..."

Stockton knew she was right. But he'd gone through the numbers three times, and he was convinced they had enough fuel left for an attack run. Probably.

"I won't order you to do it, Talon...but I think we could manage it."

"People already think I'm as crazy as you, Raptor. This should just about clinch it. I'm with you."

"Let's do this!" He gripped his throttle tightly, pausing for a few seconds. He had to be spot on here. He didn't have a drop of fuel to waste.

He moved his hand to the side, and back slightly, feeling the kick as his thrusters engaged. He slowly increased his acceleration to 3g. Then he backed off. He'd altered his vector slightly, and his ship was moving directly at the mass of bombers heading toward *Dauntless*. There were only nine left, and Federov's people were also on their tails. But he didn't think Red and Green squadrons were going to make it in time...and he and Steele were closer.

His com unit crackled to life. "Blue leader, this is *Dauntless* control. We're picking up a vector change. Please advise."

Well, that didn't take long...you'd think they have better things to do right now than keep an eye on me…

"*Dauntless* control, there is no malfunction. We have adjusted our course slightly. Umm…optimizing the flight pattern."

He shook his head as the signal moved to *Dauntless* and the reply made its way back. He knew what the control officer on duty was going to say. He could almost hear it. Waiting for the actual words was a formality.

"Negative, Blue leader. Your fuel status is critical, and your adjusted course and velocity intersect with the vectors of enemy bombers now inbound. You are to return to your original heading using minimal possible thrust."

Really? We're stumbling into enemy bombers? Oh no…

"Ah, control, we're not reading you…I'm afraid your message is breaking up."

"Blue leader, you are to revert to your original course, and return to base. Acknowledge."

"Sorry, control, there must be some kind of jamming out here…" He flipped off the comm.

"You're going to get us in trouble, you know that?" Steele's voice had perhaps a hint of concern, but for the most part she sounded perfectly willing to follow her squadron leader on his unauthorized attack run.

"Well, if we miscalculate and end up out of fuel and having to ditch, at least you can say you were just following orders. The captain will skin me alive, assuming he gets to me before Thunder." Stockton knew Kyle "Thunder" Jamison well enough to realize he was in for it, no matter what happened out here, and he didn't think the fact that the two of them were best friends would make the slightest difference. But for five months he'd been unable to push the images of the Battle of Santis from his mind. The Alliance bombers making run after run at *Dauntless*, their torpedoes pounding the ship, tearing apart the hull, killing its crew. Stockton was a pilot to his core, but he understood, perhaps more than anyone, his true role in the battleship's ecosystem.

His comm unit buzzed again, but he ignored it. If it was control again, he had nothing new to say and, if they'd kicked the problem upstairs, if that was Thunder or the captain…or God forbid, Stara, he wasn't going to put himself in the position of directly refusing them.

Stara Sinclair was a launch control officer—*please let it not have been her on that line*—but she was more than that. "Raptor" Stockton had a reputation that stretched from one end of the Confederation to the other, to every port he'd been to for shore leave. He was good-looking, just battle-worn enough, and he had sufficient self-confidence for five men. But the fighter corps' legendary playboy had met his match with *Dauntless's* launch control officer. Sinclair had ignored him for ten months, barely acknowledging his existence. Then he'd made an emergency landing during the Battle of Santis, one everyone watching had been sure would end badly. But he'd pulled it off, and he'd gone right from his damaged, burning cockpit and into her arms.

They'd both tried to write it off as relief, as nothing more than friendship, but neither of them had managed that very well. Before long they were spending so much time together, it was challenging even Stockton's ability to twist reality and continue to insist it was "nothing special."

He glanced at the screen. He was getting closer to the wave of bombers, coming in at an angle that would take him right across the entire formation. With any luck, he and Steele could take out a couple each.

He was trying to push the thoughts of Stara from his head, not to mention images of an angry Jamison and a raging captain. None of them understood him, not really. They bought into the persona he wore for everyone to see, the cocky pilot, driven by bravado and an ego that knew no bounds. But that wasn't why he was here, taking another crazy chance. He was here for them. For Captain Barron, whom he considered the finest officer he'd ever known, and a bit of a role model to replace his scoundrel of a father. Kyle, the brother he'd never had. And Stara, whom he was sure knew, despite his valiant efforts to downplay their relationship, that he loved her. Jake Stockton had always been a loner, a loner who had never had a real family. Until now. He would do anything to protect those few people who were the world to him.

"All right, Talon, here we go."

"I'm with you, Raptor. Whew!"

He jerked his throttle hard to the side and pressed his finger down on the firing control. His cockpit echoed with the whining sound of the quad lasers…and a few seconds later one of the bombers blinked off his display.

"Nice shooting, Raptor!"

A few seconds later, another bomber disappeared.

"All right, Talon!"

"I can't let you get too far ahead of me, can I?"

"We'll see about that." He pushed the throttle again, and he almost slammed it back.

No, you don't have that kind of fuel to burn…

He tapped the control, blasting his engines for just a few seconds. He had a line on another target, but it was far away. Normally, he'd have blasted his thrusters and closed, but that would burn up most of his remaining fuel supply. He squeezed the trigger, firing. Wide.

He felt the urge again to pull back on the controls, but he resisted. He was taking it to very edge, but he wasn't jumping over.

This will have to be marksmanship…

He stared intently at the screen, his eyes focused on the small dot representing the enemy vessel. The bomber was the closest to *Dauntless*. He knew any second now it would launch its torpedo. He didn't have the fuel to close faster, and he didn't have time to sit there and take pot shots. He had to hit. Now.

He squinted, his eyes locked on the target. His hand moved slightly, to the right and barely back, one tiny kick of thrust to line up the shot. Then his finger tightened, slowly, steadily. He knew in his gut, even as he heard the sounds of the lasers, that his aim had been true. A few seconds later, he got his confirmation when the dot on the scanner winked out.

He'd gotten two, and Talon had two kills as well. That was four of the bombers, four plasma torpedoes that wouldn't rip into *Dauntless*'s hull. Four deadly weapons that wouldn't endanger the people he cared about.

"Let's get back, Talon. We're out in front of the other bomb-ers. No way we can come around and target them with the fuel we've got left."

"Roger that, Raptor. And good shooting."

"Right back at you, Talon. Damned good shooting. Now let's just hope we can manage to land these things!"

Chapter Thirteen

"Damage control, report." Barron was leaning over the comm unit. *Dauntless* had shaken hard when the plasma torpedo struck, but he'd been watching as it came in, tracking its trajectory, and he doubted anything critical had been hit.

"We lost a couple cargo bays, sir. Mostly empty. Nothing vital. All things considered, we got off light." The lack of concern in Fritz's voice reinforced the superficial nature of the damage.

"Very well, Fritzie. That's good news." *For a change*, he thought, but didn't say.

"Yes, sir."

He turned toward Travis's station, but before he could say anything, she beat him to it.

"Captain, the enemy vessel is decelerating. Hard."

"Thrust vector?"

"Directly back toward the transwarp link, sir. If I had to guess, I'd say they've evaluated the failure of their bombing strike, and they're heading back the way they came."

"But they've still got fighters still out there. They're just going to abandon them?" Barron felt revulsion at the idea of the enemy leaving their surviving pilots behind, but it was followed up by a dose of hypocrisy. Confederation doctrine was not all that different in such matters, and a capital ship captain knew his primary duty was to safeguard his vessel, not to risk a battleship to recover a few fighters. The enemy ship faced a larger enemy, one with a nearly full strength fighter wing to face their own badly depleted squadrons.

He shook his head, scolding himself for not expecting the enemy to flee. *Dauntless* outmatched its foe. Barron could launch his own bombing strike, and then close on a crippled enemy to finish the job. Running was the smart play. But it had still caught him by surprise.

He reminded himself, he wasn't up against an Alliance adversary here. The reckless, almost insane bravery of Katrine Rigellus and her crew, which he had come to respect more and more, wasn't in play here. This was a different enemy, one he considered utterly evil, lacking any of the admirable qualities of the Alliance warriors he'd faced at Santis.

Now he had to decide what to do. Should he let the enemy go, or try to close before they could escape? He had the advantage here, and he had no idea what waited beyond the transwarp line in Arcturon. He felt a moment's hesitancy about leading his people into a fight they could avoid. But the Confederation was at war, and his duty was clear.

"All engines prepare for thrust at 10g. Plot a course, directly toward the transwarp point. Let's catch that ship before they can reverse their vector and get away."

"Yes, sir." Travis's tone was firm. It was clear his exec agreed with his decision.

"Issue the recall to all deployed fighters. Advise squadron commanders of our projected course and acceleration. They are to match our vector. We'll have to conduct landing operations while we're accelerating."

"Yes, sir." Travis sounded somewhat less enthusiastic than she had.

"We have no choice, Commander. Not unless we want to let

the enemy get away…and we have no idea what's waiting for us on the other side of the transwarp link."

"Of course, sir. You are right. But…we have a lot of relatively inexperienced pilots out there. Worse, they're used to landing on stationary platforms."

"I understand your concern, Commander, but our priority has to be that enemy battleship."

"Agreed, sir."

Barron sat silently for a few seconds. "Is Commander Jamison back onboard yet?"

"He is, sir. He landed about twenty minutes ago." There was something odd in Travis's tone. "He is…with Lieutenant Stockton, sir."

"I see." Travis had watched Stockton's wild show, along with virtually everyone on *Dauntless* with access to a screen. He was angry at the insubordination, but inside he was also relieved that four fewer bombers had managed to fire on his ship. Though that was something he'd never admit to his troublesome pilot.

"Ping Jamison's comm. Tell him to get down to launch control right away. Chewing out Lieutenant Stockton can wait. A lot of pilots are going to need some help with this landing, and I want him there to talk them through it."

*   *   *

"Are you crazy?" Kyle Jamison was mad, as certifiably, red-faced, searingly angry as Stockton had ever seen him. "You're a squadron commander, dammit, not some war god who can do whatever the hell he wants whenever the hell he wants. At least you're a squadron leader for the moment."

"Kyle…"

"I'm Commander Jamison to you, Lieutenant. I think the last thing you need now is any further breakdown of discipline." Jamison glared at his friend and subordinate. "Now, what the hell do you think you were doing out there?"

"We were on our way back to *Dauntless* when I realized there was a force of bombers inbound. I analyzed the situation, and I determined that the pursuing interceptors would not catch them in time to ensure that none reached torpedo range. So, as senior officer at the scene, I made a determination that, despite difficult fuel status, we should intervene. Sir, Lieutenant Steele was only following my orders."

"Look at that…you actually can sound like a military officer when you have to. I guess that means you're full of shit the rest of the time. And don't you worry about Lieutenant Steele. I intend to have one of these conversations with her too."

"Commander, Lieutenant Steele is my subordinate, and she was acting under my express orders. I must protest any disciplinary procedures directed at her, and I will oppose such, by formal statement all the way to the admiralty if need be."

"I'd be worried more about myself if I was you. I'm not sure formal statements made from the brig are all that compelling to a review board." Jamison paused, and then he exhaled. When he continued, his voice was calmer, more relaxed. "You're a royal pain in the ass, do you realize that? But you're the most goddammned loyal son of a bitch I've ever known. Steele is fine. For that matter, so are you, though for the life of me I can't explain my foolish blind spot where you're concerned."

"It's my charm, Commander. And the fact that you know I was right."

"Don't push your luck, Jake. I suspect the captain would have wanted to skin you alive, but…"

"But we got away with one minor hit, and now everybody's thinking what could those four birds have done?"

"Something like that." Jamison glared at his friend. "But don't take getting off the hook here as license to do whatever the hell you damn well please. I mean it, Jake. You're my number two on *Dauntless*. What would you do if something happened to me? Run the whole strike force like a wild pack of daredevils?"

"It was you, Kyle. And the captain." Stockton paused. It was hard for him to display sincere emotion. The defense mechanisms he'd built to survive a childhood in Valaria's poorhouses were still a bulwark of his personality. "And Stara. *Dauntless* is the only real home I've ever had. I'll do anything to keep her—

all of you—safe."

Jamison let out a heavy exhale. "Like I said, Jake, I don't doubt your loyalty, or your friendship. But you're not a hotshot pilot fresh out of the Academy anymore. And your decisions rarely affect only you. What if you'd gotten Corinne Steele killed out there?"

"I didn't order her to come, Kyle. I gave her the option…"

"What option? What pilot is going to refuse to follow the legendary Raptor? Especially one of your own Blue squadron. You may have technically given her a choice, but she didn't have one, not really. Think about that next time. And consider this, too, the next time you decide to treat your life like a disposable commodity. The people you're trying to protect…do you think they—we—believe you're as expendable as you seem to feel you are?"

Stockton didn't answer, not at first. Finally, he looked over at Jamison and said, "I understand what you're saying, Kyle." He paused again. "But where is that line? If we didn't take out those bombers, *Dauntless* might have taken two or three more hits. Would it be better if a few dozen of her crew were dead for my caution?" He took a breath. "I'm not crazy, Kyle. I *knew* we could pull it off. I *knew* we could save lives. It's not the first time I climbed into a strikefighter, after all."

"Just listen to some of what I said, Jake. Okay? Make sure you're doing things for the right reason…and remember you can't just ignore orders, even when you think you're right."

"Technically, I didn't disobey anything. It was Lieutenant Hooley on the comm, Kyle. She's a second grade, and I'm a first."

Jamison shook his head. "You're a handful, my friend, you know that?"

"Then I'm okay? With the captain?"

"Yes. He was mad, but I spoke to him, told him I'd handle you. He's focused on the enemy ship…and he recognizes that *Dauntless* might not have gotten through in the condition she's in if those bombers had gotten through."

"I'm glad to hear that. I'll take on all the squadrons the

Union can muster, but Tyler Barron is another matter entirely."

"We can agree on that much, my friend." Jamison looked at his friend. "But I wouldn't say you're off the hook completely."

Stockton stared back, a confused look on his face.

"The captain was mad, but it was nothing compared to Stara. She was fuming, Jake, and I suspect you're going to get it worse from her than you did from me."

Jamison nodded to his friend, trying unsuccessfully to keep the amused grin off his face as he turned and walked across the room. Then his comm unit buzzed.

"Jamison," he said, tapping to activate the unit.

"Commander, the captain wants you in the launch control center now. We're about to accelerate at 10g, and he wants you directing the retrieval of the deployed squadrons."

"Understood, Commander. I'm on my way. Jamison out." He paused and poked his head back. "Gotta go," he said. Then: "Good luck, you're going to need it." He nodded and then he turned and walked down the corridor, heading toward the lift.

Stockton stood still for a moment, staring at the space where his friend had just stood. Then he sat down in one of the chairs and sighed.

"Damn."

* * *

"That was the last of them, Captain. Commander Jamison reports all fighters accounted for. Total losses in the recent action, six ships. Three pilots ejected and were recovered."

"Very well, Commander." Three pilots killed. The losses were light, especially compared with the nightmare at Santis, but Barron found they hurt just as much.

"Captain, Commander Jamison also advises that he can launch a partial strike, twelve bombers with ten escorting interceptors. Squadrons became intermixed during recovery operations, but he advises either he or Lieutenant Federov can lead the strike force on your command."

"Thank you, Commander. But I don't think we're going

to be able to finish the battle in this system, not if that ship keeps accelerating like they are. And if we launch fighters, we'll have to stop and recover them before we can pursue." Despite Kyle Jamison's best efforts to direct the landing, Barron had been compelled to cut *Dauntless*'s thrust to get his fighters back onboard. The enemy ship had just abandoned their scattered survivors, and they'd continued to blast straight for the transit point. Barron figured he might get off a shot with his primaries, maybe two, but then the Union battleship would transit, and *Dauntless* would have to follow it to Arcturon to continue the fight.

"Agreed, sir. Recommend we direct the bays to prepare to commence launch operations immediately after we transit."

"Do it, Commander."

Travis turned toward her workstation, relaying the command to launch control. "Both bays report ready, sir." She paused. "Captain, Commander Jamison is requesting authorization to send Lieutenant Stockton out with the strike force when we launch."

Barron paused for a few seconds, feeling a reflexive urge to deny the unexpected request. An hour before he'd been ready to skin Stockton alive, or at least take his wings and assign him to *Dauntless*'s deepest, darkest hole to scrub out conduits. But as much as a pain in his ass Stockton was prone to be, Barron couldn't argue his strike forces weren't better off with the ship's best pilot—and top squadron leader—out there. "Yes," he said simply. Then: "Advise the commander, that Lieutenant Stockton is cleared for duty."

"Yes, sir."

Barron wanted to laugh, but he held it back. His grandfather had told him stories about the pilots who had served on his battleships, of the crazy things many of them had done. He'd never been entirely sure the elder Barron hadn't been joking, at least to some extent. But now that he had his own squadrons, he was certain that every one of those tales had not only been true, but probably understated.

"Entering primary range in three minutes, Captain."

"Very well…commence charging of main guns."

"Charging underway, sir."

Dauntless's primary batteries were two massive particle accelerators, immense guns that ran three-quarters of the battleship's four kilometers in length. They were powerful weapons, if temperamental, and they required most of the energy *Dauntless*'s reactors could produce.

Barron glanced up at one of the main screens. There was a bar graph displayed, a line of red moving steadily from left to right as the guns charged. Barron still wasn't sure he wouldn't have preferred the old primaries, powerful x-ray lasers similar to the Union's heavy guns. His particle accelerators had longer range, and they hit significantly harder, but they were also fragile and slow to charge between shots.

"Projected time until enemy vessel transits: six minutes."

Barron did some quick math in his head. He would get one shot for sure, perhaps two if his people stayed on top of things. They'd have to get the second shot off at least a minute before the enemy ship transited, and preferably a minute and a half. After that, the gravity waves around the transwarp point would throw off the targeting.

"Entering range in one minute, Captain."

"Advise gunnery crews to fire at will once we're within range."

"Yes, Captain." Travis leaned over his comm unit. "Primary gun teams, you are authorized to fire at your discretion."

Barron watched the red oval in the massive 3D display in the center of the *Dauntless*'s bridge. The enemy ship was getting close to the transit point, and the blue symbol representing his own vessel was far behind. Barron knew he wouldn't have had a chance to catch the enemy at all if the Union vessel hadn't had to first reverse its considerable inbound velocity to head back to the transwarp line.

"I want recharging to commence the instant those weapons are fired, Commander."

"Yes, sir. I will see to it myself."

Barron watched the countdown on his screen. Ten seconds.

He could feel the tightness in his stomach, and the sensation triggered memories of Santis. *Dauntless* had been engaged for hours now, but a fighter duel, especially a one-sided struggle his pilots won handily, just wasn't the same as closing into gunnery range.

Five seconds. He had confidence in his people, and he knew when to sit back and let them do their jobs. That didn't mean it was easy. A dozen things popped into his mind, warnings, reminders, an unending flow of advice he ached to unload on his bridge crew, his gunners.

They know what they're doing...let them do it...

He watched the countdown hit zero. *Dauntless* was in range.

Fire, he thought, already thinking of the recharge time between shots and the dwindling moments before the enemy vessel would be protected by the gravity well of the transwarp link. But firing wouldn't accomplish anything if his people couldn't score a hit, and that wasn't an easy task at this kind of extreme range. His gun teams were the best...in fact, he'd long ago decided he'd stack them up against any in the fleet, no matter what the stakes. They'd proven themselves in the deadly fight against *Invictus*, and he had no doubt they would do it again.

Suddenly, the bridge lights dimmed, and the spare workstation screens went blank. The sound of the massive primaries could be heard throughout the ship, a cross between a buzz and a higher pitched whine. Barron's eyes dropped immediately to his screen, waiting for the report. He had a spread of drones chasing the enemy ship, and he expected solid data on damage assessment.

A hit!

His initial excitement was quickly tempered, however, as detailed data began to stream in. Both shots had indeed hit, but they'd been glancing blows, striking the target at its extremities. Between the very long range and the non-critical locations of the impacts, Barron wasn't surprised when the assessment came in. Superficial damage.

Any hit at this range was commendable, but he still couldn't help but feel disappointment. He knew that wasn't fair to his gunners, that just connecting with both guns had been a success. But they'd spoiled him. He'd seen them make too many impossible shots at Santis, and his expectations had risen to match that performance.

"Recharge those guns, Commander."

"Recharge already underway, sir, per your orders."

Barron just nodded. He really wanted to do some damage before the enemy ship escaped. If there was nothing else in Arcturon, it wouldn't matter much, but if there were more Union forces waiting, anything he could do to wear the enemy down increased the chance of *Dauntless* surviving the encounter.

He punched at his controls, and his screen changed, the flat depiction of the space around the transit point morphing into a series of ripples—the gravity waves moving out from the transwarp point. The enemy ship was almost there, and once it moved inside the affected area, scoring a hit would move from difficult to almost impossible.

His eyes moved to the screen on the far wall, the display showing the recharge almost three-quarters complete. He felt the tension building, not only in his gut but across the entire bridge. The normal chattering between his officers had been silenced as they all waited to see if they'd get another shot.

Barron stared intently, watching as the red bar ticked slowly toward full. Full charge.

The lights dimmed again, almost immediately this time. It was clear the gunners knew as well as their captain that they were down to the last seconds to get off their shot.

Barron leaned forward, watching the data coming in from the probes. Another pair of hits, and this time they seemed better-placed. He waited anxiously for more data, but it didn't come. The enemy ship was now deep in the gravity well, and the scanners on his probes were hopelessly scrambled. A few seconds later, the icon representing the Union ship disappeared. His enemy had transited.

"Full thrust, Commander Travis. We're going in after them. I want all weapons on full alert, prepared to fire as soon as we emerge and locate the enemy. All available fighters are to be launch-ready."

"Yes, Captain."

Barron leaned back in his chair. He was nervous, concerned what might be waiting beyond the transwarp link. But he knew the Confederation was hard-pressed, more so, he suspected, than he'd been told. Their duty was clear. *Dauntless* had found the front lines, farther back perhaps than he and his people had expected, but they'd found them nonetheless.

If the Union wanted a fight, Barron was sure of one thing. *Dauntless* would give them one they wouldn't soon forget.

Chapter Fourteen

"All right, Blues and friends, this ship we're after's got nothing but a handful of fighters left. So, listen up...I want everybody to save their missiles. We take this tiny screen out with lasers and clear the way for the bombers. But we keep our primary armaments in place, understood?" Stockton was leading a hodgepodge of *Dauntless*'s fighters, about half of his own Blue squadron, with some Greens and Yellows thrown in, almost as if to emphasize the disarray sweeping the battleship's bays right now. Somehow, the launch teams had managed to switch over Federov's Reds to bombing kits, but that had left Stockton with a mix of what remained to form an escort.

He wasn't worried about the strike. The enemy ship had launched all of eight fighters, apparently the only ones it had managed to recover in the Corpus system before it turned and fled at *Dauntless*'s approach. His people could blow the meager defensive force away in a matter of minutes, and then Federov's bombers would have their way open to blast the enemy battleship.

No, it wasn't the attack on the battleship that worried him, at

119

least not *this* battleship. But the other two capital ships moving across the system had him shitting bricks.

Dauntless had emerged from the transwarp link to find its prey trying to flee with badly damaged engines. The last shot of the primaries had taken the enemy vessel near the aft, and the best the AIs could project, the Union ship was struggling with half thrust at best, and probably a good deal less. But the satisfaction had been short-lived when the long-range scanning reports came in. Two more capital ships were inbound from the Phillos transit point and leading some kind of a convoy. Within minutes, the Union battleships had changed course, and they were heading across the system at full thrust. Right toward *Dauntless*.

They're going to be too late…

Stockton knew *Dauntless* could take down its original enemy before it was engaged by the other two ships. Federov's bombers were like carnivores chasing after wounded prey, and he had no intention of letting even one enemy interceptor escape his grasp to take a shot at the them. But after the first fight was over, all bets were off. His birds and Federov's would be blown, low on fuel and ready to land…just as the two approaching battleships were sending in their own attack waves.

He pushed the thoughts out of his mind. Captain Barron would deal with it, somehow. Stockton hadn't realized how his attitude toward the captain had evolved, from respect to affection…and now to almost limitless confidence. They'd been dead out at Santis, by all rights they should have lost that battle. But *Dauntless*'s captain had proven the Barron magic still ran in his blood. At least as far as Jake Stockton was concerned.

"We're going to deploy in two lines. Evens, maintain your bearings. Odds are to hit five seconds of thrust at 4g on my mark…mark." He slammed his own throttle back, feeling the thrust as his engines fired. He counted slowly, silently. Three… two…one…

"Cut thrust now." He released the throttle and felt the pressure vanish, replaced by weightlessness. "All right, odds, you're on your own. Break formation and hunt those bastards down. Evens, hold your line. You're there for anything that gets through."

He angled his throttle, kicking in his thrust again as he picked out a target and closed on it. "Evens, use your lasers, but you can launch missiles if that's the only way to keep them from getting through. Nobody gets to our bombers, you understand? Nobody."

Even as he was speaking, he squeezed his finger on the trigger. His laser fired...and again. One of the small circles on his screen blinked out.

Seven.

*   *   *

"Captain, engineering reports both reactors are now functional at eighty to ninety percent of capacity, however they remain on minimal output per your orders. The engines are fully operational as well. Commander Merton advises against any high-g maneuvers except in an extreme emergency. Primaries are still offline, but all surviving secondaries are active. Dr. Jervis has updated the casualty reports. We have forty-one wounded in sickbay and twenty-three dead."

Sara Eaton sat quietly listening to Nordstrom as he read the updates coming into *Intrepid*'s bridge. Her people had been hiding for days now, and so far no enemy vessels had discovered her. Eaton had been steeling herself the entire time for a report advising her that Union battleships were approaching, but she was pleasantly surprised at the progress her damage control teams had managed. Her acceptance of certain death was giving away to that most dangerous of emotions. Hope.

The joy only lasted a few seconds before the casualty report brought her back to reality. There had been sharp increases in both the dead and the wounded. She knew that was mostly the figures catching up with the realty that had already existed, the finding of bodies that had been inaccessible before, or more wounded being brought to sickbay and treated. But nearly ten percent of her people were casualties, and that fact weighed heavily on her.

"Very well, Commander. Continue silent running." *Intrepid* was on minimal power generation. Eaton had taken every effort to hide her ship in the massive dust cloud, but she was still amazed that her battleship had seemed to escape pursuit. She'd dropped a spread of probes on the way into the cloud, but she hadn't dared to activate them yet beyond simple passive scans. Both the pulse to activate the scanning devices and their own operations would make it far easier for any enemy vessels nearby to locate *Intrepid*. And if the entire Union fleet was still out there, the loss of cover meant certain death.

"Maintaining silent running, Captain."

Eaton stared at the main display. It was mostly blank, with only vague light trails moving around every few seconds. The cloud that was hiding *Intrepid* was also blinding her. The ship's passive scanners were functional out to perhaps ten thousand kilometers, which was a brief hop in terms of space combat. Her active scanners wouldn't have fared much better in the dense, radioactive dust, but even if they would have, she wouldn't have dared to use them. Running active scans would be like banging a drum, begging any enemy ship within five million kilometers to locate her vessel.

"Status report from the launch bays?" *Intrepid*'s bays were a mess, damaged from the battle and overloaded with fighters Eaton had taken in. She'd ordered her bay crews to triage the birds ruthlessly, dumping any they couldn't repair immediately into space. Most of all, she'd ordered them to find a way to service twice *Intrepid*'s full complement of fighters, to find a way to refit them all, and to have as many as possible ready to launch. She expected the enemy to find her eventually, and she was sure of only one thing. When they did, they weren't going to take out her people without one hell of a fight. If she could pull it off, the launch of ninety or more strikefighters would come as quite a surprise to whatever ship or ships finally cornered her.

"Launch control reports forty-three fighters refueled and rearmed. However, the launch platforms are still crowded with extra fighters. It will be at least an hour before we'll be able to launch anything."

"That is unsatisfactory, Commander. Advise launch control I want fighters on alert and ready to launch in twenty minutes." She saw that Nordstrom was going to say something, but she beat him to it. "No excuses, Commander. I don't care what it takes, but I want it done in twenty minutes."

Assuming no one finds us in that time…

"Yes, Captain." Nordstrom's tone suggested he still had doubts. But he turned and passed the order down to the bays, silencing the objections of the launch chief as Eaton had done with his.

"Any reports from *Cambria, Astara,* or *Condor?*" The three small ships that had escaped with *Intrepid* were under orders to run silent, just like the battleship. They were operating under radio silence, exchanging messages with the *Intrepid* by direct laser comm, and only when necessary. It was a cumbersome way to communicate, especially when the dust in the cloud dispersed the lasers, reducing output by more than ninety percent. But it was almost proof against detection, and therefore the only option for her makeshift task force.

"*Cambria* reports all systems at or close to one hundred percent. We haven't had any update since the last ones from *Astara* or *Condor,* but as of their most recent report, both vessels were conducting repairs to their power systems."

"Very well." Eaton almost ordered her exec to send out a transmission, but getting the lasers through the dust cloud was difficult and time-consuming, and she felt she needed a good reason to force her people to make the effort. The commanders of the two ships would contact her when they had any material change in condition to report.

"Captain, we're picking up intermittent signals from outside the dust cloud."

Eaton's head snapped around. "Enemy ships looking for us?"

"I don't think so, Captain. It seems farther away…massive energy, explosions." Nordstrom paused. "If I didn't know better, I'd say there's still a fight going on out there."

That's not possible. The fleet bugged out days ago, and the ships that remained are...gone.

"Do what you can to amplify the input, Commander."

"Trying that, Captain, but it's still just intermittent signals. If we activated active scanners…"

"Negative, Commander. We might as well light a flare." She paused, thinking. "But maybe…" She raised her head, looking across the bridge at her exec. "Yes. Prepare to activate the probes…just the two closest to the signals you're receiving. Flash comm transmission, and passive scanners only." The probes were outside of the dust cloud, "hiding," more or less, amid the battle debris. Their passive scanners would have a better chance of picking up whatever scraps of a contact were coming through to *Intrepid.*

"Yes, Captain." Nordstrom worked his controls. Then he turned and snapped off a series of orders to the communications officer. Finally, he said, "We're ready, Captain."

Eaton almost fired off a series of questions to confirm her people had taken all possible steps to minimize the chances of detection…but they knew their business, and they had her confidence. "Do it, Commander. Activate the probes."

She knew even with the greatest precautions, the plan was a risky one. Any enemy ships near the probes would have a good chance of picking up the comm signal. But remaining in the cloud with no idea what was happening outside was dangerous too…and if there was even the chance that friendly forces were indeed out there fighting again, it smacked vaguely of cowardice to remain in hiding, enough to make that choice unpalatable to her.

"Activating probes now, Captain."

Eaton waited quietly for the data to start streaming in. But Nordstrom beat her to it, reading off his report even as she was starting to assess the raw information herself.

"At least four capital ships, Captain. Two appear to be coming from the Corpus transwarp link. The other two seem to be inbound from Phillos…and there are more contacts behind them."

"ID on any vessels? Ours? Theirs?"

"We are definitely picking up at least one Confederation beacon." A short pause. "It's *Dauntless*. She appears to be firing on the vessel ahead of her. The two other ships are too far out for specific data."

"*Dauntless?*" *Tyler Barron's ship.* She'd heard in one report or another that *Dauntless* was on the way to join the fleet. Reports of what had happened out on the Rim were still sketchy, at least at her pay grade, but it sounded like Barron and his people had fought one hell of a battle out there. *And now they get here just in time to walk into an ambush...*

She didn't doubt Tyler Barron and his crew could beat one Union battleship in a heads up fight, but it looked like at least two more were on the way in. She didn't have confirmation that the two other ships were hostile, but the direction they were coming from told her all she needed to know. *Dauntless doesn't have a chance...not unless we do something.*

She turned toward Nordstrom, but then she paused. She'd protected her people, kept them alive after she'd led them into the cloud. She'd hated herself for leaving the rest of the fleet behind, but she was grateful for her crew's lives. Now, she found the words stuck in her throat. *Dauntless* was doomed without help...but even if *Intrepid* intervened, the two battleships and their small cluster of escorts would still be outnumbered and outgunned. For the wonders her engineers had performed, her ship remained damaged, many of the repairs fragile and improvised. Leaving the cloud put her people at grave risk...but staying behind meant watching their comrades die.

Her hesitation was brief. Staying hidden was unthinkable. Their brothers and sisters were fighting out there...and without help, *Dauntless* had *no* chance. She felt her fists clench, her body tense with anger, with determination.

"Commander, prepare to bring reactors up to maximum available power. The engine room is to stand by."

"Yes, Captain." She could hear in Nordstrom's tone that the officer agreed with her actions wholeheartedly.

"I want all weapons systems activated and at full alert. Send flash laser comms to *Cambria*, *Astara*, and *Condor*…advise them to prepare to follow us into battle." She nodded back as Nordstrom acknowledged the command. Then she said, "And advise the launch bays that twenty-minute deadline just became crucial."

Chapter Fifteen

"All fighters launched, Captain. Commander Jamison reports his people are in formation and advancing to intercept incoming enemy strike force."

"Very well. Commence landing operations for Lieutenant Stockton's and Lieutenant Federov's fighters." Barron had watched as Federov's bombers savaged the battleship *Dauntless* had pursued from Corpus. Her pilots had scored no less than eight direct hits with their plasma torpedoes, and then they had linked up with Stockton's interceptors and run a series of strafing runs, picking at the great wounds they'd opened in the enemy's hull. By the time *Dauntless* had entered firing range, the Union vessel's guns were silenced, the big ship virtually dead in space. One shot from the primaries had finished the job, the stricken battleship cracking open like an egg when the heavy guns hit it amidships.

"Yes, Captain. Issuing recall orders now."

Dauntless had managed to launch about half her fighters in the initial wave, and now she had followed with the remainder, refit and refueled just as the depleted bombers and interceptors from the first strike were on their way back. He hoped to get as many as possible of the returning pilots back out into space before the approaching enemy strike force entered range, but he suspected that was more wishful thinking than rational expectation. Most likely, Commander Jamison and the twenty-six fighters he'd just launched would have to face the incoming enemy strike—over one hundred strong—on their own.

"Commander Travis, please make clear that the recall order applies to *all* pilots in the first wave." Barron had decided to let Stockton off the hook for his earlier antics, half because he liked his wayward ace and half because the scoundrel had probably saved *Dauntless* from more extensive damage. But he was running a warship, and he couldn't make a habit of looking the other way at insubordination. If Stockton pulled something like that again, he knew he'd have no choice but to throw him in the brig. And he needed the brash, gifted pilot.

"Yes, sir," Travis replied, her tone making it clear she understood just what Barron meant.

Barron sat silently as his first officer repeated his command into the comm unit, leaving no possible room for misunderstanding. He'd come to respect Travis in many ways, the majority in which they were alike, but perhaps even more the few where they were different.

Dauntless's second-in-command found it easier to be the heavy than he did. She could drink with the crew when they were off-duty, play cards with them, counter their raunchiest jokes with ones of her own as bad or worse as anything the grimmest veteran crew chief could spew. But she had no trouble instantly shedding the veneer of friendship and coming down on them like the core of a neutron star when she had to...whether she was scolding someone for a sloppy galley or sending men and women to die.

Barron liked to think he was a decisive officer, one who could do whatever was necessary. But there was always something there, a bit of guilt or hesitation, a realization that no matter how hard he worked, no matter how well he executed his duty, he'd had it easier than any of the officers and spacers under his command, that the Barron name had, at least to some extent, paved his way to the captain's chair.

Perhaps that is where Atara gets that toughness. She never had any of that privilege that blesses—and haunts—you. She had to claw her way to everything she ever attained. I wonder if there isn't a strength gained from that, one I can never share?

You would understand, Grandfather. You made the name that I inherited. I will fight, and I will do my best. I may be victorious…but I will never really understand things the way you did. The way Atara does.

"Captain, Lieutenant Stockton is leading his and Lieutenant Federov's fighters in."

"Very well…Stockton and the interceptors are to land first. Advise Chief Evans I want those interceptors turned around in record time."

"Yes, Captain."

Barron's eyes fixed on the cloud of enemy craft heading toward his ship. One hundred and four enemy fighters, almost half of them fitted out as bombers—enough destructive potential to turn *Dauntless* into a superheated cloud of plasma. And in front of the bombers were more than fifty interceptors, screening the attack…and outnumbering Jamison's fighters more than two to one.

Barron had confidence in his squadrons, and he knew they were more than a match for the enemy one on one. But two on one? Maybe…if Jamison and his people could focus on the dogfight. But he knew they wouldn't—couldn't. Jamison's pilots weren't out there to chase enemy interceptors. They were there to stop that bombing strike. Somehow.

That meant breaking off from the enemy interceptors as quickly as possible and driving toward the strike force behind. Barron wasn't a pilot, but he knew that was one of the most difficult and dangerous assignments for a fighter group. The Union interceptors would come about to close in on Jamison's flanks and rear as his people struggled to reach the bombers. Pilots would die who might have lived in a straight up fight, gunned down as they ignored the threats against them to go after the attack craft that could wound *Dauntless*.

"I want all defensive batteries armed and ready, Commander."

"Yes, sir."

Because whatever Jamison and his people do, some of those bombers are going to get through...

*   *   *

"Stay focused. We're going to hit these fighters hard, and then we're going to blast right through to the bombers. Fire your missiles against these interceptors...they're the tougher targets, and we want to blow a hole through their formation. But no dogfighting, no breaking our vector to go chasing after them. We're after the bombers. That's our priority."

Jamison knew his veteran pilots didn't need those instructions. They understood what was at stake. But half his force consisted of former garrison pilots, men and women who'd never fired at an enemy before this fight. It was natural to focus on the interceptors, the enemy that could hurt *you*. But the fighters were there to protect *Dauntless*, and their own safety, even survival, was a secondary concern.

He looked at his screen, at the incoming wave of enemy fighters. His people were outnumbered, and no matter how well his people did in the first minutes of the fight, they'd have enemy interceptors chasing them down as they tried to reach the bombers. The enemy wouldn't stop his attack, he was sure of that. But they were probably going to make it expensive.

"Typhoon, you've got the left. I'll take the right. You know why we're here."

"Roger that, Thunder. We'll get the job done."

Jamison knew Turner was one of his best, but even the ace pilot was in new territory, stepping into the big shoes of Tillis "Ice" Krill as commander of Yellow squadron.

"All squadrons, accelerate at 6g. Let's get some velocity going and blast right through these bastards."

Jamison moved his throttle, pulling it back, feeling the kick as his engines fired. He picked out one of the lead interceptors in the enemy force, and his hand slipped to the side, bringing his fighter toward his chosen target.

"All personnel, choose your targets…break."

His eyes were glued to his scanner, focused on the fighter right in front of him. The other dots on the screen were shifting all around him—his people were moving out, arcing their vectors slightly and attacking individual targets.

He flipped a row of switches on his dashboard, arming his missiles. Then he gripped the throttle, his finger poised on the firing stud. There was a loud bong from his targeting system, the AI advising that he'd achieved a final lock. But he still didn't launch the weapon. He was moving right toward his target, still accelerating, and every second not only brought him closer, it imparted more intrinsic velocity to the missile itself. He was less than ten thousand kilometers from the enemy fighter when he squeezed his finger hard, sending the deadly weapon on its way.

The enemy fighter changed the angle of its thrust almost immediately, but it was too late. Jamison had gotten close, his missile's velocity too great for the pilot to escape. Jamison imagined the frustration his enemy felt, the panic. And then, a few second later, it was over. The fighter was gone from his screen.

His eyes darted around, checking his own blind spot and keeping an eye on his pilots, even as he searched for his next target. He felt a rush of excitement as he realized his fighters had taken out seven of the enemy already. *No, eight*. And they'd only lost one of their own.

His finger closed over the trigger, launching his second missile. He fired at longer range this time, and as soon as the weapon disengaged, he angled his throttle, turning his thrust back toward his original vector. Straight toward the enemy strike group. He was at least two thirds of the way through the enemy line of interceptors. There was one more in front of him…and then clear space all the way to bombers. There were interceptors left, but it would take time for them to reverse even their modest velocity and turn to pursue his fighters. With luck, his people would reach the strike craft first…before the surviving enemy interceptors took them from the sides.

He fired his lasers, holding down the trigger, blasting away.

The enemy fighter moved hard to the side, struggling to escape Thunder's fire. Jamison knew he could catch the enemy ship. He had him dead to rights. But pursuit would turn him away from his primary targets, so he let his prey go.

He turned away, and he stared ahead, single-minded, focused. Until he saw the symbols on the edge of his screen. The fighter he'd allowed to escape...and one of his own. In one terrible second he saw that his pilot—one of the transfers from Archellia's garrison—was at a disadvantage. Caught. Dead to rights. Then he saw a tiny spec of light. A missile.

He felt his hand try to move, to turn and accelerate at full thrust after the ship he'd just let by. But he knew it was too late. He could see the scene in his mind, that pilot's terrible realization that his death was seconds away. He would know, of course, that he was caught, that he didn't have the skill or experience to break away. But there was nothing Jamison could do. He could torture himself, scream *murderer* into the mirror when he got back to *Dauntless*, blaming himself for what he had done. If he got back. But right now, he had his mission. And nothing would change that, not even the pain that hit him when the small blue dot winked off the screen. His pilot was dead.

He felt rage, almost uncontrollable. It took all he had in him not to chase the enemy he'd allowed to live a moment before. But his duty was still there, and for all the pain of imagining the death of one pilot, his mind was full of starker images. *Dauntless*, her broken hull bleeding air and fluids, great walls of flame in the landing bays, consuming everything in their path.

No, he couldn't go back. Not for revenge. Not for anything. He stared ahead, grim, his eyes focused. He would take his revenge. He would take it on the enemy bombers.

"Let's go," he said into the comm, his voice as cold as space. "It's time to kill some bombers."

* * *

"Another hit, Captain. Commander Jamison's strike force really hit the enemy bomber wing hard."

Barron didn't respond. He was gratified that his fighter commander had managed to kill so many bombers. He'd known how good Jamison was, but even he was surprised at the tally. Over twenty bombers destroyed outright, and a number more damaged. But that still left twenty-five heading toward *Dauntless*, with nothing to stop them except the ship's own defensive batteries. And perhaps a handful of fighters, if Chief Evans and his people were able to get a few of Lieutenant Stockton's birds back into space.

Hell, Stockton alone would be worthwhile. And Barron didn't have a doubt the sometimes troublesome ace had insisted his own fighter be the first one serviced.

Barron took a deep breath as he watched another of Jamison's fighters disappear. Thunder's attack had been devastating, but at the cost of leaving two-thirds of the enemy interceptors untouched. Those fighters were coming around now, ripping toward Jamison's exhausted pilots from behind and from the flanks. As they did, the casualty numbers began to rise sharply.

"Captain, we're getting several intermittent contacts from the dust cloud at 233.019.214."

Barron's head swung around to the main display. The big 3D tank was projecting the huge dust cloud, and he could see tiny lights flickering in and out as the AI tried to deal with the sporadic contacts.

"Launch a spread of probes, Commander. If we've got more enemy forces coming at us, I need to know now."

If we've got more enemy forces coming, we're dead. It's that simple.

"Probes launching, Captain."

He hadn't had much hope that his ship and its exhausted fighter squadrons could defeat two enemy battleships. But "not much" and "none" were two entirely different things. If those contacts were more enemy forces—and what else could they be?—Barron had moved firmly into the "none" camp.

Still, whether he had any hope or not, he would fight to the end. All his people would. Enemy reinforcements just forced a change of plans.

"Commander, prepare for full thrust forward. We're going to

close with those bombers and engage before they're reinforced." Expecting *Dauntless*'s point defense batteries to take out so many bombers was a fantasy, but it was also his ship's only chance. And more squadrons piling on were only going to make things worse.

"Yes, Captain." Travis turned and relayed the command to engineering. Then she looked back at Barron. "We'll take them, sir. The gun crews are ready, and they know what's at stake."

Barron was silent, but he flashed a smile at his first officer. He didn't think she believed that for a minute. He considered himself to be a cold realist, but he was a wild dreamer next to Travis's grim and clear grasp of things. She knew they were as good as dead. He was as sure of that as he was of anything. But he appreciated her efforts to bolster his morale. A captain was there to provide strength to his crew, to give them the inspiration they needed to endure the stress and fear of battle. Everyone knew that. But Travis understood something far fewer spacers realized. It was her job, the first officer's, to help provide that strength to the captain, to aid him in bearing his almost incalculable burden. And he knew she would do that as long as she still drew breath.

"Engine room reports ready, Captain."

Barron was about to respond when Travis continued with, "Captain, we're picking up solid readings now…ships emerging from the dust cloud."

Barron's eyes darted to the display. There they were. Fighters. Almost fifty of them. His eyes were locked on them, even as they moved completely free of the dense cloud and into open space. He was about to look away when he saw more blinking lights, another wave behind the first, still partially covered by interference from the dense, radioactive particulate of the cloud.

"Probes?" he snapped.

"Still too far out for better data, sir. We should have a read in a minute or two."

"Very well. Enga…"

"Captain! We're getting signals from the fighters. Identification beacons." There was shock in Travis's voice, something that

Barron knew was a rare occurrence indeed. "I don't know how, sir…but they're ours! They're Lightning's! They're Confederation fighters!"

Chapter Sixteen

Confederation Intelligence
Troyus City
Planet Megara, Olyus III
308 AC

Gary Holsten sat at his desk, staring out at the vast metropolis below. Troyus City was a monument to the wealth and industry of the Confederation. Other planets bore the scars of such progress, the dense acid smog of Pradera or the polluted lakes and seas of Grivas, but Megara was a Core world, the home of the Confederation's capital, and Troyus City itself was the very center of its vast government apparatus. Humanity had seen many types of societies—and even more, Holsten suspected, in the pre-Cataclysmic past, though few reliable records of those times survived—but he'd never heard of one that didn't lavish untold riches on the seat of its government. People prospered, or they starved. Jobs were plentiful, or they were rare. Borders were defended, or they fell. But whatever else was happening, at least until the very end, it was a dead certainty the politicians lived in comfort.

Holsten was the head of the Confederation's sprawling intelligence operation, a job he had long treated as effectively a part time vocation, leaving his nights—his *late* nights—free to enjoy the perks of his other position, that of the sole heir to one of the Confederation's largest family fortunes. At least until war had broken out. Holsten had virtually disappeared from the capital's exclusive party scene since the first shots were fired on the frontier. He was missed there, he suspected, if not by true friends who pined for his company, at least by the string of beautiful women he'd dated and the bartenders, hosts and hostesses, casino employees, and general hangers on who had benefited so greatly from his bountiful largesse. Holsten had done his best to create his reputation as a dissolute hedonist, a wastrel with little on his mind but women, gambling, and the alcohol he consumed in far smaller quantities than he led people to believe. It was a useful cover, if one he'd utterly enjoyed creating, but there had been no time for such endeavors recently. The Confederation was in real trouble.

Holsten had clamped down on the flow of information from the front, withholding vast information from the press, and some of it even from the Senate itself. He'd lost count of how many laws he was breaking, but notwithstanding the reputation he'd worked—played?—so hard to create, Holsten was utterly dedicated to protecting the Confederation, whatever it took.

He, more than anyone else perhaps, knew how corrupt the Confederation's government was, but he also recognized that post-Cataclysmic times were dominated by totalitarian regimes, theocracies, and military societies like the Alliance. The Confederation was the one place where citizens, at least some of them, enjoyed anything remotely resembling freedom. And he knew that would end if they lost the war. Life under Union rule would be a nightmare, even more for the conquered than for the despotic regime's current citizens.

"I came as soon as I got your message. I assume it isn't good news." Michael Vonns stepped into the room. Vonns was one of Holsten's top aides, and one of his few real friends.

"No, Michael," he said grimly. "It is not good news."

"From the front? Arcturon?"

"Arcturon *and* Ghallus. Union forces hit Second Fleet at Ghallus, and they almost wiped it out. Admiral Marionberg was killed, along with two-thirds of her people. The survivors fled to Belatar in disarray."

"Did the enemy pursue?"

Holsten shook his head. "No. They moved through Copernika and hit First Fleet in the flank, just as it was engaging the enemy. Admiral Winston was unable to recover the situation, but he did manage to execute a retreat before it was too late. The closest thing to good news is, he was able to extricate twenty-three of his capital ships from the trap."

Vonns stood, staring back at his friend and boss. He was an experienced spy, but he wasn't able to keep the look of shock off his face.

"Sit, Mike. You standing there with that expression on your face isn't going to change anything."

Vonns hesitated for a few seconds. Then he walked over and dropped into one of the chairs facing Holsten's desk. "I don't believe it."

"Believe it."

"How could they field two forces of that size?"

"I don't know, but one thing I'm sure of is that we really screwed the pooch. All our prewar estimates on enemy strength turned out to be completely useless. They successfully hid massive forces from us, and now we're feeling the impact of that hammer."

Vonns sighed. "And since the Purge, our intel is for shit. We really have no idea what's going on behind the battle lines."

Purge was the informal name Confederation Intelligence had given to the massive roundup of its undercover personnel on Union worlds that occurred in the days before the invasion. Within a matter of seventy-two hours, Confederation Intelligence had lost contact with virtually every one of its agents in Union territory.

Holsten paused, a shadow falling across his face. Giving the chain of events a name, even one as ominous as Purge, tended to sanitize what had happened. All across Union space, on dozens of worlds, Confederation operatives who had been sure their covers were secure were rounded up by Sector Nine agents. He tried to imagine the stunned surprise on each of their faces, the stark terror they must have felt as they realized what was happening. Some, no doubt, acted quickly enough and summoned the immediate courage to kill themselves. All Confederation agents were equipped for a suicide option. But he knew just as well that many wouldn't have had the chance, or would have hesitated, losing the opportunity.

Those men and women, he knew, had ended up in Sector Nine's interrogation cells, and there he was certain they had suffered unimaginable torment. Breaking men and women was a Sector Nine specialty and, as much respect as he had for his operatives, he was sure many of them had hemorrhaged information.

It was possible that a few of his people had survived the roundups, that they had gone deeper under cover, unable to reach headquarters with any communications, but the end result was indisputable. The Confederation had virtually no effective assets remaining in the Union. They had no idea about fleet strengths, force movements, supply status...nothing. And the fact that Sector Nine had known so much about the identities of his personnel suggested the Confederation was riddled with enemy spies. Or one highly-placed traitor.

Holsten looked up at his friend. "We have a lot of questions, and not many answers. As far as their strength is concerned, how they did it doesn't matter much, not anymore. Reports from the battle at Arcturon suggest they sacrificed an entire line of battleships as decoys. Admiral Winston was shocked, and utterly confused. But I have some guesses myself. Have you ever heard of the Blue Star Duchies?"

Vonns squinted his eyes for a moment, thinking. "Yes, I think so. Far away, no? We don't have any real way to reach their space, do we?"

"No. They're on the other side of the Union. And they're not the only ones there. I suspect the Union has not been as idle these past ten years as we suspected. Our information is sketchy, but there are indications they conducted a series of smaller campaigns in the years before they attacked us, and that they annexed many of the worlds on their far border, stripping them of every valuable resource. *That* is how they built so many ships, Mike, at least in part. And the vessels they used as bait… I'd wager anything they were former Blue Star naval vessels, or from one of the other subjugated groups."

"Would subjugated military forces just line up to fight for their conquerors?"

"You know the Union as well as I do, Mike. You might say you would refuse, but would you? If your friends, your family, your kids, were back home at the tender mercies of Sector Nine?"

Vonns didn't answer, he just looked back, the expression on his face as communicative as any words could have been.

"It's all speculation anyway, and none of it is very useful, at least not in the short term. How they put together a force as large as they did is academic. They have it, and we need to find a way to defeat it."

"How did this happen? How did we end up in this position?"

"It's our fault, Mike. The Confederation's, I mean. We've known for years this war was coming, but every request for more funding was cut down before it was approved. Every ten keels the navy wanted to lay down got sliced to five. The Senators from the industrial worlds overruled the admirals' requests, substituting the things they wanted to produce for the systems the military wanted. The people longed for peace, even though they had every reason to think war was coming, and they tried to bury their heads and ignore it."

"And now we're in the worst shape we've been in for a long time. Maybe since Admiral Barron took over the fleet." Vonns sighed. "So, what do we do now? We can't produce ten years' worth of battleships in time to stop the enemy onslaught."

"No, we're outmatched in this fight. But let me ask you this—you're ex-military. If you were a Union admiral, and you knew you had numbers, would you be doing what they are?"

"Well, what they're doing is working pretty damned well, so…"

"No, that's not what I mean. Think about it more specifically." Holsten reached over to a small set of controls on his desk, pressing a small button. A large screen on the wall lit up, displaying a map of systems and lines representing transwarp connections. There were large yellow arrows depicting the Union movements since hostilities had begun. "Really look at this. Do we even have a war plan for this level of penetration so early?"

"I doubt it. There's no way…" Vonns's voice trailed off for a few seconds. "Supply. I don't know how they could possibly be supplying such a massive offensive so far from their starting bases. That's why we don't have any contingencies. This isn't supposed to be possible."

"I don't understand it either. But that just might be something we can change. Admiral Winston wanted a decisive battle, one designed to stop the enemy advance cold. He got that, and it was a disaster. The two enemy fleets have joined together, and they'll be following up hard on Winston. He doesn't have anywhere near the force he needs to stop them. But supply… whatever they managed to work out, it *has* to be tenuous. And their whole offensive relies on it. Without weapons, spare parts, fuel, provisions…their fleet would have to fall back, and probably a considerable way. That would buy us time to regroup, and to scrape up the last reserves we can find."

"You're right, Gary. It's got to be a vulnerability, but we haven't got a clue about what they're doing or how they're maintaining a supply line that long. What can we do about it, with Second Fleet almost destroyed and First Fleet on the run?"

"I don't know, Mike. But we have to figure out something, and we have to do it quickly. They've got to have a vulnerability now, but if we give them long enough to settle into the occupied systems, they'll build up conventional supply bases and consolidate their conquests."

Vonns sat quietly for a moment, staring at the ground. "I don't know, Gary…I'm stumped. We'd have to try to get something around their flanks…" He looked over at the map. "…and there's just no way. First Fleet's beaten up, but worse, it's between the Union and the heart of the Confederation. If Admiral Winston went off on a crazy mission to try to get around the enemy fleet, there would be nothing to stop—or even slow—the enemy. They'd have an open route right into the Iron Belt."

"No, you're right about First Fleet. It's got to stay where it is, though I'm not sure it can do much to stop the enemy if they keep pushing hard."

"What then? Second Fleet is a wreck. Third Fleet is deployed to defend the Core worlds. There's no way the Senate is going to let the navy move those ships, not now. Not when they're scared."

Holsten paused. "They're scared all right...but they don't know *how* bad things really are."

"You've been censoring the reports to the Senate?" Vonns stared across the desk. "Gary, come on. I agreed with some of the earlier stuff we...massaged...but you're playing with fire now."

"I know. But I'm in it already. I knew if they got accurate reports on the enemy strength they would panic. They'd want to defend themselves, and they would have voted to pull forces back from the front. Admiral Winston was planning his stand at Arcturon and, while I had my doubts about the plan, I didn't want to see him lose any of his force right before the battle." He paused. "And, of course, one falsified report led to another..."

Vonns shook his head. "What a mess."

"Yeah, it's a mess. But I don't really care about that right now. The Confederation is teetering on the edge, Mike. We're staring into the abyss, and a bunch of chattering politicians aren't going to save us." Holsten took a deep breath before he continued. "Which is why I have activated Fifth Fleet."

"You can activate anything you want, Gary, but where are you going to get the ships to turn it from a paper formation into a real force?"

"Third Fleet, to start."

"Gary, we just agreed the Senate will never allow Third Fleet to move forward."

"Third Fleet will stay right where it is. At least the flag will."

"What are you talking about, Gary? Please don't tell me..."

"I've arranged for Admiral Striker to command Fifth Fleet… and Admiral Thompson is on board with the plan. We transfer enough ships from Third Fleet to build up Fifth Fleet…quietly."

"You're insane, Gary. How long can you possibly expect to maintain a deception on that scale?"

Holsten looked back at his friend. "However long it takes to save the Confederation, Mike. If we pull it off, I'm sure I can smooth things over." He sounded less than one hundred percent confident.

"And if the plan fails?"

"Then, my friend, the Confederation is doomed." He reached down and pulled something from a drawer, setting it down on the desk. It was a gun, small, stubby, easy to hide. Standard issue for operatives. "If that happens, I have no intention of surviving to see Foudre Rouge soldiers landing on Megara, my old friend…and it makes very little difference to me if the Senate condemns me before I blow my brains out."

Chapter Seventeen

"Launch control reports the last of the fighters are ready, Captain. Awaiting your order to launch."

"By all means, Commander. Launch at once." Eaton had always been proud of her people, but she'd never been more impressed than by the crews of her launch bays. *Intrepid* carried a full complement of forty-eight fighters, but with this last wave, she had refit and launched almost one hundred. It shouldn't even have been possible. There were too few service docks, too little space. Yet her people had done it.

She looked at the display, watching her first two waves of fighters as they moved toward the enemy strike force. *Dauntless* had launched just under thirty fighters, which Eaton knew from memory was half her complement. Whether they had lost the rest, or whether they were prepping them even now, she didn't know. The interference from the cloud was still affecting her comm.

Her wings were coming in at an angle, and they were going to hit the enemy bombers before they closed to firing range.

Which is a damned good thing, because that many bombers would have

144

hit Dauntless hard. And those two battleships would have finished her off, no question.

We're still going to have one hell of a fight on our hands, but it's one we can win together.

Her scanners confirmed that *Dauntless* had already destroyed one enemy battleship. Its shattered ruins were still floating through space, leaking radiation and residual heat, but it had only taken *Intrepid*'s AI a few seconds to determine that the vessel was lifeless and essentially destroyed.

She watched as her fighters closed the last distance and struck into the enemy bomber force. The Union interceptors, which had been fighting *Dauntless*'s remaining fighters, broke off and tried to come about to face the new threat. But they were late and disorganized, and one wing of *Intrepid*'s incoming fighters hit them with a wave of missiles. A third of the Union craft were destroyed in the first minute of combat, and the battle continued on, the results nearly as lopsided as the original exchange. Even *Dauntless*'s battered force attacked with renewed vigor, coming in from the other side and bracketing the enemy squadrons. It wasn't a battle; it was a slaughter. Finally, a few Union craft broke out and fled back toward their mother ships, *Intrepid*'s fighters right behind them.

Farther forward, the second group of *Intrepid*'s fighters crashed into the force heading for *Dauntless*. They fired their missiles and then sliced into the remnants of the group, blasting the unwieldy bombers to atoms. More than fifty interceptors tore into half as many bombers, and within a few minutes not a single attack craft remained.

She felt a wave of satisfaction. She'd put her people at risk, given up their hiding place, and saving *Dauntless* from the bombing strike made it all worth the risk.

That risk isn't over yet...

She glanced at the display, at the two enemy battleships. The massive vessels were still moving forward. Her makeshift squadrons were all equipped for anti-fighter operations. It had been miracle enough that her people got the ships into battle, but there had been no way to install the bulky bombing kits in the overcrowded bays.

That meant there would be no significant bomber attacks on the enemy battleships. The fight would be a toe-to-toe slugging match, *Dauntless* and *Intrepid* standing together, throwing everything they had at the enemy and enduring every incoming shot. Unless *Dauntless* had some bombers in their bay. She'd only seen about half the battleship's complement, but she had no idea whether the others had been destroyed, or whether they were in the bays being refit.

She'd been trying to remember everything she knew about Barron, but beyond his general reputation—and, of course his famous lineage—she had come up with very little.

Tyler Barron…the favored son of the Confederation navy…

She'd met Barron briefly once or twice, but she didn't really know him. She knew *of* him of course, everybody did. Rance Barron's exploits were required lessons in every school in the Confederation, and from what she'd heard, Tyler was a fine officer. His recent actions on the Rim had only added to his reputation, even if the details of what he had done there remained classified. She'd never second-guessed the praise she'd heard for the famous officer…but the lives of her own people had never depended as much on his abilities as they did now. She wasn't doubting him, not exactly, but she was nervous, edgy.

"Captain, we're getting a signal from *Dauntless*."

"On my comm, Commander." She reached down and grabbed her headset, pulling it over her hair, struggling for a few seconds when it caught on a few loose strands from her otherwise tightly-bound ponytail.

"*Intrepid*…this is Captain Barron on *Dauntless*. Do you read?"

"We read you, *Dauntless*. Captain Sara Eaton here."

"Captain Eaton, what can I say? We're delighted to find you here. Thanks for the assist."

"Anytime, Captain Barron. We're all on the same team." She paused for a few seconds. "Speaking of which, our team's not out of the woods yet."

"No, Captain, it's not. I've got twenty-eight fighters in my bay ready to launch, thirteen of them bombers."

"Everything I've got is already out there."

"I gathered that, Captain. Warbook confirms *Intrepid*'s complement at forty-eight. How is it you launched a hundred fighters?"

"The fleet fought here, Captain." Eaton's voice became darker. "We were ambushed. We lost a lot of ships before the main force escaped. The retreating ships couldn't pick up all their fighters. There were squadrons all across the battle line, intermixed, cut off from their motherships. We were on the end of the line, cut off from escape. I picked up as many fighters as we could cram into the bays…but I'm afraid we couldn't take them all."

Eaton felt a twinge in her gut. She expected condemnation, or at least probing questions from Barron about how *Intrepid* ended up hiding in the dust cloud while the remnants of the fleet were being butchered. She had only been following orders, but she'd been telling herself that for days with no effect on her own feelings of guilt. She doubted the explanation would carry much more weight with an officer of Barron's pedigree.

"Well done, Captain," Barron said, his voice free of any hint of recrimination. "And well done now too. Again, you have my thanks, and the gratitude of my crew."

"Thank you, Captain. You're…um…you're most welcome." She was surprised. In her experience, people, especially those among the exalted ranks of ship captains, tended to be judgmental, ready to impose their own, often highly prejudicial, viewpoints. But Barron's words seemed genuine.

"We're not done yet, though," Barron said. "There are still two enemy battleships coming…and as I see it, the Confederation navy has a debt to settle with the Union."

"Yes, Captain. It certainly does."

"Then let's get *Intrepid* and *Dauntless* formed up and make a payment on that debt."

"Absolutely, Captain Barron. Absolutely."

* * *

"We're picking up a lot of debris, Captain. Preliminary analysis suggests the battle here was truly massive. We've located at least a dozen hulks of capital ships so far."

Barron looked over at Travis. "That's why we were on our way here. But we were supposed to link up with the fleet before the battle, not get here after the fact and count the dead. It looks like they could have used us."

"From the looks of things here, and from Captain's Eaton's comments, I don't think one capital ship would have made the difference, sir."

"No, perhaps not. But I still don't like the fact that we weren't here."

"I don't either, Captain. But perhaps it was for the best. If we'd been here, *Dauntless* might have been destroyed. But now we're still in the battle…and we're looking at a straight up fight. And there isn't an even battle against the Union I wouldn't take." Travis's usually calm tone was different, unusually feral.

"I'm inclined to agree, Commander. But we've got it whether we want it or not, and it's time to strike back. We fight here for ourselves…and for all our comrades who died in this system." He paused. "Is *Intrepid* in position?" He'd cut *Dauntless*'s thrust, waiting for Captain Eaton to bring her vessel around and take position alongside his battleship.

"Yes, Captain. And her escort vessels will be in a few minutes." Barron had been pleased to discover that *Intrepid* was accompanied by three smaller ships that had also survived the battle…especially when his scanners revealed the Union battleships were each accompanied by a trio of their own smaller escorts.

"Very well. We will wait until the entire force is in formation."

Barron glanced down at his screen. The enemy vessels had stopped accelerating, but they were still coming on. He imagined the sudden destruction of their fighter wings, which had seemed so likely to overwhelm and cripple *Dauntless*, had them on edge. But he had some inkling of the way Sector Nine infiltrated Union vessels, and of the draconian punishments for officers and spacers even suspected of cowardice. He didn't suppose it was real courage that kept Union forces in the battleline, but it was effective nevertheless.

Besides, they're protecting something...

There were two dozen other Union vessels lined up behind the battleships. It was too far for detailed data, but the mass estimates suggested they were large ships. Energy readings didn't match expectations for battleships—and besides, if the enemy force included more capital ships, they would be advancing alongside the other two warships. He couldn't be sure, but Barron suspected he'd encountered an enemy supply convoy, and that the massive vessels were tankers and freighters.

Of course...supply. That's what doesn't add up here.

Something had been nagging at Barron since *Dauntless* had encountered the enemy battleship in Corpus. He'd seen the Confederation's plans for war, their force estimates and reams of scenarios. For months, his ship had patrolled the border, waiting for the outbreak of war. But now he realized something didn't make sense. There was no way the Union fleet could have moved so far so fast, not while maintaining a supply line that could support non-stop combat.

His mind flashed back to the Rim, to his struggle with Captain Rigellus and *Invictus*. Rigellus had crossed the border and occupied Santis, a major production site for tritium, the primary fuel used in warship reactors. It had been a prelude to invasion, and an acknowledgement that logistics was the key to sustaining a campaign, that without seizing the Confederation production facility, an invasion was not feasible.

How are they supplying their forces?

Conventional wisdom suggested there was no way the Union forces could have done what they clearly had. They were too far from their bases, and they hadn't had enough time to build facilities closer to the front lines. There were gas giants in many of the occupied Confederation systems, of course, spots where the invaders could build facilities to produce the reaction mass necessary to fuel their massive fleets. But that took months at least. And that didn't even account for weapons, provisions, spare parts...all the things it took to keep a battle fleet in action. He had no idea how the Union was keeping their fleets in the fight. Even the Alliance, where toughness and self-sacrifice were virtually national pastimes, had required a tritium production facility to contemplate full-scale invasion. But there was no equivalent of Santis on the Union border.

"Captain, launch control reports that Lieutenant Stockton and his fighters are ready to go on your command."

Barron shook himself from his thoughts. "Status of escort vessels?"

"*Astara* and *Cambria* are ready, sir. *Condor* is still taking position to the rear."

Condor was a scout ship, small and fast but with minimal armament. She had no place in the battle line.

"Very well. Commence launch operations. And contact *Intrepid*. Advise them we are ready to initiate forward thrust."

* * *

"Yes!" Stockton's comm microphone was switched off. The yell was only for himself. He'd led the strike force in, closing to point blank range before he allowed the bombers to launch their torpedoes. His aggressive strategy had come at a cost. Three of his bombers went down under the battleship's guns, but the others delivered a crushing barrage, their weapons tearing massive holes in the enemy's hull, ripping away entire gun turrets.

The enemy ships had sent all of their fighters forward, no doubt confident that the strike would overwhelm *Dauntless*. But they hadn't accounted for *Intrepid*…and the double contingent of fighters she carried. The massive attack from the dust cloud had virtually wiped out the Union fighters, and Stockton's people hadn't even had to face a combat space patrol.

"Interceptors, one more run," he snapped after flipping on his comm unit. "Let's see if we can't plant a few shots inside some of those hull breaches. Lieutenant Curtiss, take the bombers and head back to *Dauntless*." The fighters with the anti-ship armaments were too unmaneuverable for precise targeting with their lasers, and too vulnerable to the battleship's still-active point defense guns. The interceptors were another matter. With no CSP to oppose, they hadn't burned fuel in endless dogfighting. They had one more attack left in them.

"Roger that, Raptor. Bombers, form up on me. Let's head back to base." Curtiss was another of *Dauntless*'s longtime pilots, a veteran of the ten months the battleship had spent on the Union border and the deadly fight against *Invictus* out on the Rim.

"Interceptors, on me. Pick your targets…your lasers aren't going to do much good unless you can find a weak spot and hit them there. And watch out for their point defense turrets. They're damned dangerous this close in."

He brought his fighter around, hitting his thrust and changing his course right toward the hulking battleship. He couldn't see his enemy, of course. Space battles took place over ranges entirely too great for visuals, even when fighters were doing close in strafing runs. But his scanner displayed an image of the Union battleship, and the areas where hull integrity was lost were highlighted.

His eyes narrowed, focusing on one of the largest breeches. It was on top, amidships…near where he guessed the ship's reactors were located. His fighter's lasers weren't likely to penetrate the inner shielding protecting the massive vessel's power supply, but there would be power lines and conduits all around, stretching out to every section of the battleship, and his guns were strong enough to cause significant damage to those.

He glanced up at his display, checking the range. Four thousand kilometers. That was close by the standards of war in space, but not close enough. Stockton was going right down the Union ship's throat, and he knew the rest of his people would follow. He was determined to do some more damage before *Dauntless* closed to firing range and began the final exchange.

He adjusted his course slightly, honing his vector, lining up his guns on the target. Even for a hotshot pilot like Stockton, targeting was ninety-nine percent number crunching by his AI. It was that last one percent—intuition, gut feel, reflexes—that separated out the great pilots from the others. His ship and target were both moving, and both were changing their courses slightly, every blast of thrust affecting the targeting.

He was close, but even at point blank range, he'd be targeting a hull breach twenty meters in length from thousands of kilometers. It was an accuracy that went beyond what any sharpshooter or marksman could hope to match. And it was the only way Stockton's interceptor could cause meaningful damage to his target.

His finger hovered over the firing stud, his eyes focused on the display. Three thousand kilometers. He adjusted the throttle one more time, an almost imperceptible move. Then he fired. And again. His finger was tight against the throttle as his lasers fired over and over, at least a dozen times. Then he moved the control hard, back and to the side, blasting hard to alter his vector enough to clear the looming battleship. He'd taken his run in close, far closer than the "book" called for, but Stockton had never had much use for rules. He'd have taken it even closer, but he knew his people would have followed him all the way, and he was far from sure they all had the skill to pull it off. His blood was up, but he wasn't about to take the chance that any of his people would end up slamming into the enemy vessel.

The thrust was slamming him back in his chair, pushing down hard as his engines worked to counter his vector and velocity. He gasped for air while he maintained his grip on the throttle, holding out as long as he could—or, more accurately, as long as he thought the pilots following him could—and then he pushed forward, cutting the thrust to a more manageable 3g.

He had come around enough for his scanners to get fresh readings on the enemy ship. There were great blasts pushing out from the innards of the vessel, through the jagged tears in its hull. The fires he suspected were raging inside died instantly, of course, when they hit the vacuum of space. But his scanners displayed the great geysers of gasses and fluids ejected out of the terrible wounds torn into the giant ship. He didn't have an exact count of how many of his pilots had scored hits, but from the look of the tortured battleship, most of them had.

"All right, boys and girls, we've done our jobs, earned our

pay for this month. The rest of the party is up to *Dauntless* and *Intrepid*. Let's head back...and as soon as the fight's over, I want everybody in the officers' club. The drinks are on me!"

Chapter Eighteen

"Captain, I've got the primaries back online. Reactor A is at one hundred percent output again, but there's something wrong there, maybe a problem with the feeder mechanisms. Whatever it is, the rhythm is off…I can feel it. We haven't been able to pinpoint it yet, and we may have to scrag the whole reactor if it gets any worse. So, I'd use those guns now while you've got them."

"Got it, Fritzie. Do your best to keep the reactor online. After the battle you can take her completely apart and work your magic, but right now I need that power."

"Yes, sir. I'll do my best." Fritz cut the line. Then she turned toward the small cluster of engineers and technicians standing behind her. "What are you all doing standing around? Don't you see those battlestations lamps? You know what to do. Something's not right in the reactor, and if I have to give the captain that kind of half-assed report again, I promise every one of you will regret it until the day an enemy laser blows you to atoms. You hear me?"

There was anger in Fritz's voice, but it was mostly frustration. She drove her people hard. In fact, she had a reputation—

well earned—as the toughest chief engineer in the fleet. But for all her angry rants and her tirades, she was proud of her people, and protective of them too. She still ached from the losses the engineering teams had suffered at Santis, especially Sam Carson. The young engineer hadn't served long on *Dauntless*, but he'd quickly become one of the most popular members of the crew…and he'd been a damned fine engineer too. He'd died saving them all, braving the lethal radiation of the damaged reactor chamber to get the primaries back online at the battle's climax.

She had rarely spoken of Carson in front of the crew since then, but he still weighed heavily on her mind. For all her engineering skill and years of experience, Santis had been the first time she'd seen her people dying in action, and she was still struggling with it. Now she knew that nightmare could come again. *Dauntless* had escaped catastrophic damage in the fight so far, but she knew any second an enemy laser cannon could tear into a compartment, vaporizing some of her people or casting them out into space. And she knew if that happened, she'd have to ignore it, that her focus would have to remain on keeping *Dauntless* in the fight, on giving the captain the power and systems he needed to win.

"Billings, I want your team to go over Reactor A from one end to the other. It's working at full output now, but there's something not right. I know it." Fritz's voice was stern, almost harsh. Billings had always rubbed her just a little the wrong way. She knew the lieutenant was a good engineer, but he was always clowning around, and that clashed with her own intensity. She suspected it was how he dealt with the stress and fear of battle, and she tried to ignore it. She'd even promoted him, raising him to team leader, filling Carson's slot. Billings and Carson had been close, and she knew it had to be painful for Billings to take his friend's place, but she also knew he deserved the job.

And Sam would have chosen Walt if he'd been able to pick his own replacement…

"Yes, Commander. But it checks out on all readouts. I'm not sure there's anything to find."

"Just check it, Lieutenant, and I mean every millimeter. The internals and every feeder, every conduit…everything. I can feel there's something wrong."

"Yes, Commander." The engineer turned and jogged across the room, waving and shouting to his techs.

Fritz knew Billings didn't believe her. Most likely he thought she was imagining things…or that the accolades she received everywhere she went, the recognition as the best engineer in the navy, had gone to her head.

She reached out and put her hand on the wall. There it was. She'd felt the vibrations coming off the reactor a thousand times, and it was…different. It wasn't a big change. She wasn't surprised none of her people could feel it. But, by God, she could.

And she wasn't imagining things.

* * *

"Captain, *Dauntless* just fired her primaries again. Another hit!"

Eaton sat and listened as Nordstrom snapped out the report. That was the fourth direct hit in a row. *Dauntless* had quickly finished off the ship her bombers had damaged, and then Tyler Barron's vessel turned its fire to the other enemy battleship, the one *Intrepid* had been fighting. Eaton's people had acquitted themselves well, scoring a hit percentage just shy of fifty per-cent…well above fleet norms. But *Dauntless* had hardly missed.

She was gratified, of course. The sooner the enemy ship was destroyed, the less damage the two Confederation battle-ships would sustain. The fewer of their crews who would be killed or wounded. But she couldn't deny there was a touch of singed pride there too. She already felt guilty for hiding her ship in the dust cloud while the fleet's rearguard was systematically destroyed. Orders or no, lack of an alternative or no, it stuck in her craw. Watching Barron's crew outshoot her people was only making her self-worth take another beating.

"Maintain our fire, Commander. We've got that ship two on one, and I don't want to let up, not for a second."

"Yes, Commander."

She watched the display as her gunners fired *Intrepid*'s primaries again. A hit! Perhaps not as dead on as *Dauntless*'s last shot had been, but a solid strike nevertheless. The enemy ship *had* to be in bad shape…but it was still firing, and entirely too many of its guns remained operative.

At least their primaries are out.

The enemy ship hadn't fired its heavy laser cannons in more than ten minutes. The Union primaries weren't a match for the Confederation particle accelerators, but they were far stronger than the secondaries.

"Captain, we're picking up energy readings. The enemy vessel has engaged its engines." A short pause. "I think they're trying to break off."

"Get me *Dauntless*," Eaton snapped. She knew what she had to do, but she wasn't alone in the fight, and she wasn't about to risk any misunderstandings with Barron. Ship captains could be a prickly lot, and while she didn't know Barron well enough to gauge his attitudes, she couldn't help but think someone of his pedigree would be "by the book" all the way.

"On your line, Captain."

"*Dauntless*, this is Captain Eaton."

"Yes, Captain." It was Barron himself. She was surprised. No stuffed uniform scion of an old line naval family would answer his own comm.

"My scanners report that the enemy is trying to break off."

"Mine agree with yours, Captain. I suggest we pursue."

Eaton paused for a second. She had checked the database right after her scanners had ID'd *Dauntless*, and she'd confirmed what she'd already thought she knew. Tyler Barron's captain's commission was two months older than hers. He was her superior officer, even if only by a hair's breadth, and he had every right to issue her orders. His use of the word "suggest" indicated a far more diplomatic and careful attitude than she'd expected to find in Rance Barron's grandson. It made an impression on her, and she realized a healthy respect was growing for her comrade.

"Agreed, Captain. They appear to be blasting at 4g. Unknown

whether that is their current maximum capacity. Suggest we pursue at 6g and try to close the range."

"I concur, Captain Eaton. Commence 6g thrust in twenty seconds. Agreed?"

"Agreed."

Eaton cut the line. Despite her nagging little prejudices, she was really beginning to like Barron.

"I want 6g thrust in fifteen seconds, Commander. Course, directly toward the enemy."

"Yes, Captain."

Intrepid's bridge lights dimmed for an instant as her primaries fired again. She turned her head toward the display, just as the scanning report updated.

Another hit!

She felt a rush of pride. Her people were rising to the challenge, matching *Dauntless*'s gunners on the last two shots. Then Nordstrom turned toward her.

"Captain, the enemy ship's thrust has dropped below 2g."

Another wave of excitement took her. That last shot must have degraded the enemy's engines. She knew it was childish, perhaps, to keep a tally of damage inflicted by her people versus *Dauntless*'s, but it was friendly competition, and it did no harm. If the two crews challenged each other, drove their fellows to higher performance levels, it could only benefit both ships.

"Maintain thrust order." It was time to close. Time to finish this.

"Engines firing…now."

Eaton felt the pressure pushing her back into her chair. *Intrepid*'s dampeners absorbed some of the impact, but 6g was still uncomfortable.

"*Dauntless* is matching our thrust, Captain. We are closing on the enemy vessel."

Eaton stared at the display. If the Union ship couldn't get its engines fully back online, it was doomed. It was doomed anyway. *Intrepid* and *Dauntless* were accelerating, increasing their velocity toward their prey. The enemy vessel was thrusting at a mere 2g. Every second that passed increased the relative velocity of the Confederation battleships to their target.

"Secondary batteries, open fire. All gunnery teams, fire at will." There was no way to power the primaries, not with so much energy going to the engines. But *Intrepid*'s secondaries could fire, even if their recharges would be a bit slower than normal. And every shot that hit the Union ship wore it down, decreasing the chance of the battered vessel scoring hits on *Dauntless* or *Intrepid*.

"All turrets acknowledge, Captain. Secondary batteries are cleared to fire."

Almost immediately she heard the distant hum of the weapons. *Intrepid*'s secondary batteries were the same as *Dauntless*'s, triple-turreted laser cannons. They weren't bomb-pumped x-ray lasers like the old Confederation—and current Union—primaries, but they were the next most powerful thing. And they were quicker firing, at least when half the ship's power wasn't going to the engines.

A glance at the display confirmed that *Dauntless* was also firing her secondaries. The range was still long for the lasers, and no more than ten or fifteen percent of the shots from the two vessels were hitting. But every passing second closed the range, increasing the accuracy and power of each blast.

She watched as the Confederation ships closed, felt the bloodthirsty instinct inside as she realized the fight was almost over. *Intrepid* shook once, then again a few seconds later, a reminder that the battered enemy ship wasn't dead yet. But the hits had been from the Union secondaries, suggesting the x-ray lasers were offline. The engines were too, she realized, as she saw that the enemy thrust had dropped to zero.

"Get me Captain Barron," she snapped.

"On your line, Captain."

"Captain Barron, I think we should cut engines and divert all power to the primaries. The enemy ship is in trouble. Getting closer only makes their own remaining guns more effective. We can finish them off with our main guns."

"You read my mind, Captain. I was thinking the same thing. Let's cut thrust in ten seconds…and open fire."

"Absolutely, Captain. Ten seconds…mark." Eaton turned and looked toward Nordstrom. "You heard me, Commander. Cut thrust in…" She glanced at the chronometer. "…eight seconds."

"Yes, Captain."

She stared straight ahead, her hands digging unconsciously into the sides of her chair. "I want the primaries charged the instant the engines disengage."

"Understood."

The ship seemed to lurch briefly as the thrust ceased, and weightlessness returned for an instant before the dampeners adjusted and restored a semblance of partial gravity.

Eaton started counting in her head, waiting for the main guns to charge. She knew it was foolish, even childish, but she wanted *Intrepid* to fire first. She had begun to like Tyler Barron, but her people had been in the line during the fleet's tragic defeat here. *Dauntless* had already claimed two enemy battleships…and as far as she was concerned, this one was *Intrepid*'s.

Her eyes were fixed, waiting for *Dauntless* to fire. But before she saw the expected flash in the tank, *Intrepid*'s bridge lights dimmed. Her people had won the race, they had charged and fired their ship's primaries before their comrades in *Dauntless*. But only by a few seconds. She saw the light in the display, *Dauntless*'s guns firing right after hers…and an instant later the damage assessment from *Intrepid*'s shot.

A direct hit!

She watched as the preliminary reports streamed in…an electric feeling as more data scrolled down her screen. Massive secondary explosions, energy output dropping precipitously. The enemy ship's laser fire was silenced. The great battleship was just hanging there, floating in space.

Then the report on *Dauntless*'s fire. Another hit, but a glancing one, away from the enemy vessel's vital systems. Eaton felt bad for the pleasure she felt. She knew she should have wanted the enemy ship destroyed by any means possible…but she couldn't help it. She wanted the kill.

"Recharge those primaries," she said, unnecessarily, she

knew, even as the words came out.

"Already charging, Captain." She could tell immediately from Nordstrom's tone he understood what she was thinking…and he agreed completely.

It was petty she knew, but *Dauntless* had two kills already, plus the mysterious accolades they had won out on the Rim. It didn't matter who fired the last, killing shot. Both ships had battled side by side…indeed, *Intrepid's* fighter strike had likely saved *Dauntless* from crippling damage, if not outright destruction. But none of that mattered to her, not really. Not now. She wanted the final blow.

The lights dimmed again as the heavy weapons fired, the distinctive sound rattling from the walls and the ceiling. She waited, watching, realizing suddenly that she was holding her breath. And then, as she exhaled hard she saw it. Another direct hit, and seconds later the data she'd been waiting for. The enemy ship was torn open by massive explosions…and then it vanished, consumed by what appeared to all scans to be pure energy. Her shot had ruptured the enemy ship's containment and released the reaction before the target's AI could scrag the power plant. In an instant, the controlled fusion process that had powered the vessel became uncontrolled, consuming everything material. There was no hulk left when *Dauntless's* shot lanced through seconds later, no field of debris. Just a miniature sun that existed brilliantly for perhaps half a minute and then quickly dissipated, leaving nothing behind but a cloud of radiation and some residual heat, cooling in the frozen vacuum of space. The enemy ship was gone. Just gone.

Chapter Nineteen

"That was some pretty fancy shooting over there, Captain. Please pass on my respects and congratulations to your gunners." Tyler Barron's voice was cheerful, his words sincere. Though he knew he'd have enjoyed the killing shot as much as any captain, he was glad Eaton's people had scored the final blow. He suspected she was still punishing herself because her ship had survived when so many Confederation vessels and spacers had died. He didn't have the slightest doubt she had done the only thing she could do, nor did he have any recriminations whatsoever about her conduct, but he also knew the most brutally vicious critic was the one hiding inside an officer's own head.

"Thank you, Captain. I appreciate your words, and my crew will as well." She sounded truly grateful, and perhaps a bit surprised. Barron understood. Capital ship captains could be touchy creatures. The job required a certain amount of ego, and he could imagine all sorts of foolish rivalries over battle honors. But Barron had tasted enough of glory—and its cost—out on the Rim. He would fight this war, because the Confederation needed him, because the enemy would destroy his way of life and enslave his people if he didn't...but the only honor he wanted was peace.

The sounds of *Dauntless*'s secondary guns rattled in the background. Barron hadn't wasted any time turning his weapons on the enemy escort vessels. *Astara* and *Cambria* had been holding off three times their number of enemy frigates, and they were battered, in need of backup. The two small ships had done their duty, freeing the battleships to engage their opposing numbers. Now it was time to repay the debt. And even *Dauntless*'s secondary weapons were powerful enough to obliterate the escort ships with just a few shots.

"Things seem to be in hand here, Captain." Barron was looking at the display even as he spoke with Eaton over the comm. Another enemy escort winked out of existence. There were only two left, and he knew they wouldn't last long. "We need to discuss what we will do next."

"I believe that's your decision, Captain Barron. You're in command."

Barron had checked the dates of their respective commissions, but he'd been hesitant to assert his authority over Eaton and her people. He had a deep respect for what they had been through, and he hadn't wanted to risk bad feelings, especially since he hadn't even been part of her chain of command. But he knew a force could only have one commander, and Eaton had opened the door.

"Thank you, Captain. But commission dates notwithstanding, I would value your input and opinions."

"Thank you, sir." It was the first time she had addressed him as "sir." He suspected she was signaling him that she had no issue with serving under his command.

"That's clearly a Union supply convoy." Barron flashed his eyes back to the display, his eyes darting to the far end, closer to the Phillos transit point. There were twenty-four vessels, freighters and tankers. He suspected the ships were armed, but he doubted any of them had a beam hot enough to threaten capital ships like *Dauntless* and *Intrepid*.

"I agree, Captain."

"I can't think of any way we can aid the war effort more

than my disrupting the enemy's supply. We *have* to destroy those ships. Before they can decelerate and head back toward the Phillos transwarp link."

"Yes, sir! I agree completely." Eaton paused. "Captain, *Intrepid* is short of many supplies…and we're down to fifty percent fuel stocks. Union supplies might not be a great match, but they're better than nothing."

"That's good thinking, Captain. With the escorting forces gone, we should be able to capture a couple of those ships. As long as nothing else shows up." Barron paused. *Dauntless* could use a resupply almost as badly as *Intrepid*. But he knew an enemy task force could come through one of the transit points at any time. Indeed, it as almost certain that one eventually would. This convoy was due somewhere, and when it didn't show, someone would come looking for it.

"Okay, let's do it," he finally said. "But I want to destroy most of those ships first. If enemy reinforcements show up, I want to know we interrupted their supply, at least, even if we didn't have time to grab some fuel and ordnance for ourselves."

"Agreed. I suggest we pick out a tanker and two freighters… and blast everything else to atoms." There was a savage sound to her voice. Barron knew that tone, and he understood the feelings behind it. He'd felt them out at Santis.

"Agreed, Captain. As soon as we've retrieved all our fighters, we'll accelerate toward the convoy. We should be able to reach them before they can reverse their vectors and escape…and if we drive the bay crews hard enough, the fighters will be ready to launch again by then."

"Captain Barron…can you take a couple of my extra squadrons? Our bays were so jam packed before, it's a miracle we got a whole strike out. But it's going to slow us badly if we have to handle so many fighters again."

"Of course, Captain." Barron had almost forgotten how many orphaned squadrons Eaton had taken aboard her ship. "Send half your strays our way. We'll find room for them."

"Thank you, Captain. I'll send you the ones closest to your position."

"Very well, Captain." Barron's tone darkened, turning downright feral. "And then we'll do something about all those Union supplies."

* * *

"Look, Stara...I know you care about me. I care about you too." Stockton knew he felt more than that for her...but "care" was the strongest word he was able to force from his lips. His feelings were new ground for him—*very* new ground—but it was more than just that. He knew how much of a risk he took every time he climbed into the cockpit, and with the way the war was going, the chances of both of them surviving the next few months, let alone years, seemed pretty small. The day some Union pilot finally brought him down would be a hard one for her, and he wasn't about to make her pain worse with lofty proclamations of love and of futures together.

"If you care about me, you'll stop acting like an absolute lunatic in your fighter. Are you trying to get yourself killed?" Stara Sinclair was Stockton's opposite in many ways, circumspect, calm, calculating. But the two shared the same emotional coldness, and he suspected she could no more tell him openly that she loved him than he could tell her.

"Stara, you have to understand. I fly the way I fly. A lot of it is instinct. If a pilot takes time to think something through, nine time out of ten he's too late. That's how you end up getting blasted to plasma." He knew she doubted his words, that she suspected he would say anything to satisfy her...and he acknowledged to himself that he probably would. But what he was telling her now was the absolute truth. Pilots had different styles, and the surest way to get one killed was to try to change him. But he had no idea how to make her understand that.

She had been walking briskly down the corridor, with Stockton following behind, but then she stopped abruptly and turned to face him. "I know you, Jake. I've watched you in that damned thing for over a year now. I've stared at the screen as you tried to land an out of fuel fighter, and when the recovery shuttle

brought you back in after you had to ditch. I've felt my stomach in my throat too many times, wondering if I'll see you alive
again. It's just too hard…"

He grabbed her shoulders and pulled her toward him, kissing
her abruptly. Then he leaned back, staring into her eyes. "I don't
want to die, Stara. I want to come back, and never more than
now, when I know you're waiting here for me. But if I don't do
my best out there, I'm endangering you…and the captain and
the rest of the crew. What if the bomber I let slip by is the one
that cripples the ship? What if *Dauntless* is destroyed because the
squadrons don't do their jobs?"

She didn't respond. She just stood there looking back at him.
He could see her eyes glistening, but he knew her well enough
to be sure she wouldn't let a tear fall. "I understand all that," she
finally said, her voice soft, the anger gone. "But it's still hard.
You have to understand that."

"I do understand. I really do. But, I don't care how hard it is.
I don't want to lose…" His voice trailed off. There were noises
down the corridor, someone coming. The last thing either he
or Stara needed was a lot of gossip on the ship about their new
romance, though deep down he suspected it was too late to
maintain the veil of secrecy.

Stockton shut up, listening as the voices approached. "Hopefully the quartermaster can help. I've been wearing this uniform
for what, four days now?"

"Closer to five by now. Occupational hazard of having your
mothership bolt while you're still thousands of klicks away, fighting the enemy." There was a touch of anger in the voices coming
down the corridor. And familiarity…at least one of them.

Stockton turned abruptly and stared at the two men
approaching. He knew instantly who he was looking at, but he
still had trouble believing it.

"Timmons," he said, his voice deadpan. "Dirk Timmons."

The two men stopped abruptly. "Well, if it isn't the famous
Raptor. I thought I'd heard you were on *Dauntless*." The man had
a wary smile on his face.

Stockton forced himself to match the expression. "Warrior.

I thought you were on the flagship. What were you doing on *Intrepid*?"

"*Repulse* bugged out from the battle." It sounded like Timmons was trying to hide the bitterness in his tone, but Stockton heard it loud and clear. He and Timmons had gone through flight school together, and to say they'd been rivals was a massive understatement. But he couldn't argue with the pilot's resentment. He wouldn't have been very happy if *Dauntless* had fled a battle, leaving his squadron behind.

"From what I hear, there wasn't much choice," Stockton said, admitting to himself as he did that the argument would get nowhere with him if the roles had been reversed.

"Yeah, that's what I hear too." Timmons and Stockton exchanged intense gazes.

Stockton had never liked the other pilot, a feeling he knew Timmons returned. He'd found the man gratingly annoying since the two had been first year cadets, and peoples' insistence on telling him how similar the two of them were had only increased his animosity. He'd gotten into half a dozen fights in the Academy with other cadets who'd picked the wrong time to question his dislike by pointing out the supposed ways he and Timmons were alike.

"So, they transferred you over to *Dauntless*?" Stockton asked, not trying very hard to hide his disdain.

"Yeah, it was pretty crowded over there. I guess they split the extra fighter load."

Stockton just nodded. *They couldn't have kept you over there…*

"I'm Stara Sinclair, by the way. Deputy launch control officer." Stara stepped to the side, moving out from behind Stockton.

"It's a pleasure, Lieutenant," Timmons said. His tone of voice, utterly different from that he'd used when speaking to Stockton, triggered an angry response. It took everything Stockton had to unclench his fists…and to keep himself from giving the cocky pilot the beat down he'd owed him for ten years.

"And I'm Lieutenant Charles Aires. My call sign is Mustang, but shipboard most people call me Chuck."

"Welcome to *Dauntless*, Chuck, Dirk…or, should I say Mustang and Warrior? After all, most of our interaction will be when you're in your fighters."

Timmons nodded, almost a shallow bow. "I certainly hope that's not the only place we'll see each other, Lieutenant. That would be a terrible waste."

"Come on, Stara…we've got to go." Stockton turned and reached out, taking her hand. "Dirk, Chuck," he said, his voice frigid. Then he walked down the corridor, back the way he and Stara had come, since Timmons and Aires had been heading the way they had been going. Stara followed behind, trying to hide the amusement in her expression.

When they had turned the corner and moved out of sight, she let out a small laugh. "Not your favorite person, I guess?"

"No," he said simply, not offering any other details.

"That's strange, Jake…because the two of you seem so…"

"*Don't* say it." He let go of her hand and continued on down the hall, his pace quickening.

She laughed. "Jake…Jake, come on." She followed him down the corridor, trying to get him to stop. But she couldn't stop laughing.

*   *   *

"I know you've got more fighters than normal to deal with, Chief, but you've got extra personnel too. The captain sent you two dozen technicians from Commander Fritz's teams." Jamison was careful to moderate his tone – Nick Evans was technically outranked by every pilot in the strike force, but he was also a grizzled career navy veteran, the undisputed master of *Dauntless*'s fighter bays. Evans was a big man, physically imposing, but it was more than that. He was a firestorm of barely-bottled rage, who ruled over his team of maintenance technicians with an iron hand. But he was a creature of habit, with his own way of doing things, and he rarely deviated from that course. He was struggling to handle the extra fighters stashed in virtually every open space in the bay…and he'd had more than one unfortunate encounter with pilots from other battleships, ones who were unfamiliar with the specific rhythms of *Dauntless*'s bays.

"Commander, we're moving as fast as we can. We've got these fighters stacked up everywhere. They're in the way, and we've got to move the torpedoes and supplies farther." Evans was uncharacteristically unnerved, his voice no longer quite the imperious sonic boom everyone on the ship had become used to hearing.

Jamison, as the commander of *Dauntless*'s entire fighter wing, had always exerted at least a moderate level of control and dominance over Evans, though he was ashamed to admit, even to himself, how difficult he had sometimes found it to stand up to the terrifying chief. He'd have stood toe to toe with Evans if there had been no choice, but liked to think of himself as a tactician who could rely on manipulation instead of brute force.

"Perhaps I should ask the Captain to send Commander Fritz down here with more of her people." He flashed a glance up to the big chief's eyes.

"You don't need to do that, sir." Evan's voice was sour, as if he'd tasted something bad. "My people will get the job done."

Jamison felt a laugh struggling to burst out, but he held it in check, his eyes locked on Evans's. "Are you sure, Chief? Because I'm sure the captain will approve my request." Jamison watched as the chief squirmed. Anya Fritz was a diminutive woman, a third of a meter shorter than Evans and less than half his weight, but she was the one person on *Dauntless* who could match the chief in sheer unrelenting ferocity…even exceed him. Captain Barron had sent Fritz down to take command of the launch bays during the climax of the battle out at Santis…and Nick Evans had met his match. Fritz had enough energy, drive, and bottled rage to at least equal the chief—and she had a lieutenant-commander's rank to back it up. For the first time anyone on *Dauntless* could recall, Evans had been put into his place as Fritz seized total control of the bays. It was something the bay techs still spoke of with great amusement, at least when they were *sure* Evans was nowhere nearby.

"No, Commander. We can handle it…no problem." For the first time he could recall, Evan's voice had almost a pleading sound to it.

"Twenty minutes, Chief…not one minute more."

"Yes, sir. We'll have the whole strike force ready to launch on time. You have my word."

"Very well, Chief. Get it done." He felt a wave of sympathy for Evans's people, knowing they would bear the brunt of the chief's anger and tension. But there was no way around that. He wanted those fighters ready.

He turned and walked across the open floor of the bay, toward the pilots' prep area. He'd sent them all to get something to eat, but they should be back by now. He'd dressed down Evans, done all he could to make sure the fighters themselves were ready to go. Now, it was his turn to prepare. He had to make some sense out of the crazy combination of partial squadrons he had…and turn them into a tightly-organized strike force.

That wasn't going to be easy.

Chapter Twenty

"We go in suited up, and we stay that way, even if we think the pressurization is intact." Bryan Rogan looked out at his Marines. There were two hundred and one of them, not counting himself. He suspected there had been more than a few groans among the assembled fighters, but the Marines were in their pressure suits with their helmets snapped shut. Rogan would only hear them if they activated their microphones and spoke to him over the comm. He was grateful for that arrangement. If he'd heard the complaints he'd have had to come down on those making them. This way, he could just pretend they had cheerfully accepted the order.

Marines were technically naval troops, trained to fight shipboard actions as well as ground combats. But there weren't many boarding actions, certainly not in the large general engagements of a war like the one going on, and Rogan's people were no different than Marines throughout the Confederation service in despising pressure suits and bottled air. They preferred to fight in just their body armor, but Rogan wasn't about to lose Marines because an airlock blew out or a compartment lost life support. He hated the tight, uncomfortable pressure suits as much as

171

anyone in the bay, but he hated seeing his Marines killed more.

Rogan had seen the images of pre-Cataclysmic soldiers, clad from head to toe in great suits of powered armor, looking more like robots than men and women. He couldn't imagine the firepower and endurance of soldiers so equipped—or how uncomfortable those ancient suits must have been. But post-Cataclysmic technology wasn't even close to developing the miniaturization and nanotechnology required to build true powered armor, so the best he could do for his Marines was to make sure they wouldn't suffocate or die from the effects of sudden depressurization.

"This is an important mission. *Dauntless* and *Intrepid* need those supplies. So, we hit those target ships, and we take them. It's that simple." He paused a moment, his eyes flashing toward the end of the line. "The fighter wings are going to do everything they can to knock out any defensive weapons before the assault ships go in, but whatever defensive capability is inside those ships is our problem." He knew just what "defensive capability" would be waiting there. The Foudre Rouge. The clone soldiers of the Federal Union.

Rogan was disgusted by any government so oppressive it would create soldiers as virtual slaves. The FRs were tough, trained their entire lives to serve in the Union's wars. They didn't have personal lives. They didn't have families. They were conditioned from the moment they emerged from their crèches to serve as soldiers. Rogan knew his people were a match for them, his veterans at least. They had fought the Alliance stormtroopers and won, and those warriors had been as tough as any that had ever existed. But there was something chilling about the FRs.

His eyes locked on Ernesto Billos's. Billos had been his senior sergeant since he'd reported for duty on *Dauntless*. The career non-com had fought in the last war. He was one of the few Marines on *Dauntless* who had actually met the FRs in battle.

"Sergeant Billos and Sergeant Hargraves have fought against the FRs." Rogan gestured toward Billos and the sergeant standing right next to him. Hargraves had been one of the handful of survivors from the original Santis garrison. *Dauntless* had given them a ride back to Archellia, and every one of them had volunteered to serve under Rogan...and Captain Barron, filling at least a few of *Dauntless*'s ocean of empty slots with veterans. "Sergeant Billos will be with first company, and Sergeant Hargraves will be under Lieutenant Plunkett. Listen to them. They have faced what you are about to."

Plunkett was another veteran of Santis, the commander of the original garrison of the Rim world. He'd been wounded and sick by the end of the battle, almost dead. But Hargraves had carried his commander to safety and watched over him until the battle was won. Rogan was glad to have another experienced officer to put in command of his mostly-raw second company, and he wasn't about to split up the lieutenant and his devoted non-com.

"We're cut off behind enemy lines, but we're still in this fight. The Cap and the others blasted three enemy battleships...and now it's our turn. We've got one way to resupply...to take what we need from the enemy. And that's on us, Marines. I don't care how many FRs are on those ships. I don't care how hard they fight. We keep at it no matter what, until we take those ships." He knew his veterans understood the situation, but more than half his force had been part of the Archellia garrison, and few of them had been in battle. He was breaking up his companies, sending a veteran platoon to each ship, backed up by one of the green ones. He didn't like it, but there was nothing else he could do. After the losses his forces suffered on Santis, he knew he was lucky just to have his force up to strength.

"Any questions?" He knew there wouldn't be. Even the garrison troops were Marines. They knew what they had to do. "Okay...and remember, the FRs don't surrender. They're conditioned from ear to ear and terrorized by draconian punishments. They don't react to things the way we do. So, just keep fighting. Keep fighting until every one of them is dead."

He paused a few seconds, looking out over his force. Then he said, "Very well. You all have your boarding assignments. Let's get moving."

* * *

"Commence launch operations." Tyler Barron sat bolt upright in his chair, his voice crisp, confident. There was a fair amount of playacting in his demeanor, but that was part of the burden of command. His ship was behind the battle lines, alone save for *Intrepid* and her tiny group of escorts. He was as scared as anyone on *Dauntless*, feeling alone and cut off from the rest of the Confederation fleet. But he knew what his people needed from him, and he was determined to give it to them.

"Yes, Captain. Commencing launch operations now." Atara Travis seemed, if anything, even more focused, like a bar of dense metal that resisted bending even under the greatest pressure. Barron suspected she was also putting on a show for the crew—and him—but he wasn't sure. She had a strength of her own, a toughness born of her difficult background and the route to her current rank. It was just possible Travis truly *wasn't* afraid.

Barron hadn't been entirely sure his launch crews would have the strike force ready in time. He'd set a tight schedule— he knew enemy reinforcements could appear at any moment, and he wasn't about to waste time he might not have—and he'd taunted Chief Evans with the mention that *Intrepid* had somehow managed to prep and launch even more fighters. But then Commander Jamison checked in and reported he'd threatened the chief with Commander Fritz. Barron had almost burst into laughter, and he'd freely admitted his strike force commander had elegantly outdone him in terms of motivating the flight crews and their cantankerous leader.

Barron could feel the slight vibration under his feet, *Dauntless*'s launch catapults sending her fighters out into space. The squadrons had their orders. The two battleships were moving forward even now, closing with the freighters and tankers. With the escorting capital ships destroyed, the convoy was virtually defenseless. The supply vessels didn't have a gun hot enough to hurt a massive ship like *Dauntless*, at least not from the range where the battleship's weapons would blast them to scrap. But before the assault ships carrying his marines moved toward their targets, he had to make sure the defensive lasers were neutralized. Taking out turrets without causing significant damage to the rest of a ship was precision work, tailor made for his fighter squadrons.

He watched as fighter after fighter launched, his squadrons—and those created from bits and pieces of other vessels' wings—forming up and engaging their thrusters, heading for their targets. The launch went on for longer than usual, as *Dauntless* sent some thirty extra ships out of her bays.

"Launch completed, Captain."

"Very well."

"We will enter primary range in two minutes, sir. Should I activate the main guns?"

Barron paused. Firing the massive particle accelerators seemed like overkill. They were designed for fighting other capital ships, not for blasting freighters. But they were longer-ranged than the secondaries…and the sooner Barron could destroy the convoy, the better he would feel. It was the only way his people could aid in the war effort right now, and if enemy ships started pouring through any of the system's transit points, the opportunity could be lost.

"Yes, Commander. Contact Captain Eaton and request…" Barron was still uncomfortable assuming command on the basis of a commission a few months older than his comrade's. "…order her to power up her primaries and prepare to fire as targets come into range."

"Yes, Captain." Travis repeated the order to *Dauntless*'s own gunnery crews. Then she passed it on to *Intrepid*. "Captain Eaton acknowledges, sir." Then, a few seconds later. "Primary range in forty-five seconds. Gunnery reports the weapons will be ready to fire immediately."

"All gunnery stations are authorized to fire at will. I want targets assigned to either *Dauntless* or *Intrepid*…put our gunnery control in charge of that." Barron glanced over at Travis. "And make sure no one takes a shot at the vessels we're boarding."

"Yes, Captain."

Barron sat quietly, counting down in his head. A few seconds after the ship passed into range, the bridge lights flickered as *Dauntless* poured almost all its power into firing the massive particle accelerators. An instant later, Travis shouted out the report.

"Direct hit, sir."

Barron's eyes were on the display as the small red dot blinked out of existence, a sanitized version of what he knew had actually happened. He imagined the enormously powerful particle beams smashing into the freighter's lightly armored hull, tearing massive holes clear through the target ship. The supply vessel was large, but it wasn't built to withstand the intensity of battle, and Barron imagined it splitting open like an egg, spilling its contents—and its crew—into space as its hull broke up into pieces. He could see the images of terrified spacers struggling to don survival gear, even as they were blown out of great rents in the hull and into the frozen death of space.

He didn't like the idea of blasting freighter crews, but he hadn't hesitated to give the orders either. This was war, shorn of the pretensions of glory and other blandishments humanity had attached to the grim business of killing each other. He was here to buy time for the fleet to reorganize, to slow the enemy advance by striking at their supplies. And he would kill whomever he had to in order to make that happen.

He was still staring at the screen when another icon vanished, the victim of *Intrepid*'s gunners. He could see the supply vessels struggling to get away, blasting their engines at full to cut the velocity and vectors that were still taking them closer to their attackers. It was a futile effort—freighters and tankers didn't have the kind of thrust warships could generate—but Barron knew they had no choice but to try.

"Primaries, maintain maximum rate of fire until secondaries come into range." The energy-hogging main guns were really overkill for destroying freighters and tankers. *Dauntless* had two of the primary batteries and twenty-four of the secondaries. "Switch to secondaries at seventy thousand kilometers."

"Yes, Captain." Travis relayed the order, just as the lights dimmed again and another shot lanced out from *Dauntless*'s heavy guns.

"Another hit, sir," Travis reported, unnecessarily. Barron was as focused on the display as she was, and he'd been watching when yet another small dot blinked out.

"Maintain fire, Commander." Barron leaned back, his eyes dropping to his screen. His primaries would get off one more shot, and then *Dauntless's* more numerous secondary weapons would come into range. He looked back at the main display, checking the transit points one by one. Still nothing.

Good…this is a large convoy. It's got to hurt the enemy to lose it.

He still didn't understand how the enemy fleet was supplying itself so far from its home bases. There hadn't been time to build a forward depot, and there was no way the Union had enough freighters to sustain a supply line all the way to the front lines and back. There was something missing, some fact he didn't know…and his mind raced to come up with any idea of what it might be.

"Another hit, Captain." Travis had succeeded this time in reporting the destruction of the enemy ship before he'd noticed it. He'd been deep in thought about the enemy logistics, and he hadn't even noticed the lights dimming when the primaries fired again.

"Very well, Commander. My compliments to the gunners. Shut down the primaries. Secondaries, prepare to open fire." *Dauntless* was a strong vessel, equipped with two massive fusion reactors, but even that enormous energy production was inadequate to power all its weapons simultaneously.

"Secondaries activated. All batteries opening fire…now."

Barron could hear the faint whines of the lasers firing, and a few seconds later half a dozen icons in the display flickered. The secondaries didn't destroy the freighters and tankers with a single shot like the primaries did, but the number of guns more than made up for it. *Dauntless* and *Intrepid* were cutting through the convoy, destroying millions of tons of vital Union war supplies. It would all be over in a few minutes, the entire convoy wiped out. All except for three ships on the perimeter, two freighters and a tanker designated as off limits to the gunners on the two battleships.

He stared as a group of tiny dots approached the vessels, looking almost like a cloud on the display, and behind the fighters, a small cluster of blue triangles, the assault shuttles carrying three hundred fifty Marines, the full complements of the two battleships. Those fighters and Marines, as much as anyone in the fleet, would determine what happened next. If they could secure the enemy ships and the supplies they carried, *Dauntless* and *Intrepid* could continue to operate behind enemy lines. If not, the supply situation would quickly turn critical.

Barron had never seen a boarding action this size, much less ordered his own people to carry one out. But Bryan Rogan was in charge of the operation, and he had always had immense confidence in his Marine commander, and more since he'd seen the officer lead *Dauntless*'s forces against twice their number of Alliance stormtroopers…and win.

Come on, Bryan…we need those ships…

Chapter Twenty-One

"Blue Squadron, Direwolves, Red Eagles...with me. Yellows, Grays, Gold Shields, ten thousand klicks behind. Reds, Greens, Black Helms, Longswords, ten thousand klicks behind the second line." Kyle Jamison leaned back in his cockpit, his eyes fixed on the small display on the fighter's dashboard. He'd never led a strike this size. He'd never even fought in a battle with so many fighters on one side. He struggled a bit to keep track of so many squadrons, but the absence of enemy fighters made it easier. His entire force was fitted out for light anti-ship strikes—the fighters were carrying heavier laser cannon than usual, but not the bulky plasma torpedoes and their heavy mountings. His ship didn't handle quite as well as it did with the lighter interceptor kit, but it wasn't the pig it would have been outfitted like a bomber either.

"Acknowledged, Thunder." Stockton's reply was cool, understated. His friend and top ace didn't sound like himself, not at all. Jamison had put the two crack squadrons from *Repulse* into the first wave along with *Dauntless*'s own elite Blues. It was only after the chaotic and rushed launch was complete that Stara Sinclair had commed him and told him that Stockton and Dirk Tim-

179

mons, commander of the Red Eagles, had some kind of bad blood between them. He'd considered reordering the formation, but he'd decided it was too disruptive. Now he was wondering if that had been a mistake.

"All right, first wave…remember, we need these ships intact. You're here to pick off the weapons and disable the engines. Nothing more. *Dauntless* and *Intrepid* need these supplies, so anybody who gets carried away is going to have to answer to Captain Barron and Captain Eaton…at least after they answer to me."

Jamison gripped his fighter's throttle. "We're going in close. Really close. Take it easy. There are no enemy fighters to worry about, so take it nice and slow, and watch out for the defensive lasers." He paused, glancing quickly down at the display. Then: "You've got your assignments…one squadron to a ship. Let's go!"

Jamison moved the control to the side, pulling it back slightly and angling his thrust toward Blue squadron's position. He'd intended to go in with one of *Repulse*'s squadrons, but he changed his mind. He'd never seen the cocky Stockton sound so off his game, and he was concerned his friend would take it personally if he went in with Timmons.

Or will he be upset thinking I felt I had to keep an eye on him?

He pushed the indecision out of his mind and went with his gut, maintaining his new vector to go in with Stockton's Blues. Tactically it didn't matter. He had three of the best squadrons in the fleet leading the assault, and none of them needed him to direct their actions.

He glanced down at the scanner, watching as the image of the enemy tanker grew larger. He was less than ten thousand kilometers out, close range by normal standards…but this time he was going much closer.

Eight thousand. He shoved the throttle forward, decelerating hard, slowing his approach. The attack was all about precision. Normally, his pilots were targeting entire ships, but now they had to hit individual weapon emplacements. And any shots that hit the ships elsewhere were worse than misses. It would have been beyond easy for his squadrons to destroy the vessels, but disabling them while leaving their massive cargoes intact required a degree of precision few fighter formations could match. But if the pilots with him now couldn't do it, no one could.

Six thousand. He reached out, flipping a switch, pouring full power into his active scanners. The image on the display changed, sharpened, as the AI fed in new data. One by one he could see small sections highlighted, the locations of defensive weapons on the tanker. The supply ships didn't have any guns that threatened a battleship like *Dauntless*, but they had enough firepower to blow away a fighter, especially if the pilot got careless. This wasn't the kind of deadly fight his people had experienced at Santis, or even here against the enemy battleships, but it wasn't a milk run either. Especially since his people had to hold their fire until they were almost close enough to reach out and touch the hull.

Four thousand. The enemy guns were all marked now, courtesy of the weapons opening fire and giving away their locations. That fire had also taken its toll. Two fighters were hit, one from the Direwolves and one from *Dauntless*'s own Blues. As far as Jamison could tell, both pilots had managed to eject, though whether they were wounded or not he wasn't sure. He'd seen the recovery boats pull in the body of more than one pilot who'd been dead before he'd even cleared his stricken fighter.

Two thousand. He could hear his heart pounding in his ears, feel the sweat pouring down his back. He'd never come this close to a target before, or moved so slowly in the face of incoming fire. He angled his throttle slightly to the side then back again, putting enough unpredictability into his approach, he hoped, to shake the enemy targeting AIs. He doubted a tanker had any really skilled gunners, but at this range, even the unassisted AIs were a deadly threat, a fact that hit home again as another fighter blinked off the screen, this time without any detectable ejection.

His eyes focused on the screen, zeroing in on one of the tanker's forward guns. His hand was tight on his controls. He breathed deeply, slow controlled breaths as he stared at his chosen target. Normally, he'd have opened fire by now, blasting again and again until he scored the hit he was after. But not now. He couldn't just blast that ship all over, not without risking doing serious damage. The tritium fuel the tanker carried was highly flammable, but that was a secondary concern in the vacuum of space. Any fires would be quickly extinguished when they used up the ship's limited oxygen supply. But simply blasting open the great tanks would release the condensed liquid into space. And *Dauntless* and *Intrepid* needed that fuel.

He held his stare even as he heard a small bonging sound, his AI warning him he was less than one thousand kilometers from the target. He ignored the warning, staying motionless save for the occasional tap to the throttle. His concentration was total. There was his fighter and that gun emplacement, and nothing else in the universe. Not now. And he held that iron focus even as his AI announced, "Warning, less than five hundred kilometers to target. Collision imminent."

He ignored the warning. At normal battle velocities, he'd already be a dead man, far too close to alter his vector and clear the enemy ship. But he was moving at a fraction of that speed. That made him an easier target for the enemy fire—a risk he and his people had to take—but it also gave him time to get closer. Close enough to plant his shot exactly where it had to be.

He pressed his finger tight over the firing stud and pulled it back immediately, firing only a single shot. The targeting was ninety-nine percent mathematics computed by his AI, but that last one percent was the touch of a veteran pilot…and it made all the difference.

He angled the throttle hard to the side and pulled it back, engaging his thrusters to push his vector away from the collision course he'd been on. For an instant, a brief fraction of a second, he thought he was too late, that he'd pushed it just half a second too far. But then his fighters zipped by the tanker, coming within three kilometers of the big ship before he spun his bird around and began to decelerate.

Only then did his eyes drop to the display. He felt a rush of excitement, his fists clenching involuntarily. He'd put the shot right on target, not only hitting the laser turret dead on, but practically scooping the thing right off the tanker's hull, almost without leaving a scratch behind on the ship itself.

"Yes!" he shouted to himself. Then he glanced down at the display, watching his veteran pilots go in one after the other, scoring hit after hit, stripping the enemy tanker of every gun it had. The second and third waves would come on next, but there wasn't going to be much left for them to do except pick off a turret or two that had escaped destruction. Then the Marines could go in and take those ships.

* * *

"It looks like the fighters did a perfect job…real precision work. Remember, the ships are intact, and that means their defense forces are at full strength. They know we're coming, and they'll be waiting for us." Bryan Rogan was strapped in along the wall of the assault shuttle along with forty of his Marines. The ship was overloaded, carrying half again its normal payload, but Rogan didn't have any idea how many defenders they'd have to face, or if the enemy would be some kind of naval security force or the dreaded FRs.

"We're making our final approach, Marines. If all goes well, you'll be boarding within two minutes." Rogan frowned at the sound of the pilot's voice, not out of any animosity or concerns about his confidence, but only because the lieutenant sounded so *young*. He'd known war was coming for a long time, of course, and he was well aware that it had already begun, but listening to the junior pilot's voice reminded him that half his Marines were in their early twenties. War was a terrible thing, but it was also his business. He'd take the risks his duty required, fight with every scrap of strength he could muster. But the hardest part, he knew, would be watching the young Marines and spacers die, men and women barely into adulthood. Before this war was over, they would die by the thousands. *No, millions.*

"I want everybody ready. We move through the boarding tube quickly, quietly. We get onto that ship, and then we move slowly and cautiously. Remember, we're invading *their* ship. They know their way around, and we don't. Do your duty, but by God, I don't want anybody turning up dead because of carelessness."

He knew no matter how many warnings he gave, he'd end up in his quarters writing letters to parents and husbands and wives, but he was going to do everything he could to cut that number down to the minimum possible.

He slammed his helmet's faceplate down and gripped his assault rifle tightly. Then he sat silently, waiting as the shuttle made its final approach.

The fighters seemed to have silenced the enemy gun turrets, but the shuttle pilot wasn't taking any chances, and the small ship bounced around, its thrust pushing in one direction and then the next, making it more difficult for any weapons to get a target lock. Rogan was a hardened Marine, used to assault craft and the rougher aspects of space travel, but even he could feel the churning in his gut. He suspected that some of his people, especially the transfers from the Archellia garrison, were about ready to lose the contents of their stomachs.

A little vomit wasn't the worst thing he'd see today, but he also knew a sick Marine wasn't as alert and focused as one whose feet were firmly planted on unmoving ground. Spacesickness would kill some of his people too, he realized.

The shuttle lurched hard as the pilot decelerated rapidly to come to a stop right alongside the tanker. Then another hard shake, as the boarding tube extended and slammed into the enemy ship's hull. For an instant, there was silence, only the breathing of his Marines breaking the eerie quiet. Then a series of muffled booms, explosives piercing the tanker's hull. He knew the pilot had chosen his spot, and that the entry point was almost certainly into the ship's interior itself and not one of the huge tritium tanks…but he held his breath anyway. If that expectation was wrong, there was enough oxygen in the shuttle to feed one hell of a conflagration when the explosions set off the vapors rising from the liquefied hydrogen fuel.

He slapped his hand to his chest, releasing the harness that held him in his seat. It wasn't regulation—it wasn't even smart—

but he was going to be the first man into the enemy ship. He'd seen too many of his Marines die on Santis, and before he exposed any more to the dangers of combat, he was going to be right there himself.

"Behind me, line up by squad. We'll probably come out either in a compartment of a corridor. Whatever it is, we've got to get every approach covered immediately…and if anything shows itself, blast it. We're not after non-combatant spacers, but nobody gets killed trying to figure out who's who. So, if it moves, take it down."

He shuffled toward the heavy metal door at the end of the compartment. He could hear sounds on the other side, metal twisting, squeaking. He knew the assault tube was securing itself to the tanker's hull and filling the gaps with expandable foam sealant. His Marines had survival gear, pressure suits that could keep them alive in a vacuum for a while, and about an hour's oxygen, but that was only for emergencies. Rogan wouldn't put it past the defenders to selectively depressurize compartments and hallways where his people were advancing, and he intended to save every breath of stored air in case it was truly needed.

The door had a light above it casting a red glow over that end of the shuttle's bay. Perhaps half a minute later, it changed to green…and five seconds later the hatch slid to the side.

Rogan lurched forward, leaning down, waddling through the cramped confines of the boarding tube. It was difficult, especially with a full combat kit and survival gear, but he'd done it a dozen times in training, and twice when he'd conducted boarding actions on smugglers' vessels. He moved down the tube with a practiced waddle, and a few second later he was leaping down onto the deck of the enemy ship.

He spun around, his eyes darting back and forth. He appeared to be in a compartment of some sort, perhaps housing support systems for the destroyed gun turrets. It was empty, at least it seemed to be. He moved forward, clearing the way for more of his people to come up behind him. There was a bank of machinery a few meters away, big enough for several soldiers to hide behind. He ran forward, his gun ready, leaping around the side. Nothing. His people were alone.

"Let's go! We're getting a break, but there's no telling how long it will last, so move your asses!"

He waved his arms, a gesture to the Marines climbing through the tube and into the compartment. Half a dozen had leapt down to the deck and fanned out when he heard a metal on metal sound. A hatch opening.

His people *had* gotten a break…but it hadn't lasted long. He spun around and brought his rifle to bear, just as the shadowy figures in the doorway opened fire.

Chapter Twenty-Two

"The lead fighter squadrons are on their way in, Captain. We can confirm, total casualties in the entire strike force six ships. It appears three of the pilots successfully ejected. *Dauntless* has sent her rescue boat out to recover them."

"Very well, Commander." Sara Eaton sat in her chair, looking out over her bridge crew. The destruction of the enemy convoy was a complete success, every ship gone save the three targeted for capture. She didn't feel good about blasting poorly-armed ships with crews she knew must have been civilian or, at best, some kind of conscripted reservists, but they were hauling military supplies, and *Dauntless* and *Intrepid* had nowhere near enough Marines to occupy them all. Brutality was an unalterable facet of war, and she had no choice but to accept that.

"Status of probes?" She and Barron had launched spreads of probes and positioned them at every entry into the system. They both knew enemy forces could appear at any moment.

"Negative, Captain. No activity at any of the transwarp links."

"Very well. But I want those fighters refit as soon as they

land. I wanted them ready to launch, Commander, and I do mean in record time." It had been a risk launching every squadron to strafe the three enemy ships, leaving the two battleships without even a CSP if new enemy forces appeared. It had also been overkill as things had turned out. The first wave had almost completely destroyed the enemy defenses, and the second group had finished them off. But she and Barron had agreed they couldn't take any chances. If they lost the assault shuttles, they would have lost the Marines too, and any chance of capturing the supplies they needed so badly.

"Yes, Captain. The bay crews are on standby, waiting for the first ships to land."

Eaton looked over at the display her eyes focusing on the three red ovals, the enemy ships where her Marines, and *Dauntless*'s, were fighting even now to take control. She knew their mission was a difficult one, that they had to restrict their use of weapons and take care not to seriously damage the ships or their cargoes. It was the kind of thing Marines trained for, but also a type of mission that rarely occurred. Boarding operations were more common in peacetime, against criminal and renegade traffic. But against enemy ships in time of war, there was no telling what kind of defensive forces they would face. Whatever happened, she knew it would be bloody business.

"Any word from the boarding parties?"

"No, Captain. Nothing from the Marines. The assault ships have all reported back. All forces have boarded the respective target vessels."

"Very well." She leaned back and sighed. There was nothing to do but wait.

* * *

"First squad, stay in place and cover that entry. Second squad…around the back to the other door. Get it open, now! Blow it if you have to." Rogan was crouched down behind a large metal structure in the center of the room. It looked like some kind of control panel or workstation, but as far as the

Marine was concerned it was cover…big enough to protect him and another three of his people. He'd dived behind it when the enemy troops attacked through the room's far entrance, and he and the others had returned fire from their covered positions, driving the Union troopers back out of the room. It had been a standoff for the last two or three minutes, the soldiers in the corridor—and he had no doubts now they were indeed Foudre Rouge—holding their position and sniping at the Marines. They'd taken out three of his people before the others had taken cover or ducked back in the boarding tube. He'd gotten at least one of the FRs himself, the body still lying just inside the doorway. He thought his people had taken out one more, but he couldn't be sure. If there was another dead enemy, the body was in the hall, out of sight.

He leaned around the edge of the metal rectangle and fired a burst of shots, hitting the edge of the open doorway and sending a few out into the corridor itself. He didn't think he'd hit anyone, but his tightly-aimed shooting served its intended purpose and pushed the FRs back, shutting down their own fire for a few seconds, just as his Marines were racing around behind him, rushing for the room's second exit. He didn't know if that door opened into the same hallway the FRs were firing from, or if it led to another compartment. But he didn't really care. Anything was better than having to rush the defended doorway. He'd lose half a dozen of his Marines at least, and a lot more if there was a significant force of enemy soldiers waiting outside. He'd order the charge if he had to—the FRs were accomplishing their goal just by keeping his people penned in—but he was going to exhaust every alternative first.

"Captain, the door's jammed shut. The wall must have gotten wrecked during the fighter attack." Billos's voice was loud and clear. And calm. Rogan was struck by the matter-of-fact tone of the veteran non-com, even as enemy fire sprayed around the room.

"Blow it, Sergeant. We need that hatch open, and now."

"Yes, sir."

Rogan turned his attention back to the other door. The FRs

were pushing forward, leaning in to try and get a shot at Billos and his team. Rogan snapped his rifle around and fired, but even as he did, the enemy troopers pulled back. He saw a spray of blood—he thought he caught one of them in the arm—but the others ducked back.

"Hurry, Sergeant," he shouted, firing another burst through the open door.

"Ready, Captain…" But before Billos could set off the charge, the FRs at the door lunged forward, pouring into the room, firing on full auto as they did. Rogan was stunned, but he reacted immediately, opening fire at the advancing soldiers. He hit one, two…then a third. The Marines next to him hesitated a bit longer than he had, but they too opened up when the FRs were out in the open, taking down another three. But they kept coming, and their fire began to take its own toll. One of the Marines next to Rogan grunted and fell back hard. The captain wanted to turn to check on the casualty, but he didn't dare. There were at least a dozen FRs in the room or coming through the door.

He couldn't understand the abrupt change in tactics. The enemy had been conducting a conventional defense, taking advantage of cover and bottling up the invaders. Then, almost as if someone had thrown a switch, they'd abandoned all caution and launched a semi-suicidal charge. He figured they were after the boarding tube, that they were trying to cut it off before most of his Marines could get through. It made sense, in a sick sort of way, but he couldn't imagine ordering his people to throw their lives away with such recklessness. He'd heard enough about the FRs, but suddenly what had just been words before began to coalescence into true understanding. The Union soldiers weren't like other warriors. They were programmed, almost like machines, conditioned from birth to obey orders without question. They were charging because someone in their chain of command had decided that if enough of them sacrificed themselves, the others could cut the tube. It was that simple.

And he knew they just might do it. Unless… He was about to order Billos to blow the second door when the explosion ripped through the compartment like a thunderclap. The sergeant and his people had ducked back, away from the blast radius, but Rogan could see their movement now out of the corner of his eye. Billos leaped through the blown hatch, followed by a trio of Marines.

Rogan focused on the FRs in front of him. There were at least a dozen down now, but three of his people had also been hit. He was alone behind the control panel, and one other Marine was lying on his stomach in the boarding tube, firing out at the enemy. With Billos's people gone, every other Marine in the room was down. The sick tactic the FRs were employing was on the verge of success. One bomb tossed in the tube, and the boarding effort would be stillborn, at least from this access point.

Then the FRs stalled, and Rogan heard gunfire from the corridor. He leaned over and flipped his rifle to full auto, opening up and emptying his clip on the stunned FRs. They went down in bunches, the survivors turning toward him, rushing his position. But he wasn't there. He lunged to the side, pushing off as hard as he could, and going into a combat roll that brought him back to prone position, just as he had slammed another clip in place. He was out in the open, exposed. But he had surprised his enemies…and that gave him time. A second, perhaps two.

He fired, holding down the trigger, spraying bullets across the room. Another half dozen enemy troopers fell, but it wasn't going to be enough. He could see the weapons moving, rifle barrels turning toward him. He kept firing, for another half second or so until he exhausted his clip. Then he twisted his body, determined to dive for cover, even though he knew it was pointless. They had him.

He heard the fire…but he didn't feel anything. He sprang hard to the side, his hand moving to his chest, feeling around for wounds. Nothing.

He crashed hard into the floor and rolled across the room and into the far wall. He was stunned, but he forced himself to focus, and he pulled himself up, gripping his rifle tightly, despite the pain from what he was certain was a broken wrist. His head snapped around, looking back where the FRs stood. Where they had stood. There was no one there except Ernesto Billos and one of his Marines.

"The door came out into the corridor, sir. Right behind the FRs. They must have bypassed it because it was jammed. We took them from the flank. There were only four of them left out there."

Rogan sucked in a deep breath. "Good job, Sergeant. Well done." He didn't ask where Billos's other two Marines were. He knew. If they'd have been anything but dead, the veteran sergeant would have already turned back into the corridor to check on them.

"Let's move it, platoon. Get through that tube. Now."

Before any more opposition shows up.

He looked up, watching as his people started hopping down out and into the compartment. He reached around and pulled another clip from his belt as the rest of his people came through. He tried to snap the clip in place, but the pain from his wrist was just too much. He grunted and threw the rifle back over his shoulder, drawing the pistol hanging from his belt with his good hand.

"Okay, Marines...let's take this ship!"

*   *   *

"Keep moving...don't give them a chance to fall back to more cover." Lieutenant Luke Plunkett was shouting to the Marines jammed in the corridor, even physically pushing those right in front of him toward the enemy.

Clete Hargraves was standing to the lieutenant's side, waving his arms forward. The veteran sergeant knew they had to keep the green garrison Marines pushing ahead, and he'd told Plunkett that before they'd even left the shuttle. The lieutenant was a gifted officer, and one of the best men Hargraves knew. But he hadn't faced FRs in battle before...and Hargraves had.

The FRs were part of a system so alien to Hargraves, he could barely comprehend it. But it worked, at least after a fashion. He wouldn't rate the FRs as a match for his people man to man, or for the Alliance warriors he'd fought on Santis, but they were a deadly enemy nevertheless. The eerie, almost robotic way they conducted themselves could unnerve even veteran warriors, much less the cherries he and Plunkett were leading.

Boarding actions were always difficult. Cramped corridors, small compartments, hatches and doorways provided cover for the defenders. He'd known going in they would take heavy losses, and nothing so far had proven him wrong.

"Wounded, fall back, however you can. The rest of you, stay on the enemy. If you give them a chance to regroup, you'll only pay for this twice." Hargraves knew what Plunkett was doing, the only thing he could do. There was no fancy tactic, no bloodless way to win this fight, not against the FRs. It had to be forward, forward, forward…and damned the casualties until the battle was won. It wouldn't be won until every enemy soldier was dead.

Hargraves pushed forward, moving to the side to let a pair of wounded Marines slip past him. One had taken a shot to the chest, but from the way she moved it looked like nothing immediately critical had been hit. She was helping the other Marine, a man significantly taller and heavier than her, who was stumbling, his hand on his head, blood oozing through his fingers from a hideous wound. Hargraves had seen enough combat to recognize a mortal wound when he saw it. But he'd seen enough Marines in action to know that didn't matter at all to his comrade, who clearly had no intention of leaving the stricken man behind.

That's the difference between us and the FRs. It's why we can take them on even without a lifetime of training and conditioning. Hell, take them on…we can kick their asses…

He shoved his way up to the front, leveling his rifle and opening fire as soon as he had a clear shot. There were only a few of the FRs left, and they had taken cover. Two of them were leaning out of open hatchways, and two more were crouched down behind a pile of metal boxes they'd hauled into the corridor. The Marines were out in the open, and they were paying the price for it. Every meter of advance was gained by climbing over the bodies of their dead, but the rookies were doing it. Hargraves could see them pausing, singly and in small groups, but then he heard Plunkett's voice again, loud and clear, rallying the Marines, pulling that last measure of effort from them.

"Move," Hargraves shouted. "With me." He lunged forward, out in front of the cluster of Marines, leaping over a pair of bodies stretched across the deck. He dropped to the ground in a hard combat roll, snapping up to a prone position and opening fire on the two FRs behind the crates. He had a line of fire on them now, and his abrupt move had taken them by surprise. His rifle came to life and riddled the two with bullets, sending them both tumbling back amid a shower of blood.

He looked toward the two other FRs, dropping forward as he did, ducking below the spray of fire that slammed into the wall behind where his head had been. He pushed off with his legs, leaping as far as he could, landing hard on his stomach perhaps a meter from the crates. He scrambled forward for the cover, unsure as he did if he was fast enough. But then he heard—felt—the surge behind him, the Marines following his lead, rushing the last two FRs, and blasting the doorways with massive amounts of fire.

One of the enemy troopers dropped almost immediately. The other returned fire, long enough to take down one of the attacking Marines. But then the others gunned him down, his body hanging in the air for a horrifying second or so as dozens of bullets riddled him. He dropped hard and landed with a sickening thud.

"Well done, Marines." Plunkett was yelling, even as he raced forward toward Hargraves. The lieutenant's face was twisted into a concerned grimace, but as soon as he saw the sergeant climbing back to his feet it gave way to a look of relief.

"Are you crazy?" he asked, moving right up to Hargraves. He waved his hands and yelled, "Keep moving, all of you. We need to take this ship."

"No, not crazy, sir. I just knew we couldn't get bogged down there. I don't know how many FRs are on this scow, but I was damned sure if we let them pin us down we were sunk."

"You were right about that, Sergeant. But getting yourself killed isn't going to help us."

"A Marine can't worry about that, sir. We do what we have to do to win the fight, and we hope the gods of war spare us."

"Well, I'm glad they spared you this time, Sergeant, because I sure as hell need you." The lieutenant paused, looking at the older veteran with genuine affection. "And I'd miss your old ass something fierce."

"Marines, don't die easy, sir." Hargraves held back the wince that tried to escape as he stood up. He'd hit the ground harder than he'd intended, and he was sore. But there were a dozen Marines in the corridor dead or badly wounded. He wasn't about to whine about a few bruises and strained muscles. "What do you say we take the rest of this ship, sir?"

Chapter Twenty-Three

"Engineering secured, sir. I posted a squad on guard duty just in case we've got any enemy troops still out there."

"Thank you, Lieutenant."

"Reactor secured, Captain. I sent a detachment to occupy the engine room too."

"Very well."

Bryan Rogan stood in the middle of a room, almost certainly the bridge of the Union tanker, fielding reports from his combat teams. He imagined the room had once been clean and neat, but now its workstations were riddled with bullet holes, and its metal floor was covered with pools of slowly-congealing blood.

Rogan was standing next to what appeared to have been the captain's chair, fielding transmissions from his officers and non-coms, status reports from different areas of the ship. At first they'd been deadly serious, reports of entrenched resistance and heavy casualties. But numbers had finally told, and the last messages had been pronouncements of victory.

There were a half dozen bodies strewn about the bridge, three FRs and three ship's crew who'd resisted or gotten caught in the crossfire. Two Marines had died here as well, but Rogan had ordered their bodies removed, taken back to one of the assault ships. Rationally he knew it didn't matter what he did with the corpses, that it certainly wasn't a priority right now, but something deeper called to him to treat his Marines with respect, even the dead ones. It just felt right to him…and he knew that it sent a message to his people.

Three live crew members stood against the far wall, faces cast down, wrists shackled. They were guarded by two very grim looking Marines, who appeared more than willing to turn them into hunks of fresh meat given the slightest excuse. The boarding parties had suffered terribly in the fighting, and Rogan knew his Marines well enough to understand how they felt.

How I feel…

But Confederation Marines weren't animals. They didn't kill those who surrendered, and certainly not half-civilian spacers manning transport ships. Rogan knew well enough that a naval crewman forced to fight to the death could kill as well as die. He'd lost enough of his people, and he wasn't about to risk more when enemy forces were willing to surrender instead of resisting to the death.

He'd known the FRs would fight to the finish, but he'd been surprised that more naval crew hadn't yielded, that so many had fought alongside the Union soldiers. But looking at the terrified expressions on the faces of the captives, he suddenly understood. Their cold fear gave him all the answers he needed. He tried to imagine what Union propagandists had told their spacers about the Confederation. Did they create stories of torture and executions, a web of lies to encourage their people to fight to the death against an enemy portrayed as nightmarish?

He wondered how anyone could be so naïve as to believe such obvious lies. But then he wondered if they were all that obvious, at least to the oppressed masses of the Union. The Federal Union purported to be an egalitarian utopia, but the truth was almost the exact opposite of that lofty ideal. The people lived in poverty, and they were subject to draconian punishments for even the slightest offenses. Above them, a ruling class of politicians lived in obscene luxury, and struggled against each other to amass power. There was no media in the Union that wasn't controlled by the government, no freedom of travel, no contact with other nations—at least not for normal citizens. Education was limited, and what there was followed a strict government-prescribed curriculum.

Rogan thought about the totalitarian government of the Union, and the vicious militarism he'd seen in the Alliance troopers his people had fought at Santis. The Confederation had to survive, it had to prosper. If only because nowhere else in inhabited space did humanity live with some level of liberty and freedom.

"Cap...I've got Sergeant Reynolds on the comm." Rogan turned around abruptly. Ernesto Billos was walking across the bridge as he spoke. "His team took the computer center, sir, and..." His words trailed off.

"And?" Rogan turned his head toward Billos, looking hard at the sergeant. "What is it?"

"I don't know, sir. Reynolds doesn't know...but he thinks they found a nav control unit. One that looks like it wasn't wiped."

Rogan's eyes widened. He wasn't an expert in navigation systems, but he knew enough to realize it was standard procedure for a ship's AI to wipe them clean if a vessel was threatened with capture. It was automatic on Confederation ships—and on Union vessels too, he suspected—a safeguard to ensure that even if a captain was caught napping, vital information would not be exposed to enemy capture. But if something had gone wrong, if the failsafes hadn't functioned properly...

He turned to the side, looking across the bridge. "Sergeant Waverly...you're in charge. We've got more prisoners on the way. I want them all detained up here."

"Yes, sir."

"And, Sergeant...I do mean detained. If any of those captives end up shot, I'm going to want a damned good explanation."

"Yes, Captain."

Rogan snapped his head back toward Billos. "You know the

way to the data center, Sergeant?"

Billos nodded. "Yes, sir. I think so."

Rogan waved to a pair of Marines standing along the near wall. "You two, come with us."

"Sir!" the two Marines shouted, almost in perfect unison, as they walked up to the captain and snapped to attention.

Rogan turned back toward Billos. "Lead on, Sergeant."

"Sir?"

"To the data center. Let's see what Greg Reynolds managed to find."

*   *   *

"Captain, all boarding parties have reported in. All three ships have been secured."

Barron looked over at Travis's station. "Thank you, Commander." He paused a moment, not entirely sure he wanted to ask the question weighing so heavily in his mind. "Casualty reports?" he finally asked.

"Incomplete, sir. There is still data coming in." Travis's voice was strained, uncomfortable. It was clear she didn't want to pass on the information she already had.

"That bad, Commander?"

"We really don't have full information yet, sir. But yes...they appear to be heavy." She paused for a few seconds then added, "Very heavy."

Barron sighed softly. He wasn't surprised. He hadn't expected anything else, but there was always hope, at least until the moment it was crushed by hard data.

"Contact Captain Eaton. She is to advance *Intrepid* toward the enemy vessels."

"Yes, Captain."

Barron waited while Travis relayed the command to *Intrepid*. Then he said, "Relay orders to our engine room as well, Commander. *Dauntless* will also advance toward the captured ships. I want all cargo shuttles ready to launch as soon as we close to fifty thousand kilometers." There was no point in wasting time.

The sooner his small fleet was refueled and resupplied the better. At least if enemy ships came pouring through one of the transit points, *Dauntless* and *Intrepid* would be equipped to put up a fight.

"Captain…I have Captain Rogan on the comm, sir. He wants to speak with you."

"On my line, Commander." Bryan Rogan was one of Barron's most trusted officers. If the Marine had something he felt he had to report to *Dauntless*'s captain, Barron was ready to listen.

"Captain?"

"What is it, Bryan?"

"Sir, we've captured the tanker's nav control unit. It appears to be at least partially intact."

"Intact?" Barron felt a rush of excitement. A functional Union nav unit could contain incredibly valuable intel, including the location of all invading forces and their supporting vessels.

"Yes, sir, as far as I can tell. It looks like it might have been partially wiped, but I'm pretty sure a lot of the data is still there. I suggest you send skilled personnel to evaluate."

"I will send a tech team at once. Meanwhile, I don't want you to let that thing out of your sight, do you understand me?"

"Yes, sir," the Marine snapped back.

"Well done, Captain. My compliments to you and to your Marines."

"Thank you, sir."

"Barron out." He turned his head abruptly. "Atara, I want you to assemble a team and head over there yourself. If there's any chance of capturing Union nav data, we have to take it very seriously."

Travis jumped up from her chair. "Yes, sir…I agree completely." She walked across the bridge toward the bank of lifts.

"Lieutenant Darrow, advise alpha bay that I want one of the shuttles prepared at once for Commander Travis's team. It is to be ready in…" He turned toward Travis. "How soon can you have your team ready?"

Travis looked back at Barron and smiled. "No more than ten minutes, Captain."

"Five minutes, Lieutenant Darrow. I want that shuttle ready in five minutes."

*   *   *

"It's definitely a Union navigational data unit. It's damaged, but most of the data seems to be recoverable. It might take some work, but I think we can pull at least eighty percent of it off of here."

"Thank you, Lieutenant. What do you need to proceed?" Travis stood back about a meter, staring at the partially disassembled device in the center of the room.

"Honestly, Commander, I could have my whole team and the equipment brought over here, but I think our best bet is to disconnect the thing and bring it back to *Dauntless*. It'll be a lot easier to work on it there."

"Is there any chance you could damage it in transit?"

"A small one, I suppose, but I'm confident we can get it moved without any harm. Honestly, I'd say the risk of leaving it in place is greater. There's no question this thing should have been wiped. Some freak malfunction must have prevented the erasure…but there's no guarantee what's left of the ship's AI won't find a way to reroute the destruct signal."

"You mean the systems on this ship could still erase it?"

"Probably not, Commander. I'm just saying I think that risk is greater than the one of moving it."

"Okay, get your people ready. I just need to clear this with the captain." She turned and took a few steps away, toward the portable long-range comm unit her people had set up along the outside wall. She waved off the tech who was standing there, looking at her expectantly, and she reached down and grabbed one of the headsets, pulling it on as she toggled *Dauntless*'s channel.

"*Dauntless…Dauntless*, do you read?"

Dauntless here, Commander." Darrow's voice was loud and clear.

"Get me the Captain, Lieutenant."

"Yes, Commander." A few second later. "What is it, Commander?"

"It looks like we have a Union nav unit, sir. It's damaged, but Lieutenant Varrick believes he can retrieve substantial data."

"That's great news, Commander."

"He wants to move it over to *Dauntless* to complete the work. There's a small chance of damage in transit, but Varrick seems to believe there is a greater danger if we leave it here."

"I'm inclined to agree, Commander." Barron's voice grew softer, almost as if he was whispering. "To be honest, Atara, I feel like we're on borrowed time just sitting here. I'd feel better if that thing was here, and we could move as soon as the resupply operation is finished."

"I concur, Captain. I just wanted to confirm with you." She turned and shouted across the room, "Lieutenant, start disconnecting that thing. I want it back on *Dauntless* as quickly as possible."

"Yes, Commander."

"Atara…" It was Barron, still on the comm.

"Yes, sir?"

"While you're over there, can you see if you can light a fire under those shuttle crews? I'd really like to finish the resupply as quickly as possible."

"I'm on it, sir. I'm sure Varrick and his people can handle the nav unit without me breathing down their necks."

"I've always considered your breath on the crews' necks to be a tactical asset, Commander…though in this case, I'm inclined to agree."

"Consider it done, Captain. Travis out."

She couldn't keep the tiny smile from her lips. She'd known exactly what Barron was going to say, right down to the concern about the speed of the freight and fuel transfer operations.

"You're in charge here, Lieutenant. I want this thing on the way back to *Dauntless* as quickly as humanly possible. Understood?"

"Yes, Commander. We should be done in thirty minutes."

"Try for twenty," she said as she turned and briskly walked

out of the room.

Chapter Twenty-Four

CFS Repulse
Mellas System
Just Outside the Outer System Dust Cloud
308 AC

Three systems…through one after the other, the retreat had continued. An inexorable, disordered, unruly flight from the victorious Union forces. The most shameful, ignominious defeat in the history of the Confederation, one that had every officer, every line spacer in the fleet buried in the blackest gloom. No critic, no rival, no political enemy could have blamed Arthur Winston more bitterly or profoundly than he did himself. The navy had been his entire life, his self worth inextricably connected to his success—or failure—as an officer. He *had* failed, miserably. He had failed the spacers who served under him, the navy he loved, even the memory of his mentor, Rance Barron. And he had failed the Confederation.

Winston had been forced to fight with himself at each transwarp link, struggle to overcome the urge to turn and fight, to seek the incalculable relief offered by the prospect of death in battle. And if it had only been his own life at stake, he'd have stood and faced any odds, gratefully meeting death's embrace. But it wasn't only him. He commanded thousands of spacers. And behind his battered fleet lay the nearly one hundred worlds with untold billions of inhabitants, who had all been counting on his forces to protect them. No, a suicidal battle would be the coward's way out. Despite his shame, despite his despair, he would keep his head. He would command his fleet, and most of all he would preserve it, reorganize it, prepare it however he could for the next fight…for as long as the navy retained a force in being, the Confederation would survive.

There was no doubt retreat had been the right course of action. A fight to the finish would have been more romantic, certainly, and for an old man like him, shattered and broken, it would have been the merciful route. But he was of no concern, and the tactical realities had been clear. His fleet was depleted, low on supplies, its morale at a low ebb. Any battle would have been a slaughter, and the loss of his fleet would have left half the Confederation defenseless.

He'd already abandoned enough citizens. The stars along his line of retreat were orbited by inhabited planets, and the transwarp links from those systems led to other Confederation worlds. His retreat had pulled his forces all the way back through the systems of the Military Border and into the Provinces. Though not as vital or as populated as the planets of the Iron Belt and the Core that lay deeper into Confederation space, the worlds of the Provinces held tens and hundreds of millions. These weren't the people of the Military border, raised under the specter of war, born and bred to serve the Confederation forces and to face the brunt of invasion. The worlds of the Provinces lay far enough back from the hostile Union border that the thought of enemy conquest, of bombardments by Union spacefleets, had long seemed far-fetched. But now that reality had come.

"The supply convoy has begun to transit into the system, Admiral."

Winston looked over at his aide. Beltran had been trying hard to sound positive since the retreat from Arcturon. The admiral appreciated the effort, but it was in vain. Winston knew Beltran was as morose as the rest of the spacers of the fleet…and none was more miserable than he himself. But duty was more important than self-pity.

"Very well, Captain. I want supply distribution to begin at once. Priority to fuel and ordnance transfers, ships with the lowest stocks to be serviced first."

"Yes, sir."

The vessels of Winston's fleet had been fighting almost non-stop for months now, the last, terrible battle only the most recent in a string of defeats. The wealthy Confederation had placed massive stores of supplies on the worlds of the Military Border, but the endless fighting had burned through most of those—and what remained had been destroyed when the fleet had fallen back. His ships and crews needed rest, and they needed a morale boost…neither of which they were likely to get. But at least the worlds of the Iron Belt had managed to pour out supplies, and the massive convoy held enough—fuel, food, spare parts, weapons—to bring his wounded fleet back to full readiness, at least in terms of materiel.

He glanced over at *Repulse*'s massive 3D display tank, focusing on the cluster of small spheres pouring from the Halos transwarp link. There were freighters, dozens of them, and massive tankers he knew carried the output of half a dozen tritium production facilities. Civilian vessels moved forward as well, liners hastily converted to carry reserve troops and replacement naval personnel, as well as all manner of private craft stuffed full of whatever useful supplies they could carry.

"Resupply operations are to continue around the clock. I want every vessel fully reprovisioned and refueled within forty-eight hours."

"Yes, Admiral." The aide's voice was tentative. Winston knew what he had ordered was an almost impossible goal. But that didn't matter. The Union fleet would be coming, and his ships had to be ready. They had fled, trading space for time, but he'd already made a decision. Mellas was as far as he would go. As far as he could go. The system had four transit points, and three of them led directly into the heart of the Confederation, to the older, more populated Provincial worlds, and then to the Iron Belt and Core beyond. However outnumbered, however battered and demoralized, his fleet would have to fight here. The lives of billions depended on it.

We have to find a way to win…

His forces were weak, the fleet grievously wounded by the losses it had suffered. But at least he knew where the enemy would be coming. He could be sure that no enemy forces would emerge from three of the four transit points. Unlike the disaster at Arcturon, there was no chance he would be outflanked here. The enemy would have to take his fleet on straight up. But he *would* be outnumbered. Badly.

He stared at the bank of screens on the wall of his flag bridge. They were displaying images from probes and from the ships of the fleet. There were large freighters floating near several of his battleships, small tugs moving out from their gaping cargo doors, carrying cased fighters into the landing bays. His fighter squadrons, at least, would be at full strength, thanks to the herculean efforts of the Iron Belt factories that produced the small craft. But he knew numbers weren't everything. He'd lost a lot of veteran pilots, and their places would be taken by green replacements, "wet behind the ears" flyers who would be blown away in vast numbers as soon as the battle started.

That was tomorrow's problem. Today's was getting the fleet refit and ready for the battle he knew was coming. He'd left picket ships behind, just inside the Turas system, monitoring the transit point to Mellas. He'd know when the enemy fleet was coming, and he would make sure his people were ready.

Somehow.

*   *   *

"Admiral Striker, I have transferred *Helios* and *Discovery* to Fifth Fleet. That gives you nine capital ships, though admittedly, some of the vessels are old." Gary Holsten sat next to the hotel suite's window, his back to the breathtaking view of Troyus City's immense, kilometers-high skyline. He'd been as direct with Van Striker as he could, at least as far as he could go without outright implicating the admiral in a plot many would call treasonous. The officer had played along well enough, blithely accepting everything from the unorthodox nature of the chain of command running through Confederation Intelligence to the meetings in locations like the suite at the Royalton.

"Old is an understatement, at least with vessels like *Helios* and *Resounding*." Striker spoke firmly, no sign of fear or disappointment with the forces Holsten had managed to assemble evident in his tone. "There is more to a fighting ship than its age, however. And more to naval crews as well." Holsten knew Striker was well aware of the situation at the front. The spymaster had done everything possible to create a fighting force to support Admiral Winston's battered First Fleet, snatching what newer vessels he could from Third Fleet while he scraped up every older ship he could find in mothballs somewhere. But ships weren't the only thing in short supply now, and he'd had to hunt just as diligently for crews, ultimately activating officers and spacers who'd been retired for decades.

He'd expected resistance when he sent the notices out. He had commanded men and woman twenty, thirty, even forty years out of the service to report for active duty on a single day's notice, and he had done it with false authorizations. But the response had been overwhelmingly positive, the retirees surging forth in impressive numbers…with no one questioning the legality of the call up.

They remember the last time the Confederation was on the brink of destruction…

"We have done what could be done, Admiral. I only wish I had more ships, more crews to give you."

"We will make do with what we have, Mr. Holsten. Admiral Barron certainly did… He was also outnumbered, I will remind you, and leading a force that had been driven back in defeat."

"He was, Admiral." Holsten knew quite a bit more about the Confederation's most beloved hero than he suspected the great man's protégés in the military chose to remember. Barron had won the Confederation's survival in a series of great military victories, but he'd gained the control needed to do it through something very near a coup. If he'd been a different sort of man, if he'd craved power for its own sake, the Confederation, at least as its people knew it, would have died at his own hands.

Is that what you're doing? Forging documents, spinning a web of lies to transfer ships to the front, all to emulate the great Rance Barron?

He liked to think that was the case, though he knew military success had washed away Barron's legal transgressions in a way he could never match. He would have no such protection if the shit hit the fan. But the Confederation came first, with him as it had for Rance Barron. If he had to be a casualty of the war in his own way, that was a price he was prepared to pay for victory.

"We will make Admiral Barron proud, Mr. Holsten. We will live up to his memory…and the ideals he set for all of us."

Holsten wondered if it was seemly for the living to envy the dead. Rance Barron had been a great hero, but his stature had also benefitted from a tragic death in battle, followed by decades of retellings of his exploits by worshipful protégés. Such things whitewashed a man's memory, Holsten knew, carrying away flaws, deficiencies, all the things that made a human being *real*. Barron had been a great man, there was no question about that, but when he lived he was a *man*. Now he was a legend.

Holsten knew there was a certain amount of bluster in Striker's declarations of confidence, but there also something sincere. The navy had seen its highs and lows, but it had held off the Union for almost a century, and its personnel—including its senior officers like Striker—carried on Rance Barron's legacy. They would never yield. In that grim tenacity, in the willingness to sacrifice whatever they had to, they found the strength to fight on, and the confidence to be sure they could prevail.

Holsten was less certain, and he found himself envying the simple loyalty and courage that so effectively drove officers like Striker. He was just as determined to save the Confederation as any hero in uniform, but he was consumed by doubts, and by carefully hidden fear. He'd risked his position, his fortune, his very life to ensure the forces at the front had the best chances to win the deadly fight underway. But he wasn't sure he really believed they had that chance, and deep within his own mind, he struggled against the urge to give up.

"I will do everything possible to provide you with additional reinforcements, Admiral, but I'm afraid you cannot count on anything beyond the resources currently under your control, at least in the short term. I have transferred everything I can from Third Fleet."

Transferred…that's a nice way to sanitize outright fraud…

Holsten knew he could call it whatever he wanted, but he was well aware of the reality. He'd slipped several powerful capital ships from the Confederation's home forces without Senatorial approval. Fake maintenance manifests, forged service requests, fictional orders of battle.

"We will use it all well, Mr. Holsten. And don't worry about the old veterans. They've been in this situation before, and they fought their way to victory. They will do it again."

"Godspeed, Admiral Striker."

Chapter Twenty-Five

Gaston Villeneuve sat in his office. He had a mountain of work piled high on his desk, but he was troubled, distracted.

"You wanted to see me, Gaston?" Ricard Lille poked his head into the room. Lille was one of Sector Nine's top agents, and one of Villeneuve's few friends. Still, he hesitated to barge into the office. Friendship was a fragile thing among those who occupied the Union's upper strata. It was a culture committed almost exclusively to the acquisition of political power, and few of its players would allow anything to interfere with their own advancement. Not even friendship. More than one top Union official had advanced himself by turning in one or more of his friends, for real offenses, or simply imagined ones they could make stick.

"Come, Ricard." He gestured. "Sit."

Ricard walked across the richly-appointed office, pulling back one of the chairs in front of the desk and taking a seat. "You look unduly grim, Gaston. Unless I am far more out of the loop than I believe, there would seem to be little reason for dissatisfaction."

"The news from the front is good, Ricard, better even than we'd dared to hope."

"That doesn't sound like a problem, certainly not one requiring my particular skillset." Ricard had completed many missions for Villeneuve, including the abortive effort to bring the Alliance into the war. But killing people was his specialty—he had proven an uncanny ability to get to people who were thought to be invulnerable.

"Not at first glance, perhaps. But I have looked a bit deeper, and I do have some concerns."

"Concerns? Not from the front, surely? It seems the new supply arrangements are working perfectly…and the Confederation fleet appears to be in headlong retreat."

"That is certainly true, though I am inclined to be cautious before I count the Confeds out. The Union has had them on the verge of defeat before, but they always seem to find a way to crawl back. We should not underestimate their capabilities." Villeneuve paused. "That, however, is not my concern. I called you here on another matter, or at least one tangential to the war itself."

Lille stared across the desk attentively. "How can I be of service?"

"I am concerned about Admiral D'Alvert."

Lille stared back, his face an emotionless mask. "The admiral was one of the prime movers behind our supply 'solution,' indeed, our current success would have been impossible without his years of planning and lobbying the Presidium for the resources to implement Supply One. The war seems to be going very well under his direction…so may I assume you are thinking in terms of a post-war problem? The general's ambitions, perhaps?"

"You come right to the heart of it, Ricard. Admiral D'Alvert is not a fool, but he is not a pliable man either. The current First is ruthless of course, in his own way. But he is temperate as well, predictable…controllable. D'Alvert, on the other hand, has few inhibitions. He would be dangerous in the First's chair."

"You think he aims so high?"

"I do. It is only conjecture so far, of course. I have no real evidence. But still, it is Sector Nine's responsibility to protect the Union—and its own power. And we have never allowed a lack of evidence to interfere with our taking...precautionary... actions."

Lille's tightly-controlled expression cracked a bit, revealing a hint of surprise. He turned and glanced back at the door, a reflexive instinct. "You want me to assassinate the admiral," he whispered.

"Yes, Ricard. Not now, of course. Admiral D'Alvert's skills are extremely valuable at the moment, and his attention is fully absorbed by the ongoing war. But once the victory is won, D'Alvert will be the conqueror, the hero. He will have intolerable influence in the fleet...and a chance to transform military glory into political advancement. Perhaps even a coup attempt, one very likely to succeed. I remind you, he is a member of the Presidium as well as a fleet admiral, a consolidation of power bases that has seldom been allowed to occur, for obvious reasons. One bullet can open the First's chair, and what could be more natural than the war hero stepping into the vacancy?"

"You want me to infiltrate. To get myself in position and wait for the moment when the victory is won, when the Confederation is beaten. And then to strike."

"Precisely. As soon as the war is over. We can blame Confederation infiltrators...or perhaps traitorous elements in our own military. That might be useful in terms of eliminating any other officers we might deem too dangerous." He paused. "If I am wrong, if D'Alvert harbors no such ambitions, at worst it is a wasted effort." His tone was firm, unwavering. The notion that in such a case he would have ordered the death of an innocent man was clearly utterly irrelevant to him.

"No, Gaston...I do not believe you are wrong. D'Alvert has always been an ambitious man, and he will recognize victory over the Confederation as a unique opportunity. I would be surprised if he did not make a move. And he would act quickly. Glory is fleeting, after all, and he is smart enough to know that."

Villeneuve paused, glancing unconsciously around the room,

indulging the constant paranoia that was an occupational hazard for a man in his position. "I considered allowing things to follow their course, to stand aside and not interfere. But I decided the risk was simply too great. The current First is mostly concerned with his own luxury, and he is content to delegate the bulk of the actual work of running the Union to the other members of the Presidium and the senior ministers. That has provided a degree of, how shall I put it, security, for those of us in senior positions and a dissipation of executive power among a larger group. D'Alvert is far more energetic, more likely to upset the established order. It is just too great a risk."

"I agree, Gaston. D'Alvert would certainly be less predictable, and that alone is sufficient reason to eliminate him."

"I know this is a dangerous mission, Ricard, and difficult… but I have a reward for you upon its completion. There will be much work to do when the Confederation is conquered. Its people will have to adapt to a different way of life. They will have to learn to serve the good of the state. The job will be a vast one, and Sector Nine will need to expand massively to do it. I need a good man to take control of the overall operation. You have served me well, my friend, and you have the moral…pliability…to do what is necessary to see the job done." Villeneuve stared across his desk. "Handle the D'Alvert matter, Ricard, and the position is yours."

Lille stared back, the mask of neutrality that usually covered his face gone, replaced by undisguised shock. "I don't know what to say, Gaston. Thank you."

"You have earned it, my friend."

And you are the one least likely to betray me once you have stolen vast treasures from the Confederation and established yourself in your own power base. At least I think you are…

*   *   *

"Nothing. The supply fleet is three days overdue, and we've heard nothing. Not a thing!" Hugo D'Alvert was mad. No, beyond mad…he was positively raging, as close as a man could

come to the fiery heart of a supernova. He had the Confeds on
the run. And now a late supply convoy was keeping him from
finishing things.

"No, sir. No word, either from the supply fleet or from the
escort." Isaiah Beltran answered firmly, at least compared to
the rest of the command staff who'd been quaking every time
D'Alvert's eyes moved in their directions. The Union admiral
was a feared man, there was no question about that. But Beltran
had been with him a long time, and even a monster needed a
close confidante or two.

"I want a patrol dispatched to Arcturon now. I want to know
exactly where that supply convoy is, and why it has not arrived
on time.

"Yes, Admiral. At once."

"If Admiral Lund has been negligent in his command of
the force, he will pay dearly." D'Alvert's mind was clouded with
anger, but there was clarity below it. The supply line had given
him a strategic advantage, and had enabled him to take the Confederation by surprise. Invasions always bogged down as fleets
moved past supporting range of their bases, and it took time to
establish forward facilities on captured worlds. The Union's true
advantage in the war lay not in its numbers, not in the early victories that had pushed the Confederation forces back with such
heavy losses. It was the unorthodox system of supply, the simple
but brilliant solution D'Alvert himself had been instrumental in
creating.

But every day his fleet was forced to sit idle drained away
that hard-won advantage, the edge he'd gained through years of
work and trillions of credits in expenditure slipping through his
fingers. He'd read the history, and the intel reports. The productive capacity of the Confederation, especially of the worlds of
its legendary Iron Belt, was truly awesome. The Confederation
was easily diverted in peacetime, its inexplicably weak government bowing almost without exception to calls for funds to
be diverted from military expenditures to other, often waste-
ful, purposes. D'Alvert couldn't imagine paying mindless heed
to the wishes of the masses, of allowing the mongrels in the

street to vote for their leaders. Those who couldn't rise to power existed to serve. It wasn't his pronouncement…it was that of history. The weak had always been compelled to do the bidding of the strong, as they always would be.

He knew he had to win the war in one massive offensive. The Union had committed everything it had to the attack, leaving its home systems and other borders dangerously undefended. But three wars against the Confederation had taught a stark lesson. Once the beast was roused, the productive engine of its enemy would outproduce the larger Union. Vessels would stream from the shipyards, fighters at first, then escorts, and, eventually, even capital ships would be launched in unimaginable numbers. Fear would drive the people of the Confederation to unite, and weapons would pour forth in a torrent the Union couldn't hope to match.

D'Alvert knew his history well. The last war had almost been a catastrophe. The Union First had died, and the nation had become divided, rival claimants fighting for power. The Confederation fleets had been strong, victorious, massed on the border. But its citizens' fear had faded away, and they demanded a cessation to hostilities. In the end, that peace had only cost the Union two of the eight worlds it had conquered years before. An almost insignificant price for the time to rebuild, prepare. And a breathtakingly foolish act by the Confeds, allowing their enemy to escape to fight another day.

He couldn't understand the leaders of the Confederation making such a foolish decision, the craven nature that allowed them to cease hostilities even before reclaiming the rest of their own lost systems. He appreciated the productive capacity and wealth of his adversary, but the Confederation and his people disgusted him. They were weak…and they would fall. Whatever it took.

"Captain, contact Admiral Galt. He is to command the patrol…and he is to relieve Admiral Lund and assume command of the supply flotilla. He is to do whatever is necessary to get those ships here as soon as possible."

"Yes, Admiral."

D'Alvert knew Lund would have a long list of excuses, but he wasn't inclined to listen to justifications for failure. If the supply ships had arrived on time, his forces would already be moving against the Confeds. He might have caught them demoralized, low on ordnance, disorganized. Instead, they had more time to reorder their forces, to bring up their own resupply. He still had numbers, but whatever had knocked Lund off schedule had cost him some of his advantage. And he'd see the damned fool stretched out on an electric grid in the sub-levels of Sector Nine headquarters if his incompetence cost him even part of the gain his years of planning had created.

Nothing was going to stop him now, and he would let no weakness, no hesitation, interfere with whatever was necessary to drive his forces to the ultimate victory. Then, the hated Confederation would be gone, its rich worlds existing to serve the Union. And he would have an open route, straight to the First's chair.

Chapter Twenty-Six

Briefing Room
CFS Dauntless
Arcturon System
308 AC

"I want to thank you for shuttling over here, Captain Eaton."
Barron sat at the head of the table, his designated position as
both *Dauntless's* captain and as the senior Confederation officer present. Nevertheless, despite his unquestioned authority to
command the forces present in the system, he was making every
effort to underplay his command role, to offer his colleague the
maximum amount of respect possible. He knew his authority
here had nothing to do with the Barron name, but a lifetime of
sensitivity to the preferential treatment he had so often received
left him a bit uncomfortable issuing orders to Eaton. He would,
of course, when he had to, but he much preferred to discuss
tactics with her and gain her genuine support. Besides, he had
no idea what to do next.

"Of course, sir." Sara Eaton sat just to Barron's side. The
table was large enough to accommodate at least twelve, but
Eaton and Barron were the only two present. Unlike *Dauntless's* commander, Eaton seemed to have no problem with the
command arrangement, or at least, if she did, she was hiding it
well. She had stepped gracefully into the role of the respectful

subordinate.

"Resupply and refueling will be completed within the hour. I have ordered the remaining enemy vessels destroyed as soon as the last wave of shuttles is clear. Our respective staffs will have some extra work converting Union ordnance and replacement parts to our own uses, but there is no question we have improved our situation considerably. And all of our vessels are fully refueled." He glanced over, catching Eaton's faint nod of acknowledgement. "I believe we must now discuss our next steps."

"I agree, sir. There is no doubt we are on the enemy's supply line...and the convoy we intercepted will surely be missed. Destroying the volume of supplies we did was unquestionably helpful to the war effort, but it seems to me that we cannot stay here, at least not out in the open."

"We have both come to the same conclusion, Captain." He paused, sighing softly. "Or, shall we dispense with the formalities? I'm Tyler."

Eaton looked slightly uncomfortable, but after a few seconds it seemed to pass. "Thank you, Tyler. I'm Sara."

"So, Sara, what do we do next? It seems to me we have several considerations. What best safeguards our ships and crews? What allows us to provide maximum support to the war effort, as our duty demands? Clearly, these factors may not necessarily point to the same course of action."

"I believe we must do everything possible to support the fleet, sir...Tyler. Regardless of the risk. The losses suffered in the early battles have been severe, and we have been forced to abandon many systems. I can't believe the status of the war is anything short of critical."

"Our assessments agree. Our two ships are only a small portion of the navy, but the Confederation needs every resource it has left, including us. My first instinct was to rejoin the fleet. But there is little doubt that the enemy's main force lies between us and Admiral Winston." He hesitated. "I do not shy away from the prospect of battle...but there seems to be little advantage in throwing *Dauntless* and *Intrepid* away trying to get past thirty or more enemy battleships. I simply don't see how we can possibly sneak around the Union fleet. A small ship or two might have a chance, but two capital ships?"

"I believe you're correct. Even if we were able to stay away from the enemy battleline, it seems impossible to avoid detection. They would have left scanner buoys and probes at the transwarp points. And once they know we're there, they would respond with a force large enough to overwhelm us."

"Which brings us back to the original question. What do we…"

The door slid open, and Atara Travis came rushing into the room.

"Atara?" Barron looked up, an anxious expression on his face. He knew his exec wouldn't have interrupted him, not without good reason.

"Sir, Lieutenant Varrick and his people have decoded the enemy nav unit." Travis was as cool as they came, but Barron could see she could barely control her excitement. "They recovered the deployments of the entire enemy invasion force, sir. Forward fleets, garrisons, escorts…everything. As of three days ago."

Barron glanced over at Eaton before snapping his eyes back toward Travis. "My compliments to the lieutenant and his team, Commander. That is…impressive news."

"It certainly is." Eaton nodded as she spoke. "Though if we can't get it to Admiral Winston, it may be wasted."

"We may have to try to get through now, whatever the risk." Barron's initial excitement was fading. The discovery was of immense tactical significance, but if he couldn't get it back to the fleet it was valueless.

"That's not all, Captain." Travis extended her arm. Her hand was grasped around a small tablet. "There is information about the enemy's logistical arrangements…a possible answer to how they could be moving so quickly and staying in supply."

"What is it, Commander?" Barron had wracked his brain again and again, but he hadn't managed to come up with any way the enemy could have done what he knew for certain they *had* done. It simply took too long to build forward supply and production bases, even given suitable systems. And he'd reviewed the operations reports from *Intrepid*, scanning every grueling detail of the early defeats the fleet had suffered. It hadn't been a pretty picture, but one thing was certain. Any production facility capable of producing so much as a milliliter of tritium had been destroyed before the fleet fell back. The Union was fueling its ships somehow, but it wasn't from captured Confederation supplies or installations.

"The details are sketchy, sir, and what Lieutenant Varrick was able to decode is on this tablet." She leaned forward and placed the unit on the table. "But it appears the Union has constructed some kind of mobile logistics facility. It is referred to as 'Supply One.' Based on what we could discover from the nav unit, it is the nexus of their entire logistical tail."

Barron shook his head. "What kind of mobile installation could possibly supply enough fuel and ordnance to sustain a fleet the size of their invasion force? It doesn't make any sense." Eaton glanced back and forth between Travis and Barron. "Even if it was twice the size of a capital ship—or ten times— how could something mobile possibly carry enough materials to sustain the kind of forces the Union has thrown at us?"

The room was silent, his companions clearly as stumped as he was. Finally, Travis spoke. "Sir, I can't explain, but the nav data seems very clear on this point…and it's not like we have any other working hypotheses."

Barron took a deep breath, staring back at his first officer for a few seconds before responding. "You cut to the heart of it, Commander, as always." He paused again, a troubled look coming over his face. "Did the nav unit give us a location for this supposed supply base?"

"Yes, sir. According to the latest update, the base has just been moved forward, to the Varus system."

"Varus? That's just two transits from here."

"Yes, sir," Travis replied. Her tone was somber. Barron understood why. They all knew the third planet of the Varus system was a major provincial hub, a world with several hundred million Confederation citizens. It was one thing to think in terms of retreats and withdrawals, but quite another to be reminded about the people left behind.

"It seems we have a choice," Barron said softly. Then he looked back up at Travis. "Please, Commander, have a seat. We must decide on a course of action, and I would have your input." He looked over at Eaton, wary of any signs his fellow captain objected to inviting his first officer to their command meeting, but there were none.

"Yes, sir." Travis pulled out a chair and sat down.

"So, the way I see it, we have two choices. Do we attempt to reach Admiral Winston with the intelligence we have on enemy deployments, despite the immense difficulties in getting two battleships past the Union fleet?" He paused for a few seconds. The first option he'd laid out was dangerous enough, perhaps even hopeless. But the other thought forming in his head was downright insane. "Or do we move forward—to Varus—and attack this enemy supply base?"

Barron looked back and forth at his two companions, not at all surprised at their silence, or at the stunned expressions on their faces. It was one thing to discuss the difficulties, even the near impossibility, of sneaking past the enemy forces, but trying to return to the fleet, especially with the intel they now possessed, *made sense* at least. The idea of two battleships and a handful of escorts moving deeper into enemy-held space—and attacking some kind of phantom supply base—seemed downright insane.

"Captain...our data on the supply facility is highly speculative." It was Travis who spoke first, just as Barron had expected. His first officer was the one best positioned to try and tell him he was crazy. But he wasn't crazy. The desperation of his plan spawned from that of the situation. The cold truth was there weren't any good options, at least not any that offered a substantial chance of success. Or of survival.

"Is it, Commander? I'll admit, I can't fathom what kind of portable installation could support a fleet the size of the Union invasion force, but we have no reason to doubt the information on the enemy nav unit. In other circumstances, I'd expect deliberate misinformation, some type of counter-intelligence designed to send us off in the wrong direction. But that would require data we were likely to intercept and I can't imagine the Union high command anticipating what happened here. That we would attack and destroy a convoy behind the battle lines and escorted by multiple battleships?"

"What you say makes sense, Captain." Eaton's expression was hard, no sign of her true thoughts evident. "But what about the nav data on the enemy fleet? Doesn't our duty require us to try and deliver it to fleet command? And this supply base... wouldn't such an installation, if it exists, be well-defended? Could we hope to reach it and destroy it?"

"Could we hope to get back to the fleet with the nav data?" He paused, pushing back the impulse to edit their situation. He wasn't about to discuss the near-hopelessness of their plight in front of the crew, but Eaton deserved complete honesty from him, and he'd long ago decided there was nothing he would hide from Travis. "Any choice we make is the gravest of long-shots. For all we know, the fleet has been defeated again...or it has withdrawn halfway to the Core by now. Whatever path we choose, we must realize, the three of us at least, that we will likely fail."

He let his words hang in the almost-silent room for a few seconds before he continued. "If we head back toward the fleet, and we are intercepted and destroyed, we will do nothing for the war effort. Our captured intelligence will be lost with us. If we instead move on the enemy base...even if we fail to destroy it, we may be able to cause damage or intercept additional supply ships. Our deaths will not have been for nothing."

"It sounds like you've made a decision, Captain," Travis said softly.

"I just think we should consider our options carefully."

"Captain Barron...Tyler...both courses of action have advantages and disadvantages. It is your decision. Commander Travis and I will, of course, accept any decision you make." Eaton paused, then she continued, "I can't think of anyone more capable…to whose judgment I would be more willing to commit my ship and the lives of my crew."

"Thank you, Sara…I appreciate your confidence." His words were calm, his gratitude genuine. But inside, his gut was twisted into knots. He realized he'd wanted to discuss the matter with Eaton—and with Travis—to avoid the terrible realization that the decision was his and his alone. He was in command, and from the day he entered the Academy—no, from the day he was first old enough to understand his grandfather's stories—he'd understood just what that meant. Some part of him had tried to avoid the terrible pressure, to turn a decision it was his obligation to make into an exercise in groupthink. But he had no right to push the responsibility off onto his subordinates. He had to make the choice. Alone.

He sat for a moment, his mind going back over the details. He'd made his choice…he'd made it in the instant Travis had come into the room and told him about the enemy base. The intelligence on Union deployments was useful data, certainly. But it didn't change the fact that the Confederation fleet was battered and outnumbered, that even with the location of the enemy forces, Admiral Winston might not be able to stem the invasion. But if his people could somehow reach the enemy supply source and destroy it, or even damage it badly enough, it could change the course of the war. The enemy would have no choice but to retire back toward its conventional supply lines, abandoning almost a dozen occupied Confederation systems.

"The supply base then. We will go to Varus, and we will destroy whatever is there. No matter what it takes, we will find a way." His voice was firm, assured, the old command veneer designed to inspire his officers and crew. But the two women sitting with him weren't taken in by their commander's false confidence. Sara Eaton was a ship's captain herself, as accustomed as Barron at hiding her concerns and fears. And Atara Travis knew Barron better than any other living human being.

None of that mattered, though. They would do as he commanded, without hesitation. And if they could actually pull it off, against the odds…maybe, just maybe, they could change the course of the war.

Chapter Twenty-Seven

"That's insane, Commander Jamison. It would be suicide, plain and simple." Barron stared across the table at his strike force commander. "I can't order any pilot to throw his life away with no hope of success."

"Sir, I don't suggest that it is not risky…very risky. But I believe it's possible. Commander Fritz has upgraded a stealth suite, adding some of her own improvements. She is confident she has increased its effectiveness by over one hundred percent."

"Commander, the ability to avoid detection is far from the only obstacle to your plan. We have no idea where the fleet is, and while it may be possible to predict their line of retreat with some hope of success, we don't know how far they have gone. There's no way a fighter could carry enough fuel to travel through multiple systems, even if I was willing to allow one of my pilots to attempt transwarp jumps."

"Captain, I have reviewed the plan, and I am convinced I have come up with a way to do it. There's no chance a larger ship could sneak through the enemy forces, but I think we can make a fighter work. We strip it, remove the weapons, everything extraneous…then we pack it with extra fuel tanks. It will cut down on maneuverability, but it shouldn't be much worse than a bomber kit. Then…"

"That might work for one transit, Commander, but the fleet has likely pulled back multiple systems."

"Yes, sir, but we know the fleet retreated to the Gamalon system from here. They would almost certainly have gone to Ultara next, then Turas, falling back on the primary supply line. And Mellas after that."

"I agree with your tactical observation, Commander, but there's no way we can get a fighter to Turas from here, much less Mellas or farther."

"We could, sir, if we sent a shuttle with it. We still have cargo shuttles rigged up for fuel transfer. We could install a class five AI in one of them and automate its operation. It could accompany the fighter, and the pilot could use it to refuel."

"That defeats your entire purpose in sending a fighter, Commander. The stealth suite might hide a Lightning, but not a bulky fuel shuttle. We might as well send one of the escort cruisers."

"No, sir. The pilot will stay with the shuttle until he detects the enemy fleet. Then he will refuel one last time and send the shuttle off as a diversion. The enemy scanners are unlikely to pick up the shuttle and fighter as distinct contacts. Once the shuttle heads off in its own direction, the fighter will engage the stealth suite and disappear into the system, heading for the next transit point. It is extremely likely our fleet, or at least a detachment of picket ships will be in the adjacent system to the main Union force. Even if the fighter runs out of fuel, the pilot can transmit the data to them and then wait for rescue."

"Or suffocation," Barron said sourly. "Or death by freezing. Commander, you are one of the smartest and most capable officers I've had the privilege to command, but you've lost it with this scheme. Your list of assumptions for success is almost long enough to stretch back to the fleet. What if there are enemy forces between here and their main fleet? It won't take the entire enemy battleline to intercept and destroy one fighter and a shuttle. What if our fleet has fallen back even farther than Mellas?

There is a limit to range, even with a shuttle full of fuel…don't forget, both ships will be firing their engines. And if the fighter encounters a picketing force without any friendly capital ships, there won't be any rescue shuttles there. The pilot will be dead long before any help arrives."

"I'm willing to take those risks, sir. I understand your concerns, but can you really argue it isn't worth risking one man to get such valuable intelligence back to fleet command?"

Barron opened his mouth, but he closed it again without speaking. Jamison was right, and beneath his reaction to the risks and his concern for his people he realized it. He was risking everyone on *Dauntless*, and *Intrepid* too, in a desperate bid to disrupt the enemy supply line. Could he really justify refusing to let a pilot—a volunteer, he would insist on that—try to complete such an important mission?

"Very well, Commander," he finally said, his voice somber, grim. "But I want Commander Fritz to personally prepare both the fighter and the shuttle. I know we don't have much time, but I want her to double and triple check everything. If I'm sending someone out there, I'm damned well going to do everything possible to make sure they have what they need."

"Yes, sir!" Jamison said, nodding his head forcefully as he did. "I will get Commander Fritz on it right away, and I will get ready to leave as soon as she is done."

Jamison started to stand up, but he froze as Barron spoke.

"No, Commander. Not you."

"Sir, you just said…"

"I said I would approve the mission, not that I would allow you to fly it."

"But, sir…"

"There are no buts, Commander. You gave me all the reasons it is worth the risk of allowing a pilot to make the attempt. They all apply equally to your letting one of your people go."

"But I meant I would go."

"I know what you meant, and you can forget that right now. You're my strike force commander, the ranking pilot in both ships' fighter wings. Your place is here, commanding the squadrons, if and when we find that enemy base."

"Captain…"

"I said forget it, Commander. I know you'd rather go yourself, but it's out of the question. We have well over one hundred fighters, and your place is right here, commanding them."

Jamison was silent for a few seconds. Then he said, "Maybe I was wrong, sir. This might be too dangerous."

"Oh, it is that, Commander. It's one of the most dangerous missions I've ever sent anyone on. But you were right. We have to take the risk. The intelligence is simply too vital to the fleet."

"If I call for volunteers, half the wing will step forward. Hell, most of the wing."

"You and I both know who needs to fly this mission. I'm proud of all our pilots, but putting most of them into the cockpit on this one is no different than throwing them out the airlock."

"I know, Captain…but…"

"He's your friend, Kyle…but you'd have expected him to be okay with your going. You know he'll volunteer…and when he does, you have to let him go."

Jamison stared back silently. Finally, he just nodded.

* * *

"Why you? Why is it always you who has to do something crazy? Are you the only pilot on this ship?" There was anger in Stara Sinclair's voice, but Stockton knew it was a veneer, that fear was the true force driving her outburst.

"You know why, Stara." Stockton wasn't angry, though he knew he must have sounded like he was. Part of him was grateful to see her emotions for him so unmasked, but the fire inside that drove him to be the pilot he'd become was raging. He understood the mission, and its grave importance to the war effort. It was difficult, some thought impossible. He didn't know if he could do it, but he was sure if he couldn't, no one else could. "And you know how important it is."

"Can't someone else do it? Let another pilot go."

"You know I can't do that. What do you want me to do? Go

to one of my people and tell them, I'm too afraid to fly this mission, so I want you to do it? If you think I could do that—that I *would* do it—you don't really know me at all." He regretted the last part as soon as he said it. He was determined to fly the mission, but the last thing he wanted to do was hurt her more than he had already.

"Maybe I don't know you. Or maybe I know you too well. But I don't want you to go."

Stockton had never seen the usually cool and reserved officer so emotional. Sinclair had talked dozens of injured pilots in, directed them in safely landing their damaged fighters, and she had done it every time with a cool focus, regardless of the stress or the danger of the situation. But now she looked as though she might burst into tears.

"I know you don't. It's not that I want to go...I have to go. You know the situation the fleet is in, hell the entire Confederation. Maybe this data will enable Admiral Winston prepare for the next enemy attack. It could turn the tide and save thousands of our comrades. Millions, even billions of civilians. You know I have to do it." His voice was calm, soft, utterly at odds with his usual cocky and arrogant persona.

She stood silently, staring back at him. Then she stepped forward, burying her head in his shoulder and wrapping her arms around him. "Do you really think you can do it? That you can make it all that way?"

"I do," he lied. In his gut he figured he had one chance in three of reaching the fleet, and less than that of surviving until he could land or be rescued. But that was a chance he had to take. If he figured it at one chance in ten, or even one in twenty, he'd still have done it. But Stara didn't need to hear any of that. It wouldn't do her a bit of good. It wouldn't do anybody any good.

She pulled him tightly toward her, her fingers almost digging into his back. "Please...please be careful. Just get there...and make it back here."

"I will." He tightened his own arms, hugging her ferociously. Then he pulled back, away from the embrace. "Go now," he said, his words barely a whisper. "I launch in twenty minutes, and I need to get ready."

She looked at him, her eyes glistening, but not so much as a tear escaping them. "Come back, Jake. Come back to me."

"I always come back," he said, reverting to his normal cockiness for an instant. Then, his tone deadly serious, he said, "Really…I know how to fly that thing, Stara, you know that. I'll make it through."

"Please," she said, clearly struggling to keep her voice loud, clear. Then she turned around and walked toward the hatch. It opened as she approached, but she hesitated, for just a few seconds. Then, without another word, she walked out into the corridor, and she was gone.

Stockton took a deep breath. He already had his pressure suit on, and his helmet was resting on the table. He was ready, as ready as anyone could be for an assignment like this one. But he'd had to get her to leave. Focus would save his life over the next few days…and distraction could end it in a microsecond. He needed to prepare himself mentally. He had to be the best he'd ever been.

But first he had something else to do. He walked over to the AI control, activating his personal log. He had to put Stara out of his mind, but first he had to leave her a message, a goodbye, in case he didn't return as he'd promised. He had to tell her what he knew he should have long before, the thing he'd never been able to say.

He had to tell her that he loved her.

*   *   *

There they go.

Stockton had watched on the scanner as *Dauntless* slipped through the transwarp link, heading for Phillos. He'd launched six hours before, and he was halfway across the Arcturon system, less than a million kilometers from the Ultara transit point.

He smiled. He'd have bet a year's pay that Kyle Jamison had wanted to go, that Captain Barron had intervened and insisted

Dauntless's fighter commander stay with the strike force. He and Jamison seemed almost like night and day, at least on cursory inspection, and he knew most people couldn't understand their close friendship. He was the crazy one, and Jamison the calm, rational wing commander. But Stockton knew that wasn't the whole story. He was far more deliberative than he allowed anyone to see…and he'd seen Jamison take breathtaking risks in battle.

They all probably think I'm here because I can't pass on any risky mission, all except Kyle…

He wondered if deep down Stara understood. He wasn't doing this for glory or because he thrived on danger. He was doing it because the Confederation needed this. Because he believed he could see it through, and that it could help change the course of the war.

He was afraid, of course, for himself, but even more so for Kyle and Stara and the rest of his comrades on *Dauntless*. His mission was singular. He was alone, and that made the danger all the move evident. But *Dauntless* was moving deeper into enemy-held space, seeking a fight he was far from certain she could win. And even if Captain Barron managed to destroy his target, the small task force would still be deep behind enemy lines. They faced nightmarish odds, and he had deliberately avoided trying to estimate their chances of making it back.

"Approaching Gamalon transit point." The voice of his ship's AI pulled him from his thoughts. He turned his attention to his dashboard, grateful to have a task to distract himself. He adjusted his nav data, and he checked on the status of his fuel shuttle. It was still with him, following ten kilometers behind. It should stay with him during the transit, at least that's what all the calculations showed. He'd considered refueling before the jump, just in case something went wrong. But there was no point. One refueling wasn't going to get him anywhere, and if he lost the shuttle he was dead, plain and simple. He'd wait until he was in Gamalon.

"Three minutes to transit."

He leaned back, his eyes darting over his displays, double

checking all his settings. He'd never done a transwarp jump in a fighter before. Few had. The energies at play in the tube were deadly to anyone without proper shielding. His bird had been covered with a special protective coating, just one more modification to the fighter for this mission. Commander Fritz had done it herself, and he had enough confidence in *Dauntless*'s chief engineer to feel comfortable about it. Reasonably so, at least.

"Two minutes to transit."

He took a deep breath, thinking again about *Dauntless*, about her own dark journey. He wondered how the war had gone so badly so quickly, how a seemingly prepared Confederation had been so surprised by the strength the enemy had been able to deploy.

"One minute to transit."

None of that matters now. We're in the shit, and we've got to find a way out of it. Captain Barron knows what Dauntless has to accomplish. And I know what I have to do. If we're both successful, we might just help turn things around.

"Transit in five, four, three, two, one…"

Stockton was bathed in darkness for a few seconds, and then all around he saw a swirl of colors, light brighter and more brilliant than any he'd ever seen before. He was still alive…that meant his shielding had held, but he was distracted, unable to focus. He'd never been this…close…to the strange phenomenon of transwarp travel before. He knew he was in some kind of alternate space, removed from his own reality, but he couldn't really think about it. He couldn't think about anything. And then, suddenly, the dancing lights were gone, replaced by the blackness of space. He was through the tube, nine light years from where he'd been a moment before.

He was in the Gamalon system.

Chapter Twenty-Eight

Bridge
CFS Intrepid
Phillos System
308 AC

"Black Helm Squadron reports both enemy vessels destroyed, Captain. Gold Shields are doing sweeps out to the Varus transit point." Nordstrom's report was professional as always, but his satisfaction at the quick destruction of the target ships was evident.

"Very well, Commander." Sara Eaton stared at the display. She'd launched three full spreads of probes the instant *Intrepid* had transited into the system, and half a dozen more since. As far as she could tell, there were no enemy vessels in Phillos, save for the two frigates her fighters had just destroyed.

"Black Helms are to land for refueling and refit. Gray Squadron is to support the Gold Shields. I want every millimeter of space from here to the transwarp link scouted." The Black Helms were her best pilots, but she'd had them equipped for shipping strikes, overruling launch control's plan to send the Grays out as bombers. She couldn't take any chances on allowing an enemy ship to escape and warn whatever was waiting in Varus that two Confederation battleships and their escorts were on the way. Whatever chance they had to pull off this almost-insane operation, she suspected they had none at all if they lost the element of surprise.

"Yes, Captain."

She felt a twinge of guilt at her thoughts, at the unjustified lack of confidence she felt in the Grays. She knew *Intrepid*'s three native squadrons and their personnel well, but Gray Squadron was a new and oversized formation assembled from bits and pieces of other ships' fighter wings. They were good pilots, she knew, and some, she suspected, were excellent. But they weren't used to flying together, and regardless of the skill of the personnel, that made a difference. She'd almost held them back entirely, but she wanted to keep one of her own squadrons in reserve, so she'd held the Longswords on alert in the launch bay. Just in case.

She knew she was lucky to have the Grays, and that the pilots themselves were fortunate to be part of *Intrepid*'s extended fighter wing. Their alternative had been death in the Battle of Arcturon, either by enemy fire, or by the loss of life support.

"Scouting reports all negative, Captain. It doesn't appear that either frigate was able to dispatch a drone."

"Continue the search, Commander. We need to be sure." She didn't think the enemy had gotten off a warning either, but she was well aware that one small drone, out there somewhere heading toward the Varus transit point, could be the difference between the success of the mission and total disaster.

"Yes, Captain."

"And get me Captain Barron."

"On your comm."

"Captain, we've had no further contacts. I've got almost fifty drones deployed, plus two squadrons of fighters. I'm not saying there couldn't be something hiding out there, but we'd detect anything that tried to communicate or power up for a move." She knew she wasn't reporting anything to Barron he couldn't have surmised from his own scans and the earlier tactical reports she'd sent in. *Intrepid* had transited into the Phillos system first, and she had handled the enemy pickets immediately, launching fighters before *Dauntless* had even come through the transwarp link.

"That's good news, Captain. My compliments to you and your people for handling those Union frigates so expeditiously."

She was well aware that Barron had been uncomfortable exerting command his slight but legitimate authority over her and her vessel, and she thought well of him for that. But, truthfully, she was relieved to be part of a command structure again… any part but the top. Tyler Barron had led his ship in solo action before, indeed, his one on one fight with the Alliance flagship was fast becoming legend in the fleet, even without official recognition that it had ever happened. Eaton had only commanded her vessel in action as part of a fleet and, notwithstanding Barron's apparent concern she might harbor resentments about it, she was actually grateful to have him in command. She'd had a moment of doubt initially, a concern that the scion of the greatest naval family would not live up to expectations. But she was well past that now. She'd taken her measure of the man and found him to be utterly deserving of her respect and loyalty.

"Thank you, sir." Her eyes darted to the display, checking on the flow of reports from her fighters and drones. Still nothing. "What are your orders, Captain?"

"Let's press on, Captain. We were fortunate the enemy appears to have had no greater force in this system. I see nothing to be gained by pressing our luck, by delaying here."

"I agree, sir." She paused. "Captain, do you want to send one of the escorts through the transwarp link to scout before we go through?"

There were a few seconds of silence. Finally, Barron said, "I don't think so, Captain. I wish I knew what was waiting for us in Varus, but I don't think whatever quick scans one of the cruisers could manage would be worth risking our surprise. *Dauntless* and *Intrepid* will go through, as closely spaced as possible. If there's something there that's going to hit us, I want as much force in place as we can get."

"I agree, sir." She wasn't sure if she agreed or not. It seemed more like a coin toss to her, but she figured unity was more important.

"I want to be ready for action the instant we transit, Captain. *Dauntless* and *Intrepid* will both be at battlestations and ready for action when we enter the link."

"Yes, sir."

"Leave your fighters out to scan the system as long as possible, but I want you to recall them in time to have them refit and ready when we transit. I want every fighter ready to launch the instant we emerge in the Varus system."

"Understood, Captain."

"Very well. We should be at the transit point in just over six hours. Use the time well, Captain. Run diagnostics on all weapons systems and energy transfer points. And your reactors. Both our ships have been through a lot already, and if there's a loose connection or a compromised conduit somewhere, I want it found and fixed before we transit."

"Yes, sir. I'll see to it."

"I know you will. Barron out."

Eaton tapped the comm control, shutting down the channel. Then she looked out across *Intrepid*'s bridge. Her officers were at their stations, focused on their duties with no sign of fear, at least none any of them let show. She knew they had a great test ahead of them. Her people had been in and out of battle for weeks now, but this was different. She had no idea what awaited them in Varus. Was there truly some massive enemy supply base? And if it was there, what would be defending it? Could *Dauntless* and *Intrepid* really take it out? Or would the two battleships be overwhelmed and destroyed?

She didn't know...and she wouldn't. Not until she took her ship through the transwarp link and into the Varus system. All she could do now was make sure *Intrepid* was ready for battle.

"Commander Nordstrom, I want all weapons stations to conduct full diagnostic self-checks. And contact Commander Merton. I want him to check both reactors and every power line, especially the ones feeding the primaries."

"Yes, Captain."

She didn't know what was waiting for them, but she was sure of one thing. *Intrepid* would be ready for it.

* * *

"All stations report ready for transit, Captain. Gunnery stations on full alert, and all pilots are standing to their fighters. Commander Fritz reports primaries and all systems fully operational."

"Thank you, Commander Travis." Barron nodded grimly. He was about to lead his people into action once again…and he knew it was likely not all of them would be coming back.

If any of us come back…

"Give my compliments to Commander Fritz." Barron knew his ship was badly battered from its past fights, held together by a series of hasty, incomplete repairs. It was no small feat that Fritz and her people had managed to get *Dauntless* one hundred percent functional, and he wanted them to know he realized it. He considered it a poor reward for competence to be taken for granted.

"Yes, sir." Travis turned back to her station and relayed his words.

"I want Red squadron to launch as soon as we clear the transit point, and a I want a spread of drones deployed as well. We have to know what we're facing, and we have to know as soon as possible."

"Yes, sir. Red squadron is standing by, all pilots in their craft, and the drones are ready to launch as soon as systems come back online."

"Very well." Barron paused briefly, taking a few deep breaths. "Forward, five percent thrust. Take us in, Commander."

"Initiating five percent thrust. Project transwarp entry in forty-five seconds. Estimated length of passage, twenty-six seconds."

Barron leaned back, absent-mindedly checking his fastened harness. He didn't necessarily expect to meet resistance as soon as *Dauntless* emerged in Varus. If surprise was still on his side, it was unlikely the enemy had forces positioned right against the portal exit. But there was no way to be sure, except to go through and see what was there.

"Entry in thirty seconds."

Whatever was or was not waiting right at the other end of the transwarp link, he had no doubt there were enemy forces in Varus. He was at a loss to explain how a mobile supply base could possibly service a fleet the size of the Union invasion force, but the references to it were too clear to ignore. He believed there was something in the system ahead, and if there was a major supply nexus of some sort, there would be protection for it as well.

"Fifteen seconds to transit. All personnel, secure for transwarp passage."

Barron took a deep breath. Transits weren't what he'd call comfortable, but he was used to them by now. He knew some people were more sensitive than others to the alien nature of transwarp space. He'd never had the hallucinations he knew some experienced, but there was always some pain, and a bit of nausea.

For an instant, he wondered if he truly hoped to find the supply base on the other side...or if he secretly hoped the information gleaned from the enemy nav unit had been wrong, that Varus would be empty, or at worst patrolled by a few escort ships. But he pushed such thoughts aside. He felt fear, certainly, more pronounced for the fact that his people would be fighting deep behind enemy lines, cut off from home and from the rest of their comrades in the fleet. But he couldn't hope for an empty system. The Confederation needed a respite, and he and his people could give it to them. *If* they found a major source of enemy supply...and *if* they managed to destroy it.

"Transit commencing now..."

Barron closed his eyes, more out of habit than for any particular reason. The swirling lights so common during transwarp journeys were not harmful. In fact, they could be quite beautiful. And closing his eyes did nothing to relieve the headaches or flopping in his stomach that constituted his body's own reaction to alien space.

The bridge was silent. Sound waves didn't travel in transwarp space, at least not in any way familiar to human science. It was an odd experience, certainly, especially the first time, but Barron had made dozens of transits. Hundreds. He just sat still and waited for the seconds to slowly pass.

Dauntless was traveling at an incalculable speed, or none at all, depending on which space-time model and system of mathematics one subscribed to. Efforts to explain the technology of the fallen human civilization that had preceded the present-day nations were mostly unsuccessful. No one knew why the transwarp links functioned, much less had any idea how to construct new ones. There were many non-functioning portals too, remains of links that, by the best guess anyone would offer, had been destroyed on the other side. No one knew if there were people in those systems, trapped, or even connected to other worlds through alternate links.

Barron tried to clear his mind. His thoughts tended to wander during transits, when time seemed to lose all meaning. He knew the trip would last less than a minute, but it seemed to him as though hours had already passed. Then, suddenly, he felt his stomach heave once, and he forced back the bile rising in his throat. He opened his eyes, just as his screen reactivated and displayed the blackness of normal space.

"Active scanners on full power," he snapped. "Red squadron, launch."

"All scanners at full, Captain. Alpha bay reports launch operations underway." As if to emphasize his first officer's words, Barron could feel the light vibrations of the launch catapults as they began to send the fighters of Red squadron out into space.

"Probes launched, Captain. All weapons systems have checked in. They remain on full alert status. Primary batteries fully charged and ready to fire."

"Very well, Commander." He waited, leaning into his chair, his eyes moving back and forth from the massive display tank to his own workstation screens. Nothing. No contacts, none at all.

He realized he'd been holding his breath, and he let it out. There was nothing near the transit point, no enemy ships, no deployed fighters. Whatever fight awaited his people in Varus, it would not be here, at the transit point. That meant the other ships would have time to complete their jumps, that his small task force would have time to get into formation before the battle.

Unless there's really nothing here. Maybe that information was bogus…

He felt the urge to say something, to snap out orders to Travis, to Darrow, to anyone. But there was nothing he could do. None of them could rewrite the laws of physics. Communications moved at the speed of light, and not faster. And probes were vastly slower, despite their big engines and 50g acceleration. It would take minutes to get data from deeper in-system, hours even, depending how far the enemy was from the transit point. And there was nothing Barron could do but wait.

"Captain, *Intrepid* is emerging from the transit point."

"Very well. Advise Captain Eaton we will move forward as soon as all ships have entered the system."

"Yes, sir."

Barron sat and watched as *Intrepid*, and then the other three ships, emerged and formed up around *Dauntless*. His tiny fleet was ready…but ready for what? He still didn't know.

"Commander, the task force will accelerate at 4g, directly toward the primary." He had no idea where the enemy forces might be, if indeed they were here. But the transwarp link had dumped his ships in the middle of the system, just between the four rocky inner worlds and the nearest of the three gas giants.

"Yes, Capt…" Travis spun around, looking over at Barron. "Sir, we're getting something from the drones. Orbiting planet five. It's big, Captain. No, more than big, it's…"

But Barron didn't hear any more. His mind had gone blank, his eyes fixed on his own screen, staring in utter disbelief at what he saw.

Oh my God, how is this even possible?

Chapter Twenty-Nine

Midday to Turas Transit Point
Ultara System
308 AC

Stockton watched the small bars on his display as they moved slowly to the right. The red lights changed to yellow, as the readings moved from critically low on fuel and air to moderate levels, and then to green as his tanks approached full. His stocks had been almost exhausted before the transfer. He'd pushed his ship as far as he could before stopping again to refuel and replenish his air from the shuttle. The longer he stretched each reload, the fewer he needed. That meant less time spent immobile and helpless. He shuddered to think of how vulnerable he was, his engine offline, ship tethered to the shuttle.

He had other reasons for minimizing his refueling efforts, cool, rational thoughts quite at odds with his image as the fearless, arrogant fighter ace. He had reviewed every aspect of his mission, considered each thing that could go wrong—indeed, he had little else to do as the endless hours passed.

There was nothing to be done about the enemy…if they found him they found him. He didn't have a beam hot enough to make a piece of toast, so he wasn't about to fight his way out of any mess. But an enemy attack wasn't his only worry; there were all sorts of other things that could kill him out here, including a failure of the hastily jury-rigged system that allowed him to refuel from the shuttle.

It took precision positioning to line up the two ships so perfectly, but that wasn't his concern. He knew he could nudge his fighter wherever he needed it to go. But hooking up with the shuttle also required perfect performance from the fragile umbilicals, and the robot arms that put them in place. One failure, one part of the system slipping centimeters out of alignment, and he was dead. It would just be a matter of waiting for his air to run out.

The white lights above his tank readouts flicked on, and a small buzzer sounded. His fighter's fuel tanks were topped off, his air supply fully replenished. He'd be good for hours now…it was amazing how far a fighter's fuel went without the rapid acceleration and deceleration of combat. He only needed enough thrust to establish his vector and reach a reasonable cruising velocity, and even then he couldn't go too fast, because the cumbersome shuttle had to match his maneuvers.

He sighed as he flipped a series of switches, disengaging the fuel and air lines, and directing the shuttle's AI to pull them back into place. He watched on his scanner as the robot arms slowly retracted, waiting for the signal that the shuttle was ready. When the green light blinked on he tapped his throttle, pulling the fighter slowly away from the shuttle. He hit the maneuvering thruster, spinning the fighter slowly, orienting his engine along the vector toward the Turas transwarp link. "Four g thrust commencing in five, four, three, two, one…"

He pulled back on the throttle, blasting his engines, accelerating toward his destination. He wasn't accustomed to announcing his intentions out loud, but he'd found that the shuttle's AI was better able to follow closely if he gave it advanced notice of what he was intending. He found it annoying, but then he told himself the fuel and air on the shuttle was all that stood between him and some manner of unpleasant death.

He'd kept his thrust to a maximum of 4g, and usually even less. The shuttle was one reason, though he suspected even modified as it was to carry fuel tanks, it could pull at least 6g for a while. The enemy was the other. Ultara seemed to be devoid of enemy ships, at least as far as his fighter's limited scanning suite could detect. But he didn't dare engage his active scanners, so he was limited to data from passive sweeps. The stealth setup made his own fighter harder to detect, but even *Commander Fritz* had been uncertain how much protection the ECM device would extend to the nearby shuttle. Blasting engines at full was practically begging to be spotted, and while Stockton wasn't one to run from a fight, his lack of weapons made the prospect… unappealing.

He glanced down at the display. Fourteen hours to the Turas transwarp link. He'd thought he'd understood boredom before. Service on a battleship, especially in peacetime, involved long stretches of inactivity. But this mission had taught him the true meaning of *boredom*. It had been endless, unchanging hours of nothing. No maneuvers, no acceleration or deceleration except when his course required a vector change. Nothing but the constant blackness of space.

And the fear, the eerie feeling that any second his alarm would sound, that a squadron of enemy fighters, ships with actual missiles and lasers, would spot him. He'd imagined his death in battle many times, but the images had never been those of a trapped animal, unarmed, with no recourse but to run. He hated that vision, but he knew there was no alternative, not on this mission. He wasn't the type to surrender, no matter what the circumstances. But he knew that wasn't even an option now. His orders had been clear…get through to fleet command with the data from the nav unit. And if he couldn't, there was only one option. Under no circumstances could he allow his ship to be captured. Even if he couldn't get through, he was not to allow the enemy to discover that their locations had been compromised.

He leaned back, trying to get comfortable. It was an impossible goal, he realized. A fighter's cockpit wasn't designed for endless days of occupancy. He thought of *Dauntless*'s landing bays, imagining the walk from his fighter to the ready room, the sublime pleasure of stretching his legs. He'd been a fool, never truly appreciating that simple joy.

"Wake me up if we get any contacts." He knew the order to the AI was needless. The intelligence would ceaselessly monitor the scanners, and it would sound an alarm immediately if it detected anything, even without Stockton's specific instructions to do so. Besides, he doubted he would fall asleep. He was a natural pilot. "Born to be in the cockpit," he'd been called. But now all he wanted was to get out of the confines of his ship, to walk, to stretch out in a bed...or even on the floor someplace he could extend his legs fully.

If you want to walk across a landing bay, you need to find the fleet...

He leaned back and closed his eyes, fighting the hopeless fight for a few hours of sleep.

* * *

Admiral Van Striker sat quietly and stared out at his team. He had a few of his preexisting staffers with him, but this was the first time he'd commanded an entire fleet, and he'd had to massively expand his staff to handle the many duties of his new position. He'd had the pick of the personnel Holsten had scraped up for Fifth Fleet, but he'd found himself making his choices from among the activated retirees. These were men and women who'd seen battle before, who'd fought against the Union in the last war, and some even in the war before that.

Striker himself was among the younger officers in the Confederation's upper command structure. He'd seen action in the past war as a junior officer, but unlike the older generation of admirals, he had never served with Rance Barron. He'd never even met the Confederation's great hero. His career had been a distinguished one, but he'd long found his advancement to fleet command effectively blocked by the septuagenarians and octogenarians still riding their associations with the great admiral to the highest levels.

He'd hidden whatever resentment he'd felt...it wasn't something likely to help his career along. And he was as mesmerized by the cult of Rance Barron as every other officer in the navy.

Still, he'd sometimes wondered if the great admiral's memory had become more burden than inspiration. Barron had shattered a calcified old order, sweeping it away and replacing it with a cadre of dynamic young officers. But now, the remnants of the great admiral's followers sometimes resembled the old command structure they had replaced, at least it seemed that way to him.

"Admiral, we're approaching the Mellas transwarp link." Commander Jaravick's voice was firm, strong. The officer's demeanor exuded confidence. Jaravick had served for forty years before he'd retired, achieving the rank of Commodore before he'd hung up his stars. Striker had served under Jaravick, and when he saw the name on the list of reactivated retirees, he immediately transferred the veteran to his own team. He'd had second thoughts, concerns over how he would feel giving orders to his old superior, but Jaravick had made it as easy as possible, even insisting on reactivating as commander, a more typical rank for an admiral's aide, rather than commodore.

"Very well, Commander." It still felt strange calling Jaravick 'commander,' though, he realized, perhaps no less bizarre than giving the old warhorse orders at all. "The fleet will begin transit. *Fortitude* will take the lead. I want to speak with Admiral Winston as soon as possible."

"Yes, sir." Striker might have been uncomfortable with his old boss in a subordinate position to him, but Jaravick seemed to have no trouble slipping into a role as the admiral's aide. "Transit in one minute, sir."

Striker leaned back in his chair. He'd been flattered when Holsten chose him to command Fifth Fleet, though he was still a little uncertain how he felt about realizing just how much control Confederation Intelligence held over the force. In all the dealings he'd had to make to get Fifth Fleet operational, almost none of it had been through normal channels. Holsten seemed to be overstepping his bounds, but from what he'd seen, Striker was confident the spymaster was only doing what he could to turn the war around. It was certainly not the normal chain of command at work, but then Rance Barron had been the first one to take the established order and turn it on its head. Maybe it was time for that kind of thing again. It was certainly time for something. If the fleet couldn't halt the Union advance, the whole Confederation was in jeopardy.

"Ten seconds to transit, Admiral."

Striker leaned back and closed his eyes. The effects of transwarp space weren't particularly hard on him, save for the occasional fairly severe headache. The jump to Mellas was a short one, at least in terms of actual distance between the two stars, less than three light years. That meant no more than ten seconds in the tube, barely enough time to worry about side effects at all.

He hardly had time to think about it before the monitors displayed the inky blackness of normal space. Fifth Fleet's flagship was in the Mellas system.

He sat and waited as *Fortitude*'s scanners searched the surrounding space, and her comm system linked up with the fleet channels. Space was a massive place, and the speed of light could seem very slow when it took minutes or longer for signals to traverse interplanetary distances.

"*Helios* and *Vanguard* have transited, Admiral." Jaravick's tone was the same as before, the veteran unaffected by the transit. Striker tried to imagine how many system jumps the old spacer had made in his day.

Hundreds, for sure. Maybe even a thousand.

"Very well. The fleet is to form up as soon as all ships have transited." There was no rush. Striker would normally have sent escorts ships through first to scout the area around the transwarp link, and then reordered the fleet in sections as ships emerged. But he knew First Fleet was in Mellas, and that his entry point was deep in the rear of Admiral Winston's force. Striker wasn't one to relax his caution or the discipline he demanded from his people. But he knew they had enough challenges ahead...and he was just as aware how many would likely not return from the campaign that lay before them. He didn't need to put them through pointless effort, not when he would have to ask so much from them soon.

"We're starting to get scanner data, Admiral...and we're connected to the fleet net." Jaravick paused, and when he continued his voice carried the first chink Striker had seen in the veteran's iron demeanor. "The fleet is badly battered, sir. Half of these battleships should be in spacedock, not preparing to fight again."

"That may be, Commander…and half *our* ships should be museum displays, not active warships. But we all do what we must, do we not?"

"Yes, sir. We do." The old spacer's tone was back, as hard as polished steel. "And we *will* do whatever is needed, Admiral. Ancient ships—and crews—notwithstanding."

"I suspect when all is said and done, the enemy will be quite surprised what a bunch of old ships and spacers can do."

Chapter Thirty

Barron's eyes glazed over at the stats scrolling down the screen. He could see the words and numbers as they updated, and he knew what they meant. But it couldn't be. It simply wasn't possible. The construction orbiting the gas giant was enormous. No, such words didn't even come close to describing the thing. It was unspeakably, unimaginably, incalculably massive.

Two hundred forty-three million tons...

He read the data feed again. It still didn't seem possible, but that was what it said. He'd seen such mass figures before of course, and far larger ones, but for stars, planets, moons...never for anything manmade. Aside from the incalculable amount of work building such a structure would require, he couldn't even begin to imagine the engineering challenges that had to be overcome in its design.

Dauntless's drones were still far from the base, too far for specifics. Perhaps the data was wrong. Maybe it *was* an asteroid or some other natural phenomenon and not something built by man. But he knew even as he thought it, that wasn't the case. He stared at the screen and saw the energy readings, a level of power beyond what a hundred of *Dauntless*'s reactors could have produced.

"Captain…" It was Travis, and for once his normally resolute first officer seemed utterly unnerved.

"I see it, Atara."

He saw it, but he was still fighting to accept what his eyes told him. "Launch another spread of probes, Commander. No, two more spreads. I want that thing covered from every angle. And get all remaining squadrons ready to launch. There's no way that thing is unprotected."

God only knows what weapons it carries, beyond what ships are deployed out there in support…

"Yes, sir."

Barron's head remained fixed, his view of the scanner cast in the all too familiar red glow of *Dauntless*'s battlestations lamps. He'd wondered what kind of supply base could provide the logistical support needed to keep the Union offensive moving. Now that he saw it, he had no doubts. This hulking behemoth undoubtedly carried munitions factories and vast holds full of every manner of supply a warship needed. And its position orbiting the gas giant was no accident, he knew. The scanners hadn't confirmed it yet, but he was certain the thing was harvesting tritium from the massive planet's atmosphere, producing the fuel needed to sustain the invasion.

He watched as minutes passed, as more data came in from the probes. The small drones were accelerating at full thrust, rapidly building up velocity directly toward the base. And as they closed, the information flow increased. The station was as immense as it had appeared at first. It was in low orbit above the gas giant, and all around it smaller vessels were moving toward and away from the thing.

Hoppers, Barron realized. *Ore ships moving to and from the system's asteroid belt, providing raw materials for the production facilities.*

A projection was also forming in the main display, the AI's representation of the data the drones were relaying, the closest thing to actual video of the station. The thing was long, more than twenty-five kilometers. There were a number of nodules along a large stretch of its length…massive docking bays, Barron realized. And at every bay there was a vessel, each as large as a capital ship. Almost thirty of them. He panicked for an instant, afraid they had found a whole new fleet of enemy battleships, but then he realized, the lined up vessels were freighters and tankers.

What in the eleven hells of space is *that thing? How could they have built it? And how did they get it here?*

"Captain…we're picking up launches from the station, sir. It looks like fighter squadrons."

"Launch all remaining fighters."

"Yes, Captain."

His eyes moved toward the display, his gaze pausing on the small oval representing *Intrepid.* The battleship had emerged less than a minute before. He snapped his head toward the communications station. Normally, he relayed his commands through Travis, but she had enough to do right now. "Lieutenant Darrow, get me Captain Eaton."

"Yes, Captain." A few seconds later: "On your line, sir."

"Captain Eaton, I know you just transited, but we found what we were looking for, and a whole lot more. I need you to scramble your fighters."

"Already done, Captain. All squadrons are ready to launch. Just awaiting your order."

"Very well, you have it. Launch all fighters now."

"Yes, sir. I've got *Intrepid* at red alert. What else…" Her voice trailed off to silence, and Barron knew she had gotten her first look at the enemy supply base. A few seconds later: "My God, Tyler…how is that possible?"

"I don't know, Sara, but that's not the question we need to answer. How the hell do we destroy it?"

"Have you picked up any escorts or capital ships? Or just those freighters and tankers?"

"No, not yet. But we haven't been here for very long. There could still be a whole fleet out there for all we know."

"Any readings on the weaponry that thing packs?"

"No, not yet. If we're lucky, it's mostly production and logistics oriented. I can't explain how they could have built it at all, but there has to be some limit to what they could put into it."

"I suggest we keep *Dauntless* and *Intrepid* tight, within fifty thousand kilometers of each other. That way, if we find a weak spot, we can concentrate our fire."

"Agreed. Bring *Intrepid* up alongside us, and then we'll advance together."

"Very well, sir."

"At least we answered the question about how a mobile supply base could support their entire fleet. But what I don't understand is, how is this thing *mobile*? Doesn't look to me like it would fit through a transwarp link…so how do they move it?"

"I have no idea, sir. None at all. But I guess all we have to worry about is destroying it. Somehow."

"Let's get to it then, Captain. Barron out."

"Commander Travis, I want engines ready for 6g acceleration as soon as *Intrepid* is in position."

"Yes, Captain." Travis paused. "Sir, all squadrons have launched. Commander Jamison requests permission to…" *Dauntless*'s first officer snapped her head around. "Captain, we're picking up something from the enemy base." A short pause. "Launches, sir…looks like fighters." She turned and looked back at her screen. "A *lot* of fighters."

Barron stared at the display as clouds of small dots appeared around the enemy station, a few at first but then more and more, until ten full squadrons of fighters had deployed…and begun moving toward *Dauntless* and *Intrepid*.

"Get me Commander Jamison."

"Yes, sir…on your line."

"Kyle, I'm sending you the data feed from our scanners." He gestured toward Travis for her to transmit the information."

"I've got it on my screen already, sir."

"Link up with *Intrepid*'s squadrons, and take command of the entire combined strike force. I don't need to tell you what a strike that size can do to two battleships if there are bombers in the mix." The fighters were still too far away for detailed scans, but the fact that they were moving to engage his ships and not hanging around the station as a combat space patrol suggested they could be a threat to *Dauntless* and *Intrepid*.

"I understand, sir. We'll stop them. Whatever it takes." Jamison's voice was grim, cold. Barron knew what it would take, just as he realized his strike force commander did...and he knew what it would cost too.

"Good luck, Kyle. My best wishes to your people."

"Thank you, sir."

Barron cut the line and looked over at the display. *Intrepid* was almost in position. "Prepare engines for thrust," he said. "We're going to move up right behind the fighters, Commander."

"Sir, what if enemy bombers get through?"

"Then they get through, Commander. They'll hit us right behind the fighter screen or all the way back here...it doesn't make any difference. But whatever damage we take, our action will be the same. Close to weapons range and open fire. That thing is big enough to sustain the Union's entire war effort, and its presence here in a Confederation system is proof enough they can move it. We've got to destroy it...somehow. It may be the only way to save the Confederation."

"Yes, sir." A moment later: "Captain, *Intrepid* reports she is in position. Ready to engage thrusters on your command."

Barron took a deep breath. The fight at Santis had been the most desperate of his life, but at least he was up against a normal vessel. This thing was so colossally huge, there was just no way to know what to expect, how much damage it could absorb, what defensive systems it had.

Or what enemy ships are lurking out there...

He knew he was being reckless, that it was dangerous to advance before he could get a comprehensive scan of the system. But he also realized that no matter what he might find out there, how daunting an enemy force was waiting to fight his tiny fleet, they had to go in. It didn't matter if they were outmatched. It didn't matter if they were hopelessly outnumbered. Whatever chance they had to take out that supply base, however remote it might be, they had to take it. And the prospects of survival weren't even part of the equation.

"Engage engines, Commander. Forward…directly toward the station."

* * *

"Commander Jamison, we're picking up additional launch activity from the enemy station. No idea on numbers, but it appears additional fighter squadrons are deploying."

Jamison frowned, partially at the report that his people would be facing more enemy fighters, but also as a reaction to Sinclair's voice. Stara Sinclair was one of the top officers in *Dauntless*'s launch and flight control center, and he'd heard her on his comm hundreds of times. But now her voice, perhaps a bit off from its usual cool professional tone, just reminded him of Stockton. He'd tried not to think about it, where his friend was now, or if he was even still alive. Especially not now. He had over a hundred fighters following him, and those pilots needed his undivided attention. It was the fighter pilot's creed…in the cockpit there was nothing but the friends on your wings and the enemy in front of you. You left everything behind in the bay. But he was finding that difficult, and the slight crack he could detect in Sinclair's voice was only making it worse.

"Acknowledged, Lieutenant. Relay additional scanner data when available."

"Understood, Commander." A short pause. "Be careful out there, Kyle."

"He's okay, Stara, I know he is." It was a lie, but he knew she needed to hear it. It was also a breach of normal protocol for them to even discuss it, but Jamison didn't give a shit.

"I want to believe that, Kyle. He's so self-sure, but I could tell when he left…he was scared."

"I know, Stara. But he's the best pilot I've ever seen, and the most infuriatingly stubborn cuss I know. He'll get through it. We just have to believe."

"Thank you, sir." He thought he could hear a touch of relief in her voice. People had a way of believing what they wanted to believe. It was a trait he'd never possessed, and one he'd envied from time to time. Kyle Jamison had a coldly realistic view of things, and in his gut, he was desperately afraid he had seen his friend for the last time.

"Commander, we're getting another data dump from the probes." The instant he heard her voice, he knew it was more bad news. "It looks like they've launched another ten squadrons."

Jamison's face twisted into a grimace. He'd been watching the approaching enemy first wave, and from the fluidity of their maneuvers, he'd come to the conclusion they were all interceptors. It hadn't made any sense. The enemy station needed to defeat the two capital ships approaching it, and interceptors weren't going to get that done. Now he understood. The first wave was intended to deal with his fighters. The second would be the strike force intended to destroy *Dauntless* and *Intrepid*. And Captain Barron had committed every fighter the two ships had available. There was no CSP behind his squadrons, no defense at all, save the point defense arrays of the battleships.

And if that first group ties us up, and that second wave is all bombers...

"Stara, send me the tracking data on the second group. They're still too far for me to get a decent lock. I want to know exactly where they are at all times."

"Yes, Commander. Right away. Keep in mind a relay from the probes to *Dauntless* to you is going to put a..." Her voice paused for a few seconds. "...six minute delay on data."

"Understood, Lieutenant. And let me know if they launch anything else immediately."

"Of course, sir." She paused. "Good luck, Commander."

"Thank you, Lieutenant. Jamison out."

He cut the line and switched to the main channel. "Listen up...we've got more fighters inbound, over a hundred. That means we're outnumbered badly. But we've been there before, and this time is no different."

Bullshit...it's different as hell if we've got a hundred plus bombers moving up on us behind this interceptor screen. You can't let that strike force through. No way. Not if you want Dauntless and Intrepid to be more than two hot clouds of plasma...

"We're going to split into two forces. One to face off with

those interceptors, and the other to blast right through and take on those bombers." He didn't even know if the whole second wave *was* made up of bombers, but his gut told him yes. And that meant the enemy interceptors would fight like hell to prevent any of his squadrons from breaking through.

He had a cold feeling. His impulse was to send Stockton and the Blues to spearhead the attack on the interceptors. Even outnumbered two to one, he knew his friend and his elite pilots would make a fight of it, perhaps enough to let a few of his squadrons slip by. But Stockton wasn't there. He was off, alone in deep space. Or he was…

He snapped himself back into focus. There was no time for worrying about friends. Not now.

Timmons…

Dirk Timmons's reputation was as widespread in the fleet as Stockton's. Perhaps even more, since Timmons and his squadron had been assigned to the flagship. The thought of sending in the Blues along with Timmons's Red Eagles…sending them under Timmons's command twisted his stomach into a knot. He didn't have anything against the pilot, but he knew how Stockton felt about his rival. It seemed disloyal, and he hated himself for what he was about to do. But his first obligation was to protect *Dauntless* and *Intrepid*, and he had to stop those bombers to do that.

He thought of "Ice" Krill, lost in the fighting at Santis. He had been another star pilot, and Jamison wouldn't have hesitated to put him in command of the force engaging the enemy interceptors. But Krill was dead. Olya "Lynx" Federov commanded Red squadron, but as skilled a pilot as she was, he knew she wasn't in quite the same league as Stockton and Krill, or Timmons.

"Warrior, you will take the Red Eagles, Direwolves, Blues, Yellows, Gold Shields, and Longswords. I need you to take on those interceptors. I know you'll be outnumbered, but whatever you do, you have to keep them occupied. I'll take the Reds, Greens, Grays, and Black Helms and go after those bombers. You've got to keep those interceptors off our tails, Warrior. Or those bombers are going to get through."

"Understood, Thunder. We'll keep them busy...whatever it takes." There was a touch of surprise in Timmons's usually cocky tone.

"I'm counting on you, Warrior. Get it done." Every word cut at him like a knife, even as he said it. He could almost see Stockton's eyes staring at him from the darkness. But he had to do what made the most sense, and Timmons was the logical choice. He needed his fighters aggressively led...conservative tactics weren't going to get the job done. And Timmons was the only other crazy pilot he had with the chops to inspire the rest of the squadrons.

I'm sorry, Raptor...I just don't have a choice...

"Reds, Greens, Grays, Black Helms...with me. We're going to ignore those interceptors and blast right through their formation. We're after the bombers behind, and we can't let anything stop us. Full thrust on three...two...one...now!"

He pulled back hard on his throttle, feeling the force of acceleration slam into him like an onrushing train. It was time to win this fight, no matter what that victory cost.

Chapter Thirty-One

By the eleven hells...there they are. Right where the nav data said they'd be.

Stockton stared at the dots on his screen. According to the information from the enemy nav unit, there were fifty-three battleships, and well over a hundred escorts. The combined invasion fleets of the Union, preparing to continue their irresistible advance. It was a massive force, one that threatened the very existence of the Confederation.

And I have to get across the system...somehow...

He glanced down at his gauges. He'd refueled before he made the transit into Turas, and he'd come in on a vector he'd guessed would lead him away from the enemy fleet the nav data had told him was there. His hunch had been sound, and his fighter and the shuttle following it were heading off into the system's periphery, engines shut down, offering only the minimum energy output to any enemy scanners or probes.

There were disadvantages to his plan too. His route was longer, and eventually, he would have to fire his thrusters and substantially alter his vector. He'd have to cut the shuttle loose before he did that...the stealth suite was giving his lumbering companion some cover, but when he cut back toward the tran-swarp link, he would need every bit of ECM he could get to slip by the enemy. And that meant cutting it close with his fuel. Damned close.

If he could maintain the relatively slow course he'd set, he'd have just enough. But if he was spotted, if he had to blast his thrusters to get away, he was going to run out of fuel...this side of the jump to Mellas. He had pushed things to the limit more times than he could remember, but this one had even the legendary Raptor sweating hard.

He'd never considered what a toxic combination fear and boredom could be. He had endless hours still to go to get close to the Mellas transit point, and he knew each agonizing second that passed could be the one when the enemy spotted him. He was used to danger—even his rivals like Timmons would acknowledge that Stockton was no coward. But every man had his deepest fear, the one thing that pounded away at his psyche, unnerved him more than anything else. For Stockton, it was being helpless. He'd fight against an enemy that outnumbered him a hundred to one, and he would never lose his resilience. But the idea of being chased, hunted like a defenseless animal with no way to fight back...it shook him to his core.

He looked down at his throttle, at the firing stud that would discharge his ship's weapons. If it'd had any. The small row of controls on the panel was gone, the switches that would have charged his laser cannons replaced by plastic caps. He shook his head, wishing that Commander Fritz had found some way to leave him even one of the two pairs of guns his ship usually carried. Anything that would let him fight back.

It was all pointless, he knew, but somehow it would have made a difference to him. He could have drawn strength from the ability to resist, even when it was as utterly pointless as a fighter's laser cannons against the biggest war fleet he'd ever seen.

But you don't have that. You're not a warrior here. You're a messenger, whose only hope is sneaking past the enemy.

He felt something strange, a feeling that was new to him.

He was struggling to maintain the cool calm that made him so deadly in battle. He'd volunteered for the mission, of course. It was his nature to do so, but there was far more at play than just that. Jamison hadn't said anything about it, but Stockton was sure his friend had wanted to go himself—intended to go, he would have bet. The captain had probably quashed that idea, and rightfully so. Kyle Jamison's place was at the head of the squadrons, the combined strike force of both battleships.

He also knew that, for all the great pilots on *Dauntless* and *Intrepid*, none of them had as much chance as he did of completing the mission. He hoped he'd made his point to Stara, convinced her that it wasn't just arrogance that drove him into this lonely cockpit, and away from her. He just couldn't stand by and let another pilot—a friend, a comrade—step up and fly this mission.

Not even Timmons…

Stockton's face twisted into a frown at the thought of his rival. For all his noble thoughts about protecting his comrades, he knew Warrior was the one other pilot who would have had the same chance he did to complete the mission. And he had to admit to himself he'd had less lofty motivations as well for taking the mission. His competition with Timmons, his resentment of the other pilot…it made it impossible for him to stand aside, to let his adversary step into the shoes that were rightfully his. Stockton couldn't even remember the origins of his dislike and rivalry with the other pilot, but he felt it nevertheless, even now. Was it rational, or was it just something that had built on itself over the years? He wasn't prone to such levels of introspection, not normally, but the loneliness and boredom were bearing down on him.

"Approaching optimal thrust point."

The AI's cool voice interrupted his thoughts. He looked around the cockpit, his eyes dropping to the display. He was deep into the Turas system. He glanced at the chronometer, and snapped back to it again as the numbers sunk in. He'd been lost in thought for hours. Perhaps he'd even drifted off into some kind of waking sleep. But now there was work to be done.

He took a deep breath and rubbed his eyes. Then he reached down and grabbed a bottle of water, lifting it to his lips. He'd planned to take a few sips, but as soon as the water touched his mouth he realized how thirsty he was, and he gulped down the whole thing.

"Prepare for refueling operation," he said hoarsely, clearing his throat and repeating the words.

"Recalling shuttle, Lieutenant."

Stockton leaned forward, reaching out and flipping a series of switches. His eyes caught one of the gauges on his control panel, the gas pressure in his positioning jets. It was low, far more depleted than he'd expected, and he had no reserves. It had been difficult enough to rig the shuttle to refuel the fighter and recharge its life support systems. The gas jets were difficult to refill, even in the launch bay. There hadn't been time to rig up some way to do it in deep space, and even if there had been, it would have been half-baked, unlikely to work very well.

He'd guessed it wasn't a problem, that one charge would be enough to see him through the mission...and Jamison and Fritz had agreed. But now, he wasn't so sure. It was going to be close.

Nothing to do about it now...

He watched on his screen as the shuttle moved closer, the robotic arm extending the umbilicals toward his ship. This was mostly the AI's deal, but the whole process was so delicately cobbled together, Stockton couldn't help but watch nervously.

There was a pit in his stomach now too, one he knew had little to do with the refueling. This was it, the last recharge. After the transfer was done, he'd send the shuttle off on its own vector, completely different from his own. Then he would engage his engines and line up his course toward the transit link. This was the truly dangerous part of his mission.

A whole series of things had to go well for him to survive. Commander Fritz's jury-rigged stealth system would have to keep him hidden, even as he fired up his engines. His fuel would have to hold out...and he knew that was going to be a close one. His air was in better shape, but only marginally. If he ran out of fuel, he'd have maybe an hour's worth of oxygen remaining, a few final moments to ponder his fate.

And the fleet's got to be in Mellas, of course…otherwise you came all this way to die for no reason.

He understood all the reasons to expect that Admiral Winston and his ships would have withdrawn to Mellas…and that they would still be there. He agreed with them all, completely. But that wasn't the same thing as *knowing* they were there. Stockton had bet his life that they were, and now the doubts crept up around the edges of his mind.

Perhaps someone will find me in Mellas, even if the fleet isn't there.

The Mellas system had two inhabited worlds, but with the Union fleet one transit away, civilian traffic would be at a standstill, which meant his fleeting thought was more fantasy than reality. If he got through the tranwarp link, he'd have an hour left, maybe two. No terrified civilians waiting for an enemy invasion were going to react quickly enough to save him. No, it was either the fleet, or…

He turned back toward the gauges, not particularly caring for where his line of thought was leading him. Almost full. He'd done seven refuelings now, and he started to get a strange, almost nostalgic feeling about this being the last. The shuttle had been a faithful companion, following him on the longest journey attempted in a fighter. He felt a pang of guilt for casting it off, cynically condemning it to destruction at the hands of the enemy. He knew it was silly. The ship was an inanimate object, and even the AI that had directed it so perfectly to follow him was nothing but data.

You're losing it, Raptor. You're one step away from stark raving mad.

He watched the monitors as the fuel and air storage topped off. It was time.

He went through the cumbersome process he'd followed the other six times, reminding himself every half minute or so to be careful. He was tired, and he wasn't entirely sure exactly what to call his emotional state. He didn't jump right to crazy, but he wasn't sure he was as coldly focused as he wanted to be either.

He tapped his positioning jets, moving his fighter gently away from the shuttle with its great robot arm. There was fuel left on the vessel, and air too, something he suspected he'd remember if he found himself drifting and suffocating later. But where he was going, the cumbersome shuttle couldn't follow. The time had come to bid his companion farewell.

He reached down and tapped the comm unit, activating his direct laser link to the shuttle. "Activate navigation plan omega-zero." His voice was grim, and despite his efforts to drive off the bizarre emotions he was feeling, he couldn't quite banish the thought he was sending a friend to die.

"Omega-zero operative." The AI's voice was cool, professional, without a hint of the resentment Stockton had illogically half-expected to hear. "Farewell, Lieutenant Stockton. Good luck to you, Raptor."

The last part hit him hard, totally unexpected. Again, his rational mind knew it was just a bit of programming Fritz or one of her people had added. He was sure it was intended in the best possible way, but in his current state of mind, he found it upsetting.

He watched on his screen as the shuttle moved slowly away, operating one or two percent thrust until it was well clear of Stockton's fighter.

"Goodbye, my friend," he said softly, as the small blue dot moved farther away. He paused for a few seconds, taking a deep breath. Then he reached down and grabbed the throttle, easing it back slowly, kicking in his own thrust just a bit. He had a significant course change to make, but he wanted to be farther from the shuttle before he risked too much thrust. He had no idea how quickly the enemy would find his small tanker, but he knew they'd never get a chance to search it and discover the purpose it had served. The shuttle's AI, the string of bits and bytes he'd come so close to calling friend, had one more duty to perform. It was to evade pursuit as long as possible, lead the enemy forces away from Stockton the best it could. But it would not allow itself to be captured. Its final duty would be to destroy itself, taking with it any evidence that another Confederation vessel was loose in the system.

He waited as long as he could. Then he checked the stealth

unit and confirmed it was operating at one hundred percent power before he pulled back on the throttle and accelerated at 4g toward the transwarp link.

Toward the fleet, I hope...

Chapter Thirty-Two

FSS Victoire
Turas System
In the System Oort Cloud
Union Year 212 (308 AC)

Ricard Lille sat in the shuttle, twitching around in his seat, trying to perform the apparently impossible task of getting comfortable. The trip to the front had been a nightmare, one hideous form of barebones military transit after another. He'd suffered all manners of inconvenience and indignities on his past missions…pain, hunger, misery. But as often as not, he'd traveled in civilian circles, and usually luxurious ones. He was accustomed to danger, and he had iron control over his fear, but he found as he got older, he lacked his youthful tolerance for bad food and dismal accommodations.

There was no choice, of course. His cover was as a military attaché, an officer attached to Sector Nine as a forward scout for the eventual pacification of the conquered worlds. It was a reasonable identity, and he thought the Sector Nine connection was a nice touch. No one would expect an operative of the Union's infamous intelligence operation spying on the admiral to admit a Sector Nine connection of any kind, and they certainly wouldn't expect an assassin to do it. D'Alvert wouldn't trust him, of course, but he wouldn't particularly suspect him either. And that was good enough.

Lille had never met Admiral D'Alvert formally, but the two had been in the same room more than once. He didn't think the admiral would recognize him, but regardless, he had far too high a profile to risk being ID'd, so he'd gone to the New Face facility before he left Montmirail. The process was simple and quick…and easily reversible. His eyes were now lighter blue, his facial bones altered, his auburn hair changed to the reddish dirty blond so common on Bretaine, the home world of the identity he had adopted.

He didn't expect D'Alvert or any of his people to check him out too carefully. Sector Nine liaisons were deployed all across the front line, and advance teams had already landed on several of the border planets that had been seized. But just in case they did take more than a cursory look, he'd done his homework. There was no DNA scan of Ricard Lille in any Union database, of course, standard practice for high level Sector Nine operatives. But his genetic data *was* there now, under the name Gregoire Suchet. Lille's own Bellegeusan heritage was a near match for a resident of nearby Bretaine, close enough to fool all but the most intensive of scans. If it appeared any of D'Alvert's people were too concerned with checking him out, he could let them do it, even allow them to "secretly" get a sample of his DNA from a cup or a fork. He'd always found that something close to the truth was the easiest lie to sell.

"Check your harnesses. We're making our final approach to *Victoire.*" The voice on the intercom was cold, professional. Like most of the Union, the military operated under a harsh system of discipline, but Lille had to admit that the services managed an admirable level of efficiency.

He looked across the confines of the shuttle, at the row of soldiers sitting quietly. They were FRs, replacements, he supposed, for *Victoire's* combat losses. The troopers had been silent during the entire trip from the transport, not a word spoken, even among themselves.

He admired whoever had come up with the idea of an army of tightly-controlled, manufactured clone soldiers, and he appreciated the utility of the whole system, but the FRs made his skin crawl. They were human, of course, even if they *were* produced in laboratories, but the conditioning and training programs they went through left them seeming almost alien. Lille was merciless, a cold-blooded assassin who had taken down more than his share of enemies of the state, but even he had trouble with the icy ruthlessness applied to the FRs, the savage punishments… and the routine termination of old soldiers once their usefulness had come to an end. Such practices were practically designed to cause rebellion in almost any armed force that ever existed… save for one created and conditioned from birth to acceptance and obedience.

He leaned back and closed his eyes, breathing deeply, regularly. For all his travel, the dozens of missions he'd completed across the Union—and all the way to the Alliance—he'd never managed to shake the last twinges of his spacesickness. He was okay on large vessels like the transport, most of the time at least, but small craft like the shuttle still gave his stomach flops.

He felt the thrusters slowing the ship down and, a moment later, a lurch forward. Then nothing. He pushed back against the urge to retch at the sudden stop, sucking in another breath to calm his stomach. *We're down.*

He reached up and unhooked his harness, pulling the straps out of the way as he stood up. The shuttle was full of others, all standing up, moving toward the back as the large hatch dropped open, revealing *Victoire*'s landing bay. All except for the FRs. The soldiers unhooked their harnesses, but they stayed frozen in place, remaining in their seats while everyone else on the shuttle filed out.

Lille was the first through the hatch, his bogus colonel's rank sufficient to create deference from the mostly junior officers lining up behind him. His head moved back and forth, panning his gaze across the immensity of *Victoire*'s great landing bay. It was only one of three, he knew, the others just as massive. The Union flagship was a vast ship of war, unmatched by any save its twin, *Gloire*…and the four vessels of the Confederation's Repulse class. Three, he reminded himself. *Indefatigable* had been reported destroyed at Santis.

Lille was always uncomfortable on military vessels, perhaps because he'd come so close to a career in the navy. He'd had no intention of living the kind of life led by most citizens. Politics was the dream pursuit in the Union of course, the one that promised a life of power and luxury as the rewards for success. But the young Lille had possessed neither the education nor the temperament to make that work, and the navy had seemed like his best alternative. A bizarre sequence of events that led to his employment by Sector Nine instead. The spy agency did not take applications from would be operatives, it sought out the people it wanted. Lille had caught the eye of an agent impressed by his moral…ambivalency. After that, his cold willingness to kill had taken him the rest of the way. He hadn't been back home since, though he had heard a few years back that his father had died…in the same squalor in which he'd lived. Sixty-two years old—not bad for a member of the Union's working class, but far from acceptable to a man with Lille's ambitions.

He walked across the expanse of the bay, toward the pair of lifts that led up to the heart of the ship. Halfway there, a pair of FRs challenged him.

"Sir, if you please, Admiral D'Alvert sent us to escort you to his office." It was the first words he'd heard from one of the foot soldiers on this trip.

"Very well, Major," he said, his eyes darting to the rank insignia on the man's collar. There was a resemblance between the officer and the non-com standing silently at his side, as there was throughout the Foudre Rouge forces. They were all clones, of course, but there were over a hundred DNA lines used in their quickening, producing a heavy family resemblance rather than a corps of identical soldiers.

"Your bags will be taken to your quarters for you, sir."

And searched along the way no doubt…

Lille just nodded curtly, with all the arrogance the FR officer would expect from a colonel attached to Sector Nine. They could tear apart his bags all day, and they wouldn't find anything save mundane personal items…and a few things he'd planted to give them the impression he wanted them to have.

"That will be fine, Major."

The officer nodded curtly, and he turned around, leading Lille toward the lift.

Lille followed without another word. Everything seemed to be going just the way he wanted it, and in a few minutes he'd know for sure. Hugo D'Alvert was an accomplished military officer, and a skilled politician, but Lille was sure he could read the man, or at least get a hint if the admiral had more than the normal level of suspicion. His job wasn't to stand out here, it was to blend in…and to wait. D'Alvert was still useful. He had duties left to perform, a war to win. And Lille wouldn't move, not until all of that was done.

* * *

"Enter." D'Alvert snapped out the command to the AI. He'd called for Renault, and he was impatient to see her. The aide was the closest thing he had to a confidante. Beyond the fact that he genuinely liked and respected her, at least as much as he did anyone, she was perfectly positioned, close enough to him that her best chances at advancement rested in his coattails and not in treachery.

Sabine Renault stepped into the room, her uniform crisply pressed, as always. His chief aide was a fastidious woman, one who tended toward the cold and emotionless. He understood her, at least he thought he did—like him, she had risen from the gutter to a position of some authority. No doubt her sights were set quite a bit higher, and if she remained trustworthy, he had every intention of taking her with him when he made his bid for power.

"Sit, Captain Renault." D'Alvert had a plush office, just down the hall from *Victoire*'s flag bridge. It was large by any standards, but by those of spaceship design it was palatial. He sat behind a large desk with two chairs lined up on the other side. There was a large sofa and a round conference table off to the side, and the wall opposite the desk was covered by a large display, now black.

"Thank you, sir." Renault walked up to one of the guest chairs and sat down, her posture nearly as rigid seated as it had been standing. "Did you speak with the Sector Nine liaison?"

"Yes." D'Alvert's voice was disapproving. "He droned on for quite some time about the ways he and his teams would smoke out elements of resistance on the occupied worlds. It was a look into how the sausage is made that I didn't find terribly interesting." He paused. "Still, he's from Sector Nine, so we must be careful. We've got enough political officers in this fleet spying on us already, without having Sector Nine operatives who aren't who they say they are." He gestured toward Renault. "Have him checked out. Thoroughly. And, if it's possible, get a DNA sample...but please, be discrete. We don't need trouble from Sector Nine."

"Understood, sir. I will see to it immediately."

"Very well." D'Alvert leaned back in his chair. "Still no word from the supply convoy?"

"No, Admiral. Per your orders, I dispatched a squadron of escorts to trace a line back toward Varus to find out what happened." She paused, an uncertain look on her face. "Of course, if the problem is farther back along that line, it could be two weeks or more before they return."

"*If* they return, Captain. If something more than Admiral Lund's incompetence delayed that convoy, we have to give serious thought to what it could be. Is it possible a significant Confederation force has eluded us? That there are enemy ships operating in our rear?" D'Alvert found the whole idea hard to swallow. He'd had top-notch intelligence on the Confederation fleet before the war began, and he had a pretty good idea where all their ships were. But that didn't change the fact that his entire offensive was at a halt waiting for supplies.

"I suppose we must consider that possibility, sir, though I will admit, I have no idea how it's possible. The only known Confederation battleship unaccounted for is *Dauntless*, and our most recent intelligence reports suggest that she is badly damaged from her engagement with the Alliance flagship and still at Archellia under repair."

"How old is our last report from Archellia?"

"It is…" She paused. "I'm sorry, sir, I don't have that information with me."

D'Alvert felt a flash of anger, but it quickly subsided. Renault was an extremely competent officer, but when she wasn't prepared on something she just admitted it, directly and clearly. No miserable attempts at excuses or prevarication. He found it extremely refreshing. "Have it checked, Captain. I want to know exactly when we received that last update." He pushed a button on the small comm unit, spinning it toward her.

Renault tapped the control and leaned over the microphone. "Lieutenant Rivers, I want you to review the intelligence reports immediately. I need to know when we received the last flash update from Archellia."

"Yes, Captain. At once."

"I'm in the admiral's office. Contact me here as soon as you have it."

"Yes, Captain."

Renault looked up at D'Alvert. "I'm sorry, sir. I should have…"

"You can't have every scrap of data in your head, Captain." He found his own word strangely amusing. Whatever he'd become, he was still self-aware enough to know how differently he'd have reacted with someone else.

"Thank you, sir."

"I must make a decision, Captain. Do I press on and engage the Confeds now, while they're still disordered and demoralized? Or do I wait until we're able to resupply?" He shook his head, an angry scowl coming over his face. "Damned Lund. Everything was set. The fleet would be refit and ready to go if that fool had gotten here on time. We'd be destroying the Confed fleet even now."

"Our supply situation is not critical, Admiral." Renault paused. "It's of concern, of course, but we should have enough fuel and ordnance to sustain one more battle."

D'Alvert took a breath, looking back across the table at his aide. "Cutting it so close ramps up the risk considerably. I believe we're on the verge of victory, but what if that fool Winston is able to extricate his force again, trading space—and worlds—for time? We would be one system deeper into enemy space, and then the logistical situation would be critical to say the least."

"Everything you say is true, sir, but with all due respect, I don't believe that's the only consideration. The enemy is disordered, shaken. The longer we wait, the more time they have to prepare. They do have reserve forces, and our reliance on the caution of their Senate in committing these last resources is well conceived, but far from foolproof. Our entire war plan is based on speed, on leveraging the surprise and mobility Supply One allows us."

"Everything you say is true, Captain. And perhaps waiting is more dangerous than proceeding without resupply. I just don't know." D'Alvert rarely allowed anyone to see his indecision, but he was conflicted. The last thing he could do was allow his admirals to see him uncertain. Too many of them harbored their own ambitions, and he didn't doubt more than one imagined stepping over him to achieve their own position and power. Renault was the closest thing he had to someone he truly trusted.

"It seems we must take a risk either way, sir. Only you can determine our course."

"But if it were your decision, Captain, you would advance? Immediately?"

"I…" The comm unit buzzed, interrupting her answer. She looked at D'Alvert, who gestured for her to answer. She tapped her hand on the control. "Renault," she said.

"Captain, I have reviewed the intelligence updates. The last report from Archellia was received more than seven weeks ago. As far as I can ascertain, there has been no further contact with our operative there, though at least one follow up was expected and is now overdue."

"Very well, Lieutenant." Renault tapped at the comm unit, cutting the line. "*Dauntless*?" She looked across the desk, the concern clear on her face.

"Perhaps. In any event, we must assume so. It would explain Admiral Lund's absence."

"Would it, sir? One overdue intelligence report is hardly conclusive evidence. It doesn't even prove our agent has been eliminated, only that he hasn't been able to get a transmission out. And it doesn't change the fact that as of the last update, *Dauntless* still needed significant repairs. Even if *Dauntless* left Archellia and was able to travel all the way to intercept our supply convoy, Admiral Lund had two battleships assigned as escorts, and a third was dispatched to secure the Rim flank of our line of advance. I find it hard to believe a damaged *Dauntless* could have taken out three of our front line ships, even with the legendary Captain Barron at the helm."

"Your logic is sound, Captain. And yet, Admiral Lund is not here. His battleships are not here. His supply convoy is not here."

"What are you going to do, sir?"

"About the Confed fleet, Captain? I honestly don't know. I just don't know."

The comm buzzed again. D'Alvert answered it this time. "What is it?" he snapped.

"Admiral, one of the escort vessels on the perimeter has picked up some kind of ship on its scanners."

"A ship? What kind of ship?" His eyes darted across toward Renault.

"Unknown, sir. It doesn't appear to be very large."

"Is it alone?"

"Yes, sir. As far as we can tell."

D'Alvert slammed his hand down on his desk. An unknown ship in Turas had to be bad news. He didn't know what the Confeds were up to, but he was damned sure going to find out.

"What is the nearest capital ship, Lieutenant?"

"*Banniere*, sir."

"Order Captain Devereaux to launch a squadron of fighters to investigate at once."

"Yes, sir."

"And, Lieutenant…I want that ship captured for investigation, is that understood?"

"Yes, Admiral."

Chapter Thirty-Three

"All right squadron leaders, you've all got your assigned sectors. You heard Thunder, and you know what's at stake here. There's almost two of them to each of us, but these bastards have never seen the day they could match us. So, we hit them and hit them hard...and we don't let one of them get away. We cut a hole right through them for Thunder and his wing. If we fail, that wall of bombers will hit *Dauntless* and *Intrepid*, and I'm counting on every one of you to help me stop that." Timmons took a deep breath, wincing slightly at the pain. Doctor Stewart had fused his broken rib, but the whole area was still tender. Not that anyone would have known, listening to his steady and confident tone.

Timmons knew he was a cocky ass—he wasn't delusional enough to consider himself humble. He knew he was good, too, but now he couldn't fool himself. He was scared...not of the enemy, but of the responsibility Commander Jamison had dumped upon him. For all his normal arrogance, Timmons was overwhelmed by having more than seventy fighters under his command.

The assignment had taken him by surprise. No, more of a

soul-shaking, staggering, utter shock. By all accounts, Jamison was "Raptor" Stockton's best friend. And Timmons and Stockton had no love for each other. But Raptor was away, off on a mission that was likely to be his last, and that left Jamison looking for a stand in for the job he'd almost certainly have given his friend. Timmons was impressed that the wing commander had risen above the prejudices Stockton's enmity might have created in another man.

His eyes moved over his control panel, stopping when they reached the main display. There it was, a large, oblong cloud, well over one hundred tiny dots, so closely spaced he could hardly tell them apart. The enemy interceptors. And not far from them another cluster of tiny circles, somewhat less dense, but still numerous—his squadrons.

"Okay, here we go. Use your missiles well, all of you...and watch out for theirs!" He watched as the range on his scanner ticked down. "Break," he shouted, and he swung his throttle hard to the side, angling his thrust and moving toward a small group of Union fighters.

He flew right at the enemy, throwing caution to the wind. There was no time for elegant maneuvers, no room for long dances with selected targets. If his people didn't blast a hole in the interceptor screen, Jamison's squadrons wouldn't get through. And if they didn't get to those oncoming bombers, *Dauntless* and *Intrepid* were likely to be battered wrecks by the time the assault was over, if not dissipating clouds of plasma. A direct frontal attack would be more costly, and it would yield some of the advantage his more experienced pilots had over the enemy, but the primary goal—the only important one—was to protect the battleships.

He angled his fighter slightly, refining his targeting. Then he launched his first missile. After a quick adjustment, he released the second. He watched for a few seconds, as his targets tried to evade the weapons. Their responses were slow, cumbersome... Timmons knew his missiles would hit home.

He saw the enemy formations as they moved toward his squadrons, lining up for the fight to come. They were no match for his people, at least one on one. But the odds were almost two to one.

He could see on his scanners as his fighters launched their missiles all across the line. The deadly weapons were finding their targets, cutting down the enemy ships. He opened fire with his lasers, taking down another target, pushing on deeper, carving out a hole for Jamison's birds to slip through.

Their command is green too...they should be in a much deeper formation.

"Thunder, these guys are in a shallow line...we're almost through already. Suggest you bring your squadrons up now, before they have a chance to close in from the flanks."

"Roger that, Warrior. We're on our way."

Timmons switched his comm to the Direwolves command channel. "Mustang, these bastards are going to try to close in from the ends when Thunder leads his wing through. Take the Longswords and Yellows with your people and hit them on the port side. I'll take the other squadrons and go to the starboard. We'll create two walls, and buy Thunder the time he needs to get through. And keep your velocities down...you can't let any of these bastards past you, so make sure you can come about quickly enough to hit them again before they do."

"Understood, Warrior." A short pause. "Good luck, my old friend."

"And to you, Mustang. Take care of yourself."

He reached down and punched up the selected squadron channels. "All right, listen up...we're swinging around to the starboard, and we're going to widen this hole and give Thunder and his squadrons plenty of room to get through. Max velocity, three thousand meters per second. We've got to be able to reverse our vectors and go after any enemy birds that get by us before they can hit Thunder's force in the flanks and rear. Squadron leaders, acknowledge."

He listened as each squadron commander sounded off. Blue squadron was the last one, the slight delay more likely the cause of resentment at being placed under his command, he figured, than any sluggishness on the part of *Dauntless*'s elite formation. He didn't hold it against them. He doubted his Red Eagles would have felt any different if they'd been placed under Stockton.

He fired his lasers, and another enemy ship vanished. All along the line he could see the once-dense cloud of dots thinning as his fighters gunned down their enemies. But numbers were telling too, and their kills did not go unanswered. He'd lost two Red Eagles so far, and not one of his squadrons was unblooded. But they were holding their formations well, and attacking the enemy with savage intensity. They knew what was at stake, and they would do their duty. Timmons didn't have the slightest doubt about that.

* * *

Sara Eaton sat on *Intrepid*'s bridge, watching the fighter battle unfold. It seemed like a rout at first, the Confederation squadrons tearing into the less experienced Union pilots with unrestrained savagery. But slowly, mathematics asserted itself. The Confederation pilots killed two, three, even four of the enemy for every one that they lost. But they started outnumbered, and before long their own casualties mounted.

She winced as she saw another fighter disappear, one of hers. The Longswords had been hard hit, losing six of the thirteen effectives they'd sent into the fight. The other squadrons had fared a bit better, and they had absolutely savaged the Union first line, taking out over eighty interceptors and sending the rest into headlong flight, followed closely by the victorious Confederation squadrons.

Now it was Commander Jamison's turn. His fighters closed with the approaching enemy bombers. He'd assigned more of the strike force to Timmons than he'd retained for himself. That had impressed Eaton, and she'd agreed completely with his tactics. He'd kept the job of keeping the bombers away from the battleships, but he'd recognized that the fight against the interceptors was the more dangerous engagement, requiring whatever strength he could make available. Timmons had lived up to any expectations Jamison might have had when he'd placed him in command. His forces had shattered the enemy's first line.

Now if Jamison can just…

Her thought cut off as her eyes caught movement on the display. A blip on the scanners, coming around from behind the gas giant. Her stomach sank, accepting the realization perhaps a second before her mind caught up. An enemy battleship, a big one. And it was launching fighters.

"Get me *Dauntless*," she snapped, leaning over and holding her hand over her comm unit.

"Captain Barron on your line."

"Captain…"

"I see it, Sara. It's a big son of a bitch too. And those fighters are going to hit Jamison's squadrons just as they're fully engaged with the bombers."

"Timmons's people will never get there in time…not in any numbers." She paused. "Captain, if Jamison's fighters don't break off they'll be sitting ducks."

"They can't break off, Sara…you know that. If all those fighters get through…"

The line was silent for a few seconds, before Barron continued, "I have to split up Jamison's forces, have him detach some kind of screen to try to hold off those interceptors. We can't let the bombers get through at full strength. It's going to be bad enough anyway."

"Agreed, Captain."

Barron cut the line abruptly, no doubt to contact Jamison. She agreed splitting the force was the only alternative, but that didn't change the fact that they just didn't have enough fighters out there.

Whatever happened in the next thirty minutes, she had a feeling *Intrepid* was going to take a hard pounding. She looked over toward Nordstrom's station. "Commander, get me Commander Merton. I think it's time we got the damage control crews in position."

* * *

"Yes, Captain…understood." Jamison knew Barron was

right, that there wasn't a choice. But he hated the idea with a raging passion.

"See to it, Commander." Barron's response followed a brief pause, perhaps an extra second and a half while Jamison's comm signal traveled to *Dauntless*, and the response made its way back. "And Kyle, there's no choice, so don't beat yourself up over it. You know Raptor would be the first one to lead the Blues in if he was here."

The mention of his friend was like a sharp stab to his chest. The crisis had torn his mind from Stockton, at least for a few minutes. Now the prospect of sending his friend's Blues on a suicide mission loomed in front of him. *And whatever he would have done, he's not here.*

He flipped the comm to the Blue squadron channel. "Typhoon, do you see what's coming?"

"Yeah, Commander. I've got 'em on my scanner. Looks like four squadrons, maybe five."

"That's my read. Rick...we've got to hold them back, delay them at least, or they'll hit us just as we're fully engaged with the bombers."

"A job for Blue squadron, sir?" He sounded cheerful for a man being sent to buy time, likely with his life and with the lives of his people.

"I don't think anyone else can do the job, Rick. I'm damned sure if the Blues can't, no one can."

"You know that, sir. Don't worry...we'll see it done. Just worry about those bombers...and leave these interlopers to us." Jamison thought he heard the slightest edge of fear in Turner's voice, but if he did it wasn't much. Rick Turner was a hardcore Blue, a member of the squadron who traced his lineage as far back at Stockton himself.

"Take care of yourself, Rick." Jamison meant the comment sincerely, but he regretted it as soon as he said it. He was sending Blue squadron into a hopeless fight, and Turner was enough of a veteran—and a realist—to know that. The chances of any of them coming back seemed slim.

"Don't worry about us, Commander. Blue squadron's got

your back." And with that, the veteran pilot cut the line. A few seconds later he could see the Blues moving off at full thrust, heading to cut off an assault wave more than four times their number.

Forgive me, Raptor...

* * *

Timmons squeezed his finger tight again, loosing another deadly bolt from his lasers. The enemy fighter vanished, his fifth kill of the battle. His people had done their jobs, and done them well at that. The Union interceptor force was gutted, two thirds of its ships gone, the others scattered and fleeing in wild disarray.

Like any job well done, the victory had claimed its cost. Two dozen of his fighters had been destroyed, and the pain of the loss was only partially blunted by the fact that at least half had managed to eject. With any luck, the rescue shuttles could retrieve most of them before their life support ran out.

He slid his finger across his screen, moving the area displayed. The fight against the bombers was going well. Jamison's squadrons had smashed into the lumbering strike force, and they had gunned down several dozen of the cumbersome craft. But something was wrong. There were too few Confederation fighters there. He stared for a few seconds, confused. Then he realized. Blue squadron was gone.

For an instant, he felt a wave of panic, a worry that the Blues had been wiped out. But then he realized that wasn't possible, certainly not against a line of bombers. But where were they?

"Thunder...Warrior here. Enemy interceptors routed. My forces are pursuing survivors."

"Well done, Warrior. After you mop up, get your people back to base for refit."

"Commander...where is Blue squad..." His voice trailed off as he finally found Stockton's fighters on his screen...and a massive wave of enemy ships heading directly toward them.

"Commander, request permission to..."

"Negative, Warrior. You'd never get there in time. You'll just burn up your fuel."

"Commander…"

"I said no, Lieutenant."

"But, sir…let me take the Red Eagles. The other squadrons can handle the enemy strays, and that's enough ships to get back for refit." The line was silent for few seconds, and then Timmons added, "Please, sir…you can't let the Blues face that many fighters by themselves. We can get there in time, I know it." He was determined to go whether Jamison approved it or not, but he decided to leave that part out.

"All right, Lieutenant…but for the life of me, I can't figure out why you and Raptor don't get along. You're both a colossal pain in the ass."

"Thank you, sir." He cut the line, switching to the Red Eagles channel. "Listen up, Eagles. The Blues are out there facing off against another wave of enemy fighters. They're outnumbered and outgunned, but we're going to do something about that. Kick your engines up to one ten percent, and follow me."

He pulled back hard on the throttle, snapping off a command to his AI to override the safeties. He needed every g of thrust he could get if he was going to make it there in time.

And not getting there wasn't an option.

Chapter Thirty-Four

Stockton had watched the drama unfolding on his screen, at least the limited view he was getting on his passive scanners. The stealth suite that Commander Fritz had installed mostly prevented external sensors from picking up his fighter, but he found it also interfered somewhat with his own scans. None of that mattered, not really. The shuttle was out of his hands, though he supposed the longer its controlling AI evaded the enemy pursuers, the better it was for him. He was on a line for the Mellas transit point, his vector true, his engines shut down. He'd just make it to Mellas, as long as nothing went wrong.

He stared down at the small device Fritz had attached to his dashboard. It was the controller for the stealth system. He could still remember her standing in the launch bay staring at him with those cold, unforgiving eyes. "Don't touch this, Lieutenant," she had said. "Don't even look at it if you don't have to." It was good advice—though he suspected Commander Fritz had thought of it more as an order than counsel—but now his eyes caught something that troubled him. He didn't know much about the device, or the systems it controlled, but one of the gauges looked funny to him. The readings were bouncing around erratically...and every other time his eyes had wandered over, they had been stable.

Don't do this to me...not now...

He'd known equipment failure was one of the greatest dangers he would face on his trip. The Lightning fighters were designed for short missions. They were intended to endure the stresses of combat and return within a few hours for a refit and systems check. No fighter had ever gone a fraction the distance his had, nor remained in constant service for so many consecutive hours. *Hours? Hell, days...*

He checked his other readouts. Everything else was on the green. Whatever was wrong—*if* anything *was* wrong—it was in the stealth unit.

Great, the one thing in this ship I know nothing about.

Like most experienced pilots, Stockton had some ability to do makeshift repairs to his fighter. Combat was hard on ships, and rejiggering a damaged system could be the difference between life and death. But the stealth device was a mystery to him. It might as well have been some ancient artifact dug up on a planet in the Badlands. And that readout was definitely wobbling. In fact, he was sure it was getting worse, even as he watched it.

He his eyes darted to his display. The enemy had no ships right at the transit point.

No, you don't want to discourage transit from Mellas...you'd love it if Admiral Winston came though and attacked you...

But his route to the transwarp link took him fairly close to several enemy battleships. And if his stealth unit kicked out, there was a good chance he'd show up on their active scans.

Shit.

He tried to think of options. But there was nothing he could do. Kicking in his engines would only make him easier to spot, and any course change was a terrible gamble. There was no way to be sure he'd be able to reestablish a vector toward the jump point before his fuel gave out. And if he couldn't get out of Turas, it didn't really matter much how and where he died.

He looked back to the display. He was moving toward one

of the enemy battleships, approaching the point where he'd come closest. He stared back at the stealth system indicator. Its wobble was still increasing. "You couldn't have picked a worse time to pull this shit…"

Almost as if in response, the gauge dropped to zero. Stockton ignored the tightness in his gut, his mind focusing instantly on the situation, as he looked down the row of readouts on the stealth suite. All dead.

"With all due respect, Commander Fritz," he muttered, "you can take your orders and…" He reached out, poking at the controls, bringing up more readouts. The entire system was offline. He couldn't tell if it wasn't getting power…or if the unit itself had failed.

He looked over at his fuel readings. He still had some, not much, but certainly enough to power the stealth system. He checked the reactor readings. Green. The ECM unit was getting power.

Great.

He might have jury-rigged a solution to a severed power line, but he had no idea how this magic box Fritz had put together worked, and no idea what to do.

He looked up at the screen. He was getting close to the transwarp link…but not close enough. The enemy had plenty of time to react to him.

Plenty of time.

* * *

D'Alvert walked down the short hallway and onto the flag bridge. He'd been spending most of his time in his office, door closed, brooding over the situation—and his next move. But he wanted his people to see him now. Sitting in the Turas system and waiting was sapping the fleet's momentum, the morale boost its string of initial victories had created slowly fading away.

"Status?" he asked as he moved to his chair and sat down.

"The enemy shuttle evaded pursuit for a considerable time, sir, and when our fighters finally had it trapped, it self-destructed." Renault's report was crisp, professional. She was the only one on *Victoire* who could tell D'Alvert things the admiral didn't want to hear without sounding obsequious.

D'Alvert frowned. He'd wanted that ship intact, but he wasn't at all surprised at what had happened. "I want to know where that shuttle came from…and how it ended up in the middle of this system without any of our fleet units detecting it." He knew it wasn't an answer he was likely to get. With the ship gone, his people had precious little to go on. But he was frustrated, and they were going to feel that too.

"Yes, sir. All analysis sections are working on it now."

"Any other Confederation incursions at the transit point?"

"No, sir. Not since the last one twelve hours ago." A short pause. "I would have informed you immediately, Admiral."

The Confeds had been sending escort ships through the transwarp link for days now. They were scouts, obviously, attempts by the enemy to keep tabs on his fleet and detect any signs he was preparing to move forward into Mellas. But he wondered if there was more to them than just that.

Arthur Winston wasn't a brilliant tactician, certainly nothing like Rance Barron had been, but the old veteran no doubt had a few tricks up his sleeve.

Is he trying to tell me something? He's showing us he's still in Mellas, certainly. Is he feigning strength, trying to intimidate us? Perhaps…

D'Alvert was still trying to decide whether to move forward or not. He still had the advantage, even without a resupply before the battle. At least he thought he did…

"Captain Renault, I want a squadron of escort cruisers sent through the transwarp point. I want to confirm exactly what the Confeds have in Mellas."

"Yes, sir. At once."

D'Alvert leaned back. "And I want all capital ships on the periphery of the fleet to launch fighters. We had one mystery Confed ship pop up in the middle of this system…and I want to know if there are any more out there."

*   *   *

Stockton leaned back in his seat, trying any way he could to stretch or work out the tightness atrophying every one of his muscles. People had told him he was born to be behind the controls of a fighter, but no one had every suggested he spend every moment there. He'd worked for a few minutes trying to figure out the stealth unit before he'd given up. As far as he could see, the damned thing worked by some kind of magic.

Magic that has given out on me.

He reached down to his side, digging around in the small bag stuffed under his seat. He hadn't brought much, just the pistol he always carried, and the small charm that accompanied him on every combat mission. It was a platinum pendant, but small, worth only a moderate amount. He'd won it in a poker game in his first week at the Academy—an unsanctioned activity that could have gotten him a dozen demerits if he'd been caught. He hadn't thought much about it until the man he'd won it from was killed a week later in a training accident. Pilots were a superstitious lot, and Stockton was no different. He'd never flown again without the thing, and it had become a good luck charm of sorts.

He kept fishing around, finally getting his hands on a small tablet. He pulled it from the bag and turned it on, flipping his thumb to the side, scrolling from one page to the next. He stopped when a small image appeared, a woman with dark brown, almost black, hair. The pain, the discomfort, the fear... they all subsided for a moment, though they were replaced by a quiet sadness. He thought of all the time he'd wasted, the months he and Stara had served on *Dauntless* before either had admitted any feelings for the other. He still hadn't admitted anything, not really. Not the way he wished he had, in person instead of via a cowardly letter she'd only see if he didn't return. Now, without his stealth unit, he knew there was a damned good chance she'd end up with that final note.

He'd volunteered for the mission because it was vital, because it was worth the risk. Of everyone on *Dauntless*—and that included that blowhard Warrior—he'd realized he had the best chance. But in this case, perhaps "best" meant almost none as opposed to absolutely none. The odds were, he was going to die in this fighter, and he would never see Stara Sinclair again.

"Detecting launches from several nearby enemy battleships."

The AI's voice grabbed his attention, and he reached out for his controls, bringing up his tactical display. "They're launching all right." For an instant, he told himself they could be normal patrols, that the launches weren't proof that he'd been spotted. But they he saw the thrust vectors of the closest fighters. A direct intercept course.

Damn.

He felt the adrenaline pouring into his bloodstream, his aching muscles primed for action. His hand reached out for the throttle as the warrior inside prepared for battle. But he didn't have any weapons. There would be no fight, hopeless or otherwise. All he could do was run for it.

He looked at the display, at the distance and the speed of the enemy fighters. They were going to cut him off before he got to the transit point, no question. Unless he did something.

Do I change vector, and risk not being able to get back on line for the jump? Or do I burn the rest of my fuel and hope to outrun these bastards?

Fleeing like a terrified animal went against every instinct that made Stockton who he was. But he knew it was the right choice now. He pulled back hard on the throttle, feeling 12g of force slam into him hard. He'd shut down the dampeners, and everything else extraneous that used fuel. It made sense, but 12g was a lot of pressure to absorb with no relief. He struggled to suck in even tiny breaths of air, and he gritted his teeth against the pain.

He fought to stay conscious, even as his vision closed in, becoming a narrow tunnel, and then going totally black. He strained to focus, pouring his waning strength into holding the throttle in place. He needed every meter per second of velocity he could get, and even that might not be enough.

C'mon, baby...just a little bit more...

He could feel his consciousness slipping away, but somehow he clung to it grimly. He was lost, confused, but he was still aware, at least to some extent. And his hand was still tight on the throttle, squeezing every bit of acceleration his straining fighter could produce.

And then it was gone, the pressure, the pain. He gasped for air, and his lungs filled, easily, effortlessly. Freefall was a relief, though as his focus slowly returned he realized what it meant. He was out of fuel.

He checked his vector. Yes, it looked right. He'd enter the transwarp link...assuming he got there. His eyes darted to the tactical display. He'd done himself some good, pushed his fighter well out in front of his pursuers. There was one squadron that might get to him. He wasn't sure. Whatever happened, it was going to be close...

*   *   *

Aurore Lefebrve sat in front of her display. Her eyes were fixed, unmoving, focused on the small icon in the center of the screen. She'd thought the target was going to escape. It had been accelerating at more than 12g, heading straight for the transwarp point. But now it had cut its thrust completely. Was it some kind of deception, a trap? Or was the ship disabled, out of fuel?

She pulled back on her throttle, increasing her own acceleration. Union fighters couldn't match the 12-13g the Confed Lightnings could pull, but she figured her own 10.5g could be just enough. She might not catch her enemy...but she'd get a few shots off. And that should be enough.

Lefebrve's stature had risen steadily since the war had begun, until she'd become one of the most renowned pilots in the service. The Union fighter corps had somewhat of an inferiority complex, the result of the clearly greater skill of their Confed adversaries. The enemy had dozens of aces, and more than a few pilots that had achieved near-celebrity status as they racked up kills. That was far rarer in the Union navy, and Lefebrve was one of a select few. She'd gained rapid advancement in rank as a result of her mounting number of victories. She'd been the youngest squadron leader in Union history, and now, she'd repeated that feat with her early advancement to wing commander.

None of that really mattered to her. She was insular, a loner. She didn't crave comforts, not beyond her basic needs. Her life was flying her fighter, and becoming the best at what she did. It was all she cared about, and she let nothing interfere with her pursuit of it. Not political ambitions, not personal relationships. Nothing.

Lefebrve knew the Union she fought for was corrupt, that most of its people lived in misery and despair. That might have bothered her if she took the time to think about it, but she doubted things were different anywhere else. She didn't necessarily believe all the propaganda she'd heard about the Confederation, but if even half of it was true, her enemies were worse even than her own side.

She stared at the target on her screen, holding her focus despite the crushing pressure slamming into her. The dampeners on her fighter were small, and of typical shoddy Union manufacture. They only did so much to alleviate the strain of high g acceleration. But the effective 5g or 6g she was feeling was a big improvement over the raw 10.5g her engines were producing. It was the difference between being awake and uncomfortable, and passing out in the cockpit.

She held the throttle firmly, her fingers tense, tightening around the firing stud. It was reflex, her instinct telling her it was time to launch one of her missiles. But she didn't have any. Her fighter hadn't been prepped for launch when the orders came in. The launch command had been a surprise. Somehow the Confed fighter had just appeared in the middle of the system. She figured someone had screwed up, and she knew enough about the Union service to guess that whoever it was would pay a bitter price. Now it fell to her people to clean up the mess.

She'd sent the duty squadron out immediately, but then she'd ordered the crew chief to get her own bird ready too. She was responsible for all of *Montmirail*'s fighter squadrons, but right now only one of them was in combat…and that was where she belonged. They'd managed to get her ship fueled and ready for launch, but there hadn't been time to load the hardpoints with missiles.

She could see on her scanner that the others were falling behind. Not too far, but enough to allow the enemy to escape. She had an urge to get on the comm, to berate them all for their slow reactions, their inability to match her maneuvers. But there was no point. The under-trained Union squadrons had suffered terribly in the war to date. Fewer than one-third of the pre-war pilots were still with their fighters, and the replacements that filled the empty slots were even less prepared than their predecessors had been. There were a few exceptions, of course, but none on *Montmirail*. Lefebrve had inherited a ravaged fighter wing, one that had lost over eighty percent of its starting effectives. The ranks had been filled with raw replacements, and she knew she had a difficult task ahead of her trying to turn them into an effective force. But right now, she had her target, and that was all she cared about.

She let her head ease back into the cushioned rest on her chair. She'd never held her turbos at max power for so long before. But there was no choice, not if she was going to catch her prey.

And that was something she was determined to do, whatever it took.

Chapter Thirty-Five

Bridge
CFS Dauntless
Varus System
308 AC

"I want gunnery stations ready. Priority power to the point defense array." Barron had watched Kyle Jamison's interceptors gut the bomber force, taking out over eighty of the enemy craft. It was a victory of epic proportions, a success greater than any he'd dared hope for. But it still left forty-three bombers heading right for *Dauntless* and *Intrepid*.

"Yes, sir," Travis replied.

"And advise Commander Fritz I expect miracles from her people. However hard those bombers hit us, we've got an enemy battleship still to deal with…and we've got to destroy that station, whatever it takes."

"Yes, Captain."

Barron wasn't surprised that the station was well defended. In fact, he knew he was lucky if there was only one capital ship escort. But the sheer number of enemy fighters had taken him off guard, and he still had no clear idea what fixed defenses the facility itself mounted. One thing was certain, though. Unless he could bring his battleships through that bomber attack in at least reasonable condition, the fight here was as good as over.

The supply convoy *Dauntless* and *Intrepid* had destroyed might have bought the fleet some time, but he didn't have to look farther than his scanner to see that two dozen massive freighters and tankers were docked, no doubt loading up and preparing to move toward the front. Unless he could stop them.

"Commander, bring us within ten thousand kilometers of *Intrepid*. I want our defense networks connected."

"Yes, sir."

Barron wasn't sure how much that would help, but if one of *Dauntless*'s guns could pick off a bomber heading for *Intrepid*, or the reverse, it was worth the effort.

Barron reached down and tapped his comm unit. He knew he'd just had Travis relay orders to Commander Fritz, but he wanted to talk to her himself.

"Fritzie?"

"Yes, Captain. I've got the entire engineering staff on alert. I've positioned teams near the reactors and at all major power junctions."

"That's good, Fritzie." He paused. "I'm worried about the bays too. We're going to have to turn around a lot of fighters after the bombers go through…and you know as well as I do how vulnerable they are."

"I have standby crews ready at both bays, sir. I'm not sure what else we can do."

"I want the fuel storage moved back, Fritzie. We can't feed any fires down there if we get hit."

"Captain, I don't know how we can get that done in time."

"Then get some of it done, Fritzie. Anything will help. Conscript the science teams, the galley crew…anybody who doesn't have a vital combat role. But do what you can."

"Yes, Captain. I'm on it."

"And whatever happens, I want the fuel lines between the bay tanks and the main storage cut. I know that will slow us on the refit, but getting the bays blasted to slag will hurt even more. And I want fire retardant foam everywhere down there. Let's get ahead of this."

"I'm on it, sir."

"Do your best, Fritzie." He cut the line. His head darted back and forth as he checked on his bridge crew with something like fatherly concern. He'd led his people in battle before, and he'd watched some of them die. Now he was consumed with doing whatever he could to ensure they were ready to face what was coming and minimize the losses he knew they would take.

Losses…if we can't thin out that strike we might all *be lost…*

There were still too many bombers coming. If he'd kept back a CSP, he'd have another line of defense.

If you held back a CSP, your forward squadrons would have been overwhelmed. There were just too many enemy fighters…

Jamison's squadrons were chasing the bombing strike. They'd been forced to decelerate and reverse their vectors after their initial attack run, so they were behind. But Barron's strike force commander and his people were pouring it on, blasting at full power and closing that gap. Barron figured it was a coin toss as to whether they'd get there in time to attack before the bombers launched their torpedoes. But it was a dead certainty, Jamison and his pilots would be almost out of fuel and in desperate need of open landing platforms. Another reason he had to keep the bays functional. Somehow.

* * *

"Nice one, Condor. Best shooting I've seen in a long time!" Rick Turner knew he was exaggerating a bit. The shot had been a good one, nothing more. But he was in over his head, somehow trying to take the place of "Raptor" Stockton as Blue leader, and he was doing everything he could think of to inspire his pilots.

Blue squadron was *Dauntless*'s elite formation, but Turner knew the force he led wasn't the same one he'd served with for over a year. It wasn't the same one that had gone into the deadly fight against *Invictus* out on the Rim. That crack force had suffered significant losses, and many of those holes had been filled with replacements, transferred garrison pilots, and now, even a few strays from the fighting in Arcturon. It was still an effective force, and the veterans were stronger and more experienced for their recent struggles, but overall, the Blue squadron surrounding him had more weaknesses than its predecessor.

Then there was Stockton. The Blues' regular commander tended to be popular everywhere he went, a confident pilot, a good storyteller...everything that made him someone easy to get along with. But his pilots, the people who knew him best... they didn't just like him, they revered him. They'd watched him in battle, a terrifying force all on his own, released on the helpless enemy. And they'd seen him taking terrible risks, putting himself on the line to help one of his pilots, doing everything imaginable to get as many of them back to the bay as possible. Blue squadron without Stockton was still a powerful formation, but it went into battle without its heart and soul, and as much as he tried, Turner knew he could never replace what they had lost.

Not lost...Raptor will be back...

He didn't know if he really believed that, but right now he had to. His people needed his best, and he couldn't give that if he was devastated over Stockton's loss. He wasn't sure if he was fooling himself or not. The mission had seemed like a hopeless one, but then, he couldn't imagine Raptor failing at anything either.

We're not coming back from this one anyway...

Turner understood why the Blues had been sent to intercept the enemy assault force. They were the only squadron capable of delaying four times their number of fighters long enough for Jamison and the other squadrons to hit the Union bombers. And they had done it. Their initial attack had been so aggressive, so relentlessly deadly, they had compelled all four incoming squadrons to engage them. They'd held their own for a long time, the wingman-based tactics Stockton had taught them paying dividends as their enemies surrounded them. But now the impetus of the initial assault had waned, and the enemy squadrons had regained some level of organization. They were launching coordinated attack runs now, and despite the difference in experience between the two forces, they were starting to inflict losses.

The mission was complete, Jamison's fighters off pursuing the remnants of the bombing force. But the Blues were hopelessly intermixed with the enemy formations. Turner wanted to sound the withdrawal, to lead his people back to *Dauntless*... but he knew it was impossible. The enemy had used their numbers in a surprisingly effective manner, and they had practically englobed his force. His fighters were being attacked from every direction, and a retreat now would turn almost instantly into a slaughter. And he'd see every pilot of Blue squadron die in battle before he'd watch them butchered like fleeing sheep.

He pressed down on the firing control, loosing a bolt from his deadly lasers. The enemy fighter a thousand kilometers in front of him blinked off his screen. Another kill. His people had inflicted heavy losses on their enemies...but not enough to alter the deadly force ratio in effect. The Blues could inflict four kills for every one of their own taken down and still lose ground.

Turner's eyes caught something on the display, an approaching formation. For an instant he felt a wave of despair. Another force of enemy fighters would eliminate whatever infinitesimal chance his people had. But then he saw the direction of the approach...and the AI updated the screen, labeling the approaching fighters.

Red Eagle squadron. Timmons...

Turner lost his focus, just for a second. Dirk Timmons was Stockton's great rival, and that made him persona non grata in Blue squadron. But here he was, at the head of his squadron and racing to pull the Blues out of the fire.

He felt an instant of resentment, but he pushed it back against it. Rivalries were one thing, dislike between pilots also... but right now they were all Confederation warriors. And the real enemy was before them.

His comm crackled to life. "Blue leader, this is Red Eagle leader...we're inbound. At your location in one minute. Hang on until then, Blues. Damned fine job chewing up those enemy squadrons...thanks for leaving something for us."

Turner was surprised at the tone of Timmons's message, and he felt shame for the flash of resentment. "Red Eagle leader, this is Blue leader. You are most welcome. Thanks for the assist."

He gritted his teeth, staring at the screen with renewed ferocity. They had a chance now. He knew the Red Eagles were good…not as good as Blue squadron, of course, but pretty damned good nevertheless. It was time to show these Union pukes how to fly.

*　*　*

Barron watched as the cloud of enemy bombers moved forward. They would enter the outer limits of *Dauntless*'s defensive perimeter in a few minutes. The battleship's laser turrets outranged the attackers' plasma torpedoes, but not by a lot. That was one reason capital ships were so dependent on their own fighters for defense. *Dauntless*'s grid of anti-fighter guns was formidable, but her gunners would have two minutes, perhaps three, to inflict their damage. Then the bombers would launch their torpedoes, and the lasers would switch their targeting priorities, trying to destroy the small, far harder to target, warheads before they converted to plasmas.

Jamison's fighters were coming up behind the bombers. They were going to make it into range just in time, the result of his strike force commander's herculean efforts, and those of the pilots he commanded. But they would still be pretty far out, their shots difficult ones. They weren't going to get them all, but any bomber they took out could be the one that scored a critical hit on one of the battleships.

Barron had almost become accustomed to the feeling of battle, the tension, the tightness in his stomach. He ignored it all, focusing with iron discipline on the scanners and readouts feeding him information. His ship needed him, and he would do whatever he possibly could to bring her through this fight…and into the next one.

"All defensive batteries are authorized to fire at will as soon as targets enter range. Laser turrets have top priority for energy allocation."

"Yes, sir." Travis turned around and relayed Barron's order.

A moment later, he heard a familiar hum, faint, distant. One of the batteries opening fire. Within a few seconds, all of *Dauntless*'s point defense guns were active. A bomber vanished from the display. Then another, this one on *Intrepid*'s section of the line.

Barron's eyes moved to a faint red line on the display, the AI's estimate of the enemy's maximum launch range. The tiny dots representing the fighters moved steadily forward toward that deadly border. Two more disappeared, victims of the battleships' defensive fire.

Thirty seconds…then they'll start launching torpedoes…

The bombing strike moved forward, into the teeth of *Dauntless*'s fire. But just before they entered range, Jamison's fighters opened fire.

Barron watched as four squadrons of Confederation interceptors fired almost as one, their lasers tearing into the enemy formation from the rear. The shots were long, desperate attempts to score hits against all odds. Many of them missed. Most. But some hit, and combined with the fire from the battleships, they began to take a toll.

Bombers were winking out all across the line, ships that had traveled halfway across the system to attack the battleships falling short by a matter of seconds. Barron felt a wave of excitement as more and more of the enemy ships vanished. But then he saw a line of dots, smaller than the icons representing the fighters, indeed, barely visible in the display. Torpedoes. His people had shot down more than half of the attacking bombers, but the rest were launching their own attacks now.

Dauntless's bridge was almost silent. Every officer there understood what was happening. The laser turrets had taken their toll, and Jamison's fighters had ravaged the attacking force. But now that was over. The batteries might take out a torpedo or two as they approached, but most of the incoming warheads would survive, and when they got close enough, they would covert to pure energy, removing any hope of interception.

"I want the engine room ready for evasive maneuvers, Commander." Once the torpedoes converted, they would lose their ability to change vectors. That would give *Dauntless* a window for maneuver, and a final chance to evade the deadly weapons.

"Engine room standing by, sir."

Barron stared at the display intently, focusing on the incoming torpedoes, ignoring everything else save those horrendous warheads moving toward his ship. Coordinates ran through his thoughts, thrust levels...but he couldn't issue the orders before the torpedoes turned to plasmas.

His eyes were fixed on the display tank, each second passing like some tiny eternity, time seeming to slow until it was almost unbearable. But still, he concentrated. Then, one of the dots grew larger, the AI's way of marking a conversion. Another after that, then more until all fourteen incoming warheads had turned to searing hot balls of plasma, moving directly toward the two ships on ballistic headings.

"Full thrust, forward...three seconds," he snapped into his comm unit. Time was of the essence, and there was no time for the formal nonsense of issuing orders through Travis.

"Acknowledged," came the reply. An instant later everyone on *Dauntless*'s bridge was slammed back into their chairs, 10g of thrust hitting them too fast for the dampeners to intervene. Barron figured there'd be some injuries, muscle pulls and maybe a broken rib or two, but every torpedo he could evade saved lives.

"Bring us around to 320.098.003...thrust at 4g for six seconds." Barron's eyes were darting all across the display, his mind making snap decisions, his mouth spitting out the instructions without a second thought. There was no time to waste. Even with his best efforts, his ship wasn't going to escape from all the approaching weapons.

He watched as three of the torpedoes went by, evaded by his quick actions. But another three were heading directly for *Dauntless*, and he knew even as he started to issue the orders it was too late.

"Bring us to..." *Dauntless* shook hard, once...and then two more times in rapid succession, all three torpedoes slamming into her amidships. Barron had no idea yet what damage his ship had taken, though the hits all seemed solid. But his mind was still focused on the remaining torpedoes.

"Bring us to 123.111.234, 6g thrust for ten seconds." But this time there was no reply, not for a few seconds. *Dauntless* didn't move. Then: "Captain, the engines are offline. I don't think the damage is critical. We're working on it now."

"Very well." It might not be critical, but right now even a loose power lead could be the difference between survival and destruction. Barron watched, horrified, as three more plasmas slammed into his ship.

The bridge went dark, all except for the red battlestations lamps and their local battery power. The display projection was gone, the tank black, empty. A few seconds later the lights came back, dimmer than usual, as *Dauntless*'s reserve power came online.

"Damage report," Barron snapped into his comm unit. He wasn't even sure the communications systems were functioning, and he was relieved when Fritz's voice replied.

"It's bad, sir...but not as critical as it seems. I think both reactors are fine, but the power distribution system is a mess. The thrust damage is minor. A leak on the main fuel line caused the AI to scrag the engines. I'll have it back online in less than five minutes."

Barron felt a wave of relief. He wasn't sure he should be happy at the extent of the damage his ship had suffered, but he'd expected worse, and in battle, such things were definitely relative.

"All right, Fritzie...you know your priorities. We need power to the weapons systems."

"Yes, sir. I think the primaries are fine. As soon as I can get the energy transmission back online, they should be good to go."

Barron hesitated, just for a second. "The launch bays?"

"I don't know yet, sir. Sorry. But I don't think they're a disaster. I'm pretty sure we can keep beta bay open, at least. Alpha is reporting heavier damage."

"Okay, Fritzie...get to it. You know what to do." He cut the line.

The workstations were all back online, though the energy-hogging holographic main display was still dark, replaced by a large two-dimensional projection.

He looked over toward Travis. "Anything from *Intrepid*, Commander?" He'd forced himself to forget about *Dauntless*'s companion. There hadn't been a thing he could do to help *Intrepid*, not while she was evading incoming torpedoes. He knew the battleship was in the capable hands of Sara Eaton, and he'd left her alone to do her job.

"Yes, sir. Captain Eaton reports that *Intrepid*'s engines are at half thrust, but her people have already effected repairs. And her landing bays are fully operational. Her primaries are offline, but she expects to have them back up within half an hour."

Barron nodded. Eaton's ship had gotten off lightly, at least by comparison to *Dauntless*. He paused for a few seconds, then he asked the question he dreaded the most. "Casualties?"

"We have thirty-one dead, sir, mostly in the outer compartments where the last three torpedoes hit. Sickbay reports twenty-seven wounded, but Dr. Stewart says they expect that number to rise significantly as more cases are brought in."

"*Intrepid?*"

"Captain Eaton reports eleven dead and forty-one wounded."

Barron sighed softly. He wasn't sure if it bothered him more that over forty spacers had just died...or that more than anything else, he felt relief. Relief that it wasn't worse.

"Sir, Captain Eaton reports that she will be bringing her engines back online in..."

"No."

"Sir?"

"Captain Eaton is to...no, put her on my line." Barron's eyes were fixed on a spot on the 2D display, a red oval marking the location of the enemy battleship. The oval that was moving directly toward his ships.

"Captain Barron?"

"Sara, listen to me. I want you to keep your engines offline. I want you to keep your power output suppressed. Repair everything you can, but don't activate anything."

"Yes, sir..." There was confusion in her voice.

"Look at your display, Sara…at the enemy battleship. They think we're crippled, and they're moving forward so they can hit us and finish us off. I want them to think we're both in critical shape. Maybe we can lure them in. We've got a better chance if we can fight the battleship and the station separately."

"Yes, sir." It was clear she understood perfectly now. "Should I jettison some wreckage as well? We've got plenty of it."

"Absolutely. And keep your power output at minimal levels. Anything we can do to make it look like both ships are shot to hell." His mind drifted back to the fight at Santis. He'd used a similar strategy to lure Captain Rigellus in. And if it worked on an officer of Katrine Rigellus's skill, he was sure the commander of that massive Union battlewagon would fall for it.

"Yes, Captain."

"And, Sara…make sure your damage control crews have those primaries back online by the time that monster gets here. What's the point of setting up a trap if you've got nothing to spring on the enemy?"

Chapter Thirty-Six

"Who the hell is this pilot?"

"Identity unknown. Best estimate from scanning data suggests the fighter launched from the Union battleship *Montmirail*, the lead ship of the class, mounting..."

"Enough," Stockton growled. He'd been talking to himself, and he really wasn't interested in a lecture from his AI. Not now. He'd cleared the enemy formations, and he was on a dead line for the transwarp link. He was ripping along at one hell of a velocity, and he had no fuel left—none—to decelerate. So, if the fleet was in Mellas, one of the capital ships could send out a rescue shuttle to match course and velocity with him. And if the Confederation forces weren't there, he'd tear off into the system's fringe awfully fast. He'd only live for about an hour or so of that, but his frozen corpse would keep going, more or less forever. Unless his vector led into a planet or a star or a comet...

If, that is, he got out of Turas. He'd been sure he'd managed that, but then he realized he still had one bird on his tail. He couldn't understand why his hunter hadn't fired a missile yet. With no fuel for evasive maneuvers, he was a sitting duck. But

302

his adversary seemed to be closing to laser range. It was a break, he knew, but he couldn't understand…and that was making him nervous.

Not that nervousness was particularly troublesome over the full-blown fear and the soul-crushing exhaustion that were also wearing on him. He'd known the mission would push him to the limits of his endurance, and it had done just that. If the fleet wasn't in Mellas, he almost welcomed the frozen death that awaited him there. Anything except more hours in the confines of this fighter, waiting for the enemy, for another malfunction, for the last shreds of his sanity to desert him.

He felt the urge to reach out and grab the controls, to alter his vector, to conduct the kind of evasive maneuvers that had kept him alive in all his battles. But his instincts were pointless. With no fuel, there would be no maneuvers. He was on a straight line, and that made him an easy target.

He glanced at the display. His pursuer was still accelerating, and every passing second closed not only the distance but the rate at which he was being overtaken. He didn't have a lot of respect for Union pilots, but something told him this one was different. And that meant he was in trouble.

He waited—what else could he do? His eyes were fixed on his controls, waiting for his scanners to report the first shots from his enemy's laser cannon. If he was indeed facing a skilled pilot, it wouldn't take many shots before his adversary finished him off.

He wondered if he'd spent his last fuel well, if perhaps he should have broken his vector. But that didn't make any sense. He'd still have been trapped, and his pursuer would have run him down anyway. He'd taken a gamble, one he still knew had been the right choice, but his luck had failed him for once, and put a truly skilled Union pilot on his tail.

So close…I made it so close…

* * *

Lefebrve's eyes were tightly focused. Her target hadn't

changed velocity, hadn't accelerated or decelerated. It hadn't changed its vector at all. She understood…he was clearly heading for the transwarp link. But why not pour on more thrust? The Lightning could out-accelerate her for sure, but instead it was just moving forward with its velocity unchanged.

Her mind raced, but she could only come up with two options. The fighter was out of fuel…or the whole thing was some kind of trap. She tried to think it through, even as she closed the distance.

Why would they want to set up a trap for a single fighter?

To capture me? To try to get intel? But how? They'd have to get me through the link…and I'm going to blast this fighter before it transits.

Perhaps the pilot in front of her was a rookie, one who had no idea what he was doing.

But what would a raw pilot be doing out here all by himself?

She was edgy, but she wasn't going to let it interfere with her kill. She'd gotten a fighter shot out from under her in the battle at Arcturon, and her bruised ego had been burning for revenge ever since.

She opened her palm, moving her fingers, stretching her hand. Then she closed her grip on the throttle and brought her index finger to the firing stud. She was almost in range.

The targeting was simple. Her enemy's course was absolutely predictable. She *had* him.

Her finger closed slowly…and then her target moved.

She was shocked. She'd been just about convinced he was out of fuel. Now her mind raced. *Is it a trap?*

She angled her controls, tracking the enemy's move. It was slow, a minor shift. Almost imperceptible, but enough to make a laser blast miss.

It wasn't normal thrust. There was no energy reading on her scanner. If the fighter had engaged its engines, she would have picked up *something*. But the output was still reading zero.

She lined up her shot and fired.

Damn!

The enemy fighter changed its vector again. And once more, the move was minimal, barely a shift at all. But enough to make her miss.

This one is good...I can feel it...

She was watching, looking for any sign her quarry was trying to spin around and take a shot at her. If he really was out of fuel, it was possible his guns were dead too. But she wasn't about to get careless. She fired again...and missed one more time as her target shifted its vector slightly.

She was frustrated, the relentless g forces wearing away her focus. But she didn't let up. The closer she got, the harder it would be for her prey to escape. And she was going to get as close as she had to...

* * *

Stockton was dead. He knew it. He had no fuel, no weapons. He'd managed to use his positioning jets to buy a few extra seconds, but they were almost exhausted now too. He was close to the jump point, tantalizingly close. But not close enough. When the jets gave out, his enemy would finish him in seconds. The pilot on his tail was good...and relentless. Stockton felt like he recognized many of his own traits in his opponent.

I'm sorry, Stara...I'm so sorry...

He reached down, pawing through his kit, pulling out the small pendant. It had seen him through more than one close call, and now, if its power was exhausted, so be it. But he owed it something, and if he'd come to the end, he'd die with it in his hand.

He punched at the controls, blasting the positioning jets again. He'd had to keep his moves complimentary, to offset thrust that would push him off his vector with others that restored his heading. It was a level of predictability in his movement, but he'd had to risk it. He didn't expect to make it to the jump point, but he hadn't given up yet, not entirely. It wasn't that he had any real hope...but yielding just wasn't in his DNA.

He saw the energy spike on his scanners, another shot from his enemy going wide. Just wide.

That was too close...

He shifted one last time, expending the last of the compressed air that powered his positioning jets. The move put him exactly back on his initial heading, toward the transit point. It was only a few minutes ahead of him, but that might as well have been years. He was out of tricks, and his enemy was right behind him.

Then he saw…something. Directly ahead, coming through the transwarp from Mellas. Then, suddenly, it was there, right in front of him. A Confederation cruiser, blasting out from the jump point.

It was help, reinforcements, a vessel with more than enough power to destroy his pursuer. But it was too late. Even a moment earlier would have been on time, but there was no way the pilot on his tail would miss him now, not long enough for the cruiser to intervene.

He slapped his hand down on the comm unit. "Confederation cruiser, this is Lieutenant Jake Stockton, callsign Raptor. I am carrying vital dispatches for Admiral Winston, and I am being pursued by a Union fighter. I am unarmed and out of fuel."

It was hopeless, he knew. They just didn't have enough time. But he had to try.

If only I had one last trick I could pull out of my sleeve…

He sat for an instant, stone still. Maybe there was…but it would take flawless timing. And it would cost him most of his remaining life support.

Another laser blast ripped by his ship, barely five meters away. There was no choice. He had no time left. It was beyond desperate…but it was all he had.

* * *

"Confirmed, Commander. That's a Confederation Lightning, and his callsign and ID beacon check out."

"How the hell did a Confederation fighter get to Turas? It certainly didn't come from Mellas…we'd know if it did." Admiral Winston had ordered the Mellas side of the link bracketed with scanner buoys. If a meteor the size of a pebble came through either way, fleet command would have known about it.

"I don't know, sir. According to the fleet database, Lieutenant Stockton is assigned to *Dauntless*."

"*Dauntless*? Yes, she was supposed to link up with the fleet at Arcturon…but that was before the battle there. Could she have possibly survived?" Commander Lars Tarkus sat at his station in the center of *Stanford*'s bridge. He was shocked to find a Confederation ship in Turas, even a fighter. And what did that pilot mean, "vital dispatches?" Whoever he was, he was coming in from behind enemy lines.

"I don't know, sir…but I don't think Lieutenant Stockton is going to make it."

"We'll see about that, Lieutenant. All laser batteries…open fire. Take out that Union fighter."

"Yes, sir." The lieutenant's voice was grim. It was clear he believed they were too late.

"I want 4g thrust, Lieutenant…directly toward those fighters."

"Yes, Commander."

Stanford was a light cruiser, a vessel designed for scouting duties and for providing anti-fighter support for battleships of the line. She wasn't much against an enemy capital ship, but she had a dozen anti-fighter batteries, and now every one of them opened fire.

"Thrusters engaged, Commander. All gunnery stations active."

"Very well. Maintain fire at maximum…I want that fighter destroyed."

"Yes, sir."

Tarkus looked at the screen, at the two fighters displayed in the center. Stockton's fighter was heading straight for the transwarp point, that much was clear…but he wasn't conducting any evasive action at all. No velocity changes, no vector adjustments. He was a sitting duck that way. *Stanford* would get that enemy fighter, he was sure of that. But not in time. Not unless Stockton managed to throw off his pursuer for just a bit longer.

"C'mon, Raptor," Tarkus whispered under his breath. "Help us out, give that Union bastard a hard time of it..."

* * *

"I have you now..." Lefebrve spoke softly to herself, her eyes unmoving, locked on her prey. She'd guessed her target had been out of fuel, and that he'd used his positioning jets to evade her fire...but now that had stopped.

He's used all the compressed gas...now he's mine...

She was less than twenty thousand kilometers away, close enough, especially when the target was locked on a fixed course. The fire from the enemy cruiser was becoming bothersome, but they were too late. They were slowing her down some, forcing her to engage in her own evasive maneuvers. If she'd been able to focus on the fighter only, she knew she'd have gotten it by now. But she wasn't about to give up. She could take out that pilot...before the cruiser got close enough to overwhelm her with its firepower.

She banked hard, and then again in almost the opposite direction. The cruiser's fire went wide, missing her by over a hundred kilometers. Lefebrve was adept at executing tight, fast maneuvers, the kind designed to make enemy gunners tear out their hair. After losing her bird in Arcturon, she damned sure wasn't about to get another one shot out from under her here. No way.

She lined up her shot—the last one, she expected. It had to be...the cruiser was bearing down on her. She had to break off.

Her finger tightened, her eyes focused like lasers. But as she fired, the enemy fighter lurched hard, mostly forward, increasing his velocity. It was slight, but enough to throw her shot off. She angled her thrust, dodging a series of shots from the cruiser.

Damn!

It was hard for her to let a target go, especially one like this. But the cruiser's gunners almost had her...and unlike a fighter, the escort ship had multiple turrets, all focused on her. She was stubborn, not suicidal. She might run the cruiser's guns if she could focus on that alone, but her own course was more or less locked in by her pursuit of the enemy fighter. She could bag her prey…likely at the cost of be her own life.

She swung her throttle to the side and pulled back hard, blasting at maximum thrust, pulling away from the cruiser's grasp. She was angry, frustrated…but there would be other battles. It was time to live and fight another day.

*   *   *

Stockton could hear his heart pounding in his ears. His hands were on the throttle, but it was habit, nothing more. His tortured, depleted, half-wrecked fighter had nothing left to give. He'd compromised its final effective status as his lifeboat when he'd expelled the last of his atmosphere to push the craft forward, to throw one final bit of uncertainty toward his pursuer.

He took a breath, a shallow one. The only thing standing between him and instant death was his survival suit, and the meager amount of oxygen it carried. If he was careful, if he didn't exert himself, it might last half an hour, perhaps forty minutes. But that didn't matter, not to the mission, at least. As long as he got through the transwarp link, his message would be safe. The appearance of the Confederation cruiser was pretty strong evidence there were friendly forces in Mellas, even if it wasn't the whole fleet. The intelligence he'd carried so far would find its way to Admiral Winston. As long as he made it through the portal. With luck, he'd survive, but if he died, at least it wouldn't be in vain.

He glanced at his display, watching as the cruiser closed hard on the Union fighter. His would-be killer was clearly a skilled pilot, far beyond most of those in the Union wings…so much so he wondered how he would have fared in straight up fight, fully fueled and armed. For an instant, he thought his enemy was going to stay on his tail, despite the growing threat from the cruiser. But then he saw the icon shift slightly, pulling away, and he knew he'd made it.

He felt a wave of relief, the expectation that the laser blast that killed him would come any second fading away. But it was tempered by the realization that his situation remained desperate, that he could still die in the cockpit of his battered fighter.

He stared for a few seconds, watching his opponent blast her thrusters and flee from the cruiser. He couldn't help but respect a pilot of such ability, especially in a service that didn't produce many aces. He tried to imagine how someone of such ability could serve a monstrosity like the Union, though he knew his perspective as a Confederation citizen, even one who'd had a difficult childhood, made it impossible to imagine what life was like for that pilot. For all the helpless billions subject to the Union's brutal rule.

Whatever motivation drove his foe, he was grateful his comrades didn't have to face many adversaries like this one who'd come so close to finishing him. He was still thinking about it when his fighter slipped into the transwarp link...and out of the Turas system.

Chapter Thirty-Seven

Timmons brought his fighter around, lining up for another run across the confused enemy formation. His Red Eagles had smashed into the Union squadrons with unparalleled fury. The Blues were their rivals, or at least their respective commanders were, but they were allies too. They all had the same foe, and that enemy was before them. The savage attack had not only shaken the Union formation, it had renewed the energy of the Blues, who pounded away at every enemy fighter in their own paths, gunning them down one after another. Still, the enemy had heavily outnumbered the Confederation squadrons, and for all the desperate brutality of the onslaught, the battle continued.

The Union forces were breaking, falling back, but that only increased the bloodthirsty rage of the Blues and the Red Eagles. Too many of their comrades had died this day, and too many in the battles of the past months. They were determined to have their vengeance, whatever the cost…and they swept through the disordered enemy ranks, shooting, killing.

Timmons jerked his throttle hard—too hard, and he grunted as pain shot through his chest. He released the control and then pulled back, his motion slightly more controlled, increasing his thrust. He was going to cut through the densest part of the enemy formation, guns blazing the whole way. He knew his fuel status was becoming a problem, but he wasn't even going to consider that, not until the enemy was in wholesale flight.

He pressed down hard, firing his lasers again and again. One enemy ship erupted in flame, vanishing from his screen. The next fighter in his path took a hit far back in its fuselage, flaming out its engines, but giving the pilot enough time to eject.

Two more…

He angled the throttle, pushing his vector out to the side, lining up one last target before he had to decelerate and turn about. He fired, and missed. Then again. Another miss.

Fuck…

He pulled hard on the throttle, increasing his thrust, gasping for air as the relentless g forces pounded against his sore chest. The pain increased with every second, so much so he thought he'd rebroken the rib, but he didn't slack off, not for a second. He wasn't going to let that enemy fighter escape. Any enemy he allowed to flee was just another one who could refit and return to kill one of his comrades.

He shoved the stick as far to the right as he could, the thrust changing his vector slowly, steadily. Then the enemy moved back onto his targeting screen. He waited, watching, his finger poised over the firing stud. He pressed it tightly, discharging the five hundred megawatt fury of his quad lasers. The enemy fighter winked off his screen, another kill.

"Yes!"

He looked back at the display, searching for another target. But the enemy fighters had broken off, barely a third of their number fleeing for their mother ship. Timmons felt the urge to pursue, but he held back. He didn't have the fuel, and he doubted any of his fellows did.

His comm crackled to life "They're running, Warrior. Let's finish them off."

"Negative, Typhoon. I feel the same way, but fuel status says no way. We've still got to hit that mother ship, not to mention the station. *Dauntless* and *Intrepid* need us, and we can't end up ditching because we ran out of fuel on the way back." *And Raptor and I don't get along, but it's still on me to bring his people home...*

"Damn...you're right, Warrior. Hell of a shame."

"Yeah, Typhoon...hell of shame." Timmons shook his head, unaccustomed to feeling like the cool, rational one. He flipped his comm to the universal channel. "Okay, boys and girls...let's head back to base."

* * *

"Fritzie, I need that power available when I call for it. We're running out of time." Barron's eyes were on his screen as he spoke, watching the enemy battleship moving steadily forward toward his two vessels. He'd been sure his plan would work, convinced the enemy would do anything to protect the supply base. The Union ship couldn't risk any stray shots at the station, not if there was any choice. But Barron's stratagem would only work if *Dauntless* was ready for the fight when it came, and right now, his ship was still on severely limited power, both its primary and secondary batteries inoperative.

"I know, sir. We've replaced over a hundred kilometers of power lines and conduits. Those torpedoes hit us hard, and just because they didn't rip the guts out of any main systems doesn't mean that damage is easy to fix."

"Listen to me, Fritzie...there's no one I'd rather have down there than you, but if we're not ready by the time that thing gets into range, we're sunk." Barron knew *Intrepid* was in better shape than his ship, but the enemy battleship outmassed either of the Confederation vessels, and it was untouched. *Dauntless* and *Intrepid* had been through hell, multiple battles followed by patchwork repairs. And the three small escort ships that formed the rest of his fleet didn't have enough power to make the difference. If both his battleships could lure the enemy into range and surprise them with their combined primaries, they had a chance to win a quick fight, one that might let them vanquish the Union battleship without taking more critical damage themselves. If they couldn't pull off that joint attack, *Dauntless* and

Intrepid might still win the battle, but both ships would almost certainly be too crippled to take on the station itself. And that was all that mattered. It was why they were here.

"I understand, sir. We'll get it done…somehow." Fritz's coolness in battle was legendary, among *Dauntless*'s crew and throughout the fleet. But now, the engineer sounded like she'd been pushed to the edge of her endurance. Barron knew Fritz drove herself relentlessly, and her people too. He felt guilty about riding her…but he still did it. There was no choice. He needed that power. He needed those weapons.

"Twenty-two minutes, Fritzie. That's all we've got. All you've got."

"Yes, Captain."

Barron cut the line. Then he jumped up from his chair and walked across the bridge, stopping in front of the main display tank. "Okay, let's not waste this time. I want all gun crews tracking that ship. I want firing solutions updated every two minutes. Commander Fritz will get us the power we need, I'm sure of that…but I'll hang the gun crew that misses when we open up." The words sounded foreign to him. Barron didn't feel like himself, not when he said things like that. He wasn't a tyrant, he didn't lead his people with threats. But he understood what was at stake here. He understood it all too clearly. If his people could destroy that base, the Union offensive would be stalled. It might even collapse for lack of supply. If they failed, if the enemy could send another convoy forward, the Confederation itself could be in jeopardy.

He knew things were worse at the front than the reports suggested, that the fleet was on its last legs. Nothing as large as the Confederation died in an instant, of course, but there was a tipping point…enough ships destroyed, planets occupied…a level from which he knew his people couldn't come back. And he suspected they were far closer to that terrible moment that anyone wanted to acknowledge.

His grandfather had stared into just such an abyss, and he'd acted. He'd reached out and grabbed power, rallied a battered and demoralized fleet, and he'd saved the Confederation. The histories and legends don't recount Rance Barron threatening politicians, intimidating war profiteers under the guns of his ships, executing deserters and cowards. But Tyler was coming to realize now that his grandfather must have done such things, and more. The Confederation had made a foolish error, allowing its enemy to escape so lightly at the end of the third war, and its troops were now paying the price for it. Barron didn't compare himself with his ancestor, but he realized he was at a similar point. He couldn't save the Confederation, he didn't have the power. But maybe he could give it another chance. And the stress of it all was killing him, making him into something he didn't like very much.

How did you handle it, Grandfather? How did you endure so much pressure on your shoulders?

He'd known Rance Barron as a grandparent, a pleasant man who'd enjoyed spending time with his family, having dinner with friends. How did the man he remembered so fondly turn into the pillar of solid steel he must have been in battle? How did he mercilessly dispatch not only his foreign enemies, but also those on his own side who hindered his cause?

Barron looked around the bridge, at the eyes staring back, the looks on the faces of his officers as they perceived what he had become. In that moment, he'd have sacrificed any of them, accepted any cost, including the total destruction of *Dauntless* and *Intrepid.* Anything. Whatever it took to destroy that station.

* * *

"It's going to be a last-minute thing, Sara. Commander Fritz thinks she's got the lines and leads patched together, but we can't know for sure until we power up. And if I fire up the reactor too soon, they're going to know we're in better shape than they think we are."

"Are you sure you should be flash-starting those reactors, Tyler? Ours check out pretty well, but it sounds like yours are being held together with tape and maybe a little chewing gum."

"No choice, Sara." *And the answer is no...we shouldn't be flash starting them. But we're going to do it anyway.*

"Maybe we should open fire first...give your people time for a more controlled restart."

"No, you can see the readings on that thing as well as I can. Almost five million tons, untouched. The thing looks like it just rolled out of the damned shipyard. Both of us have to hit it, and we have to make it count. Otherwise we're either going to lose, or we're going to be commanding two floating piles of debris by the time we win."

"I'm still worried about those reactors of yours."

"You're in good company. Commander Fritz agrees with you. It's a good thing I have more faith in her abilities than she does, isn't it?"

Eaton appreciated Barron's attempt at levity, and she suspected it was as much a stress control mechanism for him as anything else. But she was still worried. If *Dauntless*'s reactors went super-critical, the results of a flash start could be disastrous.

The enemy battleship had paused to pick up the remnants of its shattered fighter squadrons, but since then it had been moving directly toward the two apparently crippled Confederation vessels. Barron had done everything he could think of to support the impression that the fighter attack had both ships at death's door...ejecting debris and bursts of fluid and gasses, maintaining minimal power levels. Even the three escort vessels were playing their parts, positioning themselves to the front, like loyal pets prepared to defend wounded masters to the death.

"You're the boss, sir." Eaton wasn't sure what she would do if the roles were reversed. She understood Barron's plan, and it was brilliant, daring. But she just wasn't sure she could have taken the risk.

"We'll be fine, Sara. We've got about ten minutes. Let's use it well. Check over your repairs, your firing solutions. In about twelve minutes, we'll know if we pulled it off." The line went dead.

Eaton sat for a moment, silent, staring off across the bridge. Then she looked down at her screen, rechecking the firing coordinates she'd calculated herself. Barron had been right so far about one thing…the Union commander *was* being careless. He clearly believed the two Confederation ships were badly battered, that they were no threat, and certainly not at the long range of their primary batteries. He hadn't even altered his approach vector…and if that ship continued to move forward with an unchanged course and velocity, it was going to greatly simplify her targeting.

"Commander Nordstrom, I want the primaries crews to conduct another practice run. Full computer simulation."

"Yes, Captain."

She'd had her people go through three of the dry runs already, but there was time for one more. Besides, she'd rather have them going through the motions and chattering about how many times she made them do it than sitting in silence, thinking about the consequences of missing.

"Get me Commander Merton."

"On your line, Captain."

"Are you ready down there, Doug?"

"We're all set, Captain. I've got double crews on both reactors. We'll be powering up reactor A and doing a full crash restart on B. Everything's been checked and rechecked. We'll be fine."

"How about the primaries?"

"We've been trickle charging them from reactor A, Captain, minimal power generation. They'll be ready to go in less than four minutes…and I'd wager everything I've got there's no way they picked it up."

"I hope you're right." She didn't *know*, of course, but Eaton suspected the enemy would have changed his approach if he even suspected he was facing functional Confederation primaries.

"We had to steal power from virtually all ship's systems. If we take significant damage, it's going to hamper the early control efforts.

"Very well. There's nothing to be done about that…so let's hit them hard before they can do the same to us." Her eyes darted to her display, checking the chronometer. "Enemy projected to enter range in four minutes, thirty seconds. That's your countdown clock, Doug."

"Understood, Captain. You should have full power within ten seconds of that mark."

"Good luck, Doug."

"Thank you, Captain. The same to you…and all of us."

She cut the line, watching as the enemy ship continued to close. She was counting under her breath, down to three minutes. Then Nordstrom turned abruptly. "Captain, we're picking up launch activity."

She snapped her head down, focusing on her screen. The reports from the squadrons had made it clear they'd had to let the enemy survivors escape or they'd risk running out of fuel. Now, those ships were coming back, refit, and she hoped the timing didn't portend disaster. The enemy ship was close for a launch, very close. She doubted that was deliberate strategy… more likely just the time it took to rearm and refuel their fighters. But if those birds were fitted out as bombers, and they advanced at full thrust from so close, she'd have…nine minutes, she estimated quickly. Nine minutes before a wave of plasma torpedoes came ripping toward the two battleships.

She reached down to her comm unit, keying up *Dauntless*'s channel.

"I see them," Barron said before she could get a word out. "There's nothing we can do. My bays are a mess. It's a miracle we managed to land the fighters at all. I may not be able to get anyone out in time. If you've got any interceptors ready to go, get them set to launch. But not until we've opened fire."

"Sir, how can I launch while we're firing primaries?" Tactical doctrine was clear. Fighters were to launch before ships entered firing range.

"Damn the book, Captain. If your crews can get anything ready to go, get them out between shots, while your guns are recharging."

"Yes, sir." She felt a surge of nausea. Eaton liked to think she was a good officer, but she wasn't as comfortable being a maverick as Barron seemed to be. Deserting the fleet, engaging in one unorthodox tactic after another, it was all too much for her.

"Commander Nordstrom, do we have any fighters ready to

launch?"

Nordstrom leaned over his workstation, flipping through status reports. "The Longswords have six ships refueled and ready. Launch control says we might have two more in ten minutes."

"Very well, Commander. I want those six ships manned and in the tubes. They are to launch ten seconds after we fire the primaries."

"Yes, Captain. Ten seconds."

She turned and looked back at her display. The enemy ship was still moving forward. Its velocity and vector had changed slightly from the launch of the fighters. It wasn't a major change, but it was enough to force her to redo the firing solution.

"Damn," she muttered under her breath. Her eyes darted to the countdown timer as her fingers moved over the screen, making the updates as quickly as she could. She wasn't trusting *this* targeting to anyone but herself.

Chapter Thirty-Eight

Bridge
CFS Dauntless
Varus System
308 AC

"I need a status report, Lieutenant. Now." Barron was hunched over the comm, speaking with launch control.

"The bays are still inoperable, sir," Sinclair replied. "I don't even know how we managed to land the fighters, but we can't get supplies through to the ships. The fuel lines are all cut, and the rail system from the cargo hold is a twisted piece of junk."

"I don't need excuses, Lieutenant. I need to know when you will be ready to launch fighters. And how many." He knew he was being unfair to Sinclair. Her people—and Chief Evans and his crews down in the bays—had performed miracles bringing the depleted squadrons back onboard, but now they had one hell of a mess to clean up. And he'd pulled almost all Fritzie's engineers away, down to the reactors and the power transmission lines. But none of that mattered. He needed fighters, and Sinclair and Chief Evans were just going to have to figure out how to get him some.

"Sir, I'm sorry. We're doing everything we can, but..." She paused. "Four, Captain. I think we can get four fighters out of alpha bay in ten minutes, but they'll launch without missiles.

That'll use up what little we have stockpiled close to the bay... and it'll be all we can do for at least an hour, maybe more."

"Very well, Lieutenant, four will have to do. I want our best pilots in those ships...I don't care if you have to draft every squadron commander to do it."

"Yes, sir."

"And Lieutenant?"

"Yes, Captain?"

"Forget this ten minutes nonsense. You've got five. I want those birds ready to launch immediately after we fire the primaries."

"Yes, sir."

"Barron out."

"Primary batteries report ready to fire," Travis said as soon as he cut the line to Sinclair. "We finally managed to get them a full charge, but we'll need the reactors on near optimal output to power them up again."

"Understood, Commander." He could hear the almost brutal severity of his tone, and he regretted it...but that didn't change anything. He was cold, his blood like ice. He was going to destroy that enemy battleship, no matter what he had to do...and then he was going to take out that station, if he had to dismantle it himself bit by bit. He was still the man who loved his crew, who looked over them with paternal pride. But some things were more important than survival. And, right now, nothing mattered. Nothing except destroying that station. That meant he had to take out this battleship first.

"Two minutes to firing range." Travis spoke slowly, clearly. She was her usual controlled self, but Barron suspected that inside she was feeling the same thing he was. Travis was as smart as they came, and she knew as well as Barron how important it was to destroy that station, and the sacrifices he was prepared to make to see it done.

He almost called up the gun crews, but he hesitated with his hand over the comm. Then he set it down. His people were good, the best. They didn't need him riding them right before they took their shot. Badgering them now would make him feel better, perhaps, but it would do nothing to help them hit the target. Distraction could only hurt his cause now.

"One minute."

Barron sat stone still, silent, wondering just how long it could possibly take for a single minute to pass.

"Thirty seconds. Commander Fritz reports all system ready for emergency reactor power up procedure."

"Very well, Commander. She is to proceed."

Barron counted down in his head. Twenty. Fifteen. Ten.

"Reactor restart now."

Nothing happened. At least nothing Barron could see on the bridge. There was no sound, no vibrations under his feet, so signs of anything happening. But then, a few seconds later, the lights brightened as fresh power flooded into them.

Barron felt a wave of relief. He had enormous faith in Fritz, but he also knew he'd given her a difficult and dangerous job, and that regardless of the skill and capability of his engineer, there had been a very real chance of a disastrous outcome. And even more likelihood that the reactors would just scrag again immediately.

"Entering range, Captain."

"Primaries…fire."

There was a pause. Barron knew it was no more than a few seconds, but for as long as he remembered that moment, it seemed like an eternity had passed. Then he heard the familiar whine, and the almost metal on metal shriek…the sound of *Dauntless*'s massive primaries firing.

His stomach tightened, twisting in knots as he waited to see if his guns had hit their target. Suddenly, Travis spun around, and as soon as he saw her face he knew.

Yes!

"Two direct hits, Captain." A short pause. "No, four, sir. Both of *Intrepid*'s guns hit as well."

"Very well, Commander." Barron's voice was cool, calm, but inside he was screaming with excitement. "Recharge primaries…and advise Commander Fritz, seconds count."

"Yes, sir."

His trap had worked. The enemy had blundered in, his course and velocity fixed, making himself a perfect target. The captain of that battleship had believed the Confederation craft were crippled, helpless...and he'd been lazy, careless. Arrogance...it was so often the weak spot. *Remember that...lest you end up in your enemy's shoes one day...*

The 3D display reactivated with the resumption of normal power, and Barron stared at the enemy ship, a large red oval floating off to the side of tank. The damage assessments were still coming in, but it was clear the vessel still had thrust capacity. Its vector was changing slowly, as it accelerated toward *Dauntless* and *Intrepid.*

Barron was disappointed. He'd hoped the first shot would knock out the enemy's engines, even for a short time. The Union vessel was still out of range of its own primaries, which allowed *Dauntless* and *Intrepid* to fire with impunity. But he knew that wouldn't last.

"Enemy will enter firing range in four minutes, sir."

Barron sighed softly. One more shot. *Maybe* two. His people would have a chance to seriously damage that ship before it could fire back, but after that they'd have to earn those next hits. The Union vessel was varying its thrust now, slightly altering its vector to make targeting more difficult. They'd taken advantage of the enemy's mistake, of the easy shot that carelessness had provided them. But the next ones would be harder.

He felt vibration under his feet. *The fighters launching. Four of them, at least.*

The enemy bombers were a danger too, one quite apart from the battleship itself. *Dauntless* was something close to fully operational, except for the landing bays, but he didn't fool himself enough to equate that with being undamaged. The power systems, the primaries, even the engines...they were being held together by patchwork and by the X factor of Fritz's engineering magic. But if that battleship opened up with its massive broadside, or the bombers got off a salvo of torpedoes, those makeshift repairs would quickly collapse.

"Primaries will be charged in thirty seconds."

"Very well. Gunnery crews are to fire at will."

Barron waited, counting off the seconds in his head. Then he heard the huge weapons firing again. His eyes darted to the display, waiting, watching.

A clean miss.

Damn!

The battleship's commander had been careless on his approach, but now he was blasting his engines in a wild zigzag approach, making his huge vessel a far more difficult target. Barron was watching a few seconds later as *Intrepid's* guns also fired. Eaton's gunners did a little better than his, but not by enough. One shot had missed, the other had scored a peripheral hit.

Barron felt the elation at the initial volley fading away. The first shot had seemed deadly, but the damage assessments suggested the impact had been less than expected. The enemy vessel was damaged, no doubt, but it appeared to generating something close to full power, and Barron suspected most of its guns were still online.

He slammed his hand down on the comm. "Fritzie, I want those primaries charged again before that ship enters its own firing range. I don't care what it takes."

"Captain, we're lucky those replacement lines are holding at all…"

"Fritzie," he roared, "just do it!" He brought his balled fist down hard on the comm unit, severing the line. He stared straight ahead, unwilling to look at any of his officers, to see the reflection of what he was becoming in their gazes. He didn't have time for any of that now. There was nothing in his mind but that enemy ship. Nothing at all.

Come on, Fritzie…I need that power…

* * *

"All right…we all know why we're out here. Now, there are nineteen of them and ten of us, but that's just math." Jamison was looking down at the screen, watching as the six fighters Intrepid had managed to launch linked up with his own four. It wasn't much of a force, less than a single squadron's strength all combined. But Eaton had ordered her own top personnel into the available cockpits, and the pilots Jamison was commanding now were among the very best who'd ever climbed into the Confederation's deadly Lightning fighters.

"We'll get it done, Thunder. Whatever it takes. We've got a few lessons left we can teach these guys."

Jamison nodded as he listened to Timmons's voice on his headset, shaking his head softly. It could have been Stockton talking. He wondered again how two men so similar could dislike each other so much. It was one of life's mysteries.

For all Timmons's bluster, Stockton knew the pilot was right. Ten interceptors, piloted by the best pilots on *Dauntless* and *Intrepid*, could take out nineteen unescorted bombers. He had *no* doubt about that. What worried him was doing it *before* the attackers fired their torpedoes. The strike force had been launched close to its targets…*very* close. That meant his people didn't have much time. And the fact that almost half his fighters—including his own—were without missiles only made it more difficult.

"Let's kick in our turbos…but be careful. Stay under ten kilometers per second. We've got to be able to come around on these guys quickly." His makeshift squadron could take out the bombers, but they'd never get them all in one pass. And if they whipped by at too high a velocity, they'd never make it back in time to prevent the survivors from launching against the battleships.

Jamison pulled back on his throttle, feeling the force of acceleration press against him. He reminded himself to direct his tiny wing with a light hand. These were squadron leaders and deadly aces he was leading, not rookies. They knew the mission, and they knew what was at stake.

He watched on the scanner as the distance closed, and then he released the throttle, reducing his thrust to zero. His hand moved halfway back to the control, a vestigial impulse to launch the missiles he didn't have. A few seconds later he saw small trails on his screen as *Intrepid*'s birds launched their weapons.

The bombers were on a direct line toward *Dauntless*, and their attempts at evasive maneuvers were clumsy, ineffective. One by one he saw missiles find their targets. By the time it was over, *Intrepid*'s birds had launched twelve missiles, and scored nine kills. That was almost half of the enemy strike force. But it left ten bombers rapidly approaching.

Jamison checked the ranges. The incoming strike craft were accelerating, doing everything they could to get into launch range before the interceptors could open up with their lasers. Jamison angled his fighter and fired. He was too far out, he knew, but they were rapidly running out of time, and he had to take any chance he could. He could see on the display that several of the others had followed his lead, firing their lasers from extreme range. They all missed too…no, not all. Timmons scored a hit. The power of his lasers was greatly reduced from the distance, and the bomber wasn't destroyed. But Jamison could see that the ship's thrust had declined considerably. So, now there were nine fully-functional bombers and one damaged one.

He picked out another target, a bomber at the front of the approaching formation. He gripped the throttle tightly, resisting the urge to accelerate. He was already moving at too high a velocity to manage a quick turnaround—the last thing he needed was more speed.

He stared at his screen, his eyes fixed on the bomber he'd chosen. He was still at long range, but he fired again anyway. His shots came closer this time, and he kept at it, one blast after another. For once, fuel and power weren't precious commodities. The fight was taking place close to *Dauntless*, and whatever happened, it wouldn't last long. He could fire at will, without concern for draining his resources.

He fired again. Then he adjusted his vector slightly and took another series of shots. A hit! He watched as the tiny icon blinked out of existence. Another one down.

He looked back at the wide area display. His comrades had taken out four ships overall. No, five…Timmons had finished off his crippled opponent. By then his makeshift squadron had zipped past their targets. He reached down, fired his positioning jets, spinning his ship around. He shot again, blasting from behind at the surviving enemy bombers, even as he decelerated hard. A miss. Then an icon blinked out, another bomber, the handiwork of one of his comrades. Then another.

Three left.

The mission had been a success by any measure, but three bombers were still a danger to *Dauntless*. Jamison knew there was a limit to how many times Fritz and her engineers could patch the wounded ship back together. And if the enemy battleship got close enough to unload…

He pulled back hard on the throttle, squeezing every bit of thrust he could from his engines. The g forces hit him hard, and he struggled to stay alert, even to stay conscious. He had no choice…and he could see several of his pilots were doing the same thing.

The heavy thrust quickly overcame his previous vector and velocity, but he was still far behind the bombers, and he kept his iron grip on the throttle. He wanted to scream at the pain, but he couldn't suck enough air in his tortured lungs to do it. He was lightheaded, and he could feel the darkness trying to take him, but he resisted with everything he had.

His head was pressed back against his chair, but he could still see—barely—the screen. He was closing now, his velocity building rapidly. He would get one chance…then he would zip past his target again. But there was no choice. If he didn't maintain the acceleration, he'd never get there in time.

He waited as the bomber got bigger on the screen, the range counting down. He had a long-range shot even now, but he held off. He'd have to cut the acceleration to fire, at least if he wanted any chance of hitting.

Then, a few second later, he released the throttle, feeling the tremendous force vanish instantly, replaced by the relief of freefall. He shook his head, struggling to restore his clarity, even as his finger moved to the firing button.

He stared at the screen, blinking several times, trying to will away the effects of the heavy g forces. His vision improved, slowly, but there were still spots floating in front of his eyes. He

tried to ignore it, to focus on the shot. Had adjusted his aim…
then again. And he fired.

A hit!

He watched the icon blink off his screen, and almost immediately after, Timmons took out another one. That left a single
bomber, heading right at *Dauntless*. He watched as the tiny ship
launched its torpedo…and then in horror as it kicked in its own
thrust at full power, heading directly toward the battleship.

Oh my God…he's going to ram…

Chapter Thirty-Nine

Bridge
CFS Dauntless
Varus System
308 AC

"Primaries charged, Captain."

"Fire."

Barron watched as his big guns shot again. Somehow, Fritz had done it. He didn't want to think of how much of an overload she'd pushed through *Dauntless*'s tortured wiring and power systems...or of the variety of cataclysms that might have caused if things had gone differently. But once again, his sorcerer of an engineer had performed the impossible.

The bridge erupted into wild cheers. The shots had hit, both of them. Solid impacts amidships. And an instant later, *Intrepid*'s fire repeated the effort.

Barron waited for the damage assessments, but even before they came in, he could see from the raw data that the enemy ship was hurt. She was bleeding air, and spewing frozen fluids into the frigid blackness of space. Her thrust had dropped, not fifty percent, not seventy percent...but completely. That wasn't absolute proof that her engines were offline, but, in the situation, it was close.

"Fritzie, I love you. Now do it again, one more time and

we're there!" He'd slapped his hand down on the comm unit, connecting to his engineer's line.

"I'll try, sir…but I'm frying kilometers of new line that we laid. This is going to set us back days on getting some real repairs done."

"Now is all I'm worried about, Fritzie. We'll think about what comes next when we get through this."

He closed the line, and turned toward the display. He'd intended to review the updated damage reports from the enemy ship, but then his eyes focused on a small dot. A single torpedo, heading straight for Dauntless. And behind it, a lone bomber. Accelerating.

He's already launched his torpedo…why is he still accel…

"Engine room," he shouted as he flipped the comm unit back on, "I need thrust now, forward…whatever you can give…"

But it was too late. The torpedo slammed home. *Dauntless* shook hard, and Barron knew immediately the hit had drawn his ship's blood. And the bomber was heading in on the same course as its warhead.

"Get me thrust…"

"Engines are offline, Captain. We lost the primaries too." Travis's hands were moving over her board so quickly, they were almost a blur. She rattled off another series of damage reports from the torpedo impact. Internal explosions, fires…casualties.

But Baron wasn't listening. His eyes were glued to the approaching fighter. He watched as it came closer…and then he saw as one of his defensive turrets scored a hit.

He felt relief…for an instant. His people had gotten the incoming ship. But then he realized the shot had come late. The bomber was destroyed, but in its death struggle, it showered *Dauntless* with debris, hundreds of chunks of metal and other components, slamming into the hull of his ship at tremendous velocity.

He heard alarms in the distance, and the bridge lights flickered again. His display erupted with reports. Power outages, systems down, crew members trapped in cut off sections…and then every screen on the bridge went dark.

He knew one thing, and he didn't need workstations or the comm to confirm it. His ship was in trouble.

* * *

"My God…did that bomber ram *Dauntless*?" Eaton stared at her screen, a look of cold horror on her face.

"It appears *Dauntless*'s defensive batteries were able to destroy the bomber before it impacted…but she was showered with debris from the blast." Nordstrom paused, reading the reports as they came in. "We're still getting power readouts, Captain, but it looks like her weapons and engines are offline."

Eaton felt the urge to comm Barron, to rush to her companion's aid. But that wasn't her job, not now. *Dauntless*'s damage left her solely responsible for dealing with the enemy battleship, and that was just what she was going to do.

"Maintain fire, Commander. That ship is ours to deal with now."

"Yes, Captain."

Eaton stared at the display. The Union battleship was hurt, she was sure of that. But she didn't know how badly. The lights flickered as her primaries fired again. Another hit. The enemy's engines were still shut down, but its heading was directly toward *Dauntless*, and it was about to enter secondary range.

If they open up on Dauntless in the condition she's in now…

"One more shot with the primaries, Commander. Then I want all secondary batteries ready to open fire." As powerful as her main guns were, Eaton knew right now she could probably do more damage to the wounded vessel with a full broadside.

"Yes, Captain." A few seconds later: "Captain, I have Commander Jamison on the comm."

"Yes, Commander."

"Captain…I can't get through to *Dauntless*. I'm going to lead the fighters on a strafing run on that battleship."

"You've done enough, Commander."

"If we'd done enough, *Dauntless*'s comm wouldn't be down. She wouldn't be bleeding air."

Eaton hadn't initially heard the guilt in the pilot's voice, but now it was coming through loud and clear. "Commander, your force did an outstanding job. It's not your fault *Dauntless* was hit." But even as she spoke, she knew it was pointless. She didn't know *Dauntless*'s strike force commander well, but she thought she understood the man, mostly because he seemed very much like her. And she knew no one's words would salve her guilt if she'd been in his shoes, regardless of how unfair it was.

"I'm the one who let that fighter through…but we're going to do what we can to help take that ship down before it does any more damage."

Eaton realized he wasn't asking for permission. He was just letting her know. She had the authority to order him to return, to land on Intrepid, but she suspected he'd only disobey…and that most of those pilots out there, the best of two Confederation battleships, would follow him. Mastering the art of command was sometimes about knowing when not to give an order.

"Good luck, Commander." She'd seen pilots throw their lives away in fits of guilt and anger. Jamison didn't seem like that type, but she'd watched it happen before, more than once with officers where it hadn't been expected. "Be careful, Commander," she added. "We need every one of you."

"Copy that, Captain." Jamison cut the line.

"Captain, *Cambria* and *Astara* request permission to advance and engage." Barron had ordered the two escorts to remain back out of range. They had no place in a duel between giant battleships. But now *Dauntless* was out of the fight, and the enemy vessel was battered, its diminished fire focusing on Barron's crippled ship. Anything that finished off that vessel before *Dauntless* was destroyed was worthwhile.

"Permission granted, Commander."

Eaton turned toward the display, just as the lights dimmed again. *Intrepid*'s primaries scored another solid hit. She watched the damage reports coming in with growing excitement. Internal explosions, massive hull breaches. She dared to imagine the enemy vessel was near the end, when it dashed her hopes and opened up with half a dozen of its own primaries, the powerful x-ray lasers slamming into *Dauntless*'s stricken hull.

"All secondaries at one hundred ten percent power. Fire!"

She heard the distant buzz of a dozen of *Intrepid*'s triple turrets opening fire, almost as one. She was taking a risk pushing an overload through her guns. *Intrepid* was badly battered, and even a millimeter of damaged power line could blow one of the turrets, killing the crew instantly and wrecking systems all around it. But she didn't know how much more *Dauntless* could take. She didn't even know what was happening on Barron's ship. She was just sure she had to do everything she could to protect her comrade and his crew.

"Maintain fire. Increase power to one hundred fifteen percent. Keep pounding at that ship."

* * *

Jamison was biting back on the rage. He wasn't prone to such intense anger, but on some level, he knew if he didn't focus his hostility on the enemy it would bounce back on himself. He knew his small team of pilots had done an extraordinary job, better than they'd dared to hope when they'd hurriedly launched less than an hour before. But the consequences of letting that single fighter past seemed so devastating, it was all he could do to keep himself from replaying those final moments, looking for any mistake, any chance he'd lost to destroy that bomber.

"*Intrepid* and *Dauntless* blasted the hell out of that ship, and now we're going to help finish the job. There are hull breaches all over that monster…and I want every one of you to send a laser blast through one of them."

"We're with you, Commander." It was Timmons again. Jamison was starting to realize he liked the brash, aggressive pilot.

Jamison adjusted his thrust, bringing his ship on a direct line for the enemy battleship. He was close now, and his screen was lit up with readings.

Damn…that thing is in bad shape.

There were plumes of energy flaring out through great rips

in the hull, and its sides were scarred where whole turrets and sections had been vaporized. Its engines weren't offline…they were mangled remnants, blasted apart by at least two direct hits and the internal explosions that had followed. But somehow there were half a dozen laser turrets undamaged, and they were continuing to fire, even as the rest of the ship seemed to be well into its death struggle. And every time those guns opened up, *Dauntless* took more hits.

"We've got to put this thing down now," Jamison said grimly. "Pick your spots, and for God's sake, make it count."

He angled his own fighter in, pulling back on the throttle, adjusting his course, heading directly at the battleship looming ahead. He was close, and he was going to get a lot closer. He understood the distances involved in space combat, even at ranges normally considered point blank. But that wasn't going to do it this time. He was going in, to knife-fighting range.

He stared straight at his screen, watching as the enemy ship grew, the projection changing from a general oval shape to an actual representation of the vessel. His gaze darted down to the range figures. Three hundred kilometers.

He kicked in his thrusters again, decelerating, bringing his fighter almost to a stop less than one hundred kilometers from the battleship. His move would normally be suicidal…the defensive turrets that were marginally effective at normal ranges could blow away a ship so close and slow-moving. But he was gambling the vessel's point defense systems were down. It was a simple bet. If he won, he'd get a devastating shot in, one that could do some real damage, even with his fighter's small lasers. And if he was wrong—if he lost—he would die.

Fifty kilometers.

He'd never heard of any fighter getting so close to a capital ship, other than a friendly one it was landing on. It went against all doctrine, all training. It wasn't even supposed to be possible. But here he was. And he was going closer.

His comm unit was buzzing, but he ignored it. His pilots were trying to reach him, afraid, no doubt that he was planning to repeat the enemy pilot's suicide run. He couldn't argue, the idea had briefly passed through his mind. But he wasn't suicidal, just coldly angry. He had to do this, for himself, for Captain Barron. And nothing was going to stop him.

Twenty kilometers.

He could see the enemy ship now. Not on his scanners, not some electronic reconstruction on his screen, but the actual ship itself, just outside his cockpit's window.

He backed off on the thrust, slowing his ship further, creeping forward, as the kilometers slowly ticked away. He saw a series of explosions—actually *saw* them—as another of *Intrepid*'s salvos smashed into the stricken vessel. And still he went closer.

The ship was growing now in front of him, and as the seconds passed he could see the gaping wounds, the geysers of fluids pouring out and flash-freezing as soon as they hit space. He could see the flickering light of internal explosions and fires, boring their way through melting sections of hull before dying at they hit the vacuum of space.

He felt a wave of satisfaction as he watched the enemy ship slowly dying. He'd never been particularly vengeful, but now he imagined the crew of the battleship, consumed by the fires, blown out of giant rents in the hull…to see if cold or the vacuum killed them first.

His eyes focused on a section of hull directly ahead of him. It was the closest one to the last group of operable guns, the lasers that were still firing at *Dauntless*. Jamison knew the captain of that ship understood he was going to die. He was targeting *Dauntless* in the hope of taking one of the Confederation vessels with him. And Kyle Jamison would be damned if he was going to give him the chance.

He angled his fighter down, coming in less than a hundred meters from the battleship's surface. His gamble seemed to be paying off. If there'd been an operable anti-fighter turret on the ship, he'd be a cloud of debris by now. Even without enemy fire, operating this close to an enemy ship was deadly dangerous.

His hands gripped the controls tightly, his sweat-coated palms sliding around on the leather-upholstered throttle. He was holding his breath, and he had to remind himself to inhale and exhale. Every centimeter of his body was tight, tense.

He saw the great tear in the enemy ship right in front of him. It was over one hundred meters across, and inside he could see a deep cross section of shattered decks. The edges were jagged, rough from where the ship had cracked open, and the armor of the hull had melted and then refrozen almost immediately.

His finger tightened, and his laser fired. Then again. And again. He could see the blasts deep inside the enemy ship as his beams impacted on the unarmored interior. He watched explosions, the previously sealed compartments blasting open, spewing air and debris—and, he suspected—crew members into space's cold embrace.

Then he pulled back on the throttle, blasting at 2g thrust, just enough to clear the enemy ship and sail past. He was about to reach down and activate the comm, to answer the calls he'd ignored on his approach. But his eyes caught movement on his screen first. It was Timmons, his fighter less than a kilometer away, following his lead, coming in slow and steady, directly toward the battleship. And behind him, Rick Turner. And Olya Fedorov. All the pilots he'd led out on the desperate mission against the enemy bombers, nine fighters in one long, slow-moving line, coming in, picking their targets as he had, and unleashing death on the enemy behemoth.

Jamison brought his fighter around, cutting his thrust, watching as his comrades followed his lead. He was still looking a few moments later when the enemy ship rolled over, and its hull began to split right down the center. He stared with morose satisfaction as the great battleship continued its death throes, huge sections coming apart, yellow and searing hot white blasts of internal explosions pouring out through the lengthening cracks.

"We did it," Timmons shouted over the comm. "*You* did it! You led us in, Commander…now take us home."

"Form up on me," Jamison replied. But the excitement was already fading from his voice. Home. *Dauntless* was home. But he doubted her bays were operational, even if Captain Barron had managed to save the ship. This had been a victory—part of one, at least—but what was the cost?

Chapter Forty

Bridge CFS Repulse
Mellas System
308 AC

"*Dauntless* and *Intrepid* both survived?" Winston sat at the head of the conference table, a stunned expression on his face.

"Yes, Admiral. *Intrepid* was hiding in the dust cloud when we emerged into the system. We were chasing an enemy battleship we had engaged in Corpus, but we encountered two additional Union capital ships in Arcturon." Stockton paused, reaching out for the glass of water a steward had placed in front of him and taking a drink. He'd been picked up by a fleet rescue shuttle literally moments before his life support gave out. He was shivering from the cold and sucking the last bits of stale breath from his exhausted oxygen tanks, when they'd hauled him into the shuttle's bay and popped his helmet. The rush of fresh air had been nirvana, a feeling he knew he would never forget.

He put the glass back down on the table. "We thought we were in for it, sir, two fresh ships bearing down on us. Then we picked up fighters coming from the dust cloud. At first, we thought they were more Union forces, but then the ID beacons came in. It was *Intrepid's* entire complement, plus almost four squadrons of refugees from other ships. They hit the enemy strike bound for *Dauntless* and almost wiped it out."

"And then you destroyed the three battleships?" Winston's tone didn't express disbelief, at least not any overt suspicion Stockton was lying to him, but it was clear he was finding the whole thing hard to imagine.

"Yes, sir. Well, *Dauntless* had already taken out the first...we'd damaged it badly in Corpus. And we had the edge on the others once their fighter wings were destroyed. *Dauntless* and *Intrepid* were able to land and refit all our fighters, just about three full wings."

"Tell us about the supply ships." Van Striker was sitting next to Admiral Winston. Fifth Fleet's commander had shuttled over to *Repulse*—without orders—as soon as he'd heard about Stockton's rescue.

"It was a large convoy, nearly thirty ships. *Dauntless* and *Intrepid* destroyed most of them while the fighters went in and disabled and disarmed a tanker and two freighters. Then Captain Barron sent the Marines to take the vessels, and we used them to resupply."

"Striker turned toward Winston. "That explains a lot, Admiral. Certainly why we haven't been attacked here yet. The destruction of their expected supply convoy might have thrown a wrench into whatever logistical system they've been using to sustain their offensive."

"I don't know, Van. With all due respect to Lieutenant Stockton here, I find this entire story a little hard to grasp."

"You don't have to believe me, sir." Stockton fought back a wave of anger. He didn't particularly care for the pompous ass of an admiral who'd already lost half the fleet calling him a liar, however politely. But Winston was as lofty as officers got, and even a pilot as wild and defiant as Stockton knew when to restrain himself. He reached into the small bag attached to his belt and pulled something out. "I brought a message from Captain Barron, and scanner data on all the ships we faced." He reached out and put a small data chip on the table, perhaps with a bit more force than he'd intended. "It also contains data on the main reason I made the trip back here. We captured a Union nav data unit. It had the dispositions of their entire fleet on it...

and it mentioned a massive mobile supply base, the nexus of the Union logistics. Captains Barron and Eaton decided to move forward and try to find and destroy the base...and they sent me back to deliver this nav data while they did."

Striker reached across the table and scooped up the data chip. "If that is true, Lieutenant, your dangerous journey—and Captain Barron's bold decision to operate behind enemy lines—could be vital to the course of the war." Striker didn't seem entirely convinced, but it was clear he was closer to it than Winston. The older admiral wasn't suspicious, not exactly, but it was obvious he was struggling with the implications.

"If Admiral Winston agrees, we will review all of this now."

"By all means, Admiral Striker."

"Thank you, sir." Striker looked over at Stockton. "You've had a difficult time of it, Lieutenant. One of the stewards will set you up in some quarters. You must want a shower, and certainly a decent meal. Maybe even a few hours of sleep. We'll send for you as soon as we've deciphered all of this. I'm sure we'll have questions."

"Yes, sir...I'll admit, a shower would be nice." He hesitated. "But, sir, with no disrespect...you'll go through it all right away, won't you? I left them all behind, Admiral, in enemy space. We've got to do something, act on that data."

"You have my word, Lieutenant. I will review this as quickly as possible. And then we will send for you again. But for now, get some rest, some food."

"Yes, sir. Thank you."

Stockton got up, surprised at how much trouble he had. He was exhausted, and he was only just feeling *how* badly. His legs had stiffened up, and he limped as he moved toward the door. He glanced back once, taking one last look at the pair of admirals, the two men who now possessed what he'd come so far to deliver. He had no choice but to trust to their judgment now... and trust was something that came very slowly to him.

He walked through the door, nodding to the steward who was waiting in the corridor.

"Right this way, sir," the man said.

Stockton nodded, and he followed the steward down the corridor to the lift. He was thinking of a number of things—the data he'd brought, what the admirals would do with it, even the shower that awaited him. He was thinking about *Dauntless*, about his comrades. Kyle, Captain Barron, Blue squadron.

And Stara. Most of all he was thinking about Stara, and what series of terrible battles she'd likely been through since he'd left.

* * *

"If you think the Confederation forces sent one shuttle into this system to lead our fighters around on a wild goose chase before self-destructing, you're even stupider than I thought." Hugo D'Alvert was raging, as only he could. He'd been getting a steady diet of half answers—and no answers—to his inquiries about the recent incursion, and he was fed up with it. "No," he continued, his voice caustic. "Something else is going on, and I want to know exactly what it is. I want every cubic millimeter of this system searched. I want every capital ship to launch fighters, and I want them doing systematic sweeps of assigned sections of space. There is something else out there—or there was—and I want to know what."

"Sir, the level of fighter operations you are proposing would further deplete our resources. Our fuel situation is…"

"Damned the fuel situation, Captain. Our supply fleet mysteriously vanishes, and then we have Confederation incursions in this system…by all accounts originating not from Mellas, where we know the enemy fleet is massed but, in all likelihood, from Ultara, which is in our rear. Where did that shuttle come from, Captain? How did it get here, and what else accompanied it? What is still out there, hiding along the periphery of this system? And why?" D'Alvert glared at the aide with withering intensity. "Until you can answer those questions, Captain, don't waste my time with concerns I can do nothing about. We have fought the Confederation before, and they have always survived despite whatever material advantage we have brought to bear. If they are planning something, a trick or stratagem, now is the time for them to spring it. I will not be blindsided by them, as so many of my predecessors were. We cannot move forward and finish this until we know what is happening…to our supply, and with these unexplained contacts."

"Yes, sir."

"Issue the order, Captain. I want all ships to maintain squadrons in space around the clock until we discover whatever is out there."

"Yes, Admiral. At once, sir." The aide snapped off a salute and hurried from the room.

D'Alvert stood where he was for a moment. Then he sat down on one of the chairs around the conference table. He was close…so close. Victory was his for the taking, a triumph that would lead him on a path to absolute power. He couldn't allow any Confederation trickery to stop him now. He'd read accounts of the earlier wars—and he'd fought in the last one as a junior officer. One thing after another had intervened to save the Confederation. Rance Barron's brilliant campaigns, the death of the Union's First in the previous conflict. D'Alvert had planned too long, taken too many chances to get here to see it all lost now.

What is it? Did the enemy somehow interdict my supplies? If so, how?

He shook his head, feeling tension taking him, paranoia building inside. He had his fleet in position, the disordered enemy so close to defeat. And yet, somehow, he felt it slipping away.

How could the Confederation have gotten to that convoy? How could they have sent a shuttle here from Ultara? It makes no sense. Unless…

He slapped his hand down on the table, his thoughts moving to the rest of the Presidium, to his other admirals. Perhaps it wasn't the Confederation at all. Could a domestic rival have intervened? He'd considered Admiral Lund to be loyal to him when he'd assigned the officer to convoy duty, but now he wondered. Was there some kind of plot in motion? Had he focused too much on the foreign enemy and relaxed his guard against those operating in the shadows, behind his back?

He wondered who he could trust. Sabine, of course. Renault was his closest aide, and he felt real affection for her, almost as a daughter.

Which was exactly where an enemy would try to strike. What could be more effective than treachery from those closest to him? *But then who can I trust?*

Suchet?

The Sector Nine liaison's name popped into his head. He didn't know the man. He'd never even heard of him before he'd set foot on *Victoire*. But perhaps that was a plus. His enemies would have moved against his friends, against his allies. It was the natural place to foment treachery. Even those closest to him couldn't be trusted. There were too many ways to suborn even unwilling traitors. Rewards, blackmail, addictions, sex, threats against family and loved ones. No, he couldn't trust anyone in his inner circle. Not now.

Suchet had checked out. He was who he said he was, and he was here for the reasons he'd stated. But he was connected to Sector Nine as well. Having the intelligence agency on his side would be valuable, extremely so.

Perhaps…

He sat for a moment, still, staring at the wall opposite his chair. Then he decided.

His hand moved toward the comm unit, hovering above the button that would connect him to Renault's line. But he stopped.

No, not through Sabine. Not through anyone.

He reached out to the small tablet on the table, his fingers navigating over the screen, pulling up the contact info for everyone on *Victoire*. There it was. Temporary channel assigned to Colonel Gregoire Suchet.

He flipped on the comm unit, entering the code by hand.

"Suchet," came the response through the unit.

"Colonel, this is Admiral D'Alvert." He paused, looking around the room and back toward the door. "I'd like to discuss something with you if you have time…"

* * *

"If this information is correct—and it certainly appears to

be—the entire Union advance depends on a massive supply and logistics center that moves forward as the front lines advance."

"How is that possible, Admiral Striker? Anything large enough to serve that purpose would be too big to fit in the transwarp links. How could they move it behind the fleet if they can't make jumps with it?"

"I can't answer that, sir, but we cannot argue that they have moved much farther and faster than our understanding of logistic would allow. They have clearly developed something we don't understand, and that being the case, I see no reason to doubt the data Captain Barron sent us. Perhaps this supply 'base' is actually a number of smaller facilities, each capable of transwarp travel."

"Perhaps. As you say, something has enabled their relentless advance. Nevertheless, even if there is such a supply base, there is little we can do about it save to hope that Captains Barron and Eaton are able to temporarily interdict the flow of supplies. Their destruction of the one supply convoy seems to answer the question about why the enemy has not yet invaded Mellas. If nothing else, their efforts have bought us a little more time. That is something." There was no excitement in Winston's voice. He sounded like a man whose execution had merely been postponed.

Striker looked across the table, his eyes probing his comrade. Winston had been a hero for as long as the younger officer could remember. The admiral had been part of Rance Barron's legendary cabal, the group of young officers who had swept away the old order, and turned the Confederation navy into the force that beat back previously irresistible Union advances. Striker had come up in the service admiring the famous officer, idolizing him almost as much as he had Barron himself.

And now he has become what he once helped to replace...old, prevaricating, nailed to his own orthodoxy. He looks at this data, at news of Dauntless's *and* Intrepid's *actions, and he sees no opportunity, only a brief respite before the end he has already resigned himself to...*

"Admiral...I believe there is much more to this data. First, Captain Barron and Captain Eaton are both outstanding young officers. It may not be possible for them to find and destroy the enemy base, but the nav data suggests the Union has moved almost all its forces forward. They are clearly unprepared for a task force as strong as two battleships to be loose along their lines of communication. It is very possible that *Dauntless* and *Intrepid* will continue to have a disordering effect on enemy supply. At least for some period of time." His last words were darker in tone. He believed in Barron and Eaton, but he was also a realist, and he knew there was a vast difference between the two captains making a contribution to the war effort by damaging enemy supply operations...and of their surviving the effort. For all he wanted to believe, he just didn't see how the two ships could make it back to return to the fleet.

"No doubt they will, Admiral," Winston said, his own dark mood seemingly unchanged. "But what does that do for us, save delay the inevitable?"

He doesn't believe we can beat them...

"Sir, I urge you to look at the situation more closely. Yes, the enemy concentration increases their strength in any battle, either in Mellas, or in Turas if we were to advance from here. But it also frees us from other concerns. Our fears that the enemy would move from Turas to Sagara and then Volland, for example—or even from Ghallus to Belatar—are baseless. They have concentrated their forces in Turas...and if *Dauntless* and *Intrepid* have indeed engaged and destroyed three enemy capital ships in Arcturon, almost all their strength is accounted for and facing us in the next system. We may also concentrate, secure that no invasion force is moving around us."

"That may be true, Admiral Striker, but it still leaves us outnumbered and outgunned, just in one battle rather than several. I do not see how that alters the situation in any useful manner."

"It is true the enemy outnumbers us, Admiral," Striker replied. "That is both a sobering reality...and perhaps an opportunity as well. We are resupplied, and they are not. It is likely they are not entirely depleted, but they must be weakened. If we advance into Turas and attack, we will be outnumbered, but we might have certain advantages as well. Beyond the data from the enemy nav unit, Lieutenant Stockton's scanners recorded considerable information on enemy dispositions in the Turas system. We know where their ships are deployed. We might be able to develop an advantageous battle plan, one that forces a longer battle—one of maneuver, of attrition, rather than numbers. That would exacerbate the enemy supply situation, exploit their weaknesses by making them expend fuel and ordnance in the protracted struggle."

"You would risk the destruction of the entire fleet?" Winston was incredulous. "You would advance against a superior enemy, throw our forces into a complex and protracted battle, one from which it might become impossible to effectively withdraw?"

"Sir, we *must* defeat the enemy. Buying time does nothing for us. We have to stop their advance somewhere. If we don't, they will continue into the heart of the Confederation. If we wait here, we cede the initiative. We give them time to—address—*Dauntless* and *Intrepid*, and the damage that has been done to their supply lines. We *have* to do something. And I think Captains Barron and Eaton, and Lieutenant Stockton, have given us an opportunity."

"I'm afraid I cannot agree with you, Admiral Striker. I am charged with command of our combined fleets, and my primary duty is to preserve them. You would risk them on a wild gamble. Such an action might feel good, Admiral, but we cannot charge off heroically into a hopeless battle. Officers in our positions must be cautious…we must consider many factors before ordering any action."

"Sir…"

"No, Admiral Striker. I will not throw away First Fleet on some wild gamble…and I will not allow you to unduly risk Fifth Fleet either. An attack into Turas is out of the question. I don't even see how we can even hold Mellas. The enemy's supply disruptions *have* given us an opportunity, however…one to withdraw, to pull out of Mellas, perhaps to Halos. Or farther back."

Striker watched his commanding officer with growing horror.

My God, he's broken. The losses, the retreats…it's been too much for him. He will run from the enemy, and his weakness will destroy the

Confederation.

But he knew there was nothing to say, no words he could utter to change Winston's mind. He just stared back, stunned, terrified at the implications. Finally, he managed to say, "Yes, sir," the words scraping over his throat like a blade.

"Very well, Admiral Striker. Dismissed."

Chapter Forty-One

Bridge
CFS Dauntless
Varus System
308 AC

"Captain…I found Commander Fritz. She says she'll have internal comm restored in most areas of the ship in a few minutes."

Barron scooped up the portable communicator and held it in front of him. He'd sent Atara Travis to track down the chief engineer, and to get an idea just how close his ship was to being a total wreck. But first, he'd broken out an emergency kit from one of the lockers on the bridge and grabbed a pair of small comm units, giving his exec one of them so they could keep in touch.

"That's good news, Commander." He paused. "How are things, Atara? Really?"

"It's pretty bad, Captain, but a lot of it is more superficial than it seems. The lifts are all out. That was one hell of a trip here by ladder. I'm just glad I was going down and not up. Though the grav compensators are out in a lot of sections, so maybe I could have just floated up."

"Any word on the reactors?"

"Commander Fritz says both reactors are close to functional.

It's mostly some minor malfunctions near the reactors rooms made a hell of a lot worse by damage to the transmission lines. It looks like some pieces of that fighter slammed into one of the major power routing centers. Still, it's not all bad news. We don't have much functional right now, but as far as Commander Fritz can tell, the reactors, the engines, even the primaries, are basically fine. It's a lot of small and scattered damage that's causing most of the trouble. There's a good chance we can get some of these systems back online pretty quickly."

"Fritzie was right to start with comms. That'll make everything easier. Ask her about ship-to-ship…and scanners too."

"Yes, Captain."

Barron could hear Travis speaking, and another voice in the background, Fritz's.

"Sir, she says she'll have ship-to-ship comm for you in thirty minutes, maybe even sooner. But scanners will be a while. There's a lot of damage to the external systems, and she's going to need to send some EVA teams out before she can finish repairs."

"Very well, Commander."

"Captain, I think I can be of some help around here. Request permission to remain and assist with repair operations."

"Do it. Hell, if I knew the top from the bottom of a polarity wrench, I'd be down there too. Conscript anybody you need, Commander. I don't care what their normal duty is. There's nothing on this ship right now—nothing—except for the repair operations. Get it done."

"We will, sir."

Barron looked around the bridge. The main lights were on, but the persistent flickering told him the power lines feeding the bridge were in less than perfect shape. The workstations were still down, but he didn't think the issue was on the bridge.

Probably in the data processing center…Fritzie will get someone on that as soon as she can.

He was uncomfortable—a massive understatement—at sitting here blind, with no idea of what was happening out in space. The enemy ship had been hit hard when he'd lost scanners, and he knew Eaton would have kept pounding away at their adversary. He'd felt *Dauntless* shake a few times as enemy laser blasts slammed into her, but that had stopped twenty minutes before. Coupled with the fact that his ship still existed, it suggested to him *Intrepid* had vanquished the enemy vessel, destroying it, or at least rendering it incapable of further attack. Either way, that bought some time to restore operations on *Dauntless*.

Barron knew there were hundreds of his people working on repairs, that everything that could be done *was* being done. But he felt helpless. He looked over the bridge, his officers all sitting around, trying with varying degrees of success to hide the fear they were feeling. It would have been easier if they'd had something to do, but with all their instrumentation down, they were just staring at each other.

"All right," Barron said as he jumped up from his chair. "Let's stop wasting time." He gestured toward Lieutenant Darrow. "You've got some engineering experience, don't you?"

"Yes, sir," the communications officer replied, somewhat meekly. "A little in the Academy, but then I changed my course of study to communications."

"Well, it's time to draw on old knowledge, Lieutenant." Barron opened one of the lockers, and leaned forward pulling out a heavy case of tools. "The damage control teams are working on the main systems, but let's see what we can do up here. I guarantee we've got some burnouts and other issues we can find and repair, so when operations come back online we're good to go." He looked around at the surprised faces staring back at him. "Let's move," he yelled, waving his arms upward. "Out of those chairs. If you don't know what you're doing then help someone who does. Check out your workstations for anything we can fix up here. If you need help, shout out for it. We've got enough combined knowledge to do more than just sit here and look at each other."

Barron didn't know how much good the bridge crew would do trying to troubleshoot and repair their stations, but he was sure about one thing. Even if they didn't fix one burned out circuit, they were a damned sight better off working on it than they were sitting around looking at each other.

*   *   *

Walt Billings pulled himself up the ladder, pausing and taking a few deep breaths. He was careful not to look down. He wasn't scared of heights, at least not too scared, but *Dauntless* was a big ship, and some of these emergency access tubes were awfully long…or tall, depending on perspective. He wasn't in any real danger of falling. The ship's engines were shut down, and without any thrust, the dampeners were providing only a small amount of simulated gravity down here. It he lost his footing, he *would* fall, but he'd drop so slowly, all he'd have to do was reach out and grab another rung. Still, he suspected the view of the two hundred meter drop would give him the sweats, and probably some stomach flops too, so he kept looking up rather than down.

He'd spent the last four hours tracking down and fixing severed power lines and replacing blown junction boxes. He had a crew of seven working under him, but he'd dispersed them all, sending them in different directions to test the lines and fix anything that wasn't functioning.

Dauntless was a big ship, a fact he sometimes forgot when comparing her to vessels like *Repulse* and *Defiant* that outmassed her by a million tons or more. But crawling around inside the endless kilometers of access tubes and corridors was definitely a job designed to make one appreciate the immensity of any Confederation battleship.

He reached up and pulled himself to the next level, turning to face a large hatchway. He punched his access code, wondering for about the hundredth time if the door would unlatch, or if he'd have to spend time and effort prying open a wracked and twisted chunk of metal.

He heard a loud click, and a smile slipped onto his face. The power was out in the whole section, so the door didn't slide open as it normally would have, but he slipped his hand into the small crack and pushed. The hatch slid open easily, and he climbed through.

He reached up, opening a small panel and pulling out a circuit board. He looked down at it.

Yup...fried.

The power feedbacks from the internal explosions had burned out electrical gear all across the ship. But this should be close to the last bit of it, at least along the main comm hub. He reached down and pulled a replacement from his sack. He pushed it in place, slipping it right into the grooves that had held the old, damaged one.

He pulled the small portable comm unit from his belt and held it to his mouth. "Commander, Billings here. We're done... at least, I think we got everything. Ready to test when you give the go-ahead."

"Do it, Lieutenant. It'll give us a chance to see how good you are."

Billings made a face at the remark. He respected the hell out of Fritz, and he considered her the best engineer the fleet had ever known, but she wasn't the easiest officer to work for. She wasn't even close. She really needed a course in the care and feeding of subordinates.

"Activating comm systems now, Commander." He took a step to the side, and reached out to a nearby workstation. He flipped a series of levers, and then he punched a code into the small keyboard. For a few seconds, nothing happened. Then the indicator lights on the panel began to come on. Green, across the board.

He tapped the small controls next to the workstation's comm unit, calling up Commander Fritz's channel. "Commander, this is Billings. Do you read?"

He waited, tense, hoping he hadn't missed anything.

"I read you, Billings. Good job."

He nodded, cracking a tiny smile. That was high praise from Fritz.

"Now, get your people down to main conduit C, Lieutenant. We've still got a break somewhere on that line, and we need to track it down."

"Yes, Commander."

He turned and moved back toward the hatch to the access tube, but then he paused and looked back at the comm unit.

Oh yeah! That's *how good I am, Commander!*

* * *

"It's good to hear from you, sir. You had us worried for a while." Eaton's voice was a bit distorted, and there was a small buzz in the background. *Dauntless's* inter-ship comm was functional again but, like many of its systems, small glitches remained.

"Thank you, Captain. It's good to hear from you too. Things looked a little grim there for a while, but it turned out a lot of systems were down because of isolated damage."

"That's good news. Honestly, better than I'd dare to hope."

"Thanks for watching our back, Sara. If your people hadn't managed to take out that enemy battleship, we wouldn't have survived long enough to get systems back online."

"Any time, Captain. Actually, there wasn't much left for us to do. Our tiny joint fighter wing did a lot of it. When you get a chance to review what happened, you might want to consider Commander Jamison for a decoration. I've never seen anything like the way he led that strike."

"I will, Captain. Jamison is one of the best, no question. And thanks for landing my strays while we were dealing with the damage." Barron hesitated for a few seconds. "What is *Intrepid's* condition, Sara? This is an extremely unhealthy place for us to remain, but we can't leave until we take out that station."

"We're in good shape. Primaries are still online, reactors close to full output. We've lost a couple of the secondary batteries, but mostly our broadside is solid too."

"How about your bays?"

"They're both operational...more or less. But we've lost one of the catapults, and there's a lot of damage to the supply delivery systems and the refueling lines. We can launch and land ships, and we can refit them, slowly. But we're far below normal operating parameters. I'm afraid to ask, but what shape are you in over there?"

"Probably better than you think. We've got lots of small glitches and malfunctions, but we're being pretty brutal in prioritizing repair operations, and most of the vital systems are at least partially functioning. Power generation is good—the reactors only suffered light damage. The power lines are still down in some areas, but we've installed some bypasses, and restored energy transmission to all weapons and to the bays as well. I've got my teams double checking the main guns, but they should be ready for action within an hour."

"That's amazing, far more optimistic than I'd have guessed. Your Commander Fritz really lives up to her reputation."

"Yes, she does. I'm very lucky to have her...and she's built one hell of an engineering team."

"So, when do we move on the station?" Eaton's voice was a bit tentative. Barron understood, and he felt the same way. Neither ship was ready for action, not really. Many systems were patched back together haphazardly, subject to renewed failure under the pressure of battle. Half of their fighters were trapped in *Dauntless's* still-inoperable bays. But none of that mattered. The Varus system was far behind enemy lines, a dangerous place for two Confederation battleships, and they'd pushed their luck far enough already. Waiting wasn't an option. Destroying the station was too important...and if fresh Union forces arrived, the chance would be lost.

"An hour," Barron said. "That will give us time to do a final check on the primaries. Then we'll move forward and engage." He hated the idea of charging in with their battered ships, and with no real idea of what defenses the station mounted. But he didn't see an alternative. "I doubt we'll be able to get the bays up and running by then...can you get your fighters launched?"

"Some, at least. We're still trying to refit and refuel them, but we've got about twenty ready to go now, and we'll have more in an hour."

Barron nodded, to himself as much as anyone. The situation seemed almost unreal to him. In the Academy they taught doctrine, how to proceed in battle conditions. But his rapidly increasing combat experience was teaching him that much of what he'd learned was useless. It was all well and good to review things under textbook conditions, but he'd found that such situations were shockingly rare in real combat. No Academy class would have discussed two battleships, both battered and depleted, attacking a massive enemy construct, with no idea of the weaponry they'd face and no useful estimate of what it would take to destroy the thing. But this wasn't a classroom, and the destruction of that supply facility could be the difference between victory and defeat, not just in Varus, but in the entire war. *Dauntless* and *Intrepid* had to go in. Barron knew that, and he was sure Eaton did as well.

"Very well. I know your people will do their best to use the hour well, as I am sure mine will. Then we go in, Captain. And we don't stop, we don't pull back until we've destroyed that thing…or it's destroyed us."

Chapter Forty-Two

"Open." Striker snapped the word, far more of his anger and frustration coming out with it than he'd intended. He was glad it was just the AI speaking to him, and not one of his spacers. The computer wouldn't take offense, wouldn't think he was angry at it.

He *was* angry, though, or, more accurately, he was frustrated. His meeting with the admiral had gone poorly. That hadn't been a total surprise. But realizing that Admiral Winston had lost his nerve, that the fleet's senior officer was shaken so deeply by the defeats he'd suffered, he was prepared to do anything to avoid risking battle again, was a sobering piece of news. And Striker had no idea what he could do about it. He'd argue his case again, of course, but he already knew that would be a waste of time.

The door slid open, and he walked through, into his quarters, pulling his hat from his head and tossing it toward the table. It hit near the edge and slipped off, falling to the floor. He turned to walk toward the small counter along the wall. He needed coffee. Actually, he needed far more than that, and for a passing moment he regretted the fact that he wasn't a drinker. The idea of really tying one on appealed to him, at least in a theoretical way.

"That bad, eh?"

Striker whipped around at the words, his hand moving reflexively toward the pistol at his side. He checked the movement before he actually drew the weapon. He was on his flagship, after all, not on a battlefield. But who the hell was in his quarters?

"No need to defend yourself, Admiral. I just wanted to have a word with you away from, shall we say…prying eyes."

Striker relaxed slightly as he recognized the voice. Holsten.

"You really have to be more cautious, Director. Someone a little more tense than I am might have reacted with combat instincts…and only find out later they'd decorated the far wall with the brains of the chief of Confederation Intelligence." He didn't bother to ask how the operative had gotten aboard his flagship without his knowledge. He suspected that had not pushed Holsten's skills to their limits.

"We all take our risks, Admiral. I have come to ask you to take another one."

"I am more than ready to face the enemy, Mr. Holsten. But that is not my decision."

"No, it is not…at present. Perhaps we have to do something about that."

Striker felt his body tighten. He didn't like where this was going. Not one bit. But he didn't respond. Something made him listen.

"Well, you haven't threatened to clap me in irons, so I'll take that as a good sign."

"If you're going to suggest what I think you are, I wouldn't be so sure."

"Admiral, what do you think of Rance Barron?"

"He's the Confederation's greatest hero."

"Yes, thank you for that answer directly from a textbook. Now, tell me what you really think of the *man*, of who he was."

Striker hesitated. "I suppose what has always struck me about the admiral's history was his courage. Not just in the face of battle, but in doing what had to be done, in stepping up when the Confederation needed him."

"And what do you think that means, 'stepping up'?"

"Taking command of the fleet, of course. Convincing the Senate to go along, rallying the officers, giving the people hope."

"Convincing the Senate? Is that what you think he did?"

Striker didn't respond. He wasn't a naïve man, and he'd always suspected Admiral Barron's actions had been more aggressive than the fawning histories suggested.

"Admiral, I am going to tell you the truth. You will have to decide if you believe me, but I trust you will not find it surprising that Confederation Intelligence knows *exactly* what happened in the middle of the second war with the Union."

Striker stood motionless, listening. Part of him wanted every detail, and part wanted to cover his ears, to flee the room.

"Admiral Barron *seized* control of the fleet. He was not appointed, he was not placed in command by a superior officer. He and a cabal of officers launched a carefully-planned operation to capture and imprison several of the fleet's highest-ranked commanders, along with hundreds of members of their staffs. He did not seek to injure any of them, though there was fighting on several ships, and there *were* casualties."

Striker moved to the side, pulling a chair over from the table and sitting down. He definitely didn't want to hear anymore, but it was like a drug, and he couldn't stop listening.

"Suffice it to say there were forged orders and a broad campaign of well-meaning deception. Many of the spacers—most perhaps—who followed Admiral Barron into that first resurgent battle did so under false pretenses. Had he lost that fight, there is little doubt he would now be regarded as the blackest traitor in Confederation history rather than the greatest hero. Assuming, of course, there would have been a Confederation without his victory."

Striker wanted to say something, to argue. His mind reeled, trying to doubt what Holsten was telling him. But somehow, he knew he was hearing the truth.

"His victories legitimized his actions, Admiral. First with the fleet, which came to almost worship him as he led them from defeat and despair to victory. Then with the people, who anointed him the savior of the Confederation. The Senate was enraged, of course, at least at first. There were bills drawn, warrants of arrest, charges of mutiny and high treason…but it became a practical impossibility to move against the admiral as his triumphant campaign continued."

"Are you saying that Admiral Barron threatened the Senate? That he dictated terms to them under the guns of the fleet?"

"No, Admiral, not precisely. Admiral Barron's brilliant leadership changed to course of the war so quickly, the Senate could not oppose him openly. The politicians were irate, but they were afraid too. We'll never know what Rance Barron would have done if he'd been pushed too far, if the Senate had declared him an outlaw and ordered the fleet's officers to oppose him. Would he have sacrificed himself, surrendered to face trial and execution? Or would he have turned his forces on the Senate? There is little doubt most of his spacers and Marines would have followed him in any endeavor. It is a credit to him that he did not use this power. The Senate quietly 'disappeared' all the actions it had taken against him, and he remained the senior admiral of the fleet as the peace was negotiated. The people adored him, and those who had voted on proclamations of treason against him began to shower him with public honors."

Striker looked across the room at the spy. "I understand why you have told me all of this, Mr. Holsten, and, while I find it all quite disconcerting, I do believe you. But *I* am no Rance Barron."

Holsten didn't move, didn't flinch. He just returned the stare silently for a moment. Then he said, "Admiral…*Rance Barron* wasn't Rance Barron, at least not what you know of by that name. He was a young admiral, sworn to follow the commands of those who outranked him. Until he realized that the Confederation he loved was on the brink of ruin. Then he acted." Holsten's stare was cold, fixed. "What will you do?"

"What do you expect me to do? I don't have a network of support, especially in First Fleet. I don't have the reputation Rance Barron had, the following. Am I supposed to move against Admiral Winston? Imprison him? Kill him?"

"I assure you, Admiral, I have no animosity toward Arthur Winston, nor any desire to see him harmed. He is a loyal officer, if one of mediocre skill. His legacy, I'm afraid has more to do with his good fortune in having been in the inner circle of a man of true capability. The loyalty he showed toward Admiral Barron was certainly commendable, as, in its own way, so is his longevity. But we have allowed the Union to prepare far too long for this war, and I confess on my part that our intelligence efforts failed to warn us of their true strength. Admiral Winston cannot stop the enemy invasion. Endless debate in the Senate cannot stop it. Any route through normal channels—any legal effort—is doomed to fail. If we are to save the Confederation, we must act…and we must act now."

Holsten stood quietly for a moment, giving Striker the chance to digest what he was saying. Then he stood up and walked across the room, extending his arm. There was a small data chip in his hand. "This chip contains orders relieving Admiral Winston and appointing you as commander-in-chief of the combined fleet. It is, of course, a forgery. But it will be weeks before any confirmation can reach fleet headquarters for confirmation. Take command of the combined fleet, Admiral. Do what we both know must be done…now, while you can. Because after this, it is unlikely I will be able to give you a second chance. If our plan fails, you will have a chance to escape the consequences. You can claim I gave you the orders, and you believed them to be genuine. I, on the other hand, likely face an unpleasant result, whether you succeed or not." He hesitated. "But it is of no matter…if you succeed, it is well worth my sacrifice to save the Confederation. And if you fail, I have no desire to outlive it."

Striker reached out and took the chip. He held it in front of him, staring at it, a look of undisguised horror on his face. He didn't react, didn't say anything. He just sat there.

"So, Admiral," Holsten asked softly, "what will you do?"

* * *

"I am sorry, Admiral Winston."

The old officer stared back across the table. There was surprise in his expression...and anger, hurt. Striker thought he saw relief as well. Holsten had crafted the false orders well. Winston was being recalled, not in disgrace, but to take command of Third Fleet, to prepare it for the defense of the Core Worlds. It didn't make sense, not really, but it was enough for Winston to save face, and that made it easier for him to accept. At least that's what Striker hoped. He was all in now, and he had Marines loyal to him just in the next room, but he was praying silently that Winston didn't push him to that.

"Why didn't this come through normal fleet channels?"

Another good question, and one that Holsten's ingenuity had anticipated. He had been standing behind Striker, silent, but now he answered.

"The document is clear on that, Admiral. Fleet channels have been compromised. That is why the order was entrusted to Confederation Intelligence at the highest levels. I considered it so important, I decided to deliver it myself."

Striker watched and waited, his stomach twisted in knots. He was ready to face the enemy fleet, to fight the desperate battle to stop the irresistible Union advance. But he wasn't entirely sure he had it in him to issue the necessary orders if Winston resisted...to watch his Marines drag the admiral away. And, even if he could, he was on *Repulse*. An attempt to arrest the admiral on his own flagship could go wrong in more ways than he could count, and any number of those could lead to open fighting between Confederation personnel.

"You will note, Admiral, that the document bears the Senatorial Seal. I urge you to request confirmation, though it will take some days for a communique to reach Megara, and as many more for the response to return."

Striker stood silently, amazed at Holsten's iron control. The intelligence director knew what would happen if that confirmation request reached the Senate, and yet he was inviting it, asking for it. Striker knew he faced the likelihood of death and defeat when—if—he was able to take over the fleet, but he still gave thanks his career had been in the military and not the spy services. He couldn't imagine playing a role—lying—so well, with such rock-solid poise.

Winston sighed softly. "No, I don't need confirmation, Mr. Holsten. The dispatch is in order, the seal valid. If the Senate feels I am needed more with Third Fleet, so be it. As I consider it, I begin to understand their thinking. First Fleet is lost, the remnants will have no choice but to retire toward the Core. This transfer will allow me to begin preparations for a last ditch defense."

Striker watched in amazement. Winston's suspicion, to the extent it had existed was being cast aside, his ego creating justifications, convincing him the transfer was a promotion of sorts, a final attempt to rely on him for salvation. He wondered how much Holsten had manipulated him into making the choice he had. He didn't think he'd been led down any path against his own judgment, but the intel chief appeared to be a master at influencing peoples' actions.

"I have a shuttle prepared for you, Admiral. There is a fast escort ship waiting to take you back to Megara to assume your new command. I'm sorry for the short notice, but the Senate was quite clear that they wanted you with Third Fleet as quickly as possible. With your permission, we can dispatch a steward to pack your things."

"No apologies necessary, Mr. Holsten. And yes, that would be fine. If you can send my belongings to the cruiser before we depart, I would be appreciative."

"Consider it done, sir," Striker said softly. "I will see to it myself."

"Thank you, Admiral." Winston looked over at Striker. "Take care of my people."

"I will, sir. With my life. I hope you know that."

"I do, Admiral Striker." He paused. "Admiral, I beseech you to exert the greatest care in your command over the fleet. We are at a terrible disadvantage here. I beg you, do not throw our ships away in a hopeless attack. You must retreat from here…you cannot win a fight now. All you can hope to do is delay the enemy advance while I get Third Fleet ready to defend the Core."

"I understand, sir." Striker's answer wasn't exactly agreement, but it sounded enough like it to satisfy Winston. He'd almost argued, telling the admiral he had no intention of yielding system after system, abandoning billions of civilians to the invaders. But there was no point. Winston was broken, his spirit gone…but his body would be gone soon too, and then Striker could set his plan in motion. He knew his attack was a desperate act, and he was terrified about the battle, about its consequences. He was wracked by guilt, disgusted with the way he'd attained command. But he knew what he had to do, and by God, he would see it done.

Chapter Forty-Three

"The primaries are online, sir. Reactors at ninety-seven and eighty-eight percent capacity, respectively." Fritz was rattling off her report, exceeding even Barron's outsized expectations of her performance. "I can get you up to 6g from the engines, anything more than that is iffy. Damage control teams positioned around the ship ready to address any malfunctions or new damage… and we *will* have issues. These systems are cobbled together the best we could manage, but it will take days to get more secure repairs in place. I couldn't get the bays operational, sir. We tried, but there's just too much damage. Even if we could have gotten a launch tube working, the rail systems to move ordnance and the fuel lines are so much junk. It will take two days, at least, to get to even partially operational status…and longer to get back to anything approaching normal."

Barron hated that half his force's fighters were stuck inside his ship's crippled bays, but he didn't lose sight of the fact that Fritz had worked magic in getting the crippled ship back into the fight so quickly. The problem was somewhat alleviated by the fact—hope, actually—that most of the station's fighters had already been destroyed. Most of what he'd *seen* had been destroyed, and nearly two hundred fifty fighters was one hell of a complement. But he didn't *know* there weren't more waiting in there.

At least Kyle's over on Intrepid, with three of the best pilots from Dauntless…

"Commander, put me on shipwide comm."

"Yes, sir…on your line."

"Attention all personnel, this is Captain Barron. We are about to move against the enemy station. Ideally, we'd have spent time doing extensive scans and sending in probes, trying to get an idea of just what we're facing. But you all know it's been some time since we've seen anything that resembles ideal. That thing is sustaining the entire Union invasion force—it's powering the advance that is killing the Confederation. If we can destroy it, or at least disable it, we can hurt the enemy far more than we can by destroying a few battleships. You all know the situation, you know the Confederation is in trouble. We can help. Fate has put us here, now…in the right place. So, whatever the station does, whatever weapons it fires or defenses it mounts, we're going to keep at it. We're going to stay in the fight until that thing is gone…or we are."

Barron paused and took a breath. He believed there were some times when it made sense to sugarcoat things for the crew, to protect them from knowledge that could sap their strength and divert them from their focus. Manipulation wasn't romantic, it wasn't honorable, but sometimes it was necessary. Not this time, though. His people would fight here for nothing less than the Confederation itself, for their families and friends and loved ones back on whatever worlds they called home…and that was—could only be—a fight to the death.

"We have battled together before. I know your quality, your courage, and your fortitude. Now, let's make sure the Union does as well!"

He slapped his hand down on the comm. He couldn't see most of his people, but from the expressions staring at him on the bridge, his speech had achieved its desired effect.

He reached down to the comm, flipping on the ship to ship line. "Captain Eaton, is *Intrepid* ready?"

"We're ready, sir."

He looked over at Travis.

"Commander, are *Cambria*, *Astara*, and *Condor* ready?"

"All escorts report ready, sir."

Barron sat silently for a moment, a fleeting thought of his grandfather drifting through his mind. *I'll try to make you proud.*

"Commander Travis…all ships are to advance."

* * *

"All right…we take down these fighters first. Not one of them gets away…not one. Then we re-form and hit that thing. Save your missiles…I want them launched at the station, not wasted chasing down these Union pilots." Jamison watched the wave of enemy fighters approaching his wing. There were twenty-three, apparently all that was left of the over two hundred the station had housed before the fighting started.

He had forty-six ships in his forces, and he'd have paired them off against twice that number of enemy craft. Still, his order about the missiles could cost some lives. His people could annihilate the enemy force with a barrage, but now they would have to endure the enemy warheads coming in with no answer of their own until they reached laser range. None of that mattered. The station had to be destroyed, no matter what the cost. And an interceptor's lasers weren't going to do much more than scratch the paint on that thing.

More than half of Jamison's fighters were stuck inside *Dauntless*'s disabled launch bays, but there was nothing to be done. *Be grateful you were on Intrepid, or you'd be hanging around pacing the corridors yourself.*

"You all know how important this mission is. So, let's do the work and get this done."

He angled his throttle, just as he saw a cluster of tiny dots moving out from the nearest enemy fighters.

Missiles.

He altered his vector, bringing his bird around, giving the incoming warheads a wide berth. The enemy missiles didn't have the range of the Confederation weapons, and the inexperienced Union pilots tended to fire too soon, before they had a good lock. The best tactic for evading them was to buy as much time as possible before they acquired, letting the warheads expend their fuel hunting around for a target.

The rest of his fighter wing followed his example, squadrons splitting up into small groups, individual pilots with one or two wingmen, moving away from the incoming missiles. An attack on an enemy battleship was often a carefully-choreographed effort, squadrons moving in tight formations, completing their runs before the next came in. But dogfights were wild, chaotic affairs, ships flying everywhere, evading enemies, chasing targets. Squadrons became hopelessly intermixed. It was the kind of thing that heavily favored skilled and experienced pilots, and Jamison knew that would benefit his people.

Still, missiles were dangerous, a fact that was confirmed a few seconds later when one of his fighters blinked off the display. Then another one.

Did they die because you told them to hold their missiles?

He knew it didn't matter, he'd done what he'd had to do, but it still hurt.

One of the enemy missiles picked him up, but he lost it easily, engaging his thrust and driving hard, right past the enemy formation. He kept accelerating until the missile ran out of fuel, and then he adjusted his thrust, gradually moving his vector toward the enemy fighters. He was behind most of them now, coming up from the rear. It took a little over two minutes to readjust his heading, and then he focused on the screen, watching as he got closer to his targets.

Two minutes passed. Three. The small circles on his display were growing, the range numbers displayed alongside dropping.

It was time to go hunting.

* * *

Barron sat silently, watching his fighters rip through their Union counterparts. Even without *Dauntless*'s squadrons, his forces out there had the upper hand. He was tense, of course, as his small fleet approached the station, though he did feel a bit of relief that the enemy appeared to be out of fighters.

"*Astara* reports ready, Captain." It was the last of the three escorts to check in.

Barron nodded, but he didn't respond immediately. The crews of the fleet's escort vessels knew, as its fighter pilots did, that defending the capital ships was always the priority. But that didn't make it easier for Barron to order the vessels forward. Risking loyal crews to scout out an enemy's defenses ran against his code of honor...but failing in his mission would be worse. Far worse.

"Escorts to move forward...acceleration at 2g."

Barron wished there was another way, but there wasn't. The only way to see what weapons that monster packed was to advance and open fire...and see what the response was.

"*Astara*, *Cambria*, and *Condor* all acknowledge, sir."

"Very well." He sat and watched as the small blips moved out in front of *Dauntless* and *Intrepid*, toward the almost unimaginably huge Union station.

"I want engines ready for thrust on my command. All weapons stations are to remain at alert. Advise *Intrepid* to do the same."

"Yes, sir."

"And launch another spread of probes. I want that thing covered from every angle. If they eject a load of garbage, I want to know about it."

"Yes, Captain."

Barron leaned back in his chair, his shirt pressing against his sweat-covered back. *Dauntless*'s life support was working perfectly, and the bridge was a crisp room temperature. But Barron felt like he was roasting.

"Sir, Captain Eaton confirms your orders. She is also launching an additional flight of probes."

"Very well."

Barron was staring at the display, but not really seeing anything. He was lost in thought, reviewing every scanning report, every scrap of data from the probes, trying to make sense of the thing he now had to destroy. He had more unanswered questions than solid info. What armament was waiting for his people? How heavily armored was the station? And, perhaps most vexing of all, how did the enemy move something that large through the transwarp lines?

Questions were coming far more easily than answers, but he knew the truth was there to be discovered. Somehow.

Suddenly, the a light flashed. He shook his head and focused his eyes back into the massive display. *Cambria* was gone, the small dot simply vanished from the floating blackness of the tank.

"Report, Commander," he snapped.

"Some kind of weapon discharge. It appears *Cambria* has been completely destroyed, Captain." Travis spoke stiffly, trying with limited success to hide her own shock.

"Scanning details, now! I want every scrap of data from the probes, the scanners, everything. And get *Condor* and *Astara* out of there now."

"Yes, sir." Travis leaned over her comm unit, snapping out orders to the surviving escorts. But before she could finish, the enemy weapon fired again. It had targeted *Condor*, but this time it missed, courtesy of the her captain's quick evasive maneuvers. The deadly beam ripped by less than three hundred meters from the small craft.

"*Astara* and *Condor* confirm, Captain. They are decelerating at full thrust."

Barron's fists clenched in frustration. The two smaller ships were still moving closer to the enemy. It would take more than a minute for them to reduce their forward momentum to zero, and more time to accelerate away from the deadly enemy station.

He felt the urge to order the battleships forward, to rush to the aid of the cruiser and scoutship. But that was out of the question. He had to know more about that weapon—power, range, rate of fire—before he could risk *Dauntless* and *Intrepid*.

But that meant sitting where he was, watching comrades die.

He slapped his hand down on his comm unit. "Commander Jamison…I need your people to attack now. Full acceleration." He didn't know if his cluster of fighters could do meaningful damage to a monster like the enemy station, but it was the only thing he could do, at least until he got some idea of what he was facing.

"Yes, sir…we're going in."

Barron just nodded. He had no idea what his fighters would be up against, how strong a defensive array the enemy facility possessed.

At least Jamison's people kept their missiles…

Barron knew holding back the interceptors' heavy weapons had probably cost three or four lives, pilots who might have survived if the wing had hit their adversaries with the weapons right away. Now he would see if it had been worth the cost.

"We're getting reports on that weapon, sir. It appears to be similar to their normal primaries, a bomb-pumped x-ray laser… just larger. Much larger."

"Estimated power output?"

"The AI's still working on it, but preliminary estimates suggest fifty to sixty gigawatts."

Barron didn't answer, he just stared over at Travis's station. He'd never heard of a laser with that kind of power. But then, he'd never faced a physical construct the size of the Union supply base either.

"Any estimate on the number of active turrets?"

"Only one so far Captain. It's on the extreme end of the facility. Analysis of the shape of the station suggests a likelihood there is a second one on the opposite end. Though there could be more than two. We just don't know."

"Range?"

"Data suggests roughly comparable to our primaries… though the power of the weapon will increase as the distance declines. Preliminary projections suggest the likelihood of catastrophic damage even to a battleship at closer ranges."

Barron nodded. That was the problem with lasers—as the

distances increased, beams attenuated, losing energy before the point of impact. The Confederation's particle accelerators hit harder at closer ranges too, but they lost far less of their effectiveness at long range. Barron couldn't even imagine the damage from a close-range hit at those energy levels. It could destroy *Dauntless* with a single shot.

"Captain, the AI suggests impact strength at our maximum primary range roughly equal to our particle accelerators. However, at secondary range, it projects hitting power double to that of our primaries."

Damn.

Barron had intended to close, to use the primaries at long range and then close to blast the station with the far more numerous secondary batteries. But now he had no choice. He had to stay outside of that thing's close range.

"Close to primary range, Commander. And I do mean extreme range. That thing is stationary, which should give us an edge in targeting. Advise the engine room I want random thrust patterns, and I want them coordinated with our own gunnery sections. Let's see if we can't maintain our aim while giving them something to think about."

"Yes, sir."

"And relay to *Intrepid*. I want both ships conducting coordinated operations."

"Yes, Captain."

The display flashed again, and this time *Condor* vanished. The scoutship was small, not a major component of the tiny fleet's fighting strength. But its crew had been fifty-three strong, and now they were all dead.

"*Astara's* status?" Barron asked, but he already knew. He could see the tiny dot in the display, blasting away at full, scrambling to escape its doom.

"She'll be outside estimated range in forty seconds, sir." Travis's use of the word "estimated" pounded home just how much they were relying on guesswork.

Barron tapped the comm unit again, more softly than he had done the last time. "Kyle, are you picking up those energy discharges?"

"Yes, sir."

"I want you to go after that location. There's a laser there, a big one. I need it knocked out. And we suspect there is one on the opposite end of the station too."

"Yes, Captain."

"Be as careful as you can, Kyle. That thing is bound to have strong close-in defenses. Break into two groups and hit both lasers."

"Understood, Captain. We're on it."

"Godspeed, Commander." *And I hope I haven't just sent all of you to your deaths...*

* * *

"That thing has already destroyed *Cambria* and *Condor*. *Dauntless* and *Intrepid* will be entering range in four minutes. That's how long we have to take it out. If we don't, it's going to start tearing apart our launch bays, our ships. So, if you don't want to sit out here with no place to land, watching your life support gauges slip down to nothing, give me your absolute best right now."

His eyes darted to the side, catching some movement on his scanner. *Astara*. The escort cruiser seemed to have made it back out of range. That was some good news. Now it was time to see if his people could create some more. Jamison had split up his force, sending half his fighters to the other side of the station under Timmons.

"Attack formation on me...remember, we're after that heavy laser turret. That's our priority, so I don't care what other juicy targets you see, hold your fire for the gun."

He stretched his hand out and gripped his fighter's throttle firmly. "On my mark...three...two...one...mark."

He pulled the control back, accelerating as he adjusted his vector, bringing him up over the station, toward the laser. He reached out, flipping a row of switches, arming his two missiles and bringing up the targeting screen.

The enemy's defensive fire had been weaker than he'd expected, but now all that changed. Suddenly, turrets opened up all across the giant station, riddling his force with harassing laser fire. He arced his throttle, moving his ship back and forth as it approached, doing what he could to confound the gunners shooting at him. It was all he could do. Breaking off wasn't an option, no matter how thick the enemy laser fire got. He had to take out that gun.

He saw symbols blinking off his display as the defensive array began to claim victims, but he ignored it. There would be time to drink to the fallen later, assuming anyone survived. For now, his people had a job to do.

He stared at his screens, evaluating the scanning data, triangulating on the exact location of the giant laser. His velocity was high, dangerously so for a ship operating so close to its target. But there was no choice. The station's point defense was gutting his attack force. His people had to finish their assault now, while they still had the strength to do it.

He leaned to the side as he kicked in his thrust to line up for his final attack run. That would be the deadliest moment, he knew, just before he launched his missiles. But that fact didn't deter him in the slightest.

He punched in the final data for his missiles' tracking systems. They were ready to fire.

He thought about going in close—crazy close—but that would be suicide. And a ship blasted before it launched did no one any good. Dying was one thing, dying for nothing quite another.

The range was less than two hundred kilometers, and the defensive laser fire was so thick it felt like he could walk on it. It was time. He squeezed his finger, launching the first missile. And then, right on its tail, he sent the second. Then he pulled back hard on the throttle, pulling his ship up and away from the station.

His eyes shot to his display, watching as the tiny dots representing his missiles moved quickly toward the station's looming bulk. The warheads slammed into the hull, exploding with all their twenty-kiloton fury…but he realized almost immediately, he'd missed. The weapons had impacted on the hull, digging a deep wound into the station's hull. But the laser was well defended, built into a deep cavity on the side of the station.

"That thing retracts between shots," he snapped into his comm. "You've got to get in there and get a missile through that opening, or your missiles will just impact on the hull."

He felt a surge of anger, of frustration with himself for not targeting his shot better. And now he watched as his pilots threw themselves at the laser, desperately trying to place the missiles exactly where they had to go. And he stared at the screen as each one of them matched his own performance, inflicting heavy damage on the target…but not hitting the sweet spot his gut told him would destroy the laser.

The last of his pilots pulled up, fleeing now from the deadly fire that had claimed a quarter of their number. Jamison pounded his hand on his dashboard, struggling to find an outlet for the rage he was feeling. The battleships would have to face the enemy's heavy weapon themselves. There was no other way now. Jamison and his people had failed.

He considered ordering his people to follow him in a strafing run, but he knew it would be pointless. The lasers on his fighters were laughably weak, and attempting to get close enough to use them to effect would cost him every one of his ships. His people had done what they could. It was time to go back.

"Let's get away from this fire," he said, trying to keep the frustration from his voice.

He pulled back on the throttle, checking on the display to make sure his squadrons were following suit. Then his comm crackled to life. It was Timmons, shouting excitedly, "We got it, sir…two solid hits. I'd bet the rest of my fuel we took that gun down."

"Well done, Lieutenant…my congratulations to your squadrons." The destruction of one of the enemy weapons was good news. At least the battleships would only have to face one giant laser as they approached…which they were doing even as his fighters were falling back into formation and blasting away.

One down…that's a lot better than none…
But it still tore at him that he'd missed that shot…

Chapter Forty-Four

Bridge
CFS Intrepid
Varus System
308 AC

Intrepid shook, and Eaton's body snapped forward against the straps of her harness. The enemy laser packed a serious punch, and she knew her ship couldn't take too many hits like that.

"Damage control, Commander." She was on her line with Merton almost immediately.

"The primaries are down, Captain. We've got serious hull breaches along sections D4 through E5. I've got reports of multiple fluid and gas leaks, and several areas appear to be cut off. Casualties are heavy, Captain, but I don't have any numbers yet."

"I need those primaries, Commander. Whatever it takes." She scared herself a little with her tone on those last three words.

"We're trying, Captain. I have half my people working on the guns right now. I think I can get them back online for you in a few minutes, but if we take many more hits from that thing, we're going to lose them for good."

"Just do what you can, Commander. As *quickly* as you can."

She cut the line. "Commander Nordstrom, I want evasive maneuver frequency doubled. We've got to evade that weapon's fire. I want random bursts of thrusts, one to ten seconds in duration. We've got to throw off their targeting…and while our primaries are down, we don't have to worry about throwing off our own aim."

"Yes, Captain."

Eaton watched the display as *Dauntless* fired her primaries again. The powerful beams lanced out and struck the station. The thing was immobile, and so big it was almost impossible to miss. But even the deadly power of the Confederation particle beams seemed to disappear in its enormous bulk. The hits caused damage, no question, but none of it seemed to threaten the overall structure. The two Confederation battleships would have vaporized an enemy capital ship by now, but the station just floated there, defiant, seeming to mock all attempts to seriously damage it.

"Captain, Commander Jamison requests permission to begin landing operations for his squadrons."

"Permission granted. Advise the commander that the bays are in pretty rough condition. His pilots are to exert all due care when landing." *Or one of them will wipe out, and the rest will be stuck out there.*

Eaton knew she was lucky the bays were operable at all. It was one lucky break, at least.

Now if Merton can just get me those primaries…

Even as the thought went through her mind, however, a troubling realization followed it.

We're not getting it done. We're damaging the thing, but we just don't have enough firepower to seriously threaten it.

The greater number of secondary batteries the ships carried might prove more effective, if not in destroying the station, at least in causing widespread damage. But closing the range was out of the question while that huge laser was still active. She was as determined as Barron to blast the thing to hell, but she was starting to lose hope that they'd get it done.

"Fighters landing now, Captain."

The fighters? Could her damaged bays possibly turn them over as bombers? The plasma torpedoes packed a serious punch…and just maybe three or four squadrons unloading could make the difference.

"Get me launch control, Commander. Now."

*   *   *

"Keep firing." Barron was standing next to his chair, the straps of his harness lying loose about the seat. It was a bad example for his people, but right now he didn't care. *Dauntless* and *Intrepid* had been pounding away at the station for over an hour. They were digging into it, tearing off great chunks of hull with each shot, but the construction was just too enormous. Barron had no doubt they were taking out factories and machine shops, fuel storage tanks, and all other manner of support systems...*but not enough of them.* That station had been built—and how it had been constructed was still a mystery to him—to support the greatest battle fleet post-cataclysmic space had ever seen. Barron knew it must contain hundreds of manufacturing facilities and vast materials storage, and his destruction of a few of those was not going to halt the Union invasion. He had to destroy the whole thing. But how?

"Commander Travis, advise gunnery crews I want that laser battery silenced." He was frustrated as hell. As much fire as his people—and Eaton's—had poured into the station, its heavy gun was still lancing out. Both battleships had been hit. *Dauntless* had suffered a glancing blow, but even that had been damaging. *Intrepid* had just taken her second hit, and reports coming in suggested she'd lost her primaries. That left *Dauntless* alone in the fight right now, and he had no illusions about how badly his ship had been hurt, or how tentatively Fritz had patched her systems back together. Time wasn't on his side. Sooner or later, fresh Union forces would arrive. Then it would be over.

"They're trying, sir," Travis replied. "That thing is well-situated. It's hard to get a line on just when it moves out."

"Then they'd better catch it deployed," he snapped back. But he knew even as he spoke, it was his frustration talking. The enemy weapon only deployed to fire, and it pulled back into its protective enclosure immediately after. He'd seen the reports from the probes. The gun was out for perhaps one and a half to two seconds each time, and there was no detectable warning before it fired. At seventy thousand kilometers, it was a quarter of a second before the light of the weapon deploying even reached *Dauntless*'s scanners. Then, it would take just over a third of a second for the particle beam to reach the station. That left barely one second to respond. The AI might manage it, especially against a mostly stationary target like the station. But there was more to targeting than deciding to fire. The particle guns took more than a second to execute a shoot order, even from full charge. That meant the only way to catch the enemy laser out of its shell was to guess when it would fire. And that wasn't a strategy that gave Barron a warm feeling.

Travis didn't respond. Barron was well aware his exec knew he wasn't expecting an answer. If anything, she knew him better than he did himself.

"Captain," Travis said a few seconds later, "Captain Eaton reports she is outfitting all available fighters with bomber kits and plasma torpedoes."

Barron was a little surprised. *Intrepid* had taken considerable damage in the battle with the station. It would be a minor miracle if Eaton could not only launch a wave of fighters, but manage to outfit them with the cumbersome bombing kits inside her tortured landing bays.

"Very well, Commander. She is to launch a strike as soon as she has the forces ready." He still wasn't sure he believed her bay crews could pull it off, but anything would help right now. Eaton had to be climbing the walls with her primaries down, and he realized his comrade was trying to come up with any way to lash out at the enemy.

Barron felt a renewed frustration at the condition of *Dauntless*'s own bays. The pilots over on *Intrepid* had to be exhausted, their ships worn down to a nub…and his squadrons were sitting around trapped on the ship, dying to get at the enemy.

"Commander Fritz is on your line, sir." Barron's head spun around. Anything from Fritz was vital right now.

"Fritzie, what is it?"

"Captain, I had a chance to review the latest scanning data on the station."

"Have you found a weakness?" Barron felt a rush of excitement. If there was one person in post-Cataclysmic space who could tear apart some kind of construction in her mind and find a way to take it down, it was Anya Fritz.

"Maybe, sir." She sounded a little uncomfortable, like she wasn't sure she should be bothering the captain with half-baked theories.

"Let's hear it, Fritzie. If someone on this ship is going to come up with something, it's you."

"Well, sir…I started looking at the thing, and I put my engineer's hat on, trying to figure out how they move it. We know they must, but it's pretty clear it wouldn't fit in a transwarp link."

"I know, Fritzie…we've all been wondering that. But that's not really a priority right now, is it?" He was disappointed. It wasn't like Fritz to waste time with off-point concerns during battle.

"Yes, Captain…I mean, I think it might be. A priority, I mean."

"How so?"

"I've been going over the schematics. We've got much better data from the probes now than we had before. I think it comes apart, Captain."

"Comes apart?" Barron was confused. "Yes, I guess it would have to if it doesn't fit, but I still don't see that it helps us that they have to disassemble the thing and rebuild it every time they move it." Barron still couldn't understand how the Union forces managed to pull that off in the time frame their lightning advance must have required.

"No, Captain. I don't think they take it apart, at least not the way you're thinking."

"I'm not following you, Fritzie."

"I think it's modular, Captain. I believe it's designed to separate into numerous sections, each small enough to be towed through a transwarp link."

"Modular?"

"Yes, sir…it's actually brilliant." Fritz's voice became animated, her engineer's appreciation for any device that met her high standards for ingenuity.

"Commander, I'm not sure now is the time to discuss the Union's technical achievement." Barron knew it was just the engineer inside Fritz reacting to something she thought was clever…but right now, in the middle of battle, he wasn't in the mood to hear how brilliant the enemy had been.

"No, sir…I mean, yes sir, I do recognize the shrewdness of the design. But that's not why I commed you. I think we can use the design against them. I think we can destroy it."

The last words hit Barron like a sledgehammer. "How, Fritzie? Tell me."

"If I'm right, that station is engineered for rapid disassembly and reassembly. I'd bet last month's salary those sections bolt together, and they come apart, probably in pieces small enough for a freighter or battleship to tow through the transit link…to another gas giant with enough tritium to support their refining operations, and a nearby asteroid belt for raw materials."

"You may be right, Fritzie, and I'm sure it's an engineering marvel, but I still…"

"Don't you *see*, sir? Those sections might be held together solidly enough for the thing to hold in orbit, and to withstand the rigors of normal operations, ships docking and pushing off and the like. But those connections have *got* to be weak points. If we target our fire there, we might be able to break up its structural integrity."

Barron felt a wave of excitement, but it almost immediately subsided. "That may be, Fritzie, but how can we find those spots? The thing is heavily shielded. We can't get any deep scans."

"I think I have an idea where, sir. I've been staring at the thing, and I'm pretty sure I've got it figured out. The Union techs who built it were clever as hell, but they still have to adhere to the laws of physics. Keeping the stresses on this thing from tearing it all apart, especially in orbit around a high-gravity planet, doesn't leave a lot a wiggle room."

"Are you saying you can tell us where to shoot?"

"Yes, sir…I think so."

"Fritzie, you beauty! Why didn't you just say that?"

* * *

"Thunder" Jamison's fighter was handling like a pig. He had no idea how Captain Eaton's crews had hauled the five-ton plasma torpedo casings to the bay, over the scattered wreckage of the rail system that usually did it, but he was definitely impressed. They hadn't been able to complete the refits, and the setups had a definite half-finished quality to them, a fact made clear with every buck and kick the fighter made as he tried to guide its course. If he'd been up against enemy interceptors, his small strike force of twenty-two refitted fighters might as well have been a wing of floating coffins. But the Union fighters had all been destroyed, and *Intrepid*'s makeshift attack wing had a clear line on the enemy station.

Jamison figured things were likely to get bad in close. The cumbersome, partially-converted bombers were hard enough to handle in open space…he couldn't imagine trying to run evasive maneuvers in them. But *Dauntless* and *Intrepid* needed all the help they could get. The attack on the station had been a losing effort so far, the battleships incapable of inflicting enough damage on their targets. Twenty-two plasma torpedoes were a powerful addition to the effort, and Jamison and his people had precise targeting instruction. If Commander Fritz was right, and if his people could get past the enemy defenses and launch their weapons, the assault could be the difference between success and failure. Between survival and death.

"Commander Jamison."

He thought he recognized the voice on the comm, but he had to check the readout to convince himself. "Captain Barron, sir." He hadn't expected to hear from *Dauntless*'s captain.

"I just wanted to wish you guys luck. If Commander Fritz is right, and if you and your pilots can pull this off, we just might be able to come out of this on top…and stop the Union offensive dead in its tracks while we're at it."

"Yes, sir. We'll do everything we can, Captain. Whatever it takes."

"I know you will, Thunder. Now get it done."

A surge of energy shot through Jamison, even beyond what he'd already felt. He couldn't let the captain down. He wouldn't. Not if it took everything he had left. Not if it took his life.

"Let's go, bombers. Beginning final attack runs. You've all got your assignments, and you know where you're supposed to hit. I don't need to tell any of you how important this is. One torpedo each, dead on the mark…and then back to the officers club. Are you with me?"

The response over the main channel was almost deafening. He had twenty-one pilots plus himself, every one of them hardened veterans. If they couldn't do it, no one could.

He directed his fighter toward the station, doing all he could with his sluggish controls to confound the enemy point defense. He was flying directly into a firestorm of laser blasts, but he managed to avoid them all, driving ever closer to his target. The station was on his display, a small white light marking his target area. Fritz had been clear about what he was looking for…and she had been brutally honest that nothing but a dead on shot would get it done. He still found it hard to believe they could blow apart something as massive as the station by hitting it at specific points, but he also knew better than to argue engineering with Fritz.

He saw a flash just outside his cockpit window, a laser blast barely missing his ship. *That was close…*

He brought his ship around and hit the throttle, thrusting right at the station. This was the most dangerous part. He couldn't swerve or mix up his vector as he had done on the way in. This was about targeting, about launching his plasma torpedo right at the designated spot. He gripped the throttle tightly, adjusting his aim. Then he launched the weapon.

He pulled away as quickly as he could after the torpedo had cleared its moorings…but he wasn't fast enough. A laser blast took his fighter behind the cockpit, near the engine. It wasn't a direct hit, but it cost him his thrust, and from the hissing sound in his ears, his life support as well.

He took one last look at his display, watching the torpedo, now a ball of super-heated plasma, heading right toward the bullseye. Bang! It slammed hard into the station's hull, exactly where Fritz had told him to put it. He felt a burst of excitement, followed by fear as he realized his air was almost gone. He sealed up his survival suit and snapped his helmet in place. He wouldn't have long out in space, perhaps an hour and a half. And he couldn't imagine how *Intrepid* could get a rescue shuttle out here, this close to the enemy.

He thought for an instant that maybe it was better to die here, in his fighter, than floating in the cold blackness of space. But Jamison wasn't a quitter. He hadn't lived his life that way, and he wasn't about to die that way. He reached out and grabbed the emergency latch, pulling hard.

The roof of the fighter, what was left of it anyway, blasted off. Jamison was sucked out by depressurization and thrown into the velvety blackness. He was just close enough to see the station, a spec in the distance. And he saw his fighter too as it careened away from him, almost the entire rear of the ship blasted away, a gaping hole where his engines had been.

Well, Jake, my friend…I was worried about you, but maybe you're in better shape than I am now. I hope you made it, brother…one of us should…

Chapter Forty-Five

Bridge
CFS Dauntless
Varus System
308 AC

"It's working. By the eleven hells, it's working!" Barron was standing in the middle of the bridge, as he had been for the past hour. *Dauntless* had taken a hard hit from the enemy mega-laser, and it had sent him careening across the deck and slamming into a bulkhead. But he'd just gotten up and brushed himself off, returning defiantly to his position, not a word from him or anyone else about his unintended lesson in why regulations required officers to be strapped in under battle conditions. Now, he was so excited, he doubted if he *could* have sat still, even if he'd wanted to.

"Keep pounding away with those primaries. And get a status update from *Intrepid*."

"Sir, Captain Eaton reports that her primaries are back online. She is charging them now."

"Yes!" Barron said, not quite as under his breath as he'd intended. He slammed his fist against his leg, hard. But he didn't feel a thing. He'd been openly insistent that his people would find a way to destroy the massive station, but inside, he'd begun to lose hope. Now, he could feel victory there for the taking, and he intended to reach out with both hands and grab it.

He stared at the display, at the projections coming in from the probes he'd sent directly at the station. The behemoth *was* splitting apart, just as Fritzie said it would, great explosions and geysers of flash-freezing fluids bursting out from multiple spots within.

The fighters had done their job, eighteen of them delivering their weapons, though six of them hadn't survived the attack. But the pilots who died had died as heroes, ripping open the great rents in the station's hull, exactly where Fritz had declared the weak points lay.

The fighters had done their part, and now *Dauntless*'s primaries were finishing the job. The deadly beams had done considerable damage to the station's hull earlier, but now they sliced into the carved out sections, cutting deeply through the unprotected spots inside and cracking apart the great segments of the Union immense construct.

He watched as *Intrepid* fired, her restored weapons lashing out alongside *Dauntless*'s and hitting right on one of the designated spots. Hull sections buckled and melted, and the ravening power of the particle beams bit into the body of the station. Then Barron saw it, exactly what Fritz had told him to expect. He had acknowledged the theory, but never truly believed until this moment. A chunk of the station, perhaps six kilometers long, broke free of the main structure, its shattered modular supports snapping from their moorings. The chunk of twisted metal, larger than any capital ship, drifted away slowly, carrying with it half a dozen docked freighters struggling to launch before they were torn to pieces by the shifting stresses of giant girders.

"Primaries, maintain fire. Engine room, I want 2g thrust... forward."

The enemy laser had ceased firing. No doubt the massive power plants were no longer feeding it the energy it needed to function. And without that deadly threat, there was nothing to stop *Dauntless* from moving forward, from bringing its entire broadside of secondaries into action and raking the enemy installation.

"Captain Eaton," he said, his hand still resting on the comm unit. "Can you close?"

"Yes, sir," Eaton replied, clearly feeling the same renewed spirit that had taken Barron. "Let's finish this thing."

"Absolutely, Captain…it's time to tear that monstrosity to debris."

"What say you, Commander Travis?" He turned toward his exec, a broad smile on his face. "Shall we blow the rest of this station to atoms?"

"Yes, *sir*," Travis responded with a sharp nod. "Entering secondary range in one minute. All batteries are ready to fire… awaiting your orders."

"Primaries…fire." He stood in place while the bridge lights dimmed again, and *Dauntless*'s ravenous primary guns ripped through space toward their dying target. Then, almost without pause, he said, "Secondaries, open fire."

Dauntless's laser turrets didn't have the direct hitting power of her massive particle beams, but she had more of them, twenty-four compared to two. And their recharge time was much quicker, their rate of fire vastly higher. The primary beams had done their jobs, ripping open the station's wounded hull. Now the secondaries would finish off the stricken enemy, pouring blasts of energy deep into the gaping rends.

"Message to *Astara*…watch those tankers and freighters. If any of them escape, they are to hunt them down." Barron had seen too many of his people killed and maimed. None of the enemy were getting away from here. His face tightened with focused rage. Not so much as a lifeboat would escape his grasp.

"*Astara* confirms, sir."

Barron heard the familiar whine as a whole broadside of laser blasts opened up, raking the target. His people had been driven almost past their endurance…they'd stared into the abyss, and no doubt many had made their own peace with death. But now victory was resurgent, and Barron couldn't move. He couldn't think of anything save standing there transfixed, watching the display.

Watching as the two battleships sliced the enemy station into chunks of worthless debris and pools of rapidly congealing slag.

* * *

"They got too cocky. They equipped the thing with a massive fighter wing, but only one supporting capital ship. The modular design was brilliant for portability, but it was a dangerous vulnerability in an attack." Sara Eaton sat in Barron's office on *Dauntless*. The station was gone, torn apart section by section along the weak points Fritz had identified. Every supply vessel that had been docked had also been destroyed, including one freighter that had gotten to within ten thousand kilometers of the transwarp link before *Astara* had taken it down.

Barron sat back, something close to relaxed. The war was still going on, of course, and his tiny fleet was several systems deep in enemy territory, but for the first time since *Dauntless* had arrived at the front, he felt there was some cause for hope. The Confederation was still in trouble, but he knew his ships had given another chance to the fleets and spacers on the front lines.

"There may have been some arrogance at play, Sara, but I think it's more that we're seeing the limit of Union resources. They did an impressive job in the twenty plus years we gave them since the last war, far more than any of us thought possible. They built that thing, *and* they got more battleships into service than our most aggressive estimates suggested was possible. But their resources had to run out at some point. They kept the station back multiple transits from the front. They figured they were safe back here. And ninety-nine times out of a hundred, they were right. When we're patting ourselves on the backs, let's not forget to give luck its due. How could they have anticipated the way our ships ended up behind the lines? That two Confederation battleships would meet up behind their line of advance, directly astride their communications lines?

"And the modular design was the only way to make the whole crazy plan work. It's all well and good to look back now, to critique it, but earlier we were dumbfounded about how they even moved the thing. The vulnerability we used to destroy it was an unavoidable aspect of its design, but we almost didn't discover it. We wouldn't have if Fritzie hadn't studied the engineering scans." *And I still don't know how she found the time to do that...*

"You're right, of course. You have one fine engineer there, Captain Barron."

"She is that. And she's very taken...so don't get any ideas about poaching." He flashed a smile across the table.

Eaton returned the grin. "Still, I don't know how they managed to build it. The cost...it must have been almost incalculable."

"At Confederation rates of labor and costs of materials. The Union is not like us, Sara. No doubt, those they conquered were reduced to virtual slavery to build that station. Forget trying to measure that thing in money...the true cost analysis there is one of human misery. How many workers killed, how many lives destroyed. How many millions lived on the brink of starvation so the Presidium could launch its war to conquer the Confederation?"

Eaton just nodded, and the two sat silently for a few minutes, each deep in thought.

It was more than a surprising level of Union production, Barron realized. It was Confederation neglect. The Confederation's famed productivity had, to a great extent, saved it in the earlier wars. The problem wasn't what a scared and mobilized Confederation could achieve when pressed against the wall...it was what a complacent and soft one did between conflicts. The Confederation fleet was only a shadow of what it could have been. But there was no way a republic could sustain public support for constant wartime levels of military production.

Barron knew the Confederation, if it survived, would face the same problems again. He had no doubt the worlds of the Iron Belt were in a frenzy of production, the terrified populations unwilling to oppose any level of military spending...now that it was almost too late. And it would *have been* too late if *Dauntless* and *Intrepid* hadn't found themselves into a position to strike the blow they had.

Barron sighed, weighed down by heavy thoughts...including one he'd tried to ignore, at least for a few moments. But it kept beating at the edges of his thoughts. They had to get back to the fleet. Somehow.

Both battleships were battered, their savaged systems pieced back together by sweating teams of engineers...and in danger of renewed failure at any moment. Now, their path led toward home, but Barron knew the bulk of the enemy's forces lay between his people and their comrades in the fleet. He had to figure some way to get his people past their adversaries, back home.

* * *

Timmons walked slowly down the corridor, lost in thought. He'd just returned to *Dauntless*, and while he wouldn't have thrown around the word "operational" to describe the launch bay, all his people had landed safely, as had the others who'd been stranded on *Intrepid*.

The fight to destroy the station had been a brutal and costly one, and he knew every squadron on the two battleships was riddled with vacancies...friends, comrades, skilled pilots who weren't there anymore. He was heading toward the officers club as custom demanded—a bit delayed, perhaps, by the extended fighting, but on his way nevertheless—to show his respect for the fallen. He and his fellow pilots would drink to them, and then, when duty called again, forget them. They would push forward to another struggle, another fight. And he had no doubt that more desperate battles lay ahead.

He'd gone through the motions many times since the war began. Too many. And for all the bluster about the "pilots' sendoff," as it was called, he remembered his fallen friends well. "Skinny" Pete Jenkins, Blake Daniels, Tony Trammel...and a crowd of other faces, staring back at him from the depths of his mind. He thought of them often. They were dead, but at least as far as he was concerned, they were far from forgotten. It was heresy, perhaps, to acknowledge that, a violation of the pilot's code, but it was true. He could lie to everyone else, but not to himself.

Are you on that list now, Raptor?

For as long as he could remember, he'd resented the other pilot, a rivalry perhaps made inevitable by the fact that the two of them had always been the best. But now, his only thoughts of Stockton were best wishes, hope that his counterpart had somehow completed his seemingly impossible mission, that he had survived against the odds.

He stepped into the officers club and walked up to the bar. Before he got halfway across the room, Rick Turner walked over to him and handed him a mug. "Red Eagle leader is here, pilots," he said, his voice so loud it was almost a yell. "Listen and listen good. The Red Eagles did the Blues a solid service in the battle we just fought." Turner reached out and put his hand on Timmons's shoulder. "We've had bad blood between us, and we'll probably have it again, but tonight you have Blue squadron's heartfelt thanks. Whatever happens, the Blues owe you one, Red Eagles, and we always pay our debts."

Timmons stared back at Turner, a smile slipping on to his face. "Thank you, Typhoon…" He looked around the room and raised his mug. "Thanks to all the Blues. You damned sure know how to fly, all of you." He raised the mug to his lips and took a deep gulp, watching as everyone else present did the same. Then he put his hand in the air.

"One more toast, friends…one that's been a long time coming for me." He paused, his smile slipping away to an emotional, almost pained expression. "To a man who is not here today. A magnificent pilot, a Confederation warrior whose courage is legendary, a man I have often been at odds with…but no more, at least not for my part." He panned his eyes around the room, lifting his mug high into the air. "To Jake 'Raptor' Stockton… and to his swift and safe return…to his squadron, and to the rest of his comrades."

Timmons drained his mug, but even as he raised it to his mouth, the applause began. He wasn't sure if it had started with the Blues or with the Red Eagles, but in a few seconds, both

squadrons—and every other pilot in the room—were screaming, slamming their hands down on the bar, on the tables. And
they began chanting, "Raptor...Raptor...Raptor..."

Chapter Forty-Six

CFS Fortitude
Turas System
308 AC

"Was it what you expected?" Striker stood on *Fortitude*'s flag bridge, amid the smoke and still-blaring klaxons and the detritus of war. The battle had just ended, but the frantic efforts to land fighters and contain out-of-control fires had the fleet's personnel still at a fever pitch of activity. There was damage control activity going on all around, and it seemed hardly less frenetic than it had moments before, when combat was still raging.

Holsten was next to the admiral, still trying to absorb everything he had seen, the mass of feelings swirling around inside him. He was afraid, certainly, and horrified at the magnitude of death and suffering. But there was something else. Was it hope? "Was it what I expected?" There was a touch of confusion in his tone.

"Yes. War, Mr. Holsten. The heat of combat. When you chose to stay with the fleet, I suspected you wished to experience it firsthand."

Holsten took a deep breath before answering. "Perhaps you are right, Admiral. My thoughts were more to stay with you, to support you if anyone questioned your right to command, as I felt responsible for your position. But perhaps there was more at play beneath my conscious thought. I had never faced battle myself, though I daresay I have been responsible many times for sending people to their deaths."

"So, what are your thoughts now? You have seen it virtually at its worst. I can't recall a more terrible battle."

"It is...not as I thought. I'd have expected I'd be more afraid, though of course I *was* afraid. But it wasn't as I'd imagined. It was more...detached."

"We all have the capacity to face more than we think we can, but we don't realize it until the need is upon us. Then, later, when the danger has passed, we wonder how we did what we did." Striker paused. "You acquitted yourself well, Mr. Holsten."

The intelligence chief nodded. "That means something, coming from you, Admiral. I don't know what else to say. Except that your leadership has confirmed my choice of you to take command."

"For as long as that lasts." Striker spoke softly, leaning toward Holsten as he did. The victory had done nothing to change the illegitimacy of Striker's command, nor the fact that there would be hell to pay when the confusion cleared. He owed his continued command to the delays imposed by vast distances, and nothing more. "Still, we won a victory of sorts here, Mr. Holsten, even if it is far from complete. Though we have paid so great a price to drive the enemy from Turas, I question whether we haven't worsened our position in terms of the relationship of total forces deployed. We may be more outnumbered now than we were before."

"No, Admiral...you have not worsened your position. Numbers are not everything. You have taken a defeated, demoralized fleet, and you have renewed its energy. You have reminded them that they can win."

"Perhaps, Mr. Holsten, but numbers matter too. That is still one massive enemy fleet we face, and unless I am very mistaken, they are now waiting for us in the next system."

Holsten just nodded, and the two men stood there, silent for a moment, the only sounds those of the bridge crew in the background, fielding damage reports and updates from the fleet.

The two forces had fought in Turas for two days, the combat almost non-stop. Fighter groups savaged each other, and strike wings launched themselves in desperate attack runs against the enemy line. The great capital ships themselves had broken up into groups, closing and raking each other with deadly fire.

The Confederation fleet had been outnumbered, and the enemy's advantage in size had almost prevailed. The Union forces had seemed like they were about to break through, to shatter the Confederation line and win the day. Then, suddenly, they retreated. Striker's plan to force them to expend their supplies in a sustained struggle had been successful, though only by the closest of margins.

Holsten had watched in stunned surprise as the Union ships dropped back toward the transwarp link and slipped out of the system, falling back on Ultara. He'd known, of course, that the enemy was low on supplies, but suspecting something, even believing it, was different than watching it unfold before your eyes.

The flight of the enemy fleet revitalized the exhausted Confeds, and all across the remnants of their battered line, ships surged forward, nipping at the heels of the enemy as they fled. They had known months of almost nonstop defeat, of endless, agonizing retreats. Now they fell on their enemies with vicious abandon, and not a ship of the Union rearguard escaped to join their fellows. When it was done, only the battered units of the Confederation fleet remained in Turas.

"Well, Mr. Holsten, at least this time we paid a cost to gain something. Perhaps not a true victory, certainly not a decisive one. Yet, not another defeat either. And that is something."

"You struck a blow here that Admiral Winston could never have matched. What you did here has given it another chance. I likely sacrificed my career, even my freedom, to place you in the position to achieve this, Admiral. You have amply repaid my trust. So, until the Senate has me dragged away to face trial, don't you think you should call me Gary?"

* * *

D'Alvert was in his office, standing, staring at the wall. His arm was bandaged and held in a sling. It would have hurt if he'd been able to feel anything but searing, relentless anger. But he wasn't.

Perfect. His plan had been perfect. His years of preparation, his meticulous execution. All spot on. He had been on the verge of breaking the hated Confeds once and for all. And now the chance for ultimate victory was lost, for lack of supplies.

He still didn't know what had gone wrong with his carefully-planned logistics. He'd heard nothing. Not from Admiral Lund and the missing convoy, not from those he'd sent looking for it. Not even from the supply base itself, though a second shipment should have been sent by now. It was maddening.

If I find that worm, Lund, I will have him skinned alive...

He was still wondering if there was more at play than simple incompetence. Was he dealing with outright betrayal? He'd always been careful, keeping his officers at arm's length, but had he watched them closely enough? Had he somehow telegraphed a weakness, encouraged a move against him?

Anyone plotting to take his place would know the final victory in the war would make him untouchable. It seemed insane that Union officers would hamper their own war effort, but there was always a delicate balancing act between the state's interest... and a desperate grab for more personal power.

D'Alvert hadn't shared his thoughts or plans with anyone. Well, with Sabine, perhaps, though only to a limited extent. He was genuinely fond of his aide, thinking of her almost as a daughter. Was that where he'd gone wrong? Had she taken advantage of his feelings and betrayed him? Who was involved in the conspiracy? He swore to himself he would find out...and when he did, there would be a reckoning the likes of which his enemies had never imagined.

He realized he was sweating heavily, that he was standing there shaking with rage. His mind was racing, images of associates whipping before his eyes, wondering whether they were part of the plot against him. He'd kill them. He'd kill them all. Whatever it took to crush the moves against him, to ensure his grip on power.

But first, he had to preserve the fleet. He had to see it resupplied, and he had to lead it back against the Confeds and secure the victory the traitors had stolen from him.

He'd hurt the Confeds, badly in Turas. That was a solace, at least, though he'd been surprised at the ferocity of their attacks. He'd thought their morale had been shattered, but the fact that they had invaded Turas suggested otherwise. Something had changed...some force had poured new hope and determination into their defeated spacers. They'd clearly been reinforced, but not by enough to explain the change in their conduct.

A new commander? Did they finally put that old fool, Winston, out to pasture?

He didn't know, and to an extent, he didn't care. Things were still salvageable. He had to reopen the lines of communication with Supply One, that was the primary concern. Once he did that, when his fleet was resupplied, he could resume the offensive. The battered Confederation fleet could never withstand his resurgent forces.

He was tempted to retire with the entire fleet, dropping back until he was able to reestablish communications with Supply One, but he discounted that option almost immediately. His enemies would certainly use it against him, seeking to discredit him in front of the Presidium. And his own spacers were shaken now, their string of relentless victories snapped at Turas. *He* could analyze the losses, evaluate the respective conditions of the two fleets...but the men and women in the ranks only knew they had retreated. That, for the first time in this war, their enemies had pushed them back. If he abandoned Ultara, fell back farther, fear would spread.

The Union didn't over-educate its masses like the Confederation did, but even the carefully-designed school curricula couldn't entirely cover up the fact that the Union had fought the Confederation three times before. No school text would state that any of the wars had been lost, of course, but it didn't take incisive brilliance to realize the need for a fourth conflict said something. He knew his spacers' morale was fragile, even in victory. No, he had to draw the line here. Besides, there was no way the Confeds could follow, not for a few weeks at least. They'd suffered too badly, lost too many ships and seen too many others badly damaged. They simply didn't have the strength to invade another system.

And by the time they gathered enough forces together, he intended to be resupplied…and ready to hit them first.

* * *

Lille sat in his quarters, his feet up on the bed, thinking. He wished there was some way to contact Villeneuve, but it was quite impossible. It would have taken weeks for a message to get through, even if he'd been able to get one off *Victoire*. His mission had been clear…wait until the victory was won, and then dispose of D'Alvert. He'd pondered his method and his timing, but never the idea that the victory wouldn't come. Now, he wasn't sure. The Union fleet was still the stronger, he had no doubt about that, but the ferocity of the Confeds had unnerved them. D'Alvert's dispatches had suggested a demoralized foe on the brink of defeat, but that wasn't what he'd seen in Turas.

Clearly, D'Alvert had suffered a setback, and just as apparently, he'd underestimated the tenacity of his Confed adversaries. It was all the more reason to move against him, but Lille was uncertain on the timing. Should he strike now? Or should he wait, bide his time, give D'Alvert the opportunity to regain momentum and finally win the war?

He wasn't in the habit of giving second chances to those who failed, and he knew Villeneuve was the same. But despite his defeat, D'Alvert was still a capable admiral, considerably more skilled than any of the fools lining up to replace him.

Lille would have preferred to simply follow orders, but he was alone, cut off. He had to make a choice himself. Killing D'Alvert now would be preferable, at least from an assassin's perspective. Even for an operative as experienced as Lille, remaining under cover was a stressful endeavor. And if he completed his mission, he could get the hell off *Victoire*, and away from the bare accommodations and unappetizing food endemic to military life. But he knew that wasn't the right choice. The war came first, and as much as he disliked the pompous ass, he would give D'Alvert time to finish off the Confeds.

Then he would strike.

* * *

"I understand, Captain Quatraine. Virtually every battleship has damage, including *Fortitude*. But the enemy's supply problems offer us a unique opportunity, one that will not last." *And I don't have much time before I am relieved...and most likely imprisoned.*

"Sir, if we could just wait another two days, it would make a major difference."

"And possibly for the enemy too, Captain, if they receive a supply convoy while we sit here repairing damage. Their engineers will be working as ours are, so if we are in better shape, so are they." Striker paused. "No, Captain, I'm sorry. We're moving out in three hours, so do what you can to have *Steadfast* ready for action."

"Yes, sir." Quatraine didn't sound entirely convinced, but it was clear he wasn't going to change Striker's mind. The admiral's voice was like steel.

"See to it, Captain." Striker cut the line and leaned back in his chair. He'd finally convinced Holsten to go back to his quarters and grab a few hours' sleep. There had been no point in the intelligence chief standing at his side, watching as he obsessed over every detail of the fleet's operation. Striker had no choice but to operate almost entirely on stims, and the meager snack he'd wolfed down a few moments before, but he'd ordered everyone not essential to repair ops to get at least two hours of actual rest. It wasn't much, but to Striker's strung out, exhausted mind it sounded like pure nirvana.

"*Fortitude* will take the lead." His flagship was in as good shape as any of the fleet's battleships, but it was more than just that.

He was driving his people hard, perhaps even brutally. Pushing them forward, less than sixteen hours after the last battle ended, right into the teeth of an enemy that still outnumbered them. His fleet was full of veterans, hardened by months of war. They knew their chances, the danger that none of them would come back. But there was no choice. They would never have a better chance than now.

"You wanted to see me, Admiral."

Striker turned to face the man who had just walked off the lift. "Yes, Lieutenant Stockton. Thank you for coming so quickly."

"Of course, sir."

"We have two squadrons on *Fortitude* without commanders, Lieutenant." He didn't say what had happened to the squad leaders, and Stockton didn't ask. "Blackwind and Iron Duke. I've got an extra fighter too. Do you think you can help us out and lead them in the fight to come?"

"Yes, sir," Stockton snapped back. "Of course, sir." Stockton had badgered the officers on *Repulse* for a fighter when the battle began, but intra-service rivalries being what they often were, no one on the old flagship had wanted to let the famous ace steal their laurels. Striker had almost blown his top when he'd found out a pilot of Stockton's talent had been ready to fight but was forced to sit on the sidelines, and he'd resolved to rectify that problem himself.

"I'd consider it a favor, Lieutenant. Though, God knows, you've done enough already."

"If there's a fight coming, sir, that's where I belong. Just have someone show me to my fighter."

"We won't be transiting for about two and a half hours, Lieutenant, so go down and get yourself something to eat first. Once we jump into Ultara, it's liable to go on for a long time without a break. We're going to push those Union bastards back where they came from, whatever it takes."

"Yes, sir!" Stockton stepped back and snapped off a perfect salute. "And thank you, sir. It feels good to be back in the fight."

Chapter Forty-Seven

FSS Victoire
Ultara System
Union Year 212 (308 AC)

"Fuel and supply transfers almost complete, sir. Priority one vessels averaging eleven percent fuel loads now, Admiral, up from five percent."

It was far from ideal, but D'Alvert's orders to move fuel and weapons from crippled and severely damaged vessels to those more combat-ready had given him a force that could put up a fight, at least for a while. Not that he expected the enemy to invade. He didn't even think it was possible. But he wasn't about to take any chances, not now.

He looked over at Renault, his eyes boring into her back as she stared down at her screens. He normally felt a rare warmth when he heard his aide's voice, but now it was displaced by a deep suspicion. Sabine Renault had never given him cause to suspect her loyalty, but she was also one of the few people close enough to him to do real damage if she did turn. He hated the idea of having to kill her, but he knew he wouldn't hesitate if she'd betrayed him. Or even if he was unable to rule out the possibility.

"Weapons status?" he asked coldly.

"X-ray laser cartridge inventory averaging sixty rounds on

priority one vessels, sir. Priority three ships have transferred all their stocks."

"Very well."

His fleet's secondary batteries were normal laser cannons. Given enough spare parts and a continued supply of energy, they could fire as long as the reactors had fuel and continued their power output. The primaries were a different matter. They were lasers, but they operated in the x-ray spectrum, and they were powered by the controlled detonation of fusion warheads. Each cartridge included an atomic bomb, and a magnetic bottle structure to contain and channel the massive energy of the nuclear explosion. Once his ships ran out of cartridges, their heavy batteries would fall silent, and they would have nothing with which to answer the devastating Confederation particle accelerators.

Assuming they've got any still functional...

D'Alvert knew the Confed weapons were notoriously fickle, and that their operation required almost all the available resources of a battleship. With the pounding he'd just given the Confeds, he wouldn't be surprised if most of their vessels were down to just their secondaries.

Not that they'd dare come at us. It was only our supply deficiency that saved them from utter defeat...

* * *

"Entering transwarp in thirty seconds." Jaravick's voice was gravelly, but the strength in it was clear. The old commodore wasn't having any trouble with his new subordinate role as Striker's aide, but the combined fleet's new commander couldn't say the same thing. For all his current rank and his crushing responsibilities, barking out orders at the old officer made him feel like a child playing a game.

"Very well, Commander. Fleet order...all ships are to launch fighters as soon as they emerge in Ultara." Striker had no idea what was waiting in the next system, how many of the Union ships were operational, or where they were positioned. It was reckless to proceed without scouting the other side of the jump point. But if he sent probes or ships through, he'd give away the fact that they were coming. The whole thing was a wild gamble anyway, so he decided to let it all ride and preserve whatever surprise he could. If he was able to catch the enemy napping, he just might gain the edge he needed.

"All ships report ready to launch, sir."

Striker just nodded. He sat back, his hands instinctively tightening on the armrests of his chair as *Fortitude* slipped into the maw of the ancient transwarp field and out of normal space.

The trip from Turas to Ultara was a long one, at least in the physical universe, almost thirty light years. In the strange alternate reality of the transwarp tube, that meant roughly one minute forty-three seconds. As short a time as that was, it was an eternity in the strange, distorted reality of the link.

Striker tried to sit quietly, ignoring the fear, and the strange side effects of the jump. He needed to be focused. His whole life had led to this moment. All the times he'd read about Admiral Barron, the endless series of memoirs by officers who'd served with the great man, when he'd heard the stories and watched the vidpics...he'd imagined himself someday in the same position as his hero. But he'd always considered that to be the wild dream of a young officer. Now, here he was, in the same situation. The future of the Confederation rode with him. He couldn't fail... he wouldn't. He needed every scrap of strength he possessed, every bit of cold analytical brainpower...and he was determined to give it all.

Suddenly the screen went back, tiny pinpricks of light appearing in the background. Normal space. *Fortitude* was in Ultara. In an enemy-controlled system.

"Launch operations commencing, Admiral. Scanning data coming in." There was a short pause. Then Jaravick continued, "Preliminary data indicates the enemy fleet is still here, sir. They're deployed back from the transwarp link. We should have time to get the entire fleet into formation."

Striker took a deep breath. It was time.

* * *

A mass of fighters moved across the interplanetary space of the Ultara system, dozens of squadrons, hundreds of tiny vessels. The first wave consisted of interceptors, lined up ahead of the bomber squadrons they were there to protect. And in the center of the formation, two squadrons in particular blasted their thrusters, heading for the enemy wings in front of them.

"All right, Iron Duke, Darkwind...I know you both fought hard—and lost hard—in Turas. You both had good commanders, squad leaders who made you proud, who led you to victory. I can't hope to take their places, nor would I try. But we're here together now...and the enemy is in front of us. So, let's fight as one today."

Stockton was relieved to be back in the cockpit of a fighter, a real fighter, one with lasers and missiles, though he was a bit wistful about his old ship. He'd been frustrated at her lack of firepower and almost insane from being cooped up in her for so many days, but she had gotten him across a vast distance and saw him through to his destination...if barely. She had given all she had to do it, and there was nothing left of her now but scattered debris, abandoned two systems back.

There is plenty to worry about here beyond a shattered old fighter...but she was a good ship, and I will always remember her...

His eyes moved to the display, passing over the serried ranks of approaching Union fighters. The enemy wings had been savaged at Turas, and they were outnumbered now. They didn't seem to have launched any bombers of their own, sending nothing but a wall of interceptors to defend their battleships against the assault. There were enough of them to rush the Confederation screen, and if they did it aggressively enough, some would get through to the line of bombers. Unless he could disrupt their formation.

"Everybody lock on a target with your first missile...but don't fire, not until I give the order." He wanted to create maximum disruption, and hitting a whole section of the enemy line with a coordinated barrage seemed likely to do just that.

He picked out his own target, flipping the locking switch and nodding at the tone that confirmed his AI had acquired the target. He waited a few seconds…the closer his people were when they fired, the likelier they were to hit. His actions were logical, the strategy itself based on pure rational judgment. But his gut was completely in charge of the timing.

"Fire," he said sharply, pressing down on his own button as he did. The fighter lurched as the missile kicked off its mounting and accelerated toward its target.

He waited a few seconds, his eyes dropping to the screen to confirm his pilots had all followed suit. Then he said, "Arm second missiles…pick out another round of targets." Even as he spoke, detonations began to appear on his display, one hit after another blasting enemy interceptors to atoms.

"Prepare to launch…now," he snapped. He'd have waited longer, but the enemy ships had begun launching their own missiles, and his people couldn't start evasive maneuvers until they'd fired. He locked onto a second enemy fighter. "Launch," he said, his finger tightening over the firing stud.

"All right, let's break. We've got missiles coming our way now, so look out for yourselves." He slammed his throttle hard to the side. Three missiles were coming right at him, the targeting a little too close for comfort. Stockton was nothing if not a confident pilot, but now he felt heat around his neck as his arm moved wildly over the controls, veering off on a wild escape route.

The Union missiles were inferior to the Confederation weapons, with significantly less range and endurance. But Stockton still had to evade for at least two minutes, and with three separate warheads, he had to take care that escaping from one didn't put him into the path of another.

His eyes darted to his screens, even as he raced to escape from the missiles. He had twenty-one other pilots, and they were all his responsibility. He knew they weren't all going to make it—a fact that hit home when one of them vanished from the display, a victim of a missile the pilot couldn't evade.

Damn.

He swung around again, angling his thrust, responding to the missiles' pursuit. One of the weapons had already lost its lock, and the second one had exhausted its fuel far short of his position. But the third one had stuck with him, stubbornly matching his every evasive maneuver.

He reached down next to his seat, his fingers feeling around for the switch he knew was there. He slipped his finger under the lever and pulled it, releasing the safeties on his thruster. He needed more power, even if he risked blowing out his entire reactor. That would be bad, but no worse than getting picked off by the missile still closing on his tail.

He blasted hard, feeling 12g of thrust slam into him. He gasped for breath, struggling to fight off the blackness, just for a few seconds. It was hard to concentrate, but he held on, counting down in his head. Then he released the throttle and felt a wave of relief as weightlessness replaced the crushing pressure. He'd gotten the distance he needed, and he watched as the missile's thrusters died and the weapon continued on its final trajectory. He tapped his throttle a bit to the starboard, moving him comfortably away from the weapon's course.

He inhaled deeply, fighting off the tension. He hadn't expected to be so sorely tested by the enemy missile attack. A quick look at his screens confirmed his fears. Four of his fighters were gone, and worse, he couldn't detect a single escape pod.

There was no time to think about that now. There were enemy fighters to destroy, and some of them were already pushing through, trying to break out toward the bombers.

And Jake "Raptor" Stockton had no intention of letting that happen.

* * *

"The forward line is engaged, Admiral."

Striker heard Jaravick's words, but his attention was on the display, on watching the very vessels his aide was referencing. He'd ordered the eleven ships with operational primary batteries to the vanguard, and now they were firing, their deadly particle accelerators lancing out, striking the enemy battleships facing them.

The enemy's maneuvers had been sluggish, unimaginative. He'd have guessed their commander was one of limited ability, but he knew better. He'd read Confederation Intelligence's report on Hugo D'Alvert, and he'd studied the Union admiral's actions in the war to date. According to the dossiers Holsten had provided, D'Alvert was almost a pure sociopath in human interactions...but no one could call him an unskilled admiral.

So, why are you just sitting there?

Striker knew what he thought, what he hoped. But he was reluctant to let himself believe the Union forces were *that* low on fuel.

The lights on the flag bridge dimmed for a second. *Fortitude* was one of the eleven ships with operational primaries, and Striker had rejected all suggestions that the flagship hang back from the forward line. The Confederation was in a struggle for its life, the fleet was making its stand. He would be nowhere, he'd declared angrily, but in the thick of the fight, just as Admiral Barron had been years before.

His hand clenched unconsciously into a fist as he saw *Fortitude*'s shot on the display, the particle beams slamming into an enemy vessel amidships. Low on fuel or not, the Union forces still outnumbered him badly, and he knew his people needed every hit they could get.

"Activity at the transwarp link sir. Something is coming in from Gamalon."

A cold feeling took Striker's stomach. The intelligence Lieutenant Stockton had brought hadn't shown any enemy forces within supporting distance, but he'd been concerned nevertheless, too cautious to completely believe the Union nav data. He'd bet his people could take out the larger, but poorly-supplied Union fleet. Just. But if enemy reserves were moving forward, he knew his people were finished. He could order a withdrawal, and the enemy's fuel status might even allow most of his ships to escape. But then a reinforced Union fleet would be right behind him...and new ships would probably bring fresh supplies with them.

He was angry with himself for allowing his ego to convince him he could handle this level of command. He'd let himself dream of saving the Confederation…now he would go down in history as the man who lost it all. His only saving grace that there would be no history, at least none the Union censors didn't write.

"Admiral…" There was something in Jaravick's voice, a sound that pushed aside his normal hoarse growl in favor of something more…optimistic. "…we're picking up ID beacons from the ships at the transwarp. They're ours. It's *Dauntless* and *Intrepid*, sir. And they're both launching fighters."

Chapter Forty-Eight

"All squadrons launched, Captain. *Intrepid* reports the same."
Travis was nailed to her chair, her hands outstretched over her
workstation, her eyes locked on her screens.

Barron had expected his people to face an almost impossible
journey to get back home, an insurmountable effort to get past
the enemy fleet. But instead, his people had transited into the
middle of a battle, a big one...obviously a major fleet action.

They were still on the far side of the enemy formation, and
Barron knew that beyond the risk of battle, his people still faced
an uphill fight to survive. But even if they were to die here, it
was far preferable to do it helping the fleet win this fight. Helping them turn back the Union onslaught.

"Advise *Intrepid* we will be increasing thrust to 6g, Commander. Set our course...directly toward the nearest section of
the enemy line."

"Yes, Captain."

Barron knew the fight his people faced. They'd come a hair's
breadth from destruction in Varus, and then they'd chased a
squadron of Union escort ships all the way back to Arcturon,
before catching up and destroying them. Now they were going

back into battle.

"I want primaries charged and ready to fire as soon as we enter range."

"Yes, sir. All gunnery stations report ready."

"Get me Commander Fritz."

A few seconds later: "On your line, sir."

"Fritzie, give it to me straight...are these systems going to hold up?"

"Yes, sir, at least until we start taking hits. We made good use of the time it took to get here, Captain. I'm not saying she doesn't need time in spacedock for some real repairs, but we're a lot less fragile than we were in Varus."

"You're a treasure, Fritzie. I don't know what I'd do without you."

"Neither do I, Captain...neither do I."

"Have your people ready, Fritzie, because we're heading right into the shit again."

"Where else would they be, sir? Where else would *we* be?"

"Good luck down there, Fritzie."

"And to you, sir."

"Captain," Travis said, "entering primary range in ten seconds."

Barron just nodded. Back into battle.

*   *   *

"On me...we've got to hit that wave of fighters, and we've got to do it now." Lefebrve was already bringing her ship around, and she swore under her breath at the sluggishness of the pilots under her command. The battle in Turas had been a holocaust, and she'd lost half her people there. She liked to think those that remained were seasoned for the exposure to such a terrible fight, but she suspected stunned was closer to the mark. Fear had taken hold, its cold hand gripping their spines. They'd launched, of course. An open display of cowardice in the Union was a ticket to the airlock. But their fighting spirit was gone.

"Let's move it!" she screamed, anything to wake them from

the funk they'd all been in. They had half loads of fuel, and that was the last the fleet had to give them. They had to make this fight count. It was the only chance they'd get.

She knew she didn't have the fuel to burn, but she pushed her engines close to maximum thrust anyway. Most of her people were falling behind, but a few—likely the best ones, and certainly the bravest—were coming close to keeping up. It didn't matter anymore, not really. Beneath the bravado, and the cold-blooded focus on her job, she knew this was her last mission. She didn't have enough fuel to fight a battle and return to base, so that meant this was a one-way trip. And she intended to make it count.

Her eyes locked on her screen, watching the wave of fighters coming at her. It looked like two Confed battleships had transited into the system, right in the rear of the fleet. It wasn't a large force, but their position was dangerous. The line ships didn't have the fuel to come about to face the new invaders, so her people had been sent to buy time. Somehow.

She'd already fired her missiles, so there was nothing to do but push forward to laser range. She glanced down at her fuel readings. Not good. But crawling forward through the enemy's missile range wouldn't have been any better.

She punched in her turbos, accelerating to the side, trying to sweep around the flank of the enemy formation. A few of her pilots followed her, but most were blundering forward, serving themselves up as targets for the Confeds. Her stomach tensed, and she ached to help them…but there was nothing to do. She had to get around the interceptors and take down as many enemy bombers as she could. The battleships were always the priority.

The pressure of her thrust pushed her back hard into her seat, but she kept it up until her course brought her around the end of the Confed formation. She could see the enemy pilots, some of them at least, reacting, blasting toward her position. But she was going to get to the bombers first. Her, and two maybe three of her people.

She'd have two minutes, she figured, maybe three…and then the enemy interceptors would react, and she'd be overwhelmed.

But every bomber she could take down in that time was a plasma torpedo that wouldn't hit one of the battleships. Every one she stopped could save dozens of lives, even hundreds. And that kind of math was appealing. It made it easier to face the near certainty that she wasn't coming back from this mission.

* * *

"Let's go, Blues...follow me. Red Eagles and Direwolves too. We've got to cover the bombers, now! We're already too late, so let's not waste any more time." Jamison had watched the Union fighters slipping around the flank, but he hadn't taken it seriously at first. He was used to facing overwhelming Union numbers, but now he realized too late that he was up against a capable tactician this time...and one hell of a pilot as well. "Yellows and Black Helms, hold the line here. Don't let any more groups break off."

He kicked in his thrusters, gulping a breath as the g forces pounded into him. He had no time to waste. He was already late. Whoever that pilot was, he was damned good. And the thought of a flyer *that* skilled attacking the almost defenseless bombers made Jamison's blood run cold.

He'd had been a little shaky when he'd first launched, but his chops had come back quickly. He'd been moments from death in Varus, down to the last breaths of air when the rescue shuttle had plucked him out of space. He'd been sure he was dead, absolutely convinced. But, against all odds, *Dauntless* and *Intrepid* had managed to destroy the station. He'd heard the plan had come from Commander Fritz, that she had identified a weakness in the design. He had intended to find her and thank her when he got back to *Dauntless*, but she'd been busy around the clock on repairs, and he hadn't seen her anywhere. Every place he'd gone he been told, "she was just here." or "she's down at Reactor A." And, of course, when he went there they told her she'd just left for somewhere else.

"We're with you, Thunder." Charles Aires was one of a minority of pilots with a calm demeanor. His friend Timmons had often spoken of him in jest, calling him a robot...but Jamison knew Warrior respected Aires's abilities, and he took Warrior's opinion very seriously, at least when it came to judging piloting skill.

"Roger that, Mustang. I think your people are actually closest. But be careful, that Union ship is being flown by somebody who knows what he's doing."

"Got it, Thunder. Don't worry...we'll take care of him."

Jamison didn't like the sound of that. He knew a large number of pilots who tended to be a little wild, and a few downright crazy ones like Timmons and Stockton, but he'd run into a lesser number of the stone cold killer type, men and women who considered comparisons to computers to be compliments. "Ice" Krill had been one of those. But Jamison never seen one of the latter lose his cool edge without disaster resulting. War could wear a man down, he knew, and the tightly wound types like Aires were sometimes susceptible to it. But it usually got them killed.

"Mustang, wait up a few seconds. I can be up there in less than a minute."

"We don't have a minute, Thunder. You said it yourself. We'll hit them hard...don't you worry about that."

Jamison opened his mouth, but no words came out. He had a bad feeling, but that wasn't justification to allow the enemy an extra minute loose among the bombers. Finally, he just said, "Be careful, Mustang. That pilot's dangerous."

"I'm always careful, sir."

Jamison frowned. The Red Eagles were even farther back. If anyone was going to get up there and support the Direwolves, it was him. He pulled back the rest of the way on the throttle, maxing out his thrust.

* * *

Lefebrve fired, then again...two lasers blasts, and two bombers destroyed. The cumbersome ships were trying to flee, but her throttle was like an extension of her arm, and she whipped her ship around, firing in multiple directions as her vector took her right through the heart of the strike force.

Her wingmen were there too, and each had a kill of their own. All together, her attack had taken out six bombers, cutting a wide swatch through the enemy formation. She wanted to decelerate, to come about and launch a second run, but there were enemy interceptors inbound, and she could see they would get to her first.

"We've got visitors," she said into her comm. She'd always been a cool customer, but now her calm was almost eerie. She'd never felt as much one with her fighter, and it had never been more effortless to target her shots, to put the deadly laser blasts exactly where she wanted them.

She fired her thrusters again, adjusting her vector, setting herself up to face the attackers coming in. She was outnumbered, badly, but at least they were coming in waves. If she could take enough of them down, maybe the rest would break off.

No…these are veterans. I can tell by the way they fly. I may kill a few, but then they're going to get me.

The thought was almost clinical, as if it had already happened, as though she were reviewing the details of her own death, like some flight instructor narrating a training video.

Her fingers closed around her firing stud. The deadly lasers fired again, and they claimed another victim. She held her thrust, her turbos burning through the last reserves of her fuel as it brought her course around, directly toward the new attackers. She fired again, and a second interceptor exploded. There were half a dozen ships left in the squadron coming at her…and then one of her wingman hit another. A few seconds later, one of the enemy ships fired, and she lost one of her companions.

Her eyes locked on that blip on her screen, marking the ship that had fired the killing shot. He was skilled, she could see that watching his maneuvers.

That's got to be the squadron leader.

She adjusted her vector, bringing her fighter to the side, around the enemy interceptor. Her eyes darted back and forth to her fuel readings. Her maneuver would use up most of the rest of what she had, but she was going to do it anyway. Her plan relied on deception. She was heading right toward another enemy fighter, one deployed farther back, giving every indication she was bypassing the lead bird, that she was making a mistake, leaving herself exposed.

She waited, watching, as focused as she'd ever been in the cockpit. For an instant, she thought her adversary wasn't going to take the bait. But then the energy readings shot up as the Confed fighter blasted its engines, its vector coming around, moving right toward her.

She smiled. *I have you now…*

* * *

"Mustang!"

Jamison heard Timmons's voice on the comm, a frantic scream that echoed through his cockpit.

"Get out of there, Chuck…now! Blast your thrust!"

Jamison saw it too, the trap…and the Union fighter moving to spring it. But it looked like Aires was blind to it. The Union pilot, the one that had captured Jamison's attention, was luring the Direwolves' leader in. It was brilliant, hard to detect, but a trap nevertheless. Aires should have seen it, but he didn't. He was too focused on saving the bombers from taking any more losses.

"I'm fine, Warrior." Aires's voice was calm, unconcerned. Then, a few seconds later: "Shit."

Jamison gritted his teeth against the pain as he continued at full thrust. He had to get there…he had to save Aires. But even as he jammed his throttle back full, he knew he wasn't going to make it.

"Shit…shit…"

"Get out of there, Mustang," Timmons screamed, his frantic voice reverberating in Jamison's cockpit as it blasted out of the comm. "Now!" But it was too late.

Jamison watched on the screen, almost as though it was happening in slow motion. The Union fighter spun around, still thrusting hard, opening fire as it did.

The laser blasts flew all around Aires's ship, bracketing his position, even as his attacker moved in a sweeping arc behind his ship. The lasers fired again…and again.

Jamison was moving right toward the enemy fighter, firing his lasers already. But pressing the firing stud didn't change the fact that he was still out of range. He watched in stunned horror as the Union ship fired another burst of shots, each one closer than the last had been.

"I can't break…" Aires's voice was cut off, even as Jamison watched the small dot disappear from the screen. He felt the bile in his stomach rising, as he stared at the scanner with fading hope, looking for a transponder signal, any sign that Aires had ejected. But there was nothing at all, just a cooling cloud of dust and debris where his fighter had been.

Then his cockpit erupted, as Timmons's primal scream blasted from the comm.

*   *   *

Lefebrve watched as the Confederation interceptors closed. She was still savoring the victory, likely her last, she realized. The enemy pilot had put up a fight in the end, but she'd outmaneuvered him. Now she would be outnumbered, surrounded…if she didn't run out of fuel first.

The lead fighter coming toward her had been firing from well out of range. She'd expected him to be her next opponent, and very possibly the one who took her down. But now there was another ship on the screen, accelerating at the almost unimaginable rate of 14g.

He must have blown out every safety feature on his ship…

She wondered how he was even maintaining consciousness, but he kept coming on, the massive thrust relentlessly continuing.

That is a skilled pilot. If I'm going to die, this is a worthy opponent to face for the last time.

She moved the throttle, adjusting her thrust, trying to get

herself in a reasonable position to face her new enemy. She didn't have the fuel for an optimum approach, but she would do what she could. She could accept death if need be, but she'd never go down without a fight.

She'd never seen a fighter flown so aggressively. She had killed dozens of enemies, but it had always been cold, impersonal. This pilot was after her blood.

She thought of the ship she'd just destroyed. *A brother, a friend?*

Yes, it made sense. Lefebrve had always been a loner, but she'd seen others who'd formed attachments, and she'd watched the pain of loss that so often accompanied such relationships. It seemed somehow appropriate that she, who fought neither for patriotism nor for hatred, should be killed by a pilot consumed with vengeful rage. But if he wanted her, he was going to have to earn it.

She tapped her thruster to the side, and then she fired the port positioning jets, bringing her ship around, targeting her lasers on the enemy fighter streaking toward her like a bullet. It was poor tactics, suicidal even, but she knew *that* pilot wouldn't blunder forward into her range.

He's going to break one way, just before range…and then he's going to trust to his aim to take me out quickly. But which way will he go?

She watched carefully, knowing that if she waited until she could see his movement, it would be too late. She closed her fingers around the throttle, ready to adjust her angle. She wasn't a creature of instinct like so many of her fellows, but there was no place for cold logic in this choice. It was a guess, a random chance of being right. She waited until the last possible moment…and then she tapped her jets to starboard, an instant before she saw the enemy fighter breaking to her port. She fired, her beams lancing through empty space, even as her enemy's shots came right at her.

The first blast missed, but the second hit, tearing the tail section clean off her fighter. Her helmet slammed down automatically, and her portable oxygen supply started feeding her air, even as the atmosphere of her cockpit blew out into space through the massive breach. She saw the next incoming shot on her still-functioning screen. The chunk that had been blown off the fighter saved her, the change in her vector from the impact moving her away from what would have been a direct killing shot.

She almost resolved to stay where she was, to die with her ship. But something made her reach out and pull the escape lever, and she was pushed out into space, to float there helplessly, waiting to see if the Union won the fight…or if death would finally take her.

*   *   *

"Primaries…fire!" Barron was leaning forward in his chair, sitting at least, instead of standing in the center of the bridge. Even in his chair, though, his harness still hung loose under him.

Nothing happened. No familiar sound, no scanner report on the shot he'd just ordered.

"I said fire, Commander."

"Gunnery reports primaries down, sir. There seems to be some sort of power interruption."

"Fritzie…" Barron was on the comm in an instant.

"It's reactor A, sir. It scragged."

"Fritzie, this is a bad time…"

"I'm on it, Captain." Barron could hear the frustration in her voice. She'd been saying for the last two weeks that something was off in the reactor, but she hadn't been able to find anything, no matter how many tests she'd run. He'd hoped she was just imagining things, but he knew her too well to really believe that. The thing couldn't have picked a worse time to finally fail.

Dauntless shook hard, as the Union battleship it was facing moved into the range of its own heavy guns and opened fire. Then again. The Confederation primaries were more powerful than the Union guns, and longer ranged. But the enemy ships had more of the x-ray lasers, and they packed a potent punch.

"Forward thrust, Commander…whatever we can manage." He had to get into secondary range, whatever it took. But with one reactor down, he knew his engines couldn't give him much. Reactor B was powering the entire ship, and it was chewed up pretty badly itself.

"Engine room reports maximum thrust 1.8g, Captain." Travis looked down at her screens for a moment, running calculations. "That will be eight minutes until secondary range."

Too much. Dauntless *can't take eight minutes of that pounding. But our vector's already in that direction. It would take even longer to pull back out of range.*

He moved his hand to the comm controls, but then he stopped. Fritzie would do everything humanly possible…all he could do was distract her.

The ship shook again, and the lights flickered.

If they knock out Reactor B, we're done…

He'd known all along that getting his people home was a long shot, but dying within sight of the fleet…it was just too much…

"We've got fighters coming in, Captain. It's Commander Jamison and Lieutenant Timmons."

Barron's interceptors had escorted *Dauntless's* and *Intrepid's* bombers toward the enemy line—and he'd watched as they'd fought a sharp battle with a small group of Union ships that had hit the strike force hard. Now they were coming back in, and Jamison was leading them against the enemy battleship.

Barron felt a rush of excitement watching his squadrons, but he knew they weren't going to be enough. If Fritzie couldn't get Reactor A back online—and she'd been trying to find the problem for days now—his ship was in trouble. The rest of the fleet was on the other side of the enemy forces, too far away to intervene…"

"Captain, *Intrepid* is moving up on our port." A wave of excitement slipped into his first officer's voice. "She's firing, sir."

His eyes darted to the scanner, just as the readings updated. Eaton's people had scored a direct hit.

Well done, Sara!

The incoming fire from the enemy vessel slowed considerably, perhaps half as many guns firing as before. Then his comm buzzed.

"Captain, I'm going to restart the reactor. I still don't know what's wrong with it, but I think I can get it back online."

"Do it Fritzie."

"There *is* some risk, sir. I've covered every…"

"Do it."

"Yes, Captain. Restart in ten seconds."

Barron just nodded, waiting. Ten seconds wasn't a long time, but it seemed like it sitting there on the bridge. His officers had heard Fritz, they knew what was happening, and there wasn't a word spoken, not a sound save the occasional buzz or ring from a workstation.

Then, there was a high-pitched whining sound, and the lights brightened. Fritz's voice blared through the comm. "Back online, sir, at eighty-nine percent. I think it's going to need a total replacement, but for now I've got it working."

"You're a genius, Fritzie!" He spun around toward Travis. "Cut engine thrust…charge primaries now."

"Yes, Captain."

Barron felt the g force pressure disappear as the engine shut down. A few seconds later, *Intrepid* fired again…another hit.

The enemy fire lessened again, down to two or three batteries. Then it stopped entirely.

Barron didn't understand. The enemy battleship hadn't taken another hit. Why had it stopped firing its primaries?

"Gunnery reports ready to fire, Captain."

Barron put the thoughts out of his mind. It didn't matter. There was only one thing on his mind now.

"Fire."

Chapter Forty-Nine

CFS Victoire
Ultara System
Union Year 212 (308 AC)

D'Alvert sat in the center of *Victoire*'s flag bridge, watching the chaos unfolding around him. He still outnumbered the Confeds, and his forces had inflicted heavy losses on their foes. Another six enemy battleships had been destroyed, and there wasn't one out there that wasn't badly battered.

His own vessels had suffered as well, his losses even greater. But he'd started with more. He knew the war could end right here in the Ultara system. The enemy commander—almost certainly not Winston anymore, he'd decided—seemed committed to a fight to the finish. It was tailor made for his purposes... save for the fact that he didn't have the fuel and supplies to see it through.

He knew he had to order a withdrawal. If he didn't, his ships were going to begin to run out of fuel. Half his line had already gone through all the cartridges for their primaries, and the rest were down to their final few shots. The battle was lost...lost for lack of the ordnance and fuel to fight through to victory. If he didn't retreat now, if his ships ran out of fuel in the face of the enemy, he'd lose the entire fleet. At least if he pulled back, the war would go on. But his dreams of a quick victory, of smashing through to the Confederation's Core worlds, of bombarding the Iron Belt factories before they could churn out an endless stream of new ships and weapons…they were gone.

He had no idea what had happened to his carefully-designed supply line. The two enemy ships that transited from Gamalon… could they possibly have destroyed all his convoys and their escorting battleships? Could they have taken out Supply One? It seemed impossible. Yet, what else could have happened?

No, that was inconceivable…this had to be more than the work of bad luck or enemy effort. It had to be betrayal. They were plotting against him, all of them. He looked over at Renault. The officer was hunched over her workstation, seemingly focused, as always. But she had betrayed him. He knew it. His enemies had found his weak spot, the one person he hadn't suspected. It had to be. It was the only way they could have gotten to him.

He'd lost everything. A lifetime's work, the backstabbing, the brutality, the careful planning…it had brought him within reach of absolute power, and now he was watching it slip away.

"Admiral, the task force commanders are all calling. They are reporting critical fuel supply levels and requesting permission to withdraw to Gamalon."

D'Alvert heard the words, but it wasn't Renault's voice. It was a shrieking, evil hiss, the very sound of betrayal. *How could she have done this to me? How could she have helped my enemies destroy me?*

He stared at her, at the back of her head, her neatly-cropped brown hair extending just below her collar. She had been his mistake. Such an innocuous misstep, to trust someone, to seek a friend, a protégé. He felt his hand moving toward his waist, gripping the sidearm and pulling it from his holster.

His eyes bored into the back of Renault's head, hatred welling up from deep within him. She turned and looked over at him. "Sir, what do you want…"

He aimed the pistol at her head. "Why, Sabine? Why did you betray me?"

The flag bridge was silent, save for the sound of Renault's

increasingly frantic breaths. "Admiral, I don't under…"

"Don't lie, Sabine. It's far too late for that. You could have risen with me. I would have ruled the Union…and you could have been there, at the very seat of power. What did they give you? What was the price of your betrayal?"

She stared back, her face a mask of terror and confusion. "I don't know what you're talking about, sir, but…"

"It's time to pay the price for your betrayal, Sabine…"

"Admiral, no…please…"

A loud crack echoed across the bridge, and Sabine Renault slipped from her chair to the floor, a single bullet hole in her forehead.

D'Alvert leapt up from his chair. "Who else?" he shouted. "Who else was plotting against me?" He panned his vision around the bridge, pointing the pistol at each officer in turn. "You, Girard? You, Nicolas?" There was naked insanity in his voice, in his crazed stare.

"I should just kill you all," he shouted. He turned and aimed the pistol toward the closest officer, just as the lift opened on the far wall. D'Alvert turned abruptly, in time to face Ricard Lille, Gregoire Suchet to him. The operative stepped onto the bridge, a small pistol in his hand.

"Suchet, what are you…"

Lille fired, and the admiral snapped back, falling over his chair to the deck below. The assassin's shot had been perfect, precise. Hugo D'Alvert was dead.

"I'm from Sector Nine," he snapped quickly. "Ricard Lille, senior operative. Charged with the termination of Admiral Hugo D'Alvert." He knew his words were no proof of who he was, but he was also aware of the fear the mere mention of the Union's spy agency could cause. And he just needed to control the situation, to forestall some officer or guard from shooting the man who had just killed the admiral.

He turned to an officer at the communications station. "Contact Admiral Beaufort, Lieutenant. Advise him Admiral D'Alvert is dead, and inform him he is in command. He is to extricate the fleet from this fight at once and retreat."

The officer stared back, a look of stark terror on his face.

"Do it," Lille roared. "Now!"

The officer spun around and carried out the command.

Lille just stood where he was. D'Alvert had come close to achieving his goal...but he'd fallen short. The dream of a quick war was gone, and the reality of a brutal, sustained conflict was slowly taking its place. The Union fleet had to fall back now, probably several systems, to reestablish its supply lines. They'd be hampered by lack of fuel, and they'd have to move slowly. Fortunately, the Confederation forces seemed to be in no condition to pursue.

There would be a lull, he knew, an extended period while both sides licked their wounds and reorganized...but the war was far from over.

He looked down at D'Alvert's body, eyes still wide open staring back at him.

It was far from over.

*   *   *

Lefebrve sat quietly in the shuttle, her hands shackled in front of her. She'd been resigned to death, floating in space on the edge of the battle. When the Union fleet withdrew, it had taken her last hope with it, leaving her with nothing but a final few moments before the end came. She'd been shocked when the Confederation rescue shuttle locked on her transponder. Nothing she'd ever heard of the enemy suggested they would save an enemy pilot.

She'd almost killed herself then and there. There could be only on reason the Confeds would rescue a Union pilot. And she far preferred solitary death to Confederation torture chambers and interrogation. But there was something in her that intervened, that almost physically constrained her from harming herself. She knew she'd be better off dead, but she just wasn't capable of giving up. She would die if need be, but she would be defiant to the end...and her enemies would have to kill her. She wouldn't do it for them.

She glanced down at the bandage on her hand, recalling her surprise when the medic treated her wound. *What kind of sadistic joy do they get out of healing me so they can torture and kill me?*

She'd heard all about the Confeds, and while she didn't believe all the propaganda she'd heard as a Union officer, she had no reason to expect anything better from her captors. She had killed dozens of their people, gunned down their pilots without mercy.

"*Dauntless* is closest…our orders are to dock and drop everybody off. Then we're to refuel and head out to make another run." She could hear the pilots talking the cockpit.

"Estimated time to docking, six minutes." A pause. "We're getting an advisory…*Dauntless*'s flight decks are in marginal condition. Exert caution on landing."

Lefebrve listened, taking a deep breath, realizing she was just moments from the enemy battleship. She had always been considered calm, cold. She was a warrior, through and through…it had been her life. But now she was something else, something new.

She was afraid.

* * *

Stockton brought his fighter around slowly, carefully. He remembered the wreckage of *Dauntless*'s bays when he'd left, and he doubted the fights she'd been through since had done anything to improve the situation. Admiral Striker had offered him an assignment as *Fortitude*'s strike force commander. It was a big step up to the command of every fighter on one of the fleet flagships, but he'd politely declined. He'd had nothing but good things to say about the pilots he'd commanded in the battle, and he'd stayed long enough for the traditional sendoff for those who hadn't come back. But, as he'd explained to the admiral, *Dauntless* was more to him than an assignment. She was his home. And as welcome as he'd been made to feel on *Fortitude*, he was anxious to get back. Blue squadron was waiting, and Kyle Jamison…and Stara.

Dauntless was only taking select traffic into its bays while repair operations continued, but Striker had been only too willing to give the needed authorization, showing there were no hard feelings for Stockton's refusal of his offer.

The pilot liked Striker, he liked him a lot. He found he respected the admiral in a way he never had Winston. The fleet commander was a lofty officer, lord and master of the entire combined fleet, but in many ways, he seemed like the next guy in the wardroom. He lacked the formality of someone like Winston, and he seemed willing to find time for any of his people, from senior officers to the lowest-ranked spacers working in the recesses of engineering.

Stockton had always been a warrior who focused on his immediate world, his ship, his squadron. Now he realized he had a new optimism about the war, about the Confederation's prospects. The fleet was a wreck, but the enemy had also been roughly handled, and *Dauntless*'s destruction of their supply line had compelled them to fall back half a dozen systems. The Confederation still faced a dangerous and damaging war, but it was no longer staring over the brink. And Stockton felt good about his part in that.

He shifted his throttle slightly, lining up with the entry to *Dauntless*'s alpha bay. He was anxious to see his friends. Still, he found himself trying not to think about it. *Dauntless* had been through hell, and for all Stockton knew, Kyle, Rick...even Stara...could have been lost. He'd tried to check on the fleet database from *Fortitude*, but the information was spotty, and *Dauntless* and *Intrepid* hadn't even connected to the fleet network yet.

His fighter slid into the bay, and he brought it down gently in the open space that had been cleared amidst the debris. He felt a pit in his stomach, tightening with every second. It was one thing to think about friends and loved ones, to worry about them. But he was back now, after what seemed like months. In a few minutes he would know how they all had fared. He would know if they had lived...or if they hadn't.

He popped the cockpit and scrambled out, handing his

helmet to the tech instead of tossing it as he usually did. He climbed down the ladder and hopped onto the deck, his boots clacking loudly on the smooth steel surface.

"By the eleven hells, look who decided to grace us with his presence."

Stockton turned around, a wide smile bursting out on his face. "Kyle," he shouted, lunging forward and hugging his friend. "It's so good to be back."

"It's good to have you back, my friend. I'm not afraid to tell you, I was worried about you. Hell, worried? I was scared to death."

"Me too. About both of us."

The two men laughed. "Seriously, Kyle, it sounds like you've all been through one murderous fight after another."

"It's been a rough couple of weeks, that's for sure, though I suspected hardest of all on you." He paused. "Jake, there's something I need to talk to you about."

A cold feeling went through Stockton. "Stara?" he asked, barely gasping out her name.

"No…no. Stara is fine, Jake. She got bruised up a bit when a support gave way in launch control, but she's fine. Rick too, though we did take our share of losses."

Stockton felt an onrush of relief. "What is it you want to…"

"Jake!"

Stockton heard the voice behind him, and he knew instantly who it was. He spun around, extending his arms as Stara Sinclair raced across the debris-strewn deck and threw her own arms around him. All thoughts of discretion, of keeping their relationship a secret, were gone, and the two of them, a senior launch control officer and the fleet's reigning celebrity pilot, created quite the scandal by kissing in the middle of the battleship's crowded alpha bay.

"I was so worried about you," she said as she pulled back and looked up at him.

"I told you I'd be back, didn't I? I could never stay away from you, no matter what it took to get back."

He turned around, looking over toward where Jamison had

stood. "Sorry about that, Kyle, you wanted to…" But Jamison was gone, and Stockton realized just how good of a friend he had in *Dauntless*'s strike force commander. "I guess it was something that could wait," he said softly. Then he added, "Good."

He pulled Stara closer to him and said, "Let's go find someplace to talk. There's something I have to tell you, something I should have told you a long time ago, and I don't want to wait any longer." And he led her off the launch bay and into one of the lifts.

Chapter Fifty

CFS Dauntless
Ultara System
308 AC

Stockton walked down the corridor toward the officers club. He was anxious to see his Blue squadron comrades, or at least those who had survived. He'd had a chance to check the roster, so he knew who was still there, and who hadn't made it. The ship's data net had told him something else too, and he didn't know how he felt about it. He knew how he would have reacted before, but things had changed over the past few weeks, and he was different as well.

He turned and stepped into the room, and a second later the place erupted into applause. Blue squadron was there, of course, as were the rest of *Dauntless*'s fighter jocks. And standing right in front of the bar were Captain Barron and Commander Travis.

Stockton snapped to attention. "Captain. Commander."

"At ease, Commander...for the love of God, at ease."

Stockton looked back, a confused expression on his face. "I'm sorry, sir...did you call me Commander?"

"You don't miss much, do you?" Barron had a broad smile on his face. "You turned the admiral down, Jake, and I can't tell you how thrilled I am to have you back. But we couldn't let you walk away from your promotion too, could we? I was all ready

428

to dust off the Barron name and take it for a ride, demanding you get the bump in rank, but the admiral said yes right away. Apparently—somehow—you made a good impression. Don't take it personally, Commander, but you wouldn't be my first pick to grease the brass, so to speak. Still, congratulations. That trip you made will almost certainly get you a medal as well as your clusters, but for now you'll just have to be happy being the second highest ranking pilot on *Dauntless*."

"I am, sir. I really am. Thank you. I can't tell you how good it feels to be home."

"We're thrilled to have you back. Now, how would you feel about drinking with your captain?" Barron turned back toward the bar. "A round for everyone."

The room echoed with a loud cheer as the bartender started handing out mugs.

"Jake," Barron said softly, "there is one thing I wanted to discuss with you."

"Timmons." He looked up at the captain and then at Jamison. "He led the Blues while I was away." Stockton took a deep breath. His people were nothing if not loyal. Half a dozen pilots had already told him what had happened, urging him to make amends with the Red Eagle leader...but assuring him if they were forced to choose between the two, they would always be Stockton's. "We've had our differences, but I'd never say he wasn't one hell of a pilot...or a squadron commander."

"It's not just that." Barron flashed a glance to Jamison and then back. "We took terrible losses, Jake, and that was on top of Santis. We need to replenish our ranks, and I'd rather not have to deal with an influx of raw trainees. So, I asked Lieutenant Timmons and the Red Eagles to stay permanently, to bulk up our roster. I'll have to get the admiral to approve the transfer, but I suspect he owes us one for taking out the enemy supply station."

"Did Timmons accept?"

"He said he would stay...but only if you were okay with it. He lost his best friend in the last battle, and he's taken the survivors of the Direwolves into his squadron."

"Captain, I'd have probably said something very different a

couple weeks ago, but a lot of things have changed since then."
He looked across the room to where Timmons was standing,
and he waved his hand, gesturing for the pilot to come over.

"Yes, Commander?" Timmons said, clearly uncomfortable.

"We've had our differences, Warrior. We both know that.
But maybe it's time for all that to end. I can't even say I remember why we ended up at odds all that well anymore. So, let's start
over now, clean. And if that's good for you, it's good for me."

"It's good for me, Raptor."

Stockton extended his hand, and Timmons took it enthusiastically. "Welcome to *Dauntless*, Warrior. And you don't have
to thank us for getting you off that massive flagship. You've
swapped the most prestigious ship in the fleet for the best one."

Timmons nodded, and he even cracked a tiny smile. "No
argument there, Raptor. And we'll do whatever we have to do to
keep it that way!"

Confederation Intelligence
Troyus City
Planet Megara, Olyus III
308 AC

"I wasn't sure I'd ever see this office again, my friend." Holsten sat behind his palatial desk, staring across at Vonns. "It was
an…interesting…experience being with the fleet during a battle
like that, but I think once was enough for me. I was able to keep
from soiling my pants, which was a Godsend for my dignity,
but I don't think I should push my luck. Besides, with Admiral
Striker securely in place, I believe the fleet is in good hands."

"I still don't know how you managed to extricate yourself
from the hole you dug. The Senate retroactively approved all
your actions. You're in the clear, and while we've still got one
hell of a war to fight, at least we're not staring into the abyss anymore." Vonns seemed genuinely surprised. "How did you pull it
off with the Senate? I was waiting for word you were arrested."

"I just reasoned with them. Nothing but cold logic."

No one except Holsten himself ever need know the extent of the threats and deals and outright intimidation it had taken to secure the support of enough Senators to ratify what he had done. Fortunately, those who'd screamed the loudest for his blood and expressed the greatest outrage at his 'betrayal,' had turned out to be the ones with the longest lists of financial improprieties and illegitimate children and illicit affairs, all neatly categorized and documented in Holsten's private files.

No politician could idly make an enemy of a man who'd occupied Holsten's position, and so it had been with the Confederation's Senate. A man like Holsten had his secret resources, and he'd made sure the politicians realized he would retain most of them, even when he'd been stripped of his post and charged with a long list of crimes. If his machinations had failed and the fleet had been defeated, perhaps he would have had a harder time, but the Senate was overjoyed that the Union forces were no longer advancing inexorably toward them. They'd found it relatively easy to get over their outrage, courtesy of a judicious combination of relief, blackmail and bribery.

"So, what is next? We averted disaster, but if the reports I've seen are any indication, the fleet is in bad shape."

"It's far worse than you imagine. But the Union forces were badly damaged too. I suspect there will be a lull while both sides recover. But based on the resources they committed in building their fleet and that supply base, I'd say the Union is in it to the end this time. I fear we face a long and difficult fight."

Vonns just nodded. Then he asked, "What about Tyler Barron? This is the second massive victory he's won. I know he is young, but should we be considering a move to flag rank?"

"We probably should...but not yet. He and that ship of his are a unit, unlike any I have ever seen. His people are devoted to him, and they seem uniquely able to achieve the impossible. I'm reluctant to separate them, at least so soon. Tyler Barron may yet prove to be his grandfather's equal, but with Striker in command, we can be patient. Our new commanding admiral brings a whole generation of officers with him, and a fresh energy.

Striker is willing to promote Barron to task force command now, but I asked him to wait. To give Barron and his people and his ship a bit more time together. I think they've earned at least that much."

CFS Dauntless
Ultara System
308 AC

"Commander Fritz has worked wonders, Captain. It gets old saying it so often, but she really is the closest thing to a miracle worker."

"I think Fritzie would badger a miracle worker to the verge of insanity. All this time together, and I still can't say for certain that the woman sleeps. Ever." Barron flashed a smile at Travis. The two were in his quarters, just catching up on the latest reports. He appreciated the quiet, and the company.

Dauntless still carried a fair number of scars, but the battleship was more or less fully functional. Barron knew she could use a long stretch in spacedock, but he also realized there were other ships in greater need. The opening battles of the war had been the fiercest and most costly ever known, and the fleet had a tremendous amount of repair and rebuilding to do.

"We're in good shape, Ty…considering. The Red Eagles will go a long way toward bringing our squadrons back to top readiness. And even for all our losses, the pilot roster looks like an all-star assembly."

"We're very lucky, Atara…if that's something we can say after all we've been through." Barron paused. "This war isn't over, not by a long shot. As soon as the Union gets their fleets refit and resupplied, they'll be back at us. And we'd better be ready for them when they come."

Travis looked at him, an iron look on her face. "We will be, Ty. We will be."

**Coming Spring 2017
Blood on the Stars Book 3**

Ruins of Empire

Captain Barron and the Dauntless's crew of must make a desperate journey to the ghostly worlds of the Badlands to stop the Union from discovering an ancient relic, a pre-cataclysmic weapon of unimaginable power, one that could shatter the balance of power and allow the Union fleets to crush the Confederation once and for all.

Also By Jay Allan

www.jayallanbooks.com
www.bloodonthestars.com